RUNE OF THORNS

TALES OF EDENIA

ENCHANTED SHADOWS
BOOK 2

KELLY N. JANE

18TH AVENUE PRESS

Title: Rune of Thorns, Enchanted Shadows, book 2 (Tales of Edenia)

Copyright © 2025 by Kelly N. Jane

Published by 18th Avenue Press

Cover by Rebecca Frank, Bewitching Designs

Editing by The Enchanted Quill

Map by Cartographybird Maps

to view the map in color visit www.kellynjane.com/edenia-map

ISBN (Paperback) 978-1-947695-30-6

ISBN (eBook) 978-1-947695-29-0

Join Kelly's newsletter and get a fun book for free!

http://www.kellynjane.com/join-the-warrior-circle/

For my Libby

AETERNUS SEA

THE ENCHANTED LANDS
OF
EDENIA

GALLINAR SEA

RULAVA
PENUMAR
KAZNA
KUR
MORTUS
THE BARROWS
ORA
AETHERCREST
SIGHTLESS VALE
SAGANUS
FANGHOLT
VEILRUNE MOUNTAINS
ANOMIE
HAVILAR
ACLANUS
SYLPH BAY
BAILARA
VATARA
THALASSAR
KESTURU
ZANDIRI
ILLUSION PASS
TIXAMAR
THE BLUFFS
ERIDAR

KRUOS
RANTZA
WHITE FANG
MOUNTAINS
IBERN
VELMEG
FORSA
OMANE
SING
OSAR
HERGIL
BOLSTA
SKANDAN
STRAIT
PULMA
CORVUS
THON
TH
FELL
GE
BELYSE
CITADEL
PANON
HYRCANI
LURENE
ARSA
SAVASAY
MOUNTAINS
FARRADAR
DASHIR
TIRI
CARRATHU
THE KELSON SEA

PROLOGUE

The fae remained divided after the Chasm, so Osric, the Great Guardian of Caelus, created the land of Edenia. He then foretold a cryptic prophecy that would come to pass after two Burning Moons occurred eighteen years apart.

A millennium passed without such an event, and the prophecy faded from memory, spoken of occasionally in hushed tones as folklore or delusion.

Until seventeen years ago, when the first Burning Moon occurred . . . on the same day as The Reaping.

The sparrow of silver fire will strike the owl from above and below,
when thrice the seven gather before the prime goes dark

1

ROWENA

DREAD COILED in Rowena's gut. She ground her teeth to stop the bile from rising, but the taste of failure already coated her tongue.

Moons. What had she become?

A month ago, she'd laughed at fear. Stood tall, blade in hand, as if born to it. Hadn't she argued, fiercely, to anyone who'd listen that she was ready for battle? That she craved adventure? That she was a warrior?

What a lie.

Her hands balled into fists, nails digging deep into her palms.

Not a warrior. Just a child aching for her mother.

A mother gone. A father dead. A home reduced to rubble and ghosts.

A choked sound clawed up her throat, but she swallowed hard and forced it back.

No.

She *would not* break.

With a growl, Rowena seized the sodden dish cloth and slapped it into the basin. She scrubbed hard, more demanding than necessary, as if scouring the grime could erase what she'd become. She had to be stronger. Skandan needed a queen, not a broken princess trembling at the wind.

Her breath quickened. Vision blurred. She hated this place. Hated that Bram dragged her through shadows while more kings died among the ruins. And worst of all, for leaving Safi behind.

She hated herself most. For not fighting harder, for not being enough, for knowing, deep down, she feared the door.

The world outside no longer belonged to her.

Had it ever?

"Inhale." Bram's voice, soft and steady, drifted across the room. "Exhale."

Her chin dropped to her chest. Her lip quivered. She exhaled, trembling.

"This will pass." Bram spoke from just beyond reach.

Moments ago, he'd stood across the room. His silence needed more than a keen ear to follow. She wasn't unaware, just anxious. Exhausted. Defeated.

She leaned into the table for support. A single tear struck dishwater, sending it rippling. "How can you say that?"

His fingers brushed her shoulder. An invitation, not a demand. Rowena spun and threw herself into his arms, tears finally spilling. She'd grown used to his quiet touch. Craved it. He never pushed. Never crowded. Always near, never too close.

One arm wrapped around her; the other stroked her hair. "You haven't had a moment's peace these past days. Much has happened. Much was lost."

"I cried many nights as Uther's slave." Her breath hitched; she sniffed hard against it.

Bram leaned in, resting his head atop hers. His whisper stirred her hair. "Planning vengeance is not the same as healing."

She spread her fingers over his chest, leaning back to meet his gaze. Swirling amber burned with fierce intensity.

"Time will heal your grief. With me, you need only rest." His palm cupped her face, fingers skimmed the line of her jaw. As his thumb swept a tear from her cheek, she fought to hold the rest back.

Rowena rested her head just below his collarbone. From the moment they'd arrived, he'd let her unravel, giving her space when she needed it, and standing by her when she fell.

She didn't deserve his kindness. "Safi only has until Masah is full. That's less than a month . . . and I am afraid to walk out the door. She is suffering because of me—maybe dying."

"We'll find Fidessa. We'll reclaim the sword. I promise."

She believed him. But what then? "And after that? Will you give it up to save Safi if you must?" She knew losing the sword gnawed at him. He never spoke of it, but more than once she'd caught him standing alone in the meadow, his fists clenching and unclenching at his sides. Perhaps it wasn't just the weapon. Perhaps it was all the time she wasted, drowning in her own turmoil.

She shook her head. It had to be the sword. Whenever they spoke of it, his lips thinned, and his amber eyes frosted over like winter ice.

It was his duty to find and protect the moon-born, to guard her, and gather the Armor of Caelus piece by piece.

And the one piece he'd found, Rowena lost. To her aunt, the mad queen, Fidessa.

"One step at a time."

Safi was the only family she had left. Rowena refused to claim relation to Fidessa. That bond had severed before it ever grew. Rowena would never sacrifice Safi to save a sword.

When she closed her eyes, she was back in the feast hall at Velmeg.

Safi, sitting silent and dazed under Fidessa's spell.

Daenon dragging her away.

Fidessa vanishing with the sword.

Rowena tucked herself tighter against Bram's chest, letting silence fall between them. Even the formidable Seeker had no comfort strong enough to wipe away the truth. Safi would remain trapped under Rowena delivered the Sword of Justice to Daenon. And with every moment spent in the cottage's safety, the task grew harder. More dangerous.

Rowena wasn't the only one hiding.

Fidessa's smokescreen departure could have led her to any corner of Edenia.

Rowena huffed out a breath.

"What's amusing?" Bram asked, tracing slow patterns through her hair and down her spine.

"How can I find Fidessa if I don't even know where I am?"

Several heartbeats passed before Bram answered. "We are in Havilar."

Rowena leaned back, gaping. "With the dryads?"

"Yes."

She twisted from his arms and bent over; hands braced on her knees. "Then I am lost as well."

Why had he brought her here?

She'd trusted him to protect her. The only thing holding her together.

And perhaps . . . perhaps that had been her worst mistake.

"This is the safest place you can be."

"Ha!" She flung her hands into the air. "How can you say that? Every story says those who enter the forest uninvited are lost forever. And the dryads invite no one."

Rowena stomped to the center of the room. She had survived her first visit to the cottage, when only a lonely chair sat before the fire.

Now a long sofa stretched along one wall where Bram had slept each night. His blankets were folded neatly at the end. He'd given her the only room with a door.

And a lock. One she'd never used. One he'd never tested.

"As Seeker, I'm allowed anywhere in Edenia." He slid over and perched on the table's edge.

She stared at the far wall, refusing to meet his gaze. "That's fine for you. What happens to me if you're not here?"

She wished he stood before her in his Seeker form. The horns. The claws. The glow of runes across his face in the fire-light. Those had become a comfort when fears threatened to overtake her.

Foolishness.

She forced herself back to reality.

"Why would that ever happen?"

"Don't be foolish, Bram." Rowena hugged her herself and stared at the floor. Everyone leaves. "Things happen."

"I am not going anywhere."

"You will." She kept her back to him. Whether he admitted it or not, facts were facts. "It's inevitable. As Seeker, you have a duty to all the moon-born. I'm just the first you've found."

A chair scraped against the wooden floorboards. Rowena peeked from the corner of her eye. Bram sat stiffly on the hard seat, staring into nothing. He understood. Just as she did.

They had no future together.

Their fragile time in the cottage only added another knot to the tangle in her heart.

"What you say is partly true. I must help the others. But I'll find a way for us to stay together. I won't leave you."

She twisted and found him hunched over, elbows on knees, forehead cradled in his palms.

Here, in this solitude, it was easy to believe nothing could tear them apart. Her chest ached at the sight. She wanted nothing more than to stay with him. To help him gather the others, just as he had helped her.

The thought drew a wry smile, but reality crushed it before it could take root.

She eased toward Bram, crouching before him, and took his hands gently from his face.

"As much as I want to dream of our future, that isn't the path either of us walks. Duty and love, enemies of peace. Enemies of each other." Rowena drew a steadying breath. "We have limited time together. We have to accept that."

He caught her gaze with a fierce intensity that pierced straight through her. "This isn't how it was supposed to be. I never . . . never planned . . . never expected you."

Her heart swelled, crushing the breath from her chest. Why had she ever doubted him? She tightened her grip. "Bram—"

"Don't. Don't tell me how wrong this is. How it will never work." He turned his face away. When he spoke again, his voice barely reached her. "How you could never truly love someone like me."

He made no sense. She was the impulsive one, the reckless one. All she'd wanted was vengeance against Uther. And through it all, he had protected her.

Rowena inhaled his smoky oak scent that clung to him. His warm brown gaze locked onto hers.

She rose and perched on his thigh, never letting go of his hands. "You've saved me, more than once. No one has your skill, or your care."

"I am the shadows. The darkness to terrify others into compliance."

"You are brave and kind." She bit her lip, fighting a grin. "And you're not that scary."

He narrowed his gaze, leaning so close their noses nearly touched. "I have horns."

Rowena's gaze dropped to his lips, a flock of sparrows taking flight in her stomach. When she spoke, her voice rasped out in a whisper. "They're beautiful."

He sat back with a heavy sigh.

Rowena leaned her side against his chest. Neither of them spoke. The silence wrapped around them—a fragile respite from the world outside.

Bram brushed a stray lock from her cheek. "No matter what . . . we'll stay together."

Hope sparked through her like a moonbeam. But it slipped away like mist in the night. "We don't know what's coming."

His fingers stilled against her shoulder. "You doubt me?"

She leaned back to meet his gaze and shook her head. "Never. I mistrust everyone else."

That was the truth. It's why her breath caught, why her arms shook, why sweat soaked her skin whenever her hand brushed the door latch. Inside, with Bram, there were no dangers. Outside, terrors waited.

Bram could not fight them all.

"Those who should have loved my parents killed them out of jealousy and ambition." The look on her father's face before he'd died haunted her dreams. Despair shadowed his eyes as he watched his daughter loose an arrow. Not the one that pierced his heart, but he would never know the truth until she reached the hero grounds herself. "I trusted others who either died or lied. I faced beasts that flew wild and attacked without reason. There's no control over anything. I see that now, clearer than ever now."

"You're safe with me." He rubbed his thumb across the back of her hand.

"I believe you. For as long as I'm with you. But I can't hide behind you forever. And you can't stay by my side when there are others to find." She swallowed, clinging to her composure.

Bram pulled his hand free and cupped her cheek. "I would never stand in front of you—only at your side. You are a capable warrior. You deserve the freedom to become the queen you were meant to be."

"Will I . . . become queen?" The idea of taking the crown without her parents to guide her sent terror through her chest. But the alternative was worse. She would not let Goetz, her father's traitorous advisor, seize Taesing. He'd burned the longhouse, trapping those loyal to her inside. What horrors had he unleashed on the survivors while she was gone? "What happens after I have the sword and the Lunastone?"

Bram's mouth tightened. "I'll have to find the others. You'll need to keep the Armor safe until then. As Queen of Skandan, you'll have that authority. Whatever happens, I swear, I'll keep you safe. Trust me."

She wanted to trust him, with every beat of her heart, and leaned into his touch. "There are dangers that could hurt you, too. This form is not immortal."

His lips quirked in a faint smile. "That's true. But since the Heptad made me this way, it's not likely they'd kill me."

The thought of Bram dying sent familiar unease rattling through her chest. She swallowed, but it only grew. She shot to her feet, shuffling out of Bram's reach.

He rose and followed. "I'm sorry. I shouldn't have made light of it."

"It's fine. I'm fine." Her skin crawled. She didn't know what to do with her hands. The walls seemed to close in. "Talk about something else."

Images battered her mind—Bram full of arrows, tumbling off a cliff. Just like Hann. Bram cold and lifeless in her arms, chest split open by an axe. Bram across the room, fading, eyes glassy and unseeing.

None of it real.

Yet her mind whispered that it could be. That she should believe it.

She raked her fingers through her unbraided hair, letting it fall in a blonde curtain across her face.

"Your safe. Breathe." Bram's threaded through the chaos of her mind.

"We have to go. We have to get to Safi." It was the only way to make things right. The only way forward. Bram had done so much for her, but it was time she stood on her own.

His duty was to the moon-born.

Hers was to her cousin. To her people.

"We will." Bram closed the space between them. "Tonight, when Masah is out."

That made sense. Masah's energy would steady her. Fill her with the calm she needed. "That will be good. But where will we go? Do you know how to find Fidessa?"

"The sword has a vibration I can sense, though it is not precise. That's why I had to follow such a winding path to find you. But once we set out . . . I'll find her."

The sword called to Rowena, too, but never from far away. "Perhaps together, we'll feel it faster."

"I'm sure of it."

The plan helped steady her breath. She glanced at the door again.

Tonight.

She would leave after dark.

2

BRAM

BRAM LOVED the way Rowena's eyes lit when she smiled. It washed a warmth over her face, only to vanish like moonlight slipping through storm clouds. If only he could hold it there. Help her see herself the way he did.

No matter what he said or did, her joy never lasted more than a breath. She needed time. Time she deserved.

But she was right. They didn't have that luxury. Fidessa still had the sword. Wait too long, and she'd disappear deeper into Edenia, beyond reach. If Rowena could trust herself again, they could go together. That would be best. She was his duty as well, after all.

Duty.

He pinched the bridge of his nose. What a hollow word.

It wasn't duty that made him stay. No one could have predicted this; least of all the Heptad. They'd chosen him to be terror in the dark. A hunter. A force to drive the moon-born toward their fate. They must have believed there was no other way. How could they have foreseen a stubborn, powerful Lunara would find him handsome instead of fearsome?

And yet.

"What's that look for?"

Bram flinched, startled from his thoughts. "What?"

Rowena arched a brow. "You've got a silly grin on your face."

"I'm sure I don't."

Her lips curved, an unguarded smile blooming, fleeting but real. Amusement danced in her gaze.

His chest tightened. Caelus help him. He'd do anything for her. "It was nothing."

"Mm-hmm."

She crossed the small space, returning to the dishpan. The moment was gone, slipped away like so many others. He watched her work, the fragile calm settling over her again.

He hated how easily panic gripped her. Hated even more the reasons why.

Bram liked Safi. He really did.

She had a warrior's heart, and a swagger to match. She cared for Rowena in a way few could.

But she wasn't part of the prophecy.

No matter how fierce, how important to Rowena, she would not be the one to save Edenia when the next Burning Moon arrived.

The thought curdled his stomach. But he didn't let it linger.

His gaze drifted back to Rowena. She still moved stiffly, hesitating at ghosts that weren't there. If she couldn't leave tonight, he'd have to go alone.

Just for a little while. He would search while she slept.

She'd never even know he was gone.

He probably should have done it already.

A splash of water, a shift of movement . . . she was at his side, her fingers slipping between his.

A ray of hope.

"I'll be ready tonight, I promise."

Bram stilled.

Had he been so easy to read? The tightness in his chest made it difficult to respond. He licked his lip. His heart whispered one truth: stay. Wait. Give her more time.

But duty pressed harder. Under three months until the Reaping and the final Burning Moon.

Rowena drew her hand away, retreating to the counter. She braced herself against the wooden surface. Distance. Silent. A wall reformed between them.

"Are you upset with me?"

The question struck like an arrow in his ribs. Not undeserved. He should have known better. Even without using her Lunara skills, she saw straight through him.

"I'm not angry," he admitted. "Like you, I want to move on. But I don't know how."

She exhaled sharply, rubbing her fingers against her temples.

"Safi is my cousin, Bram. She's the only family I have left." Her voice trembled, but she forced it steady. "I haven't even had enough time to know her. Not really."

Bram shifted toward her, but she lifted a hand, halting him.

"I know I'm being ridiculous. I should be able to move on. I should be stronger." Her hands curled into fists. "But she needs me."

"You're being exactly as you need to be." The words escaped before he could stop them. "There's nothing wrong with that."

Her throat bobbed, but she didn't look at him.

"Grief has no time limit," he added. He wanted to go to her, to wrap her in his arms. But she was like a frightened animal. He had to be patient.

"She's not dead."

Her words sliced straight through him. He lifted his hands. "That's not what I meant to imply."

But maybe it was. Maybe she heard the truth neither of them dared say aloud.

Rowena turned away. Her hand seized the dishcloth by the basin, knuckles whitening. She slammed it onto the table, scrubbing with too much force. Not cleaning. Purging. As if she could scrub away the helplessness clawing at her from the inside.

Bram exhaled and shoved the chair aside, crossing to the fireplace. The logs were blackened and cold. Burned to nothing.

A fitting image.

Some things could not be rekindled.

Rowena's voice floated across the room, quiet, but certain. "I can't keep wallowing."

Bram kept his back to her. Maybe she needed something different from him. "Are you in pain, or just feeling sorry for yourself?"

The sharp inhale behind him told him he'd struck a nerve.

"How can you ask me that? You just reminded me of all I've lost."

Maybe he'd chosen the wrong approach. But he'd try anything if it meant helping her. He schooled his features before turning to face her. "I said nothing you don't already know."

Her expression hardened. "That's cruel."

"It's the truth."

Rowena's hands clenched tighter around the cloth, knuckles white. "You think I don't know what I've lost? That I don't see their bodies every time I close my eyes?" Her voice cracked, but she didn't falter. "I had a family. I had a home. And now all I have left is—"

She cut herself off.

Bram stepped closer. "Is what?"

She swallowed, hard. But she didn't continue. She didn't have to.

Bram saw the war waging behind her eyes—grief, pride, and something else neither of them dared name.

Still, he didn't let up. If she needed to hate him, to pour all her rage and pain into him, he would bear it.

"You have a choice, Rowena."

Her chest heaved. "What choice?"

"To keep standing. To stop letting fear rule you. To fight for what's still yours."

She scoffed. "And if I fail?"

"You will."

Her head snapped up, anger flashing hot in her eyes. "Then why even bother?"

"Because failing doesn't mean you stop trying." He stepped closer, easing the space between them. "You've been knocked down. That's not where you stay. It's not who you are."

Her lips flattened, then quivered. The battle within her was clear as glass. Her breath shuddered out. "You make it sound so simple."

"It isn't. It never is."

Her hands trembled. She stretched her fingers, only to curl them back into fists. No words came. Or maybe there were too many. . . and none strong enough.

Bram waited. Hoping.

Then, a flicker of something.

Not acceptance. Not yet.

But understanding.

Silence stretched between them. Thick. Heavy.

Until it shattered.

A shadow crossed the window.

Bram's senses sharpened.

He reached for her, one heartbeat before the door handle rattled.

Something was outside.

Havilar was a land of secrets; trust given sparingly, if at all.

The old stories whispered in Skandan had been exaggerated. But not by much. A tempest of fear had to be brewing inside Rowena. He couldn't blame her.

The dryads were not merciful.

And yet, someone had come to their door.

Another shadow flickered past the window.

Bram moved before Rowena. Laying a hand on her arm, he bent close to her ear. "Say nothing."

She went rigid beneath his touch. Not from fear. Not entirely. More likely from the weight of those stories. Stories she didn't yet understand.

A voice sliced through the silence, smooth as steel. "Show yourself, Seeker. The Heptad demands answers."

A woman's voice. Commanding. Expecting. But not one he recognized from the council.

Bram inhaled slowly. Not the dryads, then. "Hold tight."

Rowena clutched his waist as the shadows curled around him, familiar as breath. His form shifted, runes flaring against his skin, horns throwing dark shapes along the walls. His fingers elongated into sharp-tipped claws. But he did not release her. And she didn't let go.

She pressed closer, her heartbeat a frantic rhythm against his ribs, seeping through the layers of black leather.

"And bring the moon-born who hides with you."

Bram exhaled through his nose. They knew he hid her. No point delaying now. They'd probably come because of the lost the Sword of Justice. He and Rowena could simply walk through the door to stand like scolded elflings . . . But he refused to show weakness.

He wouldn't make excuses. The reasons for the sword's loss were legitimate. And he would stand by them.

He bent low, his voice steady and unyielding. "No matter what we face—stay at my side. Hold tightly."

Rowena's fingers dug into his tunic before he even finished speaking. Trust. Silent. Instinctive.

He wrapped his arm around her waist and stepped forward. The world shifted, weightless and dark. One heartbeat suspended. And then they reappeared outside the door.

Sunlight. Pine.

Air charged with power.

And *two* women waiting for them.

Bram's gaze swept them instantly, reading every inch of their stance, their presence, their intent. One: the expected druid. The other: a dryad. Princess Ida wearing a subtle sneer.

His stomach tightened. This was not a coincidence. His gaze locked onto the druid first.

No weapons. Copper robe twisted between knuckles. Gold band over her forehead. A paritor, and one he remembered. The Heptad had not come themselves, but sent one of their assistants. Lhoris.

She was still a true druid. A Primary fae bearing the full power of Caelus. His jaw clenched. He'd expected someone from Saganus to check in . . . eventually.

He turned his focus to Ida. She held his attention longer. Did she remember their agreement? Or had she chosen to forget?

Where Lhoris exuded authority, Ida radiated something sharper. Animosity.

She stood rigid, almost indistinguishable from the surrounding forest. The bow at her back spoke of skill. The flex of her fingers, ready to draw, spoke of experience. She shifted slightly, and the morning light caught the sharp edges of her face. Assessing. Measuring.

Weighing him as he weighed her.

Rowena stiffened beside him.

Bram shifted forward, subtly placing between Rowena and Ida. Forcing the dryad to acknowledge him first.

They were deep in dryad lands. And Ida wanted them gone.

3

———

ROWENA

"You have violated our lands."

The woman's tone carried no warmth. No welcome. No space for negotiation.

She had to be a dryad.

Her green tunic seemed woven from leaves and moss.

Her trousers matched the color of bark. Was it bark?

A bow poked over her shoulder, slicing through her black hair, falling in a silky curtain to her waist, as dark and narrowed as her eyes.

Rowena stiffened, her shoulders curling inward before she caught herself.

She edged back, bumping against Bram's boot.

Heat burned up her neck.

Bram didn't move.

Arms crossed over his broad chest, horns shimmering, dark and rippling like a river catching moonlight, even though it was still morning.

He didn't glance at her.

Didn't even flinch when she pressed against him, just for a breath.

His focus locked on the dryad.

The air between them thickened, charged with power.

It pressed against Rowena's skin, heavy as damp wool.

She, too, had power.

The thought whispered through her mind, distant. Almost laughable.

Against these three, her strength felt like a flickering candle caught in a storm.

"Explain yourself. Why have you hidden in these lands?" The druid seemed every bit as angry as the dryad.

Bram finally broke his silence, his tone even; edged with steel.

"Only if you do the same, Lhoris." His gaze didn't waver. "I am following my orders. Why are you interfering?"

Rowena inhaled sharply. They knew each other. This wasn't chance.

Bram said nothing.

Rowena nearly dropped to her knees. Nearly begged for mercy.

But he didn't flinch.

Rowena's gaze darted between them, searching for signs.

Lhoris was nothing like Asta. Asta had scared her; an Oraku, disavowed but still strong.

But this woman . . .

Power radiated from Lhoris, equal to Bram's, flooding the air like unseen waves.

Her cinnamon-colored hair rippled like silk against a copper robe. She was beautiful in a way Rowena hadn't thought possible. Ethereal. Untouchable.

How long had they known each other?

How deep did it run?

Rowena studied every subtle shift, the familiarity woven into their words. A tremor rolled through her, but she held her ground.

A shadowy mist curled along the ground, slipping over her boots. Instinct screamed: move.

Retreat.

But she clenched her jaw and squared her shoulders.

She was not a coward. Not anymore.

"You have brought an intruder into our lands." The dryad's bow slid into her hand, effortless, lethal. No arrow drawn.

Not yet.

But it wouldn't matter. If she reached for one, Rowena would already be dead.

Rowena ignored Bram's earlier warning, keeping her voice steady. "I meant no disrespect. My injuries have healed. We can leave."

Bram's weight shifted. A silent warning. Clear as a blade against her ribs.

Too late.

Lhoris turned to her then, assessing. A frown creased her brows. "This is the moon-born?"

Rowena's fingers twitched. Power or not, the woman's tone sliced, judging her and finding her wanting.

She lifted her chin, meeting Lhoris' gaze head-on. "Yes."

Bram's tone remained unreadable. Unaffected. "No realm may forbid me entry. Queen Alona has known of my presence here since I first occupied the cottage."

The dryad's expression darkened, her mouth twisting as if the words tasted foul. "My mother does not interfere in your Heptad affairs. However," her gaze flicked to Rowena, sharp as a blade's edge, "our concern lies with this one. Our realm is sacred, unblemished by careful effort to keep it isolated. No one crosses our borders without the Great Guardian's blessing.

This one. Rowena's stomach turned.

Not a name. Not a person.

Bram stepped forward. "I approved her, Princess Ida."

Did he know everyone? Understanding settled in her gut like a rock. Of course he did.

Reality clicked into place. Royalty.

Rowena should not have been surprised. Enchanted royals drew the most power from the Primary Spring, feeding it into their realms' heartstones. Ida carried herself with the weight of command. The certainty of someone never denied.

"She holds no heartstone," Ida countered.

"Nor do I see a piece of the armor," Lhoris added, folding her hands into her sleeves.

Rowena rolled her eyes. "Maybe it's hidden inside?"

The words left her sharper than she meant them to. But she was done being spoken around. Done being ignored. "I am the Queen of Skandan."

A flicker of something . . . amusement? pity? . . . crossed Ida's expression.

"That is yet to be decided," Lhoris said. "For now, Taesing remains under the control of the realm's former advisor. Without the armor, there's no evidence you are the true one to hold the Lunastone."

"I assume there are Lunara royals in Penumar who claim the heartstone as well," Ida added.

Rowena twisted the fabric of her trousers into fists. Her grandmother had fled Penumar because of a coup. A stolen crown. Rowena was her only living descendant. Her claim was stronger than any of the theirs.

"Goetz is a usurper," she said, her voice low, steady. No one would take that from her. "I will remove him and take my place as soon as I am able."

A sound. Small. Almost imperceptible.

Bram.

Rowena twisted sharply, catching his gaze. He had cleared his throat, the faintest sound. But she caught it. A flicker of doubt.

He didn't believe her. He doubted her.

A slow, simmering heat curled through her ribs. Her fingers tightened, nails piercing fabric until one seam gave.

Did he think her incapable? Did he think her weak?

She swallowed the frustration. Swallowed the sharp edge of betrayal.

Bram held her gaze, calm. Unreadable. "That is a secondary concern. When we secure the heartstone and armor, all will be right."

A dismissal.

Rowena's pulse pounded in her ears.

She wouldn't argue now. Not in front of the others.

Her breath came sharp and slow, but she forced It out, unclenching her fists.

This wasn't the time.

But he would understand. She would make him understand.

"Whether you rule the northern island is of no consequence," Ida said, her voice sharp as frost. "Only those who possess a heartstone when crossing into Havilar may return. Others remain forever—one way or another."

Rowena's blood chilled. Like a foolish elfling, she had hoped the stories weren't true. She turned to Bram, her pulse a dull hammer against her ribs. "Why did you bring me here?"

"My presence will suffice as well as the Lunastone."

Ida scoffed.

But Lhoris raised a hand, silencing her. The pause stretched, thick and heavy, before she spoke. "And when you leave?"

The words struck deep. Rowena's insides shriveled. But she forced her spine straight. He'd said he wouldn't go. She had known better, but she'd let herself hope.

Everyone leaves.

She flicked her gaze between the two women. Neither cared what happened to her.

One wanted her forgotten.

The other wanted her destroyed.

Bram's voice stayed steady. "I have my duties. And they are to this moon-born. I will not abandon my responsibility."

Duty.

That was all she was to him? A duty?

Her chest tightened, but she said nothing.

What had she expected?

That the nights they'd spent together, him holding her when sleep wouldn't come, catching her tears when they wouldn't stop, had meant something more? That she had mattered to him beyond his druid-be-damned mission?

He had worried she couldn't love him. Had he never considered that perhaps he couldn't love her either?

Rowena swallowed hard. Forced herself to speak. "I can take care of myself."

"Then you accept the consequences of being in our lands." Princess Ida tilted her chin, waiting.

A familiar movement. Rowena's mother had used that same commanding gesture.

Rowena stared at the ground, her throat thick, clogged. "I . . . uh . . ."

"Don't say anything," Bram said, low, dangerous. He shifted forward, shadows already stirring to strike.

But Rowena had had enough.

She wanted to dart back into the cottage. Bar the door. Refuse this conversation. But instead, she squared her shoulders, forced her breath even, and lifted her chin.

"Yes," she said. "I will accept whatever happens."

Bram moved in front of her. A barrier. A wall. Just as he had always been. "She will stay with me. Where she is, I must remain." He lifted his hands, runes glowing faintly across his skin. "My utmost priority is to protect all moon-born. And the armor."

Rowena's gut twisted. There it was again. Not her. Not Rowena.

The moon-born. The title. The prophecy.

The duty.

Ida did not look impressed. "Dryad business will be done without your interference, Seeker."

Rowena's fear and hesitation burned away, replaced by something colder. So, this was protection? A cage disguised as care? She stepped closer to Bram, placing a firm hand on his arm.

He hesitated. Then shifted aside with a low grumble.

Good. She was done being protected.

"What is it you want from me?" she asked, voice calm, even as her pulse roared in her ears.

Ida's nostrils flared. For the first time, she seemed uncertain. "Our queen must decide your fate."

Lhoris intervened, her voice like steel wrapped in velvet. "I will take him." She turned to Bram, extending a hand. "Come, and we will let the Heptad decide what happens next."

A muscle in Bram's jaw tightened. "What do they need me to explain that I can't tell you here?"

Lhoris cut in, voice like steel wrapped in velvet.

"I will take him." She turned to Bram, extending a hand. "Come. We will let the Heptad decide what happens next."

Rowena's breath stilled. "He didn't exchange it!" The words tore from her throat, wild, unthinking.

Bram twisted toward her. A glare. A silent warning.

She glared right back. Did he expect her to say nothing?

Lhoris ignored the outburst. "The Heptad questions your ability to continue your mission; your right to be the Seeker."

Rowena's stomach dropped.

"Can they take that away?" She hadn't meant to whisper, but the words came too weak to stop it.

Bran did not answer at first.

She studied him. The rune on his cheeks. The horns arching back from his head. The golden glow of his eyes.

This was him. The Seeker. The thing that made him Bram.

He sighed, a sound of resignation. "I must go."

He must go.

Her hands clenched into fists, nails biting deep into her palms.

His gaze softened. "Regardless of missing the Lunastone, I don't believe the dryads will harm you. Just remain calm—"

"I have been nothing but," she snapped.

Bram tilted his face to the sky, his eyelids sliding closed. "Yes. Please continue in that way."

She wanted to scream. This was the pattern. Leaving. Always leaving.

Everyone she loved.

He had said he wouldn't. She should have known better.

"You promised." Her voice betrayed her, catching halfway through. She wanted to sound furious. Instead, she sounded broken.

Bram hesitated. Just for a second.

Then he hooked a finger under her chin, tipping her face toward his. "Remain here. Wait for me. No matter what happens, wait." His voice softened, as if it might make this easier.

It didn't.

"I will return."

Rowena's throat ached, but she said nothing. Neither of them should make promises like that anymore.

She studied his face, memorizing it.

And then, instead of answering, she only nodded.

Bram brushed his fingers down her arm, careful of his claws. A lingering touch. One that should have meant something but didn't.

Not now.

Then, without another word, he turned to Lhoris. "Let us leave with haste," he said, already distant. Already gone. "So, I may return with equal speed."

And then he disappeared. Shadow melding into brilliant light.

Leaving her alone. Again.

Rowena stared at the empty space where Bram had stood. Her fingers searched her arm where he had touched her. A foolish, meaningless habit.

He wasn't here. No warmth lingered.

Deep, sinking loneliness spread through her. Swallowed her whole.

"We have nearly a day's journey to reach our destination," Ida said.

Rowena flinched at the interruption. Reality swept in, sharp as a viper's bite.

She turned, just in time to see the dryad reach behind her shoulder. Pulling free a rope of braided vines.

Binding.

Her stomach turned.

"This will ensure you don't fall behind," Ida said. "Or get lost."

Rowena slid a step backward. Her voice came hard. Cold. "You will not restrain me. Nor will I go anywhere else. I will remain here to wait for Bram."

Her breath hitched. Fool. Hopeless fool. She had no reason to believe he would hurry. No reason to believe he'd return at all.

For the first time since leaving Ibern, she reached inward, calling for her power.

A mistake.

The moment she did, she felt it. Weak. Flickering. Listless.

She had spent too long indoors, away from the moons. The glow she needed was gone.

A tingle whispered through her arms, then silenced in a heartbeat.

Nothing.

"If you are to remain in Havilar, you must have the queen's permission," Ida said simply. "And you are not a prisoner. The binding is a precaution, so you do not become lost."

Rowena wanted to scream. Wanted to rip the sky open and demand answers from Caelus. Why did she never have control over her own life?

She had been bound before. Controlled.

Told where she could and could not go, what she could and could not do.

She would not become anyone's captive again.

Her chest ached. Her temples throbbed. She forced herself to remain calm. She would not let the dryad princess see her falter. She straightened, forcing steel into her voice. "I'll keep up. Skandan is a rugged island. I'm quite capable."

Ida didn't seem impressed. Her grip on the rope tightened, her copper-colored knuckles paling against the dark vines. "You must follow in my footsteps. Exactly. Touch nothing I do not. You will not defile the forest."

Rowena blinked, trying to comprehend the demand. "You want me to traverse a strange forest without touching anything? Is the path so clear we won't encounter a log or a steep hillside? How can I promise such a thing?"

A flash of memory overtook her. A rainy trail. A body slipping away. Hann's hand, shoving her to safety without concern for himself.

Her pulse kicked faster. Her throat tightened.

No rain. The sky was clear, soft blue. Unbothered by the chaos inside her.

Rowena inhaled, long and steady. She had survived worse. She'd been a slave. She'd faced a frost dragon.

She could run lightly through the blangdang forest.

"Are you well?"

Rowena lifted her gaze. Forced her body still. The princess watched her like a predator. "I'm fine. Lead the way."

"If you need help, call out."

Rowena almost laughed aloud. Help? From the dryad? Doubtful.

"In Havilar, everyone is connected to one another," Ida continued. "What hurts one hurts all. You must be respectful."

Rowena studied Ida's clothing, woven from the forest itself, as if it had grown around her rather than been sewn by hand. The dryads weren't just in the forest. They were part of it. Every vine-strangled stitch, every rough patch of bark in Ida's attire was a reminder that Rowena didn't belong.

Rowena flexed her fingers against her own tunic. The fabric rough and lifeless in comparison.

There was less than a month left. Less than a month to find Fidessa and retrieve the sword. Then, track down Daenon, and hope Safi was still alive.

Still fighting. Her cousin was the stronger one between them. Rowena wouldn't let her down.

Not again.

She squared her shoulders. "I will do all I can to respect your lands, princess."

"We do not use titles here." Ida slid the rope back onto her belt, adjusting the bow at her shoulder. "Is there anything you must retrieve from inside?"

Rowena twisted toward the cottage. Her chest hollowed at the sight.

It looked small. Lonely.

This had been the last place she and Bram had shared. The last place she had felt even a sliver of protection. She'd risen each day. Dressed in her tunic and trousers, sewn from Velmeg's battle. Knotted her bootlaces. Ready to leave.

Then hadn't.

There was nothing left for her there.

"A full waterskin," she said, quietly.

"We will stop and share a drink with the river." Ida turned, already moving. "Come."

She jogged into the meadow; her steps effortless.

Rowena hesitated, only a moment. Then she followed, careful with every step. Knowing there would be no one to catch her if she fell.

No one to come back for her if she was left behind.

ROWENA'S BREATH CAME SHARP, ragged. Her legs burned with each step. Ida moved effortlessly, not a foot out of place on the forest floor.

In contrast, Rowena was no more graceful than a baurun, dragging a cart. Every step offended. Every stumble earned a sharp hiss that slithered through the trees like a warning.

Her boots caught on a hidden root. She lurched forward, catching herself against the prickly bark of a sturdy tree. Her palms stung. Her knees threatened to give out. Stars flickered in her vision. Dizzy.

She clenched her teeth, refusing to ask for a break.

After the third time she disturbed something, a mushroom, a patch of moss, Ida finally slowed. Not out of kindness, Rowena suspected.

Out of some cold, unspoken judgment.

The slower tempo gave Rowena a chance to take in her surroundings. There were evergreen trees, like in Skandan. And, for a moment . . . a pang of homesickness.

It was short-lived, though. This forest was nothing like her homeland. The trunks were so vast, ten men standing side-by-side could hide behind them. Their tops soared a hundred feet or more into the sky without a single bend. Straight-backed sentinels.

Guarding Havilar since Edenia's first breath. Their scent was softer. Sweeter. Not smell the tangy bite of Skandan's pines.

The women continued through the underbrush without a break. Small creatures chittered at them in greeting not warning. A massive beast with flat, spreading horns and a humped back chewed cud like a cow and ignored them as they ducked under its high belly.

Rowena darted a glance over her shoulder. The beast didn't follow, but she shivered all the same and kept within an arm's length of Ida. If that was a gentle animal, she didn't want to face the menacing ones.

True to her word, after an hour, Ida stopped at a river for a drink. Rowena had no flask. Her throat burned. Dizziness overcame her.

Her legs shook. Her chest ached.

When Ida crouched down to scoop a handful of water, Rowena fell to her knees with a thud.

"Clumsy orek." Ida rose, towering over Rowena. "You must respect the land and all that grows upon it."

Ida turned, whispering something. Rowena craned her neck

to respond, only to realize Ida wasn't speaking to her. Ida's hand rested on a branch. After she touched two fingers to her forehead and the back to the tree. She pinched three large green leaves away.

A flask, woven from the leaves, appeared over Rowena's shoulder.

"Fill this. If you have a bond with the living world, it will help you when you ask."

Rowena took the vessel without hesitation. Hands shaking, she plunged it into the river. Cool, clear water rushed in.

She gulped it down in greedy mouthfuls, some dribbling down her chin. Only after the sharp ache in her throat eased did her mind catch up with her actions.

She turned the flask in her hands. The woven leaves were sturdy, and the stopper crafted from a tight bundle of greenery. It was impossibly well made, as if it had grown into shape rather than been constructed. Her brows knit together. How—?

She exhaled through her nose. Not the time. Questions could come later.

Rowena rose, refreshed from the cool water, and comforted by the ability to carry more. She tucked the flask into her belt, nodding her thanks to Ida.

Ida gave her an approving tip of her chin, then turned away. A moment later, they jogged into the cool shadows of the towering pines once again.

After another hour, Ida allowed Rowena a short time to sit on a flat rock and rest, before pushing on. After a third, perhaps fourth hour, Rowena lost track. The forest changed.

Not in the trees. Not in the inhabitants. But in the feel.

It grew quiet, reverent in an odd, unsettling way.

Without warning, Ida halted and spun. Rowena nearly plowed into her. Only by skidding did she stop in time.

They both studied the disturbed ground.

"You shouldn't have stopped so fast." Rowena arched a brow, hiding the guilty twist in her gut.

Ida pinched her lips. "In the forest, you must be prepared for anything. Anticipate what might happen, so you can react if it does."

There was no way Rowena could guess what everything around her would do. The woman expected the impossible.

"We have reached the sacred glen. Only my mother may grant your stay in our lands. She will only speak to me. I must listen to her voice. It is imperative that you make no sound. As keeper of the scroll, she is in permanent silent contemplation, absorbing wisdom."

Rowena glanced around. "If she can't speak, how will you hear her?"

"There are many ways to communicate. Come." Ida held up her hand. "I will show you where to sit. In silence."

She repeated the command as if she didn't trust Rowena. Which wasn't completely offensive. Ida couldn't know she had ignored suggestions from other royals before.

She would follow along this time, though.

There was an alluring presence about the dryad princess. It welcomed like a hug. And terrified like an executioner.

Rowena would stay silent.

Ida strode toward two tall willows, branches hanging as full green curtains. They shouldn't have survived under the imposing pines. Yet they flourished with shiny leaves, gleaming like polished emeralds.

The dryad ducked through the drapery and disappeared.

Rowena hurried to follow.

She stepped inside, where more willows created a wide circle. But it was the oak in the center that stole her breath away.

Its majestic canopy soared higher than any other tree. It spread at least seventy feet in all directions. Sweeping limbs kissed the ground, then rose, twisting into a tangled crown. The trunk, wide and gnarled, anchored it all.

When Ida pointed to a root, rising out of the ground, twenty feet from the nearest branch. Rowena perched against the make-shift seat. The moment she touched the rough bark, the leaves of the oak's canopy rustled, though there was no breeze.

The air in the glen remained calm, peaceful.

Ida faced the oak and dropped to her knees and bowed her head.

Time seemed to hold its breath.

4

BRAM

Not since Bram had become the Seeker had he experienced such an intense burning in his chest. When he melded with the druid, the white light of the Primary Fae was like stepping into a crucible. His skin lit on fire. Burned to ash.

Reformed in Saganus.

A side-effect of his transformation, no doubt.

The pure primary form would not mix with his shadows.

Light versus dark. Competitors, not allies.

Though Bram had returned to his elven form, the Seeker scratched beneath the surface. Whether he traveled in light or dark, the Heptad forever changed him.

No longer a druid. No longer an elf. Yet still both.

The painful experience hadn't been his alone.

Lhoris had ripped her hand away the moment they arrived. She doubled over, hands braced on her knees, gasping. It took long moments before she stood upright.

Even then, her face stayed pale, brow sheened with sweat.

They'd arrived at Aethercrest, the massive ziggurat with the Heptad's cylindrical Tower of Enlightenment, rising over all of Saganus.

"Wait here. I will confer with the Heptad and return. You can slip that over what you're wearing." She nodded to a ceremonial robe hanging from a hook on the wall; the blue silk of his former sentinel order.

Lhoris' hand still trembled as she slipped through the twenty-foot oak doors, carved with ancient Caelus symbols.

Bothered that he needed approval to enter, Bram stared at the blue robe.

A tightness grew inside his chest. Being back in the druid homeland twisted something deep. As if he was still that naïve youth, eager to be a hero. As if what had happened to him could be swept aside.

Ignored.

When they arrived, his clothes had shifted with him. The blue tunic and black trousers, the uniform of a sentinel.

His old life.

But the robe was more appropriate for a meeting with the Heptad.

Disgust mixed with regret surged through him as he closed his eyes and slipped the robe over his clothes.

Bram ambled to a window and rested his hands on the ledge. The Radiant Garden, encircling Aethercrest, providing beauty and greenery. Hedges twisted in intricate patterns. Scattered ornament trees dotted each triangular, sprawling lawn.

To the south, the city spread below. Ordered, narrow streets. Thatch-roof homes of dried mud-brick. A dull gray-brown quilt beyond the brightness of the Garden.

It seemed more crowded than he remembered.

High palisade walls ringed the island. A shield against dangerous ocean storms. And a barrier.

To ensure privacy. Or was it seclusion?

Only those invited dared approach the druid homeland.

Like Havilar.

He had to believe the dryads had allowed Rowena to remain at the cottage. He'd go mad if he didn't. He had to keep his wits. Clear his name and get back to her side.

Those few allowed to trade goods were scrutinized mercilessly before earning an entry pass. They had to learn the endless maze of rules in Saganus.

Difficult enough for druids, impossible for visitors.

Bram had devoted himself to law and order, even as the Heptad spun endless new regulations. Since he'd been gone, they'd most likely added several more. Rules they would judge him by.

He had accepted so much out of blind loyalty.

That was why they had chosen him to become the Seeker. He had valued dedication. Loyalty. Above all else.

Which made questioning him now sting worse.

The dryad queen would recognize Rowena's Lunara powers. Would allow her to stay. Alona had not changed out of her oak form in a millennium, it made sense she hadn't come herself.

But why send an emissary at all?

He never should have left. He should have made Lhoris wait.

As if he had any say against the Heptad.

Bram shifted his weight, leaning his shoulder against the cold stone wall.

Muscles coiled tight. His fingers drummed against the hilt of his dagger.

Restless.

Irritated.

It wasn't his fault. But he hadn't kept his word to Rowena. It tore at his gut.

She expected him to fail her. And he had.

Respecting druid customs, he waited. Like an errant elfling. His temper grew with every heartbeat. When the door finally cracked open, and only Lhoris emerged, he fumed.

"What is taking so long?" Bram's teeth squeaked in his ears as he growled out the words. A pang of regret followed when she winced. She followed the Heptad's commands, just as he did.

"You are welcome to wait inside. However, the council has retired to their small meeting chambers for private discussion before they hear your testimony." Her voice was calmer now. The demanding tone stripped away now that they had returned.

Bram clenched his fists at his sides, inhaling once then spoke. "Why summon me here with such urgency only to play games? I have left a moon-born in a precarious position for their convenience."

Lhoris held up her hand. "I'm aware of the situation, and I'm afraid I have no answer for you. The only consolation I can offer is that I have been ordered to retrieve her. The Heptad did not make it clear to me that if she was with you, I was to bring her as well."

Concern quickly swallowed the brief rush of relief. Rowena wouldn't be left alone with the dryads, but she would be terrified traveling with a stranger. She would resist. She would be furious when she arrived in another foreign place against her will.

At least he could greet her when she arrived.

If she would even want to see him.

"I will go with haste before any others can reach her."

Bram leaned back. Others? "What do you mean by that? Who else is searching?"

The druid blanched. Her mouth opened, then closed again.

Why did she struggle?

"There have been reports, but you should speak with the council. The Heptad will have the most up-to-date information."

"Tell me what you know." The Heptad demanded answers from him, bur made him wait for theirs. He needed answers now.

Lhoris' lips parted, then flattened into a thin line.

A quick glance over her shoulder. Fingers twitching inside her sleeves. She was hiding something.

Bram's jaw locked.

"There are rumors the King of Mortus has sent scouts."

Fire flared through Bram's chest. "How would Ha'mon arrange that? He's imprisoned under the barrows."

Lhoris fidgeted. "He has ways of sending messages. The Heptad hasn't uncovered how. What is known is this: He believes if his followers gather the armor pieces . . . and he gets hold of a moon-born . . . he can unlock the gates and free himself during the Reaping."

"Word has spread, then? I understood information about the moon-born was secret." Bram raked his hand through his hair, staring blindly over the landscape. "It's even more important now to finish this business. And get on my way."

Lhoris twisted her lips. "It is not just Ha'mon."

Bram snapped his gaze back to the paritor. "Explain."

"Tanith also has spies, too. She's searching for anyone of noble blood, and the right age. Her vendetta against Ha'mon makes her just as dangerous to Edenia. Just as dangerous to the moon-born."

Bram gripped the window ledge until his knuckles shone like bone. "We cannot afford this delay."

Lhoris forced a weak smile. "It's true. The scent of change is in the air. We must keep faith that the Heptad has the best plan for everyone."

Bram closed his eyes. He wanted to believe that. He had volunteered to become the Seeker because of faith in the Heptad's guidance.

Before everything went sideways.

And now they called him away from his duty. Duty they had

insisted he race to complete. For what? To accuse him of failing them?

It made no sense.

"This is a reckless. They have to understand that."

Lhoris cleared her throat, nervous or frustrated. He couldn't tell.

"I must go. I will return as quickly as I can. You are welcome to step inside the outer chamber and wait. That way, you'll know the minute the Heptad returns."

She didn't wait for his answer, hurrying down the open-air, curving staircase that encircled the tower.

Why hadn't she just left through the light? Aeternus was massive; sprawling. What did she have to retrieve before she left?

So many things were not adding up.

Lhoris was the newest paritor. He shouldn't have been so short-tempered with her. As one of seven apprentices-in-waiting, she trained for the day one of the Heptad fell. Whatever they bid her to do, she could not question.

Their orders had to be she raced through the ziggurat on foot.

Bram rubbed the spots on his forehead where his horns sprouted in his other form. With Ha'mon and Tanith in pursuit, it was more urgent than ever to retrieve the sword from Fidessa.

He doubted she would hand the armor to anyone from Mortus. Would she?

He had to think it through. What advantage would Fidessa gain by aligning with the king? Or with Tanith?

That thought gave him pause.

Tanith's daughter created the first witches. Tanith still called herself Queen of Mortus, Mother of Witches, and ruled from her throne in Anomie.

Surely, she wouldn't ally with a mage?

Finding the moon-born had just become much harder.

Sawel slipped toward the horizon. The day waned as he waited.

Lhoris had made a fair point. He needed to be available when the Heptad returned. Bram pulled open the heavy door and stepped inside.

Sage and sandalwood assaulted his nose. His stomach lurched. He had to brace himself against the wall. The scent dragged him back to the day of his transformation. The day he became the Seeker.

He rolled his neck.

Forced his mind back to the task at hand.

Open tomes and unfurled scrolls littered the semi-circular table, where seven high-backed chairs waited for the council. No one else could sit in their presence. Petitioners stood alone, exposed, in the room's exact center.

Bram wandered the dark-paneled room while he waited. The back wall held only one door, leading into the private meeting chambers. Easy to know when they entered. Twelve shelves, stretching fifteen feet high, lined the two side walls, each crammed with tomes and scrolls.

Bram scanned the titles. Most were journals documenting misdeeds and punishments. He huffed under his breath. He pulled down a volume and flipped to a random page. Lines of text chronicled ridiculously minor infractions that were punished with overwhelming severity.

One story told of a city merchant, late to a meeting because a loose vulugoat wrecked his shop. A few minutes' delay. Still, the Heptad found him guilty of disrespect.

Ordered him to pay a full month's wages—to the Heptad.

The second, slighted, merchant, received only two mynts.

Bram shoved the book back onto the shelf. A heavy pressure

sank into his gut. He was no mere merchant selling pots and jars.

But would they strip him of his position just as easily?

A journal lay open on the Heptad's table. Bram edged closer, wondering what crimes filled its pages now.

He tilted his head to read it upside-down. Not current. Not petty disobedience.

An account of a disavowed druid; one who had refused to give her elfling to the pedagogue over twenty summers ago.

The vivens trained all elflings. It had been that way for centuries.

Why would she risk everything? And why was the Heptad dredging it up now?

Every druid, elfling or grown, devoted themselves to protecting the Primary Spring.

No other race had that privilege.

Without druids guarding the Spring's distribution of power to the heartstones, there would be no enchantment at all.

If elflings weren't housed in the pedagogue, the rites and traditions of Saganus would collapse.

That destruction would spill into every other realm, dragging all of Edenia down with it.

Elflings needed strict instruction. The kind only the vivens could give.

No wonder the Heptad dealt so harshly with any who defied them.

There were disavowed in every realm he'd crossed, searching for the moon-born. Searching for Rowena.

He unwittingly brushed his fingers over his chest.

The disavowed were marked forever for all to see. White hair, like his Seeker form.

But silver eyes. Not gold like his.

And they were trapped in their elven forms.

The room grew too warm. Bram pressed both hands against both temples; vision blurring.

Bright lights burned overhead.

He lay in the lazaret, broken.

They'd promised it would be simple. A minor diversion of the Primary Spring's powers. A faster way to travel through the realms.

Easier.

Instead, a fever raged through his body. Bloodied bandages covered his hands, where claws ripped through his skin. A headache hammered at his skull where horns had torn from his brow bone.

Any movement made him retch as if his body was being torn in two.

Mereb came to his side. Once. She laid a tentative hand on his arm. "Is the pain bearable?"

He'd swallowed. Once. Twice. Finally forced out a whisper. "Yes."

"It wasn't supposed to happen this way," she said. "The enchantment flared . . . we couldn't control it."

"Fix it." His voice, breathless. Hoarse.

She dropped her hand into her lap. Her voice turned somber. "I'm afraid it is your expectations that must change."

Instead of a heroic quest through the light, he tore himself apart as shadows, terrifying the chosen into obedience.

The chamber door swung open, snapping Bram back into the present.

He crossed his arms over his chest, refusing to step back as each hepta entered.

"You know where to stand, Seeker," High Hepta Achan said. The oldest of them; sharpest points to his ears, longest lobes that wobbled when he shook his head.

Bram didn't move. He held his ground. Jaw locked.

A challenge? No. A demand.

The silver-robed heptas flanked Achan's sides. Waiting. Silent. Expecting Bram's disobedience to end.

Anyone allowed inside had to stand dead center on the small circle embedded into the stone. The Mark of Testimony. Three lines carved deep: truth, justice, respect.

The values demanded of all. Council and petitioners alike.

Bram pinched his lips together. A churning ball of acid boiled in his gut, rising through his chest.

He believed in those values. He questioned if the Heptad did.

He waited, silent. One heartbeat. Two.

Forcing his fingers to stretch at his sides. This was the ruling council of Edenia. Deemed by Osric, worthy to care for all the realms. Maybe it was his own heart; his hubris to be great that tainted the procedure. That birthed the shadows inside him.

Had he wanted glory more than truth? More than justice? The least he could do now was offer respect.

If he could tame the restless anger, clawing at his ribs.

He exhaled. Forced his feet to slide back. Deliberate, slow . . . until he stood atop the mark. But he did not wait for the Heptad's permission to speak.

"I've had time to do some reading while I waited." A muscle ticked in his jaw. "A late arrival, it seems, is a punishable offense."

"Insolence will not help you here today." Hepta Nasir, fifth, tall, hulking, arms nearly dragging the floor, scowled down at him. A brow so heavy it made him look perpetually brooding.

Ignoring the rebuke, Achan gave a slight gesture to the others, then sank into the largest chair at the table's center. The others followed, silent shadows settling into place.

"You are here, in part," Achan's voice cut like cold iron, "to explain why you chose to form a physical bond with the moon-born, Rowena."

Straight to the point. Bram could almost admire that.

"Which then caused you to cede the Sword of Justice to a Telana mage," Folas added. He leaned his arms on the table, beady eyes darting from one council member to another, never once landing on Bram.

"I received no instructions forbidding attachment. Rowena is the first moon-born I discovered, and I protected her as I saw fit. I can recount every step, where I found her, what's happened since, but it will take time. Would you like to hear the truth?"

"Do not be flippant. This is a serious charge." The newest hepta, Siora, sat straight-backed, her blonde hair slicked into a tight, severe bun.

"We are seated. The proceedings have begun, Hepta Siora." Mereb's voice cut across the room, calm but sharp. "Must I remind you that only the Triad may question until we sequester?"

Mereb, second only to Achan, sat stiffly at his right. Bram's only true ally among the seven. Her gaze simmered against the younger hepta, full of silent warning.

Everyone knew: Only the Triad, Achan, Folas, and Mereb, held the right to interrogate.

Siora lowered her gaze in silence.

"My duty is my priority." Bram kept his voice even, though fury boiled under his skin. He did care for Rowena. A great deal. That was none of their concern, nor did it hinder his performance. "These questions don't require my presence. Lhoris could have delivered my report. Instead, I was forced to abandon Rowena in a dangerous situation."

"She is being secured from the dryads." Folas waved a cold, dismissive hand.

Bram steadied himself. "That has been shared with me. Has Lhoris returned with her yet?"

A low shuffle across the table. No one rushed to answer.

"If the dryads forced her out," Mereb said at last, voice even, "she may be harder for the paritor to retrieve."

Bram's stomach twisted.

If Rowena had been expelled, stripped of her protection, she would be trapped, hunted, lost.

"Is it true that Ha'mon and Tanith both have scouts searching for moon-born?" Bram could not believe that was not the top priority of this council.

"We have heard rumors of such," Mereb said. "Though nothing has been substantiated."

"We must deal with these matters first," Achan said, tone heavy with finality. "Then we will dispatch whatever actions are necessary. To the dryads, and any others that need to come to heel."

If the situation was so easy to deal with, why did they need Bram? What good was the Seeker. There was more going on. But what?

"He has not even answered the first question put forth." Folas glanced to his right and left at each of the others. "How are we to trust he will cooperate? Someone else, an eye witness, brought these concerns to us. They are not frivolous charges."

"You speak true," Achan answered. "Of bigger concern, Seeker, is the accusation that you are actively persecuting those from other lands. Involving yourself in other realm's affairs."

Bram grit his teeth together so hard the muscles in his jaw popped. He may have broken a tooth. They didn't care that every second they debated, endangered Rowena's life. "My purpose is to aid in Edenia's preservation, not weaken it."

"Yet you involved yourself in Ibern's battles," Siora said, lifting her pointed chin higher in defiance.

"I will not warn you again," Mereb said, her voice losing its calm demeanor. "If you are unable, or unwilling, to adhere to protocol, recuse yourself."

Bram ignored their squabble over procedure. He addressed the hepta's statement. "To protect Rowena and the Sword of Justice."

"So then, a mage did not disappear with the Sword as we've heard?" Achan leveled his narrowed stare at Bram. A glint in his eye told Bram the high hepta already had the answer.

"The former Queen of Ibern possesses the sword. That is true. Which is why I should not be wasting time defending myself in this chamber."

"You have failed, then." Folas leaned forward, his gaze finally landing on Bram with an unwavering, searing glare. "We believed in you when you pleaded to become the Seeker. But you were not strong enough after all."

Bram's temper snapped.

Too many emotions.

Rowena. Alone. Waiting.

Insults.

Betrayal.

He transformed.

Shadows exploded from his skin.

Billowing across the floor, crawling like dark vines toward the council table.

Every hepta leapt to their feet. In a blink, seven bodies of pure white light flared across from him.

"How dare you bring that form into this chamber!" Achan's voice came from his form but filled the room with so much power that Bram stumbled backward. He had never challenged a Primary Druid before. What was he thinking?

He wasn't.

He should have kept his temper in check. No matter what.

He closed his eyes, slowing his racing heart. The Seeker receded and Bram returned.

Several heartbeats after that, the council members also returned.

No one moved to sit. Siora stared wide-eyed, her chest heaving. Achan and Folas glared, and tears glistened on Mereb's cheeks.

"We are done for today." Achan's voice cracked with rage. "We will sequester, and decide your fate."

He spun away, storming into the antechamber.

The others followed.

All except Mereb.

5

EVORA

Evora knelt behind the cascading veil of a willow, her breath slow, controlled. The weeping branches swayed in the whispering wind, cloaking her as she watched the outsider.

Golden-haired. Sun-kissed. Unrooted.

Her grandmother's vast, twisted roots had risen from the earth to form a natural seat beneath the girl. Strange, to see an outsider sit so still, waiting for a sentence that could never end in her favor.

Evora pressed her palm against the damp soil, reaching, listening. The heartbeat of the land thrummed beneath her fingers, the gentle hum of the ancient trees, the murmur of leaves brushing against one another, the whisper of the wind through the towering canopy.

Everything connected to the land made itself known.

Everything except her.

Evora frowned. Even the smallest insect had a place in the forest's rhythm. Even the moss beneath her knees, the tiniest sprout of green, pulsed with life's minerals.

But the stranger?

She was something else.

Evora crept closer, moving with the forest not against it. Each step precise, her bare feet silent against the land.

The outsider's clothing baffled her. Unlike her living garments, these didn't breathe or pulse with life! No woven bark that shifted with movement, no vines that curled with the day's warmth. The fabric just sat there stiff, silent on the elf's body.

How strange! Evora tilted her head, fascinated.

The material seemed like it had once been part of nature, but had forgotten its roots. Why would anyone wear something so disconnected from the forest's song?

And her hair. Evora's eyes widened. The woman's braid reminded her of sunlight through leaves, twisted like the vines Evora trained along the elder trees. Did she weave it herself each morning? Did she whisper to it as it grew?

A bubbling excitement swelled in Evora's chest. Where had this stranger come from? Did she hear the trees singing their morning songs? Had she ever lain on her stomach, feeling the soil's heartbeat thrum through her bones?

Evora couldn't resist. She had to know more.

Without thinking, she darted forward, her fingers brushing the odd braid. Dry. Brittle. Yet warm, like sun-heated stone.

A sharp gasp.

Evora's heart lurched.

The woman spun. Eyes wide, startled.

Instinct took over. Evora pressed a finger to her lips. A silent plea.

The stranger didn't move.

Their eyes locked—green to gold.

Recognition. Not of the face, but of something deeper.

A connection.

A sharp crack split the air, striking Evora's backside. She yelped.

The outsider clapped both hands over her mouth, stifling her own cry.

Evora's stomach twisted. Who had caught her? Her mother? Or worse, her grandmother?

She didn't dare look away. The stranger's presence should have felt wrong, but it didn't.

For the first time, Evora defied the sacred commands. Had broken something old and holy.

And yet ... she did not regret it.

6

ROWENA

IDA JUMPED TO HER FEET, hands on her hips, and glared, thankfully at the other woman, not Rowena.

The closest willow parted its green curtain and remained that way, providing a swift exit, but no one moved.

Ida rolled her eyes and made a sharp shooing gesture.

The other woman lunged, snagging Rowena's sleeve to tug her forward. Rowena started to protest until the root she sat on sank into the soil, dropping her into the dirt.

Ida gestured for Rowena to leave as well. Stunned, she scrambled to her feet and stumbled after her new captor.

Once beyond the willows, away from the sacred glen, they halted.

"What land are you from? How did you get here? I'm called Evora. Do you have a name? You must have a heartstone. Which one?" The questions tumbled out in a single hurried breath.

This dryad did not act like Ida at all, though she appeared a younger replica. Same loose, dark hair, same copper-toned skin, same deep brown eyes. Whoever she was, Ida had allowed her to take Rowena from the glen. She would answer her questions, if she could remember them all.

"My name is Rowena. I'm from Skandan, and I arrived here with . . ."

Who was Bram to her? A friend? A guide?

More?

Her heart pinched. Thinking of him reminded her how far they'd been torn apart, and how long it might be before they found each other again.

"Is there someone else in the forest? We must go find them."

Rowena touched Evora's arm, halting her frantic search. "You ask too many questions. No one else is with me."

Evora giggled. "We don't get visitors. Not ones who are granted an audience with my grandmother, anyway."

"You're Ida's daughter." Interesting. Where Ida was stoic and stern, Evora blazed with restless light.

"Why did you interrupt? I don't want your mother blaming me for that." Rowena twisted toward the glen, fear curling in her chest. Angering the princess, or worse, the queen, was not a mistake she could afford.

Evora waved the concern away. "Mother knows it was me. Grandmother told her I was there right before she reprimanded me. It was Grandmother's idea to let you leave with me."

"You speak to the trees like your mother?" Rowena's skin prickled. It unnerved her, the idea of a forest whispering secrets she couldn't hear.

"Anything that holds the land's minerals, we share a sylvatic link with. But my mother isn't speaking to a tree; she's speaking to my grandmother."

"Who is a tree?"

Evora grinned. "My grandmother is a dryad, like my mother, like me. We have both elven and tree forms. You said you were from Skandan. That makes you Telana, right?"

Rowena's cheeks warmed. She should have made the

connection sooner. "My mother was Lunara and my father Telana. I am both."

"Elves do that? Mix themselves up? Strange. Is that why you were sent here?"

Rowena stiffened. "I was not sent here. You make it seem as if I'm corrupted. I am not. I am elven. There's no difference, only whether we carry enchantment or not."

"I meant no offense. It's just different from how we do things here."

"Different doesn't mean wrong." Rowena's throat tightened at the insult. She twisted to stare at the willows. "Perhaps I should go back."

"No, please stay! I apologize again. I'd love to get to know you. I promise I'll try to rein in my questions." Evora bounced slightly. "I never talk this much, really! It's just so exciting having an outsider among us."

"I'm not sure I am staying." Rowena rubbed her arm, wary. "That's what your mother and grandmother are deciding."

The willow branches parted. Ida strolled toward them, her presence cutting through the glen like a blade.

"Alona has offered you an invitation," Ida said, surprising Rowena.

"She has? That's wonderful!" Evora seized both of Rowena's hands, practically vibrating. "Now you can come with me, and tell me everything about your lands."

Ida lifted a hand. "You are to finish your daily rituals, Evora. This has nothing to do with you."

"But what is she supposed to do?" Evora jabbed her hand onto her hip, stubborn.

"Not your concern." Ida's brow arched, patient and lethal. "Off with you."

Evora twisted her lips. "It was nice to meet you, Rowena. Perhaps our paths will cross again. Be well."

It was such a final statement.

Ida stood with her arms crossed over her chest. Rowena said nothing, only giving a small wave to Evora.

Once Evora disappeared, Ida turned fully to Rowena. "Mother Alona has insisted you stay. And I must train you. It is a rare gift, one you must not waste."

Train? In what?

The idea of speaking to the trees intrigued Rowena, but she didn't have that kind of time. "I only came for permission to stay in the forest. I have to return to the cottage."

"That permission may come later," Ida said. "For now, you will stay and train. You are unprepared for our lands. You are not allowed to travel through them alone."

Rowena gritted her teeth. "There is a task I must complete before Masah is full again.

"Only you will determine how long you stay," Ida said "Learn quickly, and you are free to go. Follow me. See what awaits."

Rowena hesitated as Ida marched off. She could find her way back to the cottage. If Bram arrived first, he would search for her. Then they would find each other, and leave on their own terms.

"Rowena," Ida's voice cut through the clearing. "If you refuse this training, Mother Alona will insist you remain in Havilar for all time. As others have who tested her patience."

Rowena scanned the ground, checking for roots ready to slap or drag her under.

Her heart pounded. Her palms itched.

She needed a way to convince the dryads to let her leave, without enduring endless lessons. Rowena hurried to catch up with Ida, planting each step carefully.

If being the perfect pupil was what it took, then so be it.

Rowena found Ida, standing on a stone outcropping, staring at a vast pattern traced in the meadow below. White stones outlined winding paths, coiling toward a center filled with small semi-circular openings—then mirrored the journey outward.

"You must walk the labyrinth."

Relief flooded Rowena's chest. If that was all the they required, she'd be free within the hour. "Let's get down there."

For the first time since she'd met Ida, a corner of the dryad's mouth tipped into a grin.

By the time they reached the labyrinth's entrance, evening had fallen. The fist-sized white stones that outlined the winding paths shimmered faintly under the deepening sky.

No trees blocked the wide-open sky. Masah's pale, waxing gibbous hung low on the horizon. Ghostly, waiting to spill its silver light.

Rowena's skin prickled with anticipation.

"Enter here," Ida said, pointing to the opening at their feet. "Follow the path to the center. Walk deliberately, never run. At each of the six archways, contemplate what you have learned. When you reach the center, retrace your steps exactly. Stay within the marked path. Do not disturb the stones. I will wait here."

"What happens if I bump one?"

"You must drop to your knees and spend five minutes in contemplative silence before continuing."

What a ridiculous waste of time. Rowena set her jaw. She glanced from the labyrinth to Ida. "All I have to do is follow the circle?"

Ida dipped her chin, solemn. "When you have searched inside your heart and uncovered your inner strength, you will have completed the task."

The woman spoke in riddles. Rowena doubted a thousand winding steps inside a rock-made circle would uncover anything she didn't already know. But if completing this foolishness earned her freedom, Rowena would play along. She'd finish it. Return to the cottage. Maybe Bram would already be there.

Worried, waiting for her.

Rowena lifted her foot to step forward, but Ida's hand clamped onto her arm, stopping her.

"Before you enter, focus on your breathing. Find your center. Let your awareness expand beyond yourself, so you can hear the guidance you seek."

Rowena offered her a tight, brittle smile and obeyed. She inhaled deeply. Exhaled slowly. Then strode into the labyrinth before Ida could halt her again.

It wasn't a difficult task. The path was flat, the way simple, though narrow enough that she had to place her feet toe-to-heel to stay within it. A strange wind picked up, curling around her braid like a mischievous elfling. Rowena stiffened. She bit back a growl, resisting the urge to swat at nothing like a fool.

Her fourth veer left brought her alongside the open center. Rowena eyed the stones. One leap, and she could cut the task by half.

A shift in the air. Rowena froze. Ida's gaze pinned her in place, sharp as a blade. Her arms remained folded; her head tilted in silent warning.

Rowena grumbled under her breath. So much for shortcuts. One foot, another. Follow the path. She stole a glance at Masah. The calm moon would guide her through the forest, and restore her powers. Perhaps, if she arrived before Bram, she'd start a fire, roast some potatoes. Pretend this whole mess had never happened.

Rowena navigated a long curve hugging the labyrinth's outer

edge. As she passed near Ida, she forced a polite smile, hiding the seethe curling in her gut.

Was the dryad buying her show of sincerity? Rowena didn't risk glancing to check. Instead, she made a sharp right turn, putting her back to Ida, and rolled her eyes, exhaling a long, slow breath of frustration. There were a hundred better ways to spend her time, yet here she was, walking in circles.

Ida had said walk, but she hadn't said how fast. Rowena quickened her pace, setting each foot down sharply, as if daring the stones to challenge her.

The path twisted unexpectedly, doubling back when she thought she understood it. One moment, the center gleamed ahead, tantalizingly close, the next, the trail yanked her sideways, spitting her back toward the edge.

Her temples throbbed. A headache bloomed at the base of her skull as she squinted at the winding, endless trail ahead. When she finally reached the center, the world tilted under her feet, subtle at first, then stronger until she had to plant her boots wider to stay upright.

The rounded archways fanned before her, silent, expectant. Rowena stepped into the first one. Reflect, Ida had said. Rowena closed her eyes. Nothing. Her mind stayed stubbornly blank. No revelations. No spiritual insights. Only the gnawing sense of precious time bleeding away. She would invent something suitably profound for Ida by the time she finished.

The journey outward should have been familiar. A simple reversal. Instead, each turn jolted her, corners sharper, twists more abrupt than she remembered.

Shadows stretched across the path, darker and longer, reaching for her feet. The sounds from outside the labyrinth—birds calling, branches creaking—pressed against her ears, unnaturally loud.

Rowena's breath quickened. Her chest squeezed. By the time

she stumbled free of the labyrinth, her heart pounded against her ribs.

Ida stood waiting, arms crossed, face unreadable.

The sky deepened to the rich, velvet blue, the last breath before true darkness. The towering trees would soon devour the moonlight completely. Rowena glanced upward. She would need to stay under the moons as long as possible, draw every scrap of energy they could offer. Whatever waited between these ancient trunks, she would not face it drained.

"What wisdom have you gained?" Ida's gaze bored into her, unblinking, unrelenting.

Rowena shifted under its weight.

She straightened her shoulders. Stared off to the left, buying time to think. "The path to a goal is not always a straight line." A faint, unbidden smiled touched her lips. The memory of her mother's voice surfaced, unexpected, bittersweet.

"Very good." Ida clasped her hands in front of her and waited.

"So, I can leave?" Rowena rocked up on her toes, poised to bolt for freedom.

"Have you aligned your inner heartwood with that of the outer world?"

Rowena wrinkled her nose. "What did that even mean?"

Ida settled deeper onto her heels. "Then you have not completed your task."

7

BRAM

Despite everything else, the moment Bram stood in front of Mereb alone, something inside of him unlocked. A quiet knowing that he didn't bear the world's weight alone. She always had done that for him. Through everything.

"How are you feeling? Truthfully." Mereb's face softened, faint lines creasing her forehead as she studied him.

All the fight drained from Bram. He let his chin drop. "I'm better. The changes aren't so difficult. The pain is gone."

"I'm glad to hear that." A wobbly smile flickered across her lips. "I'm sorry that you have to do this alone. I'm sure it isn't easy."

He wasn't alone, not anymore. But that had gotten him here, facing reprimand. "Would it be so bad . . . if I had someone to care about?" Someone who cared about me, he wanted to add, but the words lodged in his throat.

"It's unfortunate that you found the Lunara first. There's so much we don't know about the moon-born. What they can do, why they can do it. To be so close to one who can manipulate emotions," Mereb shrugged, "how would you know if she's being honest with you or just using you for some purpose that could tear the realms apart?"

Rowena would not do such a thing. "She hasn't fully developed her skills. Her mother was the only other Lunara in Skandan. She died before they had time for training."

"All the more reason to be cautious. And to keep your heart out of your duty."

A vice clamped around his throat. He only nodded, hoping it seemed sincere.

"Without more knowledge we're all vulnerable. That's why your mission is so critical. The end of the Age is upon us. No realm is safe."

"Are we certain about the timing? How can we be sure the next Burning Moon will arrive with the Reaping, just because it happened that way once before?"

"Queen Albruna herself came to deliver the news. Failure is not an option." Mereb pinned him with a thoughtful expression. "Have you told this moon-born there are others?"

Bram swallowed. Mereb always read him too easily, knowing more about him than anyone. Even as an elfling, during walks outside the pedagogy, or quiet games of Peril, she'd figure his strategy early and counter to win. He'd beaten her only once. The last time they ever played. Right before he volunteered to become the Seeker. There was no use lying now.

"Yes."

"That was a mistake. It is imperative to keep this information out of the wrong hands. That would cause panic among all the realms. The moon-born would be hunted relentlessly, ruthlessly. It could thrust us into another Chasm. If the prophecy fails, Edenia will fall. You must prevent this."

"I understand. However," he closed his eyes, "isn't my time here taking away from that purpose?"

"It is a necessary interruption to ensure you stay on task.

Your lapse of judgment concerns us. We need to decide if we've made the right decision, before any more time is lost."

"How can you believe the word of a spy in this situation? Who could be so credible their word outweighs mine? No one but Rowena knows my identity."

"She's learned who you are?" Mereb pressed her fingers to her temples. "Bram, you cannot continue in this way. You are the Seeker, a force of power like no other. You must remain neutral. Determined. Nothing is more important than securing the moon-born and every piece of armor. No other moon-born can witness your elven form. Is that understood?"

"Yes."

"There is also a rumor that the Sword of Justice is missing the Lunastone. Is it true?"

Where was she getting her information? "How do you know that?"

"I have many sources throughout Edenia."

"Most realms are either vying for power, or isolated. How do you find anyone trustworthy to cooperate?"

"We are Primary Fae. We are not hindered by realm boundaries or petty squabbles. It's only prudent to gather information through sources beyond the Spring. We must understand all perspectives."

"Even from the Oraku?"

"The disavowed who serve royals and nobles sometimes provide assistance. But there are other, anonymous, sources who have proven the most valuable. Don't let that concern you. Just remember your duty."

Mereb patted his arm with a soft smile, then paused at the council door and twisted to face him. "And Bram, when Rowena is recovered, she will remain here. We can't risk her exposing your identity. Even by accident."

Bram stood frozen as Mereb vanished behind the door. That

could not happen. He promised Rowena protection, and being trapped in Saganus, hidden by the Heptad, was no more than another cage. She wouldn't stand for it. And he would make sure she didn't have to.

Somehow.

He scrubbed his hand over his face. The air seemed to squeeze closer from all sides. He needed to get outside, walk it off. There was time before the Heptad made their decision. The market would serve as a perfect distraction.

Bram descended the curving open-air stairs along the outside of the Heptad's tower until he reached the smallest square of Aethercrest. The paritors' residences. Each lower square of the ziggurat grew wider until the bottom formed the receiving hall, where the Heptad heard public grievances once a month. That was where Bram headed.

The hall stretched sixty feet on each side, divided into thirds by massive twenty-foot-high columns supporting the upper levels. Open-air windows ushered in the sweet scents of jasmine, hazel, and elderberry from the Radiant Garden beyond.

His footsteps echoed against the tile. There had once been tables laden with food, seating for those waiting to petition the Heptad, or simply needing time to reflect, to honor Osric and Caelus.

Now, the room now stood empty.

A lonely monument to how much had changed in the short time he'd been away.

Twilight veiled the sky as he strolled along the graveled walkway to the front gates. Evening prayers at the Well of Reflection had ended, leaving the manicured gardens, fountains, and statues lining the main path in quiet respite. From the tower's politics and the bustling markets outside the walls.

An entire day gone with nothing gained.

Yet, Bram's mind kept circling back to Rowena and what

might happen to her next. She had endured enough. Now the Heptad wanted to become another captor.

So lost in thought, he almost collided with two sentinels barring the tall, iron gates.

"The gates are closed until Morning Blessing," one sentinel said. Tall and thin, he met Bram's gaze squarely.

Bram still wore the blue robe of their order. It should have marked him as one of their own. "I wish to find a meal in town."

The second guard, younger, blinked nervously, glancing between Bram and his partner. He took in Bram's attire, then snapped his gaze straight ahead. "Apologies, sir. We have our orders."

"Why are the gates locked at all?" Another change since he'd left.

Both sentinels exchanged a look, each silently urging the other to speak. Finally, the first answered. "The Heptad wishes to prevent the town from disturbing the Garden at night."

"The Garden is a place of refuge for all druids."

"With your pardon, sir, it seems you haven't visited our realm for some time. A curfew has been instituted because it's not safe to move about town after dusk." The second sentinel stood rigid, uniform crisp. Perfect posture. His first post out of training, most likely.

Was that what he'd become—a visitor?

Interesting that neither Lhoris nor the Heptad had mentioned the restriction. Apparently, they hadn't expected him to leave the tower.

"It would be best if you returned to your room. Meal will be served inside," the first sentinel said.

It wasn't an order, but Bram bristled at the commanding tone nonetheless. "Perhaps I'll do that after I visit the Well. My meeting kept me from Evening Blessing."

He would leave another way. The sentinels didn't need reprimanded because of him if he pulled rank.

"You must wait until morning to offer your blessing," the younger sentinel said, seeming surprised by Bram's wishes.

"I'll just take some time for quiet contemplation, then retire to my room." Bram turned on his heels and strolled toward Aethercrest's front doors.

They needed to believe the ruse. With so many changes, what had happened in the town? He had to find out for himself.

He would use the hedges for cover, slipping through the shadows unseen.

Only about a thousand druids lived in Saganus. And after Mereb's comments, he bet *every* hepta had spies watching, everywhere. Merchants, sentinels, the rare healer . . . probably reported to someone. As far as Bram knew, his other form was the only officially guarded secret. Everyone had heard of the druid-turned-Seeker, but no one knew it was him.

The Heptad had insisted the mystery would serve him well.

For now, he appreciated that he could stroll the streets without anyone shrinking from him in fear. They would feel free to speak the truth about the new rules.

Before he left, sentinels patrolled the streets, more helpers than peace-keepers. There had been no disorder in Saganus. Even the basalt pavers gleamed, merchant shops stood tidy and orderly.

But as he slipped from the shadows, ready to savor his freedom, the stench of refuse met his nostrils.

Dirt and soot stained the streets. Missing or broken stones caused an uneven surface. Most buildings sagged, their mud-brick walls crumbling. Thatch that should be a golden-brown, had dulled to a lifeless gray. Nothing was as it should be.

Bram's shoulders tensed, a knot forming deep in his muscles.

It was still early enough that the streets should have been

full of life. Vendors calling out their wares. Shoppers bustling, baskets brimming with supplies for the next day.

Instead, only a handful of others drifted along the street. Shops that should have been lively stood shuttered. Others were boarded over entirely.

His stomach rumbled at the scent of spiced meat coming from a small brasserie. The only place still open.

Lanterns hung from the roof corner, giving the place a pleasant glow, but the timbers holding a tattered covering leaned dangerously, as if one stout breeze could topple them. The vendor had his back turned, busy stoking a fire under a brick oven when Bram arrived. Several baskets sat empty where apricots, plums, and other fruits should have overflowed.

"What's the puzzled look for?" A female voice startled Bram from his inspection.

He recognized the woman at once, an old friend he'd grown up with in the pedagogy. "Farryn! What a pleasure to run into you."

Dressed in a green healer's robe, Farryn nudged his arm playfully. "Where have you been hiding these last few months?"

Their conversation caught the vendor's attention. He hurried over.

"Two knish orders?"

Thankful for the interruption, Bram hoped Farryn wouldn't press him further.

"That would be wonderful," Farryn said.

The vendor quickly filled paper cones with three meat-filled pastries each. More of a snack than a meal, but Bram wouldn't complain. He was eager to speak with his old friend.

"Would you also have a dragonfruit that my friend and I can share?" Farryn asked as the vendor handed over their food.

The vendor hesitated, then slipped behind a curtain. He returned with a rectangular package.

"Thank you." Farryn fished two coins out of a purse that hung from her belt and dropped them into vendor's waiting hand.

Another change.

Saganus rarely used mynt. Their system had been built on a trade-first philosophy. Skills offered freely, knowing the courtesy would be returned in time of need.

"Thank you," he said to Farryn. "I've not been updated on many of the new changes."

Farryn offered a smile and nod of acceptance.

Bram devoured half of his first knish in a single bite, savoring the spicy flavors, as he and Farryn strolled down the cobblestoned street.

Farryn tore a hole in the top of the package, and offered Bram a piece of speckled white fruit.

"Why so perplexed?" Farryn asked.

"These don't grow in Saganus. I'm curious about how they came to be here."

"The Heptad opened limited trade with Tixamar recently," Farryn answered. "It has brought some new opportunities—and tasty treats."

Bram frowned, contemplating the Heptad's decision. It went against many of the covenants Saganus stood upon. He wasn't opposed to interacting more with other realms of Edenia, but strangers within the druid city had the potential for dangerous repercussions.

"It's hard to envision pixies in Saganus." He shook his head, but still enjoyed the delicacy from the jungle lands.

"They are required to remain in elven form," Farryn said.

"How would anyone know if they honored that?" Bram chuckled.

Farryn raised a shoulder with an upward palm. "There are

many who question the Heptad's decisions." Her voice lowered to a whisper. "Though it is risky."

After his meeting earlier, Bram believed that easily.

"You never answered my question. Don't think I didn't notice." Farryn nibbled a bite of knish, gaze steady on Bram, brows raised in silent urging.

"I was given a task by the Heptad. One that took me away from Saganus. I'm only back for a short time."

"Away from Saganus." It wasn't a question, just a contemplative murmur. Farryn busied herself with her food, but Bram didn't trust the silence. His friend was a healer, knowledgeable in countless subjects, proficient in all of them. Questions would come. Of that, he had no doubt.

"Well, I should head back to the dispensary. It's nearly last bell. Curfew's coming."

Bram froze, knish midway to his mouth. No questions?

"You've been missed, my friend." Farryn wiped the corners of her mouth with a handkerchief from her purse. "If you've been away so long our food upsets your stomach, stop by my shop. I'm sure I can find something to help."

She patted Bram's hand, and in doing so, slipped something small into his palm. The movement was so practiced, so discreet, it stunned him.

"What is this about?"

Farryn chuckled. "It was good to see you. Be well."

Bram watched her disappear around the corner, forgetting to offer a farewell. He released a long breath and studied the token she had slipped him.

Laurel leaves curled around the edges of a flat tin circle, roughly the size of a low value mynt. But this wasn't currency. It was too light, too hollow to be worth anything.

Why had she given this to him? With so few on the streets,

what were the odds he'd run into an old friend at the first place he stopped? Or that she would seem so prepared for him.

What had he stumbled into?

He twisted, staring at the spot where Farryn had disappeared, the token cold in his hand.

No.

He had to stay focused.

Clear his name. Get back to Rowena. That was all.

His duties as Seeker had nothing to do with Saganus politics. The Heptad could manage their own troubles. The druids cared for the Primary Spring, and the enchantment flowing from it. But any unrest in Saganus would ripple across all of Edenia.

He growled under his breath and quickened his pace.

His mind wouldn't settle.

Unrest in Saganus, while Ha'mon searched for a way to escape Mortus. While a deposed queen in Anomie hunted for moon-born. And now, an old friend slipping him a cryptic message.

Bram didn't believe in coincidence. Edenia was shifting.

That much was certain.

Would it be for the better, or worse?

That he couldn't answer.

BRAM SLIPPED BACK into the Radiant Garden unnoticed. Now, inside the empty receiving hall, jaw clenched, he waited, trapped by the Heptad's timeline instead of his own.

The curfew bells Farryn mentioned had rung hours ago, their echo long faded into silence.

His gaze kept drifting to the high window, tracking Masah's path across the sky. When Lungol finally rose on the horizon,

Bram's muscles tensed. The sight of both moons only sharpened every thought of Rowena, alone and vulnerable. Without allies. With each passing mark, the distance between them gnawed at him.

He paced the hall again, boots echoing off cold stone. Hours of enforced idleness had worn his patience thin. The urge to abandon the Heptad's orders and vanish back to Havilar clawed at him.

Only his oath, and their threats, kept him rooted.

But with both moons now shimmering overhead, a restlessness surged through him. Rowena would be drawing on their energies. She had been so vulnerable lately, in ways no one else understood.

She was capable—more than capable.

Under normal circumstances, he wouldn't worry. But these weren't normal times, and his instincts screamed to be at her side.

For safety and support.

Pain constricted his heart. He exhaled slowly, peeling back the tactical facade. He missed her. That was the truth.

And it burned through his careful restraint.

The distant creak of doors snapped his attention to the far end of the hall. Lhoris approached, lantern swaying with each step.

Bram didn't wait, closing the distance at a jog.

"Have you brought Rowena?" The question tore from him before Lhoris had even stopped walking.

Lhoris inhaled deeply, her expression guarded. "She was not in the cottage when I arrived. I did my best to negotiate with the dryads, but they gave me no information. I had to return."

The dryads had her. They had to. "Queen Alona gave me assurances I could use their lands without issue. Did you speak to her?"

"I didn't." Lhoris stared at the floor. "The High Hepta says there are other resources the Heptad can use to retrieve her. He is working on it as we speak."

What other resources could the Heptad have?

Not even disavowed druids lived in Havilar. It was why he'd asked the queen to shelter him. It was the one place where he could plan how to find the moon-born, alone.

Paritors carried council authority into other realms. Lhoris had proven that well enough when she came for him.

"There is another message." Lhoris blinked rapidly, staying well out of arm's reach. "The council sent word. They won't speak to you until tomorrow."

"They must not delay me further. Come find me again once they've made up their minds."

When the first licks of shadow surrounded Bram's boots, Lhoris lunged and grabbed his sleeve. "There is more. You can't leave or you will be disavowed."

That seemed redundant. There was little left they hadn't taken from him.

Except, they'd threatened to remove him as Seeker. What would that entail? Could it even happen?

They could be bluffing.

Mereb had insisted he stay in Seeker form to find the others. She still wanted him searching.

Unless that was their plan all along. To bind him forever in Seeker form.

He yanked his arm free.

"You don't need to be present for them to bind your power." Lhoris voice wavered. "They have ways."

If he stayed locked in Seeker form, he would lose everything. His anonymity, his ability to walk among the moon-born without fear.

He would only be the nightmare.

Would Rowena still want his company if he had to stay that way forever?

"Why would they do this? They know the danger they're causing. Rowena is alone among the dryads. A rogue mage holds the Sword of Justice. This is a dereliction worse than anything I've ever done."

"Only the council can explain." Lhoris once again backed out of reach. "We are called to obey. If you'll follow me, I'll show you where you can rest."

Bram hesitated, heart hammering. If he had any chance to continue his mission, he had to keep his abilities.

All of them.

Beyond Fidessa and the dryads, there was Ha'mon. Tanith. Who would they send to capture the moon-born? The weight of the realization crashed onto his shoulders.

He had to stay.

He nodded stiffly to Lhoris and forced his feet to follow.

8

———

BRAM

LHORIS LED Bram to guest quarters on the third level of the ziggurat. Most rooms had been sealed; their furnishings packed into storage since the days when all of Saganus lived inside the massive structure. Lhoris said the majority had been closed, with all furnishings removed to storage. The only room she could offer sat on the service floor—among the cooks and maids.

"I'll be back to collect you for Morning Blessing." Lhoris left so quickly he didn't have time to grunt a response.

The room must have belonged to an elfling. The bed was a head too short for Bram, and it only took him two paces to cross from the door to the mattress. Four paces from end to end. He would do better sleeping on the floor.

After an hour of trying, and failing, to get comfortable, Bram left the cramped room for a walk, leaving his blue robe on a peg.

A stroll through the gardens might settle his frazzled nerves.

Once outdoors, he had a moment to breathe. But the tall iron gates, shut against the town beyond, reminded him of Farryn. The tin token she'd given him rested in a pouch on his belt.

What had his friend wanted to share with him?

A sentinel ambled past, twenty feet down a gravel path.

"If you're not on duty, it's curfew." The guard called; voice flat.

"Just needed some air," Bram said. "I'll go back inside shortly."

Bram offered a friendly wave. The sentinel nodded and moved on.

Bram eyed a patch of lilac-covered wall. The Heptad may have had spies, but not even they could watch every shadow.

He pretended to study the purple flowers, counting to thirty under his breath once the sentinel moved on.

Bram reached Farryn's dispensary moments later in his elven form. He stood at the building's side, cloaked in darkness, and listened.

Distant voices floated from a window a street over. A goat bleated in a pen nearby. Otherwise, the night held its breath.

No lanterns flickered from the upper floors where the healers lived. Farryn held the highest rank, but the healers were the smallest, and most mysterious order. None understood more about the natural elements of Edenia than they did. Their healing herbs, and powerful connection to nature, kept the druids strong.

He considered slipping inside to listen unseen, but the risk was too great. To his knowledge, no one in Saganus beyond the Heptad knew the Seeker's true identity. And he meant to keep it that way.

He crept to the back door and knocked, most likely the kitchen, and far more private.

When no one answered, he moved toward the front, keeping to the shadows. Even hidden from the street, he didn't want to linger. He had just rounded the corner when a soft click echoed from the back door. Bram hurried back and caught Farryn peeking through the narrow opening.

She gasped, then sighed in relief. Farryn opened the door wider and waved him inside. "I wasn't sure you'd come."

"Perhaps I misunderstood. Should I have knocked on the front?"

"No." Farryn lifted a hand, voice dropping to a whisper. "You did well coming to the back. Do you still have the token?"

Bram opened his palm, revealing the tin circle. "Why so clandestine? What is this?"

She grinned and gestured for him to tuck the token away. "Let's talk first. Perhaps it's nothing." The smirk she gave made it clear she knew otherwise.

Bram's curiosity prickled sharper than the hair standing at the back of his neck.

Against the back wall, a waist-high cupboard stood oddly angled. Farryn shoved it back into place, then pointed for Bram to sit across from her at a simple table with four chairs. The tabletop was cluttered with jars, herb bundles, near a mortar and pestle. Crushed mint perfumed the air.

Bram took the offered chair, careful not to disturb the medicinals spread across the table. "What is all this?"

Farryn lifted a shoulder in a half shrug. "Just keeping my remedies fresh for anyone who may need them."

All sentinels studied rudimentary physics in case they needed to tend wounds in the field. Alongside with mint, Bram recognized comfrey, calendula, and goldenrod, all common in wound care.

"Perhaps we should be candid. My time in Saganus is limited, and you seem to have something specific to discuss."

The sentinels' comments at the gate, and the council chamber records Bram had read, left him uneasy. If discord brewed in Saganus, he couldn't be part of it.

Once he'd been idealistic, eager to make his mark on the realms. He understood better now.

"Your ability to speak plainly is what makes you a great sentinel." Farryn said. "But I also believe you understand justice. That sometimes the spirit of the law isn't matched by its punishment. Sometimes justice means offering mercy. Does memory serve me well, or has nostalgia clouded it too much?"

Of course, he understood leniency. There were always extenuating circumstances to weigh. Unbidden, his mind conjured Yralissa, the druid from Velmeg, who begged for mercy, after the battle. And he had been harsh instead.

That had been when emotions were high, and knowledge of her situation was scarce. The memory's sudden return only deepened his discomfort.

Perhaps he hadn't changed much after all. He should have stayed in his room.

He leaned back in his chair, forcing his focus back to the conversation. "I'd like to think of myself that way. What is this truly about?"

"I need reassurances." Farryn said, voice low. "That we can speak freely. That this is a private conversation, not official."

Farryn didn't blink, waiting for his answer.

"Am I right to assume that our meeting wasn't as accidental as it seemed?"

Farryn only smiled, sliding a jar of herbs idly across the table.

"I won't report what you say to the Heptad, if that's your concern." A flash of pain pierced his chest sharp as a needle.

Duty above all else. The mantra he'd lived by, believed with his whole heart. And every day, something new chipped at that foundation.

This was dangerous territory. He had one mission, and all realms relied on his success, whether they knew it or not.

His responsibilities were clear: Protect Edenia. Safeguard the moon-born. Gather the armor for the prophecy's fulfillment.

Nothing more. Nothing less.

Yet, he remained in his seat. Curious, yes, but it was more than that.

Right and wrong had once been simple. Follow orders. Maintain justice. Protect the realm.

Now, nothing was so easy.

His heart hammered against his ribs. If it cracked open, he would deserve it for daring to question the path he'd sworn to. He had to keep a clear mind. Listen to Farryn. Hold judgment, on her, and himself.

"It's clear you're preparing for wound care." He nodded toward the table piled with herbs. "I understand Saganus may need to grow . . . change. And I'm willing to listen. But I have limits, especially if there are plans for violence."

"To have anyone who could make a difference even listen would be more than we've had before." Farryn straightened the cuff of her green robe, then hesitated. "I know who you are."

"We've known each other a long time." Bram stayed perfectly still, though his heart pounded.

"There are rumors the Heptad made you their emissary."

An interesting way to describe it. "All rumors carry a grain of truth, until they lose it the wider they spread. If you're searching for a way to keep me in your debt by knowing who I am it's not a good strategy."

Farryn gave a wry chuckle. "I endeavor to keep those in my care safe."

"As do I."

Silence joined them. A quiet judge, waiting to pass sentence.

At last, Farryn spoke. "There are those who are angry; who believe no one will listen. I want to show them there's hope for a peaceful solution."

"That is always the best plan."

Farryn rose from her chair. "Let me offer the first step toward that goal. I am taking a risk. But someone must go first. Will you join me? It's only a conversation, I promise."

Bram stood too, pushing his chair neatly under the table. "I will listen."

To his surprise, Farryn returned to the crooked cabinet he'd noticed earlier.

She slid it aside, crouched, and pressed her hand to the stone near the floor.

A hidden door creaked open, revealing a stairwell plunging downward.

"If you wouldn't mind pulling that flush to the wall before closing the door behind you?" Farryn pointed at the cabinet.

Bram dipped his chin in acknowledgment and followed. He pulled the cabinet flush as asked. Darkness swallowed them when the hidden door snicked shut.

His vision adjusted almost immediately. One benefit of living between shadows.

The stairs ended on a landing before twisting left and diving deeper. A familiar tightness coiled in Bram's chest. The same tension he always felt entering unknown territory without proper reconnaissance. But this was Farryn. They'd grown up together. She cared, deeply, fiercely, for others. If she believed this risk necessary . . .

Farryn pulled a torch from a bucket and struck a flint along the stone wall. The flare of light caught the worry etched deep in her features. "This way. Stay close."

"You want to tell me what we're walking into?" Bram kept his voice low, falling into step behind her.

She shook her head. "Soon."

Bram followed her deeper, resisting the urge to rest his hand on his dagger. The air thickened, like damp, cool fingers, wrapping unseen around his skin. The path narrowed, twisting through what appeared to be an old lava tube. Unexpected for such a small island. Bram's gaze darted to each side passage, his mind cataloging potential escape routes.

When they reached a dead end, his muscles coiled tight. Had he misread the situation?

But Farryn knocked three times against the stone wall, and a hidden door opened. A male druid appeared in the gap, candlelight flickering behind him.

He gasped when he spotted Bram over Farryn's shoulder rising onto the balls of his feet, ready to spring. "What have you done?"

"He's with me, Niven," Farryn said, her tone brooking no argument. She twisted toward Bram. "Show him what I gave you."

Bram's fingers tightened around the token in his pocket. Every instinct screamed caution. The space beyond the door was tight, likely without another exit. If the Heptad ever learned of this place, it would be a slaughter.

Bram's gaze locked onto Farryn's, searching for reassurance. Searching for the friend he had once trusted as an elfling.

Something in Farryn's eyes, determination, perhaps desperation, made his decision. Rowena would have pushed forward without hesitation. The thought of her gave him the incentive he needed.

He leaned around Farryn and placed the token into Niven's outstretched hand.

"How do I know he didn't force you to give him this?" Niven turned the stamped circle over and over in his palm, suspicion sharpening every line of his face.

Farryn planted her hand firmly on Niven's chest and shoved him back. "Because I say he didn't."

Bram followed, ignoring the stranger, every sense alert and ready.

The cavern stretched wide, candles flickering across walls slick with shadows. The scent of tallow hung thick in the tunnels beyond. But it was the druids who held Bram's attention. Two dozen sets of eyes locked onto him. Wary. Waiting.

A hint of movement near the back. Someone reaching for a weapon? No. Just a healer adjusting a satchel. Most were merchants and vendors, except the other green-robed healer. No others wore blue.

"This is Bram. He's been away for a while," Farryn announced. "I invited him because, as a sentinel, he's in a unique position to help us."

"You've brought a sentinel here?" A male's shout cracked against the cavern walls.

"You'll get us all disavowed before we even act!" a woman shouted from the crowd's center.

"Bram is not here officially. He is my friend." Farryn glanced at Bram, exhaled and continued. "We all risk everything every day. If we're to make any real changes, we can't just whisper about troubles among ourselves. It's time to move forward. It's time to be heard."

"That's what I'm willing to do—listen." Bram raised his hands as muttering rippled through the crowd. "I can guarantee nothing, since I just learned you're here. But you are safe to speak freely."

"Why should we trust you?" A merchant in the front stood tall, his chin raised.

"Why did you go away from the city?" A woman added, wringing her hands and darting glances between Farryn and Bram.

"I've been traveling throughout Edenia on a task for the Heptad." Bram waited, searching for signs of fear or surprise.

None. A good sign his Seeker identity remained hidden. "Being away has enlightened me to other realms. Trust, however, must be mutual. We all seem to have a concern for safety in common."

The silence filled the cavern, thick as smoke. Then—

A wail split the air, raw, aching, primal. It clawed straight into Bram's chest. His spine locked, muscles seizing before his mind even caught up.

He spun to face Farryn. "You've kidnapped an elfling?"

She held up her hands, shaking her head. "We've kidnapped no one." She pointed toward the cries.

Bram followed her line of sight, an elfling, no more than eight, peek out from behind the nervous woman in front. Others followed, small faces appearing alongside adults, or cradled in their arms, slipping out of the tunnels like shy shadows.

"Why are they not in the pedagogue?" Bram asked.

"Because they are ours, our blood, and we've chosen to raise them ourselves," Farryn said.

This group didn't want to discuss change. They'd already rebelled against a fundamental druid way of life. And had been doing so for years. Bram's chest tightened until he could barely breathe. "Why would you do this?"

"Because of your mother." Farryn smiled softly, as if he should understand.

He did not.

9

———

ROWENA

ROWENA OPENED HER MOUTH, ready to say something, anything, that might sound enlightened. But the dryad princess raised a brow and crossed her arms, dismissing her excuse before it left her lips.

"The light is fading," Ida said. "It's no use continuing now. We'll begin again in the morning. This way."

Rowena exhaled, dropping her chin to her chest. No leverage to argue. No way to leave. She followed.

Evora slipped her arm through Rowena's, practically bouncing at her side.

"This will be fun. You can stay with me and tell me everything about the outside world. I need all the details. Start with whatever you want. We can talk until dawn."

Great.

Tired. Hungry. Worried. The last thing Rowena needed was an enthusiastic dryad determined to interrogate her until dawnlight.

"I don't know much," Rowena muttered. "Only Skandan."

Somehow, she doubted that would matter.

Evora's grip tightened. "That's perfect! I want to know every-thing about it."

Rowena sighed. It was going to be a long night.

She glanced around. The labyrinth was gone, replaced by a meandering path through towering trees. Uneven ground sloped steeply, then leveled again. Shadows stretched long and twisting, but Rowena was careful, *very careful*, to step only where Ida walked. The warning from the cottage was still burned fresh in her mind. "Where are we going?"

Evora lifted a shoulder. "Wherever Mother decides."

Rowena frowned. They could be trying to confuse her. It didn't matter, she was already thoroughly lost. "We're just wandering around in the dark? Don't you have a home?"

Evora halted so suddenly Rowena stumbled to a rough stop; their arms still entwined. Evora stared at Rowena with such confusion, as if she'd declared the sky was green and the land blue.

"The whole forest is our home," Evora said, her words slow and well pronounced, as if explaining something to a very small elfling.

Rowena's stomach tightened. "Yes, but don't you have a place? Somewhere safe to return to?"

Evora stared. Long. Unblinking. Then, to Rowena's discom-fort, a slow grin spread across the dryad's face. "What a strange idea. If we returned to the same place every night, we would damage the soil."

Rowena clenched her jaw. Of course, what was she thinking?

"We are part of the forest," Evora continued. "We have no things but what is provided. When we rest, our roots anchor into the ground, and the land nourishes us."

Right then, Rowena's stomach growled. Loudly.

Evora jumped. Her grip tightened on Rowena's arm. Eyes wide. "Was that one of your inner rings?"

Rowena blinked. "My what?"

"Your rings." Evora placed her hand against her stomach. "I've never heard mine like that. What did it say?"

Rowena arched a brow. "That I'm hungry."

Evora gasped.

Rowena immediately regretted her answer.

"Mother," Evora shouted ahead. "Do you understand this?"

Ida didn't slow her stride. "It is a primitive way to nourish her body. We are heading somewhere that will meet her needs."

"Primitive?" Rowena muttered, but before she could complain further, Evora tugged her forward again.

"Does your sap diminish as you move about?" Evora's head tilted, her stare unwavering. Too long, too searching, as if she were trying to unravel Rowena piece by piece. "What will you need to keep your body strong? This is fascinating."

Rowena grumbled. This was worse than being questioned by her parents in the longhouse. The thought brought a pain to her chest, and she stumbled.

"Keep up, Evora." Ida called, her voice floating around them like the wind itself.

The dryad giggled. "We'd better hurry. Mother doesn't like bothering the wind when I get distracted. It makes her grumpy."

"She's not already?"

"Not yet."

Rowena sighed again. At this rate, she was going to lose her mind before she ever saw Bram again.

Evora stopped short. Too short. Rowena's momentum carried her forward. Her foot caught on a root, and she lurched. She managed to twist at the last moment, bracing herself before she could crash into Evora's back.

She lifted her gaze, and froze like a varsler deer hiding from a hunter.

A willow tree rose before her, where she was certain one had not been before.

Not just any willow.

It was massive. Thicker, fuller than any Rowena had ever seen. Its branches cascaded to the ground, pooling like a living curtain. And through its silver-green leaves, small blue lights danced and blinked, shifting in a rhythm too fast, too strange.

Blink. Blink-blink. Blink-blink-blink. Blink.

Rowena's pulse raced. The rhythm felt . . . unnatural. As if it played her heartbeat like a flute.

A strange pull tugged at her, deep under her ribs.

"Careful." Evora's light touch broke the trance. "The wisps are beautiful, but they play tricks. It's best not to stare too long."

Rowena swallowed hard.

Wisps.

She'd heard tales of them. Mischievous, fleeting creatures, twisting paths and stealing travelers away until they never found home again.

Rowena shoved the fear down hard.

She would return home. She had to. Bram would come for her. Or she'd find her own way. She would not be lost forever.

"The wisps guard my mother as she revives through the night," Evora said.

Rowena pinched her brows. "This is your mother?"

Evora grinned.

The branches parted. Wisps danced between the leaves, their glow illuminating the area under the willow as brightly as if both moons huddled near the tree's trunk.

Rowena took a hesitant step forward.

A single branch lifted behind her. It pressed gently, firmly, against her back. Nudging her inside.

Evora strode forward, utterly at ease.

The air shifted. The forest's darkness fell away, replaced by a soft, golden glow as the wisps dimmed.

A soft rustle overhead. Then something thudded near Rowena's feet. She flinched. A ball of leaves.

Evora bent and peeled back the layers, revealing a bundle of berries and nuts.

"Mother says you'll be able to eat this."

Rowena hesitated, then accepted the offering. "Thank you."

Evora smiled. "You can thank the forest for providing what you require."

"Thank you . . . forest?" Rowena exhaled, awkward and unsure whether Evora meant it literally.

The leaves overhead rustled in a whisper that seemed to accept her gratitude.

Evora beamed.

Rowena had either just made a friend. Or agreed to something she didn't understand.

Evora settled cross-legged on the ground, facing the willow's trunk. She pointed to a soft-looking patch of moss. "Sit. Be comfortable."

The spot was at the base of the trunk, between two exposed roots.

Rowena glanced around, but moved over to where Evora directed. The moss and roots acted like a chair filled with furs and the smooth bark curved just right for her shoulders. It was a pleasant surprise.

"Is this like the meals you have where you live? How many others live in your lands? Is it far?" One of the long vine-like branches snapped in the air over Evora's head. She halted her questions. "Sorry. I will not interrupt your meal."

"Are you not going to eat?" Rowena popped a black berry half the size of her thumb into her mouth, stifling a groan over the sweet juices.

"I will root with the soil later, but I must find a different spot. It's been three years since I could fit under my mother's shelter."

Rowena studied the area where they sat. The willow branches, Ida's branches, provided enough room for at least twenty to lounge in comfort. That would be about the same number to share a meal in the longhouse each night.

A sharp pain stabbed Rowena's chest. The longhouse had burned. She'd watched the smoke rise, black and heavy, into the sky as she sailed away on Uther's ship. It seemed like years had passed since then.

The berries turned sour in her stomach. She set the leafy trencher on the ground beside her.

"Is something wrong?" Evora leaned over to check on what Rowena had yet to eat. "Do you need something different?"

"I'm sorry . . . It's not . . . I was just thinking of something. I'll eat some more in a little while."

Evora propped her chin in her hands, her face eager.

Rowena stared at her fingers, purple stained from the berries. She had a feeling it wasn't going to be a restful night.

10

EVORA

It was strange, and thrilling, to sit beside someone from another realm. Few had ever entered the forest, and none had stayed long, so Evora had heard. She had never even glimpsed them. And *no one* spoke of where they had gone. She yearned to know everything Rowena could share, but she didn't seem to enjoy all the questions.

Evora could wait. Let Rowena decide when she was ready to talk.

What if she didn't want to?

Evora had to join with the soil soon or she'd not be able to keep up the next day. Surely, asking a few things wouldn't be too intrusive.

"Would you mind if I asked? . . ." Evora trailed off, twisting a leaf between her fingers.

Ida's willow branches swayed above. Her mother's presence weighed heavily on her, but Evora pressed on. "That is, I need to join with the soil soon, to rest. Is that . . . something you're familiar with? Do others outside our forest do this too?"

She held her breath, waiting for any flicker of annoyance

from Rowena. The question seemed safe enough - practical, even - but was she being a bother? A small vine near her foot curled inward reflexively, quivering like her insides.

Rowena's presence was like a glimpse through a doorway into the wider world, and Evora desperately wanted a peer through before it closed again, possibly forever.

Her mother's teachings echoed in her mind: don't be forward, don't be demanding, don't draw attention. But questions burned in her throat, twisting like tangled vines.

She swallowed them down. Mostly. One small question couldn't hurt. Did it?

Rowena tilted her head, studying Evora with an expression that was more curious than annoyed. "Join with the soil?" she asked. "You mean like sleeping on the ground?"

Evora nodded, grateful that Rowena seemed interested rather than put off. "Yes, we merge our essence within the land to restore ourselves. It's when we share nutrients and revive our enchantment." She paused, wondering if she should explain further.

The willow branches swayed again. Her mother's silent warning not to reveal too much.

But Rowena was already shaking her head. "Most people just sleep in beds; raised platforms with soft coverings. Unless we are traveling, then we lay our coverings on the ground."

"Raised platforms?" Evora sat up straighter, fascinated. She raised her gaze to the branches overhead, trying to picture what Rowena meant, while also weighing the risk for more information. She had to know. "How would you reach the branches without the roots?"

Rowena's chin dipped, her lips twitching. Was that amusement? Evora adjusted her position, uncertain if she had said something foolish.

"We don't climb into the tree branches," Rowena answered. Her eyes were soft, not teasing. "We just build a frame about this high," she gestured near her shoulders, "so we're away from the dirt and the cold. Then we can fill the frame with a mattress stuffed with husks or feathers so it's comfortable."

Evora nodded. "Like the birds . . . in a nest."

Rowena lifted a shoulder. "Sort of, I suppose."

"But why reject the soil? It provides sustenance and life." Evora pinched her brows. She would be lost without the warmth of the forest's minerals flowing through her.

"The Lunara way to replenish our enchantment is to absorb the rays of Masah and Lungol."

Evora tried to imagine feeling moon rays on her skin. That seemed so odd. "It's difficult to understand. There are many differences between us."

"For me as well." Rowena rubbed her hands on her thighs.

It seemed she also had questions, but held them inside—just as Evora's mother expected from her. But she had started now, and Rowena didn't seem to mind, so she would use the time she had while it lasted.

"How do you get this frame to stay off the ground? If an apple no longer holds the branch, it falls to the ground. Is that not the same where you are from?"

"We nail pieces of wood together, so there are posts that sit on the ground, leaving space between the ground and the mattress."

Evora eyes bulged wide, growing dry from the air. "You harvest fallen trees and abuse them for your comfort?" The vine at her feet coiled tighter. Tingling licked up her legs—the first warning of her transformation under stress. Taking a deep breath, she forced herself to stay present, not to retreat.

Ida's branches twisted sharply, whipping through the still air.

Evora scooted closer to the trunk, closer to Rowena. *I'm just trying to understand, Mother.*

If you continue, you will not enjoy her answers. Outsiders act in barbarous ways. She will fill your mind with gruesome images.

What could that mean? Instead of scaring Evora away, her mother only made her more curious.

"What happened?" Rowena asked.

Evora pulled a strand of hair across her mouth. What should she say? If she admitted what her mother said, she would be calling their guest a barbarian. But she couldn't ignore that her mother had interrupted their conversation for a reason.

She smoothed her hair back into place. "My mother is just concerned that some of your customs may be troublesome to understand."

Rowena scanned the branches over her head, pulling her knees to her chest. "What will she do to me?"

"Oh no, please! You are safe."

"What if I make her angrier? I don't even know what offended her."

"She is not angry with you." Evora paused. That was mostly true. "She's just worried about the questions *I'm* asking."

"Oh. So, she doesn't want to turn my blood to sap for her tree?" Rowena wrapped her arms around her knees, making herself into a tighter ball.

"Of course not. None in Havilar would do such a thing. I can't even imagine how that would be done." Evora bit her lip, shaking her head, coming up with nothing to understand Rowena's fear.

"That's one of the stories I've heard in my homeland about yours."

"It is not true." Evora chuckled. "Is your home, Skandan, far?"

"Yes. It is north. An island that does not touch the continent."

"I have never left Havilar, so I don't know what that means."

"Ever?"

Evora stammered, feeling bark roughen her fingers. No, not now. She forced herself to take slow, steady breaths. She'd sounded so foolish. "I don't really know about . . . elsewhere. We have all we need here, so there is no reason to leave."

"That is the opposite of my home. We must get many supplies from other lands. Our soil is very rocky, making farming difficult. We do raise sheep and cattle, but mostly we trade for what we need."

Evora's fingers curled against her knees. Farming. The word was strange on her tongue. Unfamiliar. She hesitated, but the question pushed forward, anyway. "What is farming?"

That is enough, Evora. You must join the soil, or you will not have enough time to revive yourself.

"I apologize for becoming intrusive. I'm just so curious. However, it is time for my joining."

"I don't mind the conversation, but I am tired as well."

Evora exhaled slowly, her shoulders loosening. She hadn't embarrassed herself or bothered Rowena. Good. "I enjoyed our conversation. Perhaps we can resume again tomorrow?"

"If there's time. I still have to walk the labyrinth again."

Oh yes, Evora almost forgot. "Hopefully. Until the sun rises." She dipped her chin and slipped through her mother's flowing branches.

She ambled to a patch of soft, rich soil twenty paces away. She had visited with a stranger and it was marvelous. Rowena had been so interesting. Not a realm-destroyer like the stories said.

Evora wriggled her toes into the cool dirt, sinking down,

letting soil embrace her. She would make sure there was time tomorrow to speak with her new friend. Could she call her that?

Evora slowly twisted, her skin crackling into bark as she thought.

Yes, she would call Rowena her friend.

A moment later, her branches sprouted, and her mind focused on listening to the forest, leaving all else behind.

11

BRAM

NO ONE SPOKE.

Not even the infant cried.

Farryn's claim that the group's motives stemmed from his mother made no sense.

Bram scanned the cavern, searching for anyone to contradict her. But all he found were eager faces, waiting. Expecting.

A pit hollowed in his stomach.

"I lived in the pedagogue with many of you." His voice stayed firm. A reminder. A line drawn between them. He turned to Farryn, spreading his hands, palms up. "We are druids of Saganus. Each of us a branch of the same tree. The vivens guide us, protect us. I have no mother."

Farryn flinched, as if he'd struck her.

"That's how we are raised." Her face hardened, her voice tightened. "But did you never yearn for something more? Never reach for an absence where there should have been . . . someone?"

Bram clenched his jaw.

Farryn continued. "There are vivens who offer kindness.

They mentor, they teach. But that is not the same as love shared between a parent and an elfling."

"It is efficient." Bram straightened, instinctively standing ready as a sentinel. "Equal. Every elfling is given the same amount of care. When we enter society, we understand we are all one, and care for one another."

Farryn scoffed. "It is cold and impersonal."

"It is fair."

"It is survival." She threw out a hand, eyes flashing with crackling anger he'd never seen from her before. "That is all it is. Enough to keep us alive, but never enough to make us whole."

Bram's fingers flexed his fingers against his side. "I've seen lands where some live in abundance, while others starve. Where some are abandoned for their weaknesses, left to rot because they failed. We do not have that here. No one wants for anything."

Farryn's expression softened, but not in surrender. "There have been changes since you left."

The dirty streets, the scent of rot, the empty baskets at the brasserie flashed in his mind. It was not the healthy town he'd left. He couldn't deny that.

"What of individuality?" Farryn asked, pain lacing her voice in a quiet plea. "Creativity? Love? What if we wish to form a lasting mate bond? To choose who we care for? To build connections of the heart?"

A dangerous flicker twisted in Bram's chest.

Rowena.

He had fought it. The first stirrings of something beyond duty. And yet, hadn't he been drawn to her from the moment they met? Even before he knew what she was?

Hadn't his heart reached for more?

No. That was irrational. He forced the thought away.

"You would be selfish," he said instead. "To build a life only for yourself while others suffer because they do not make the same choices you do. That is heartless."

Farryn stepped closer, closing the space between them. "Is that what you tell yourself? That you fight for equality? That you sacrifice for the good of others?"

Bram said nothing.

She tilted her head. "Or is it because you're afraid to admit you want something more?"

His spine locked. "I serve Saganus. We are stronger together. The Primary Spring fuels all of Edenia, and as caretakers, we have a responsibility to live in harmony. Not as scattered seeds, but as one garden. Bound by duty, rooted in tradition."

Farryn's expression twisted. Not in anger, but in sorrow.

"You speak of harmony," she murmured, "but you refuse to hear the discord."

Bram gritted his teeth.

A woman stepped from the crowd; an infant cradled to her shoulder. "We do not have to relinquish our elflings for the Spring to flow."

Bram's stomach twisted.

Another voice rose. Niven, the man who'd tried to stop Bram at the door, slid nearer to Farryn. "Your mother knew that, too. That's why we're here."

Was she disavowed for that choice? If so, she had decided her own fate.

Bram's breath stilled. He scanned the cavern again. Their faces. Their stories. Their hope. It filled the space like a haze, perfumed by anticipation.

"She lost her elflings," Niven said. "That's why we hide in these caverns. We choose a different path."

Another reference to the woman Bram did not know. Why was he even considering the idea of a singular mother? The vivens raised him. They were enough.

Most before him were adults, but the young ones stood out. Eight within view, ranging from the babe-in-arms to a girl on the cusp of adolescence, stared at him. Their skin was too pale from the darkness, their expressions wary.

"How long have you lived down here?" Bram's voice came quieter than intended. "Have these elflings ever been above ground?"

"It is too dangerous," Niven said. A girl, no more than four or five summers, peeked around him, clinging to his hidden hand. "We take turns bringing in supplies, and we must divide our work duties to keep up with the rising fees and assessments the Heptad continues to levy."

Bram drew in a slow breath. "You've built your own pedagogy."

He expected outrage. A denial. What good was it to rebel if they ended up changing nothing but the danger?

Instead, the woman with the babe smiled softly. "This is my son. Not a charge. Not a shared duty. When he is sick, I stay with him. I comfort him. No one else."

Farryn nodded. "We do share responsibilities, when needed, but it is a choice."

A choice. Bram turned away. Why did that word feel like a blade slipping between his ribs?

"You all risk so much." Bram studied the little ones. The girl stayed clutched to her father but peeked at Bram with wide-eyed wonder. The babe sucked on his fingers, content and sleepy. Others stayed near the back but climbed on tables for a better view of the stranger in their midst.

"And you don't?" Farryn met his gaze, then crouched down to stroke the young girl's hair. "Come meet my friend."

Farryn lifted the girl to her hip, and kissed her temple. Bram backed up a step. "She's my daughter, not a threat. Mila, this is Bram. He's an old friend of mine. Can you say hello?"

Mila's light brown curls swung side-to-side, and she hid her face. "Scary," she whispered into Farryn's robe, but Bram caught it.

He stiffened. If she understood, if any of them did, they would have run long ago.

"He might help us."

"I've agreed to nothing." The situation was foolish. The pedagogue existed because elflings needed order and instruction. Merchants and vendors and healers were not trained for that task.

"You live by the Heptad's will. But in all your travels, Bram, have you never seen one of our kind in the other realms? One of the disavowed?" Farryn asked, rocking gently from foot to foot as she rubbed the elfling girl's back. The soft, caring gesture tugged at his heart.

He hesitated, uncertain what she was getting at. "Not many. The ones accepted as Oraku, yes. Those who trade their gifts for protection."

"And the others?" someone standing nearby asked. Bram wasn't sure who.

"They live as outcasts. If they're lucky, they find a place. If not . . . they survive. Barely."

"I knew it wasn't true. They are no more than slaves." A boy, thirteen or fourteen summers, sauntered from the nearest tunnel. He leaned his shoulder against the dirt wall and glared Bram's way. Lanky, and dressed in plain brown trousers with a simple linen tunic, he wore no insignia of his order.

Bram's throat tightened. He thought of Rowena. Her defiance when she'd been forced into slavery.

This was different.

"Have you been assigned an order for your profession?" Bram had already earned his apprentice robe by the boy's age.

"We choose our own path down here. Or we will when we go topside." The boy lifted his chin and met Bram's gaze.

"How will you fare? What are your propensities? Have you been tested?" Bram admired the boy's mettle, but his fists clenched at the thought of instilling such chaos into the next generation.

"It's antiquated ideas like that, holding all of us back." A man who'd stayed quiet in the back stepped forward. "We are all capable of many things, but we're shoved into boxes others decide are best. Only a handful of duties are deemed worthy enough for a druid of lower orders."

"The vivens told me I was wonderful at helping the elflings with their studies." The woman who spoke had been near the brasserie earlier. He had seen her inside Aethercrest also. Brawny with a wind-worn look to her face. She was easy to recall. "But a post in the pedagogue is for life, by the Heptad's decree. You'll have no home, no friends, no life outside those walls. I wasn't about to live in that place for the rest of my life."

"You'd be better off to clean the streets," someone shouted.

"I wish I would have had that choice," the woman answered. "Because I refused their offer, they sent me to work on the shore. My days are spent pulling in heavy nets and gutting fish. They tell me it is an honor to work with my hands since I chose not to use my mind."

Bram listened as more voices rose.

One after another exposed a Saganus he had never experienced. He also learned that besides the older boy, Killian, others of similar age were ready for the topside, as they called it. Their impending prime days created the urgency behind the rebels' need for change.

Unrecognized druids could not simply arrive in the city. The Heptad would send sentinels searching every corner for more.

Bram's stomach rolled. Had he not become the Seeker, he would have been one of the hunters.

When they finished with their stories, silence echoed through the chamber. The weight of what they were doing settled against his chest.

Once more he chided himself. He shouldn't be involving himself in this situation. If the Heptad found out he'd spoken to a group of rebellious druids, they could prevent him from returning to Rowena. They could strip from him the Seeker.

Farryn's voice came softly. "You may not want to accept that you had a mother, Bram. But she inspired every one of us in these tunnels."

Bram scanned the cavern again. He met every gaze, memorized every face. Another memory surfaced alongside those he made. The entry from the Heptad's chamber—about the druid, disavowed for refusing to give up her child. The air grew too thick to breathe. He shoved the implication away and stood tall. The situation at hand. That was all.

He had no mother.

"When I left the pedagogue and entered service, I apprenticed under another healer who helped this community," Farryn said. "She had no elfling of her own, but she longed for one. When she was sent away, I took up her cause."

So many had had their lives stolen from them. For what? Loving too much? Breaking the rules?

Choosing their own path.

The Heptad proclaimed their rules kept everyone safe, but had it really been about control?

The Heptad!

Bram gasped. "How do you gauge time in this space?"

"We have orbs." Niven used his chin to direct Bram toward the device suspended in a round cradle, where a steady stream of sparkling black sand dripped from one glass orb into another.

The higher orb was almost empty. "It is nearing dawn above. Those who work through the night will return shortly."

Bram had gotten so engrossed in the conversations, and the situation, that he'd paid no attention. If anyone came to wake him in the tower and found him gone, it would cause too many questions.

"I must leave. You've given me much to consider." He smiled at Mila, who surprised him by returning the gesture. "I'm not sure what I can do. My duties will again take me far from Saganus. For now, I urge all of you to consider other options. Speak with the Heptad. Pursue change that doesn't risk your lives."

"A pretty thought. That you have listened is perhaps a start," Farryn said. "I will escort you back and make sure the exit is secure."

His mind warred over what he'd heard. But his heart had already begun to whisper differently.

Bram hurried through the door with Farryn close behind. He jogged through the tunnel, fighting the urge to slip through the shadows. No one in the caverns knew he was the Seeker, and he wanted, needed, to keep it that way. Most likely, they never would have opened up to him otherwise. Though Farryn came close, believing him an emissary.

Inside the dispensary, Farryn hurried to secure the secret door and adjusted the cabinet before she faced Bram. "Thank you. I . . ." she trailed off and flattened her lips.

"What else?" He was so concerned about returning to the tower, his words came out harsher than he intended. Through the windows, the sky was beginning to lighten, and he was anxious to get back.

"While you were gone, there have been stories about another Burning Moon during the Reaping this year. That the prophecy will be fulfilled and everything will change." Farryn ran her fingers along the edge of the herb-filled table. "I want my daughter to see the sky. To experience Sawel's light on her face before that takes place."

Bram's instinct urged him to assure her that he'd do his best. But he held back. "The stories are true. But for now, it would be best if you kept that information to yourself. If there is a way for me to help, I will, but I can make no promises."

Tears glistened in Farryn's eyes as she attempted a wobbly smile that barely touched her lips.

There was nothing more to be said. He strode out the door and down a back street until he found a dark area without any overlooking windows. Bram was about to slip through the shadows when movement across the street drew his attention.

Someone ducked behind a pile of crates.

He'd been followed.

If they were hiding, they likely weren't much of a threat. Bram stepped away from the side of the building and into the center of the cobblestoned street. "Come out and face me."

Nothing happened and there wasn't any movement, but a quiet breath rasped from the shadows.

"I know you're there. You breathe as loud as an oxvark." Bram would give whoever it was another moment before he went in after them.

"I don't know what that is." Killian rose and crossed his arms over his slender chest. "Perhaps I would if I lived topside."

Bram grumbled deep in his throat and bit back an inappropriate response. The kid hadn't followed him and Farryn. They would have heard him. There had to be another exit.

"How often do you sneak up here? Seems you might have learned a lot by now." Bram strode closer. "Like not to lurk in the dark where you might get caught."

"Hasn't happened so far." Killian dropped his hands and ambled out into the open.

"Until now." Bram strolled toward the end of the street as if he didn't care about Killian's actions.

Killian hung back for a moment, but then hurried to catch up. When he settled in at Bram's side, he shoved a thumb into his belt, trying to seem casual.

From the corner of his eye, Bram noticed Killian pulling his shoulders back, mimicking Bram's posture and gait. The action tugged at something in his chest. Recognition. The boy reminded him so much of himself at that age; impatient, eager to prove himself, chafing under restrictions he didn't understand. Duty and honor had been abstract concepts then, not the pillars they'd become.

"Your actions don't just affect you." Bram forced his tone gentler than he'd use with an adult fae. "What would happen to the others if someone found you?"

Killian kept silent for a moment. "I'm careful."

"You sure about that?" Bram stopped and held the boy's gaze. To his surprise, Killian maintained eye contact longer than expected—before his shoulders slumped.

He kicked at a loose stone; eyes fixed on the ground. "I just want to do things. Important things. Down there it's the same every day. Nothing matters."

"I get it." Bram began, remembering his own frustrated youth.

"No, you don't." Killian threw up his arms. "No one does. They're all like, 'it's too dangerous,' 'you're not old enough,'— but they're wrong."

"Sure." Bram let his agreement hang between them, watching Killian's surprise register. He remembered his own mentors. Their patience had shaped him when rigid rules alone would have driven him to rebellion. "But they mean well, and they know things you don't. I didn't believe that once either, but it's true."

"You go everywhere. I heard them say you're an emissary, whatever that means, along with being a sentinel. You're helping people and keeping order. Doing things." He stalked over to a barrel, picking at a loose splinter. "My parents tell me I can be anything I want . . . someday. That's nothing but a dodge."

There was admiration and envy in his voice. The idea plucked at Bram's heart. Had he earned such esteem? The weight of responsibility settled across his shoulders. This wasn't just about keeping the boy safe now. It was about guiding him toward understanding the value of tradition and duty that had taken Bram years to appreciate. Things Killian would learn if he was part of the pedagogy.

With Rowena, he'd speak of tactics. With Farryn, strategy. But with this elfling, he needed something different.

"I wish I could tell you things will be different right away, but I can't." Bram moved closer, leaning against a rough plastered wall. He softened his voice, not out of weakness, but as a deliberate choice; the way his own mentor, had once reached him. "What I can say is that I'll help however I can. What your parents are doing . . . it's against tradition. Dangerous. But there are reasons for those traditions that I didn't understand until I was older than you are now."

"How is it dangerous? We aren't a threat to anyone."

"Anytime there's change, it takes away familiarity. That makes some afraid they won't know how to live with the new ways." Bram raised his shoulders. "But tradition is also a good thing. It keeps things grounded. Those from the past and those from the future can understand each other."

The more Bram spoke, the more his convictions tangled. He didn't like that he might be resistant to change, but he also believed in the Saganus traditions and rituals. It kept everything orderly.

"That's ridiculous." Killian kicked the barrel. "Everyone

should do what they want. Some can keep doing the old things. Let others do new things."

"If everyone did the right thing all the time, there wouldn't be a need for sentinels." Bram grinned. "Then what would we do?"

Killian rolled his eyes.

He was a fine young druid trying to find his own way. Bram appreciated that. He hoped he'd been able to help him in a small way, but he needed to get back to his room.

Footsteps on the cobblestones echoed between the buildings. It was still within curfew and they could only be sentinel night patrols.

"We need to go." Bram peered around the corner of the building, scanning the empty street that ran in front of the apothecary. His instincts prickled. So much had changed. The enforcement of curfew seemed excessive, unnecessary. "See that? We're out after we should be. It's easy to get things wrong. It's a lot harder to do the right thing all the time. Everyone makes mistakes."

Killian scoffed, a look passing over his face that Bram recognized. The barely concealed pride of someone who believed they'd already mastered what they were being taught. The boy followed nonetheless as Bram hugged the building's shadow and hurried away.

They'd nearly made it to the corner where they'd turn toward Farryn's shop when a voice called out behind them.

"Ho! Who's there?"

"Run!" Bram called, sprinting around the corner. Killian's boots slapped against the cobblestones behind him, the rhythm too steady. Too confident.

If secrecy wasn't crucial, Bram could have moved them through the shadows to Farryn's shop within seconds. As it was, they'd have to find a different route to avoid bringing suspicion to her door.

"This way," Killian called, racing past Bram with practiced ease.

Bram's eyes narrowed as the boy easily navigated the streets. This wasn't the hesitant movement of someone in unfamiliar territory. Killian moved with the confidence of someone who had done this many times before. His footfalls quieted as they reached rougher terrain, adjusting automatically to minimize sound. A sentinel's awareness. Or a practiced rule-breaker's.

The shouts behind them grew more distant, but neither slowed their pace. Killian led them through a sharp turn, then toward a stack of crates positioned too neatly against a wall. The boy sprang up first, feet barely touching the wood before he grabbed the ledge and hauled himself over. No hesitation. No wasted movement. Not his first escape.

Bram followed, landing harder than intended. The crates wobbled beneath him, a crack splintering through the wood. He gritted his teeth and launched upward, gripping the ledge just as boots pounded in the alley below.

Killian stopped abruptly on the rooftop and lifted what appeared to be a commonplace grate. Beneath it lay not sewage or rainwater channels, but a hidden entrance. Bram crouched beside him, eyes still scanning for pursuit while his mind processed what this meant. The grate's edges were worn smooth from use.

Killian caught his gaze and lifted his chin with a hint of defiance. "There's a group of us that come out at night. We have a lot of exit points."

The pieces fell into place. Killian's movements, his eagerness to prove himself, the knowing way he'd navigated the streets. This wasn't elfling rebellion; this was organized resistance. Bram glanced away, pinching his lips together to hold back his immediate reaction. Part of him admired their ingenuity; the part bound by duty recognized the danger.

"Do me, and everyone in the tunnels, a favor," he said, low and controlled. "Don't come back out for a while. Tell the others. Let me work out a way for you to come out with freedom, so you don't get hurt."

Killian twisted his lips, the gesture somehow both elfling and weary beyond his years. "I doubt they'd listen to that."

"Make them. Promise me."

"I'll try, but I can't promise."

A man of his word, even when the truth was inconvenient. Bram respected that. "I like you, Killian. Trust me when I say I'll help. And stay home for the time being."

"Fine." The word carried reluctance, but Bram detected sincerity behind it.

"I'll watch for a while and make sure no one saw us come up here." The skies were starting to lighten, and Bram was in danger of getting back on time himself.

Killian nodded and disappeared down a ladder into the dark, pulling the grate closed over his head.

Rebels in Saganus. He would never have guessed it could happen.

Bram kept low and hurried to the edge of the building. Below, sentinels searched a block away, rifling behind barrels and crates. He slipped back into the alley and hurried away unnoticed.

A moment later, he was back in the small bed chambers he'd been given in the tower—without a moment to spare.

The handle clicked as someone cracked open his door.

12

ROWENA

Rowena woke to a pair of eyes staring too close to her face. Instinctively, she swept her arm through the air, slammed into her intruder, and bolted to her feet.

Evora sat on her backside, stunned, eyes wide.

Rowena groaned. "I'm sorry." She extended her hand to help the dryad to her feet.

"Is that a typical morning greeting in Skandan?" Evora asked.

"When someone startles them by staring a finger width from their face—yes."

"I will remember that." Evora chuckled. Her good nature made it difficult to stay angry.

Despite a restless night's sleep, worrying about other dryads appearing and draining her blood for sap, Rowena had managed some rest. She was ready to go back to the cottage right away.

"Mother is waiting for us," Evora said. "It's been a while, so we should hurry."

The leaf bundle with nuts and berries still lay on the ground near where Rowena slept. Except now it was in the middle of a patch of dirt with no willow in sight. At least she'd be able to break her fast. She snatched up the food and hurried after Evora.

"You want me to go through again?" Rowena folded her arms. Why? She had followed every instruction the day before, even lingered in the center longer than necessary. And now Ida insisted she do it again?

The dryad met her frustration with calm indifference." This time, you must use a slower pace. Perhaps it will offer you a more honest revelation."

Rowena huffed. She should argue. She wanted to argue, but what would it change? She couldn't leave. If she ran, where would she go?

She had no leverage.

With a sigh as her final protest, she once again turned to the labyrinth.

The white stones gleamed brighter this time, as if they were in on some cruel jest. What was she supposed to learn?

"This is nonsense."

Ida tilted her head. "What one learns in the labyrinth is uniquely akin to the path they travel in their life journey."

So nothing.

Rowena exhaled with a growl and strode between the first set of stones.

The moment her foot touched the path, the wind returned. Stronger. It shoved against her shoulders, pulling at her braids, tugging as if trying to slow her down.

Rowena gritted her teeth and leaned into it. She wouldn't stop. She wouldn't be pushed around by wind and riddles.

The air shifted. A scent, faint and warm, wafted past her nose. Clove.

She slowed. Not clove; coral root. The woody plant grew in Skandan, under the pines. She hadn't noticed that before.

A flicker of warmth bloomed in her chest. Taesing. Home. She let the scent settle around her, filling the space between her ribs. For the first time, she didn't fight the labyrinth. She let herself remember.

Taesing's busy harbor with fishermen gathering their supplies or fixing nets. Shop owners calling out about their beads or hair combs for sale. Her mouth watered at the thought of Grandma Myrna's minced meat hand pies.

The path wound inward, and before she realized it, she was at the center again. The six archways curved around her, waiting in silence.

Her peace shattered.

Smoke. Other memories, darker, struck like a blade.

The longhouse burning.

Uther's ship.

The sails swallowing the sky.

Chains cold around her wrists.

Her breath hitched. Her pulse throbbed against her neck. She didn't want to do this. No good would come from just standing there, reflecting. There was too much to remember. Too much pain.

Her fists curled so tight, her nails bit into her palms. Her entire body trembled with the effort to stay still.

She refused to cry. She refused to break. She had to leave.

Rowena tore through the six spaces like a honeybee in an overgrown field of flowers. She wouldn't listen. She wouldn't feel.

The path blurred under her feet. The wind rushed past her ears, deafening now, like voices whispering too fast to understand.

She had to get out.

Her boot bumped against something. Rowena stumbled,

catching herself a moment before she fell. She glanced at the offending object.

A bullfrog.

It sat in the center of her path, the size of her face, unmoving.

She could just step over it. But she didn't. Her breathing slowed.

The frog breathed too fast. Despite its stillness, its sides pulsed erratically, rising and falling with rushed inhales.

Stillness and chaos at the same time.

Rowena's heartbeat matched the frog's rhythm.

Too fast.

Her anger lessened . . . by a blade's width. A wave of exhaustion washed over her, heavier than before.

Rowena released a slow, controlled breath. Then carefully stepped around the frog.

For the first time since entering, she moved with patience. That was at least something, even if she didn't fully understand the point of the trial.

And that was enough.

Wasn't it?

She picked up her pace toward the exit, eager to be free of the winding path, and its meaningless contemplation.

When she freed herself beyond the final stones, she turned to Ida, lifting her chin. "I did what you asked. Now what?"

She forced more confidence into her voice and posture, than flowed through her veins, but she met the dryad's gaze, unwavering.

Ida's expression remained unreadable. Until the smallest tilt of her head sent a cold twist of unease down Rowena's spine.

She wasn't finished here.

Not yet.

"Before you attempt another quest, come with me." Ida

strode away from the labyrinth's entrance, disappearing into the trees without another glance.

Rowena lingered, peeking at the circular path, half expecting the glowing stones to shift—to trap her. She sighed, then followed.

They stopped before a dense thicket, huddled in the long shadow of an ancient pine. Ida knelt. The soil folded around her as if to welcome her, soft and yielding.

Rowena sat beside her, though only cold and dampness seeped from the dirt beneath her knees. It screamed one thought—foreign.

"Everything living creates a vibration in the aether," Ida said. "For you, the moons fill you with power, refreshment, and life. For my kind, it is growing things. The roots. The leaves. The Primary Spring provides the forest with a pulse that flows through everything. "

Rowena pinched her brows. It made sense, in a way. She'd never truly thought about how the different fae connected to the elements. In Skandan, there were no enchanted outside of her family. After her grandmother's death, other Lunara who had lived in her village moved on. To where Rowena hadn't learned. Only she and her mother remained.

She had never considered how others lived with power.

But she should have. She should have asked. A good queen would have.

"How is it decided?" She forced herself to risk the question, but her confidence drained as she spoke. "That some connect to one element and others to something different?"

Lines furrowed across Ida's forehead. "After the Chasm, the Great Creator, formed Edenia from the Primary Spring, giving life to all the elements. You must know the tales."

Rowena hesitated. She did know them . . . in bits and pieces. She should have listened better, but she hadn't. She lifted a shoulder, studying the dirt instead of Ida's expectant gaze.

When the dryad spoke again, her tone had softened. "The Chasm forced the fae from Caelus, severing them from their Primary forms. The Great Creator created conduits, heartstones, within the Primary Spring cavern, distributing them among the six races given guardianship of Edenia."

Rowena had been so focused on her own survival, her own struggles, that she had never considered the balance of power across the lands. "I've only been able to access my enchantment for a short time." She hadn't even tried to touch it since she'd gone to the cottage with Bram.

"What matters," Ida continued, "is that you keep working to grow your Lunara abilities."

Her hand settled over Rowena's.

"Our similarities make us fae, but our differences bring harmony. The Primary Spring fuels us all. No element must overpower another. Balance must be maintained.

Rowena exhaled. Good. She had too many battles ahead. She had no interest in chasing more power than necessary.

Ida scooped up a mound of soil, cupping it in both hands. "To some, this is simply dirt. But for me, it sings. Just as you must bathe within the rays of Masah and Lungol, I must become one with the soil, the leaves, the life throughout the forest."

She took Rowena's hand, turned it over, and let dirt spill into her palm.

A thrill jolted through Rowena's arm.

It startled her. She squeezed her eyelids closed, concentrating. The sensation grew. It wasn't a hum, wasn't a whisper . . . it was movement. Something swimming beneath her skin, flowing through her veins like a river breaking loose from a dam. The only other time a similar sensation—The sword!

Her pulse quickened. Her lungs tightened. Sparks flashed behind her eyes.

A blur of shadows.

Branches.

A face; half-hidden.

Watching. Anticipating. Curious.

Rowena gasped, jerking her hand away from Ida.

The vision shattered. It hadn't been pointing her to the sword as she hoped. But there was something.

Her heartbeat thundered in her ears. That was not normal. Heat crawled over her skin, warming her cheeks.

"I don't know what happened." She rubbed her chest to steady herself. "It was like my enchantment found something and wanted to grab it."

Ida sighed. "Very good."

Rowena blinked. That was good?

The dryad rose, placing her hands on her hips. "Come out, Evora."

Rowena's head snapped up.

From behind a nearby tree, Evora emerged. Or had she been a tree?

Rowena's breath hitched.

The younger dryad grinned, unbothered.

"Have you been there the whole time?"

"Not the—"

"Evora." Ida's tone snapped like a dry twig, carrying the warning of an approaching predator.

"Fine. The whole time." Evora lifted a shoulder, shameless. Her grin widened. "I had to. We never have visitors."

Rowena shook her head. A little shaken. A little impressed.

Evora studied Rowena like a plant she wasn't sure would bloom, but there was a glint of eagerness in her expression. "You didn't speak to the trees. I would have heard. How did you find me?"

Rowena glanced at Ida, but the dryad offered nothing.

"A sensation surprised me." She pressed a hand over her chest. "A warmth."

"Fascinating. You're so strong, but use so little of your abilities. Are all outsiders like you?"

Rowena bristled, but before she could snap a response, Evora leaned closer and sniffed her hair.

"Get back!" Rowena lashed out with the side of her fist. Years of training to fight, guiding her instincts.

Evora dodged to the side, her grin unwavering. "I was ready for you that time."

Ida, her gaze lifted to the sky, offered no interference.

"You seem like an oak," Evora mused. "Growing alone, never allowing anything close, or you'll be choked and die. Like my grandmother."

Rowena's stomach twisted, frustration replacing whatever fragile peace she'd gained.

"Why is that?"

"I'm not a tree," Rowena shouted. "Or any part of the forest."

She faced Ida and the dryad's gaze settled on her.

"I've done all you asked. Can I leave now?"

"Enter again," she said. "And listen more closely."

No. I can't do it. Rowena's resolve ebbed away like the tide.

Evora beamed, bouncing on her toes, like this was the most exciting day she'd ever lived.

Blood throbbed through Rowena's ears.

Again? Did she have a choice?

The answer clear enough, but her mind tried to ignore the truth. She inhaled, holding her breath for an extra heartbeat before forcing it out in a gust.

Then, with an internal grumble, she spun toward the labyrinth once more.

For the third time, Rowena stood at the labyrinth's entrance. The final time. She could stand no more.

Ida watched her, steady as ever, hands resting over her forearms. Beside her, Evora fidgeted, shifting from foot to foot, her face alight with anticipation, like she was about to witness something magnificent.

Rowena huffed through her nose. What did they see she didn't?

"There is one thing to do before you enter this time." Ida bent, gathering some fallen leaves. Her fingers twisted the stems together deftly until they formed a wide, woven band. She stepped closer. "This time, your sight will not distract you."

Rowena had no time to react before the band settled over her head, resting atop her nose. Warmth spread across her face, the leaves molding as if fusing to her skin, locking her eyelids shut.

Panic clawed up her throat.

She reached up, fingers digging at the edges. It wouldn't budge. Her breath came in bursts. Her knees threatened to buckle. She was trapped.

Enslaved.

"What . . . what have you done?"

Ida's hands enclosed her own, a grounding touch. "It will only come off when you finish. Feel the breeze on your skin. Let it refresh you. Listen to the veeries sing in the brush. You are not confined. You are free to let your other senses guide you."

Rowena breathed in.

Hold.

Exhale.

She could almost believe Bram stood beside her, gentle fingers guiding her through her panic as before. His soft whisper, 'this will pass.' Her pulse slowed. Her mind cleared. She could do this.

One more time.

She straightened her shoulders, mapping the pathway in her mind. She would not fail this time.

With deliberate steps, Rowena crossed the threshold. The wind was there immediately. A whisper against her cheek. A tug at her braid. She let it pass through her, slowing her pace.

She listened. Bees hummed straight ahead. The air shifted with the flutter of butterfly wings. A soft laughter of leaves rippled from the trees. She breathed in the crisp scent of pine and damp soil.

The labyrinth was alive. And for the first time, she was part of it.

Rowena reached the middle and everything stilled. No wind, no birds, no rustling leaves. Not an absence. Not an abandonment.

Peace.

She turned in a slow circle, waiting. Listening. Which alcove, which petal, would call to her first?

A pulse.

Not from her, from the ground. It thrummed beneath her feet, soft but insistent. Unbidden, her steps moved.

The first archway. Then another. She let the rhythm guide her, staying within one until she was urged to the next. By the fifth, her body was weightless, her mind free.

Then in the final space, a presence unfolded around her.

Vast. Ancient. Unmistakable.

All will be gathered in time after they have followed their path.

The voice did not speak. It resonated. Rowena stiffened. Her heart thudded once, hard.

The crown you seek is larger than you expect and will require sacrifice. Remember, sometimes the blade that cuts, may also heal.

Rowena shuddered. Sacrifice? She touched her face, startled to find a single tear slipping from under the mask and down her cheek.

Let your heart dwell on this, and remember that great things are most often done in small moments. When the time comes, your choice will decide your destiny.

Understanding flowed over her. She knew who spoke. Her lips parted. "Queen Alona?" she whispered.

Yes, dear one.

A warmth spread around Rowena like standing in sunshine. It wrapped over her shoulders, unending and comforting.

You have completed your training, and your heartwood is solid. You are ready to move forward on your journey.

The snug shawl that had draped over her within the labyrinth dropped to the dirt, replaced by a chill to her bones.

She wasn't ready. Not yet. Her hands curled into fists. "I need to return to the cottage. To wait for Bram."

That is not possible. Your time in Havilar is complete.

Rowena shook her head. "But how will he find me?"

When your paths reconnect, it will not be in Havilar.

The certainty in the queen's voice left no room for protest.

We have been generous in allowing your stay, but that is now ended.

A lump lodged in Rowena's throat. She would have to find another way to let Bram know where she'd gone. But where would that be? "Where will I go?" she asked.

The one you seek is in the Veilrune Mountains. But when you arrive, remember to ask the right questions.

Another riddle. Rowena's brows furrowed. Why did everything have to be so complicated? She'd seen one of her father's maps of the continent once. There were several mountain ranges. How was she to know which was the Veilrunes?

You'll have to choose, dear one.

The warmth shifted. Rowena tensed. Choose? How? Just point and pick?

You are Lunara and Telana. One side follows the moons, the other the spirit.

Rowena trembled. The queen wasn't speaking of maps.

You cannot follow both.

Her pulse thumped against her ribs, but before she could ask what another question, the presence withdrew.

"My grandmother speaks with great wisdom," Evora's voice came suddenly, close.

Rowena yelped. "Don't startle me like that."

Evora gave a quiet laugh. "I'm sorry. I've been by your side for a while, and didn't realize you were unaware."

Rowena's lips parted. It couldn't have been that long. Rowena was just in the labyrinth's center. Wasn't she? She turned her focus outward. The world pulsed with life; birdsong, rustling leaves, the wind curling through the trees. Everything. Evora's heart thumped the loudest. But there were many others.

Creatures skittering through burrows beneath the roots. Eyes wide, blinking, watching from branches. Tiny wings buzzing and fluttering, stirring the surrounding air.

Everything was alive and in perfect harmony.

Water bubbled to Rowena's right. She twisted to listen. "Can we drink from the water nearby?"

"Yes. You are doing very well to have heard it." Evora took her hand and led her to the rippling creek.

"This is a good place to rest for your journey."

Rowena exhaled, releasing the last of her resistance. She had changed. Even if she wasn't sure what it meant yet.

Evora secured a waterskin to Rowena's belt. She ran her fingers over the shape, from vines and leaves, just as Ida had made before.

Evora had grown more subdued since Rowena completed the labyrinth trial.

Rowena crouched near a stone to brace her foot as she blindly tightened the laces of her boots.

Evora's voice, thoughtful, broke the silence. "Why is it that elves intermix together?"

Rowena's fingers froze, mid-knot, the laces of her boots cutting into her palm.

Again, the dryad raised the topic like Rowena was unnatural. Intermix.

This time the word landed heavier than it should have, curling in her gut, twisting.

She'd never had to explain it before. Never had to justify it. At home, no one questioned that her parents, one enchanted, one not, belonged together. No one had ever asked if she belonged.

Slowly, she straightened, tense. "The way you say 'intermix' . . ." The words strangled her, but she held her voice steady, "makes it sound like a corruption. I've explained this to you already."

Evora gasped. "That is not how I meant it. I have only ever known dryads. There are no other races in my realm. Your heritage is interesting, that's all."

Rowena returned her attention to her boots, grumbling to herself. "The dryads need to leave their lands more often, and stop thinking of themselves as better than others. Then you'd know the difference."

Silence.

Evora's constant chatter disappeared, and the stillness grew unnerving.

Finished with her boots, Rowena waited. The dryad had not left. Her heartbeat still thrummed an arm's length from Rowena's side.

"We don't see ourselves as better." Evora's voice wasn't timid, just . . . quieter. More thoughtful. "We don't leave because these are our lands. We are part of this forest. It is our home."

It was alright to love your home and still wish to explore. Rowena's fingers trembled. She checked that the waterskin was secure . . . again. "You have never wished to go anywhere else? To see other cultures and landscapes?"

"I love the forest." Even without sight, Rowena could hear a smile in Evora's words, soft and sure. "I find you fascinating and would love to know you better, yet it doesn't make me love my home less."

Rowena had yearned to travel. Since she was small, she had begged her father to take her with him. To collect rents, sail to the continent, see new places, meet others. She longed to taste foods from distant lands, hear stories of other realms. But there had always been the understanding.

One day, she would stay. One day, she would rule.

One day, that may never come.

"My home means everything to me. It's why I'm determined to go back."

Again, Evora paused. Silence settled between them.

"When you return, what will happen?

Rowena busied her fingers, tidying her braid. Evading.

"Will everyone wish to hear your stories?" Evora's foot brushed against the dirt. "I will tell everyone here of the time I met a half-Lunara."

Rowena's shoulders stiffened.

Again! Not Lunara.

Half.

No doubt Evora hadn't intended it to wound, but it did anyway. As if Rowena was something else. Something . . . less.

Rowena forced her jaw to unclench, swallowing back a bitter response eager to spew. But Evora's next words struck harder.

"Will they welcome you?"

Rowena's breath caught. A memory surged forward with brutal clarity.

Smoke. Fire.

The burning longhouse.

The shore pulling away as Uther's ship carried her toward slavery.

Her father's men slaughtered.

Her pulse thundered. The taste of ash filled her mouth.

When she recovered, she pulled her shoulders back. Tall. Unshaken.

"There is no one to welcome me home any longer." Her tone stabbed the words like honed steel. "When I return, it will be to destroy the usurper sitting on my throne."

Evora gave no reply. Distance crept between them, though Evora's fingers spread against Rowena's back, guiding her onto the path away from the creek.

After that, Evora spoke of the trees, the creatures, or the flowers along their way, but she didn't elaborate with her usual exuberance.

Rowena hadn't wanted to sever their bond, but she would not apologize for standing her ground. Not for this.

Still, she wondered, if they ever met again, could they still be friends?

After some time, no more than a full mark, Rowena guessed, the air grew warmer. A sweet floral scent mixed with the pine, thickening with each step.

Sweat gathered on Rowena's brow. Even Evora seemed affected. Her breath quickened and her steps became sluggish.

Rowena frowned, the leaf mask over her eyebrows protesting the movement. "Are you well?"

The dryad hesitated. When she spoke, there was a sadness in her tone. "Yes, but I will miss our time together."

Rowena exhaled through her nose. It had taken most of a day to reach the center of Havilar with Ida. Surely, they still had plenty of time to spend together; for Evora to resume filling the quiet with her own type of birdsong. A heaviness wrapped around Rowena. She hadn't expected to, but . . . "I will too."

Evora sighed and stopped walking.

Rowena halted beside her.

"I can go no further," Evora murmured. She seemed as if she wanted to say more, but stopped herself. Instead, she placed a hand on Rowena's shoulder. "Keep alert. I don't know what you may encounter next. May you be well rooted."

A strange tingling sensation washed over Rowena's skin. She shivered. Before she could say another word—silence.

Evora was gone.

A dull hum of heartbeats remained, but Evora's was missing.

The air thickened.

Rowena took a step, then another.

The leaves on her face grew dry. Brittle. Scratchy. She brushed her fingers over her cheeks. The leaf mask crumbled to dust. Rowena inhaled, blinking from the light, her sight restored.

The forest had changed. No longer tall pines but smooth barked trees that seemed to crowd around each other. Vines looped in all directions like too many errant ropes on a ship.

She was not in Havilar.

She was alone.

13

EVORA

EVORA STOOD ROOTED to the ground in her yew tree form, watching Rowena disappear into the pixie lands. The moment her friend vanished; uncertainty wrapped around her like clinging ivy.

She had done the right thing. Hadn't she?

The sun began its descent while she waited. For what? She dared not even allow the answer to form in her mind.

With a heavy heart, Evora let go of her tree's stillness, shifting back into her elven form. Warm air kissed her skin, but it felt foreign.

She should stay. Return deeper into Havilar, to her mother, to her grandmother.

And yet . . . Rowena's words twisted through her thoughts.

"The dryads should leave their lands more often."

It had seemed an offhand remark. But it had planted a seed. For all her grandmother's wisdom, for all her mother's guidance, had they ever truly considered leaving? The answer was an obvious no.

Her grandmother insisted their borders stay locked.

Evora had glimpsed the jungle countless times from Havilar's border. She had heard stories, nightmares, of what lay beyond. But she had never known for herself. Never questioned.

What if she had led Rowena into terrible danger?

What if the jungle was filled with wonders none in Havilar had ever seen?

What if Evora never found out?

A scream split the air from the jungle side. A sharp, raw sound cutting through the treetops. It was probably an animal.

Communicating. Friendly.

Probably.

Evora didn't recognize its call from any in her lands. Her friend could be in trouble, and Evora had led her to it. It was the final push she needed.

Her feet moved before her mind could catch up. One step, then another. Then she was running. Branches lashed against her arms. Vines snatched at her ankles.

The jungle swallowed her whole, its breath thick and damp against her neck.

Strange sounds echoed all around her. Chirping insects, rustling wings, distant howls.

Evora's pulse quickened. She'd listened to similar chords many times. There was nothing to fear. But there was a different cadence; strange, unfamiliar.

She'd never felt so small. Never felt so lost.

Evora shuddered. The jungle pressed in, loud, chaotic, unfamiliar. Her sap churned, her instincts screaming for stillness.

For safety.

For home.

But she had grabbed her chance to explore. To gain independence. Her first steps beyond the border. She couldn't turn back already. Not yet.

She closed her eyes, begging herself to remain calm. She could do this.

It was so different. What had she expected?

The shift overtook her before she could stop it. Her skin hardened, stiffening as bark curled up her arms. Roots burst from her feet, anchoring her in place. The hum of the jungle faded, replaced by a deep, steady rhythm. Even in a new realm, the land provided harmony. Her breath slowed. The world muffled in green stillness.

Safe. Unseen. Untouched.

Then a voice sliced through the cacophony, battering at her thoughts.

Evora, I see you.

Her sap froze.

You stand out in the middle of all this madness. Turn around and face me.

Her mother. Here.

Her roots tightened.

Her grandmother had spent a millennium as a tree, never shifting, never leaving. Maybe she could do the same. Remain like this forever, hidden amid the chaos.

Alone. The only one of her kind.

Evora, face me. Return now.

Ida's voice was steady. Unyielding. A frayed vine, ready to snap.

Evora's branches shuddered.

She *was* homesick. The sun had not even moved, and she already longed to rush back across the border.

Her branches grew heavy, like stone. Her sap boiled, searing beneath her bark.

With a final tremor, she let go. Slowly, she twisted, returning to her elven form. Her feet settled onto the jungle floor, damp and unfamiliar. She kept her gaze low, staring at the jumbled vines near her mother's feet.

Ida waited in silence.

It grew harder for Evora to breathe, between the thick air and her mother's disapproval.

"What made you do such a thing?"

The words were not harsh. Not angry. But they held weight. Evora swallowed her shame.

"Have you never wondered what else is out there?" she asked in a whisper. "She's all alone, braving this realm by herself. I thought . . . maybe I could go with her. Guide her. Strengthen what she learned from us."

The jungle buzzed with unseen life, but between mother and daughter—silence.

Evora continued to avoid her mother's gaze. A heartbeat. Two.

Ida exhaled.

"There are reasons we stay within our borders." Her voice was gentle now. "Safety is one of them."

Evora flinched. That was understandable for themselves. Except, didn't others deserve safety as well?

"We cannot predict what will happen to those who live in the dangerous realms outside our home. We can only take care of ourselves."

Evora repeated the words to herself. It wasn't a rebuke. It was a truth. It was the way of Havilar.

"Now, come with me and return home." Ida reached out her hand.

Evora stared at it. Part of her ached to refuse. To stay and prove she could survive in a different realm. That she could root to more than one soil. But . . .

She'd already proven otherwise.

She laced her fingers with her mother's.

The moment she did, warmth wrapped around her. Like stepping back into the sunlight after standing too long in the shade. She had already missed it.

Together, they strode back toward the border.

The jungle faded behind them, wild and unknown. Evora didn't look back, but as she crossed the border, her heart whispered—soon.

14

———

BRAM

Remnants of wispy shadows scurried to the corners as dawnlight filtered into Bram's room.

"Bram?" Lhoris' whisper barely stirred the air.

"Am I not allowed privacy?" he scoffed, startling the apprentice hepta into a stumble. Her copper robes snagged in the slim opening of the door.

"I apologize," she said, slipping inside with a tray of food. "I grew concerned when you didn't answer my knocking."

Bram cringed inwardly but forced a neutral tone. "I finally fell asleep after struggling most of the night."

Lhoris darted a glance to the tightly made bed as she set the tray on a side table. Her brows knitted. "You straightened your coverings?"

"It is warm in here. I slept on top." He nudged the conversation forward. "Has the Heptad retrieved Rowena?"

She held his gaze for a moment and then stepped aside. "The council has reconvened and wishes to speak with you. They offer apologies for missing the Morning Blessing. They didn't share any other information with me. You have time to eat, then they insist I escort you straight to their chambers."

Would they tell him if they had found her? Bram shoved the thoughts of Farryn and the rebels aside. He couldn't let Rowena's safety suffer because their cause had rattled his loyalties.

"Have you eaten?" He didn't like the thought of eating while she stood watch.

"Yes, some time ago. But thank you for asking," Lhoris said with a small, surprised smile.

The food was still warm, and he downed it quickly, uncomfortable with Lhoris having to stand by and wait.

Once finished, he brushed down the front of his tunic, and caught the smear of dried mud on his boots. Surprising it hadn't fallen off during the scramble through the streets with Killian.

"Lead the way," he said, gesturing to Lhoris.

He closed the door behind himself and fell into step behind her. As they wound up the curving tower stairs, Bram discreetly knocked his boots against the edges of the steps, scraping away the last traces of his night underground.

Lhoris opened the council door and slipped inside, leaving a gap for Bram to follow. To his surprise, the Heptad was already seated, their faces as hard and cold as the tower's basalt walls.

"That will be all, Lhoris," Achan said. "I'll expect that report about the rebel rumor immediately after Morning Blessing."

"Yes, High Hepta," Lhoris said, bobbing a quick bow before hurrying out.

"Rebels? Here or elsewhere?" Bram lifted one eyebrow in mock surprise. His feigned indifference seemed to work; several heptas dropped their gazes to the table or darted uneasy glances at one another. High Hepta Achan, however, held his stare from the center seat.

"That is not your concern."

"I would think it should be." Bram eased himself into a casual stance, stretching one leg farther than the other. "Wouldn't the Seeker be more effective at quelling a resistance? Though, if it's only a rumor, then there's no threat at all."

Of course, the Heptad knew about the old lava tubes winding beneath the island like an ant colony. Clearing those caverns would take an army of sentinels. But why risk it when he alone could be more effective? He could slip warnings to Farryn, protect their identities, and stage a failed assault to appease the council.

"We are sorting out the situation. You have other duties to attend." Something strange threaded through Mereb's voice. Hesitation? No—resignation.

"Entertaining the disavowed's information is a waste of time." Folas braced his arms on the table, darting glances between Achan on his left and the brooding Nasir on his right. "If only true spies weren't so costly."

"Which is why we keep reading their messages." Achan lifted his hands in a motion of weary dismissal. "This discussion isn't why we're here. Let's get to the task at hand."

So many lies. No one wanted to disobey, if they could help it. At least, that's was what Bram believed . . . before.

The more the Heptad spoke, the more their words twisted. Oaths of duty, of order—yet every decree served only themselves. He had spent his life enforcing their will, believing their laws protected Edenia. But now? He wasn't sure of anything.

"Have you retrieved Rowena from Havilar?"

"That is irrelevant to our discussion," Achan said.

"Not if you wish me to cooperate." Too forceful. Too exposing. Too dangerous.

Silence slammed into the room. Every gaze sharpened, fixed on him.

"The dryads will release her when they see fit. This meeting concerns your indiscretions," Achan said, his expression carved from stone.

"There will be no punishment, provided you retrieve the sword from the mage," Mereb said. "All the pieces of the armor and the heartstones must be brought under druid control."

A growl rumbled in Bram's chest. He expected support from her.

"I've committed no indiscretions that require punishment. The armor wasn't exchanged or bartered or given. It was lost in battle. You've interrupted my plans just to demand I finish what I was already doing."

"Watch your insolence." Folas laid his hands flat on the table, poised to rise.

Bram forced his shoulders to loosen. His neck throbbed with tension, a warning to hold his tongue.

A slow breath. Steady. Measured.

Control. Always control.

This entire business was nonsense. His time in Saganus had dragged him from Rowena, exposed Heptad scandals, and endangered innocent druids. He released his clenched fists, forcing his body into stillness. Too many emotions warred inside him. He had to cling to logic. To reason.

Collect Rowena. Retrieve the sword from Fidessa. Find the Lunastone.

He straightened and dipped his chin solemnly.

"My apologies. I will leave at once to continue recovering the armor."

Achan narrowed his eyes. "Not quite yet—"

The door burst open and Bram dropped low, instinct taking over as he readied for attack.

A sentinel burst into the chamber, Lhoris stumbling at his side.

"I apologize," Lhoris wheezed. "I tried to stop him, but he insists he must speak with you right away."

Bram straightened, glancing over his shoulder, waiting for Achan's command.

"Let him in." Achan's smug expression glinted with the thrill of a secret he couldn't wait to reveal. The hair on Bram's arms prickled. Something was deeply wrong in his homelands. "Then go into the city. Bring me that report."

Lhoris slipped out the door as two more sentinels dragged a male between them. The homespun clothes and frail body made Bram's stomach twist. A warning sparked through him. Stop. Protect.

"We found one of the rebels, your graces," one of the sentinels said.

Bram didn't catch which sentinel spoke. His gaze locked on the fist tangled in Killian's light brown hair, jerking the boy's bruised face into view

"Stand up, filth." The sentinel yanked Killian's hair, forcing the boy onto unsteady feet.

Why hadn't the boy gone home as he'd promised?

Bram's stomach lurched. He should have escorted Killian all the way to safety.

When Killian wobbled, Bram lurched forward and steadied him. "Was this treatment necessary?"

Killian flinched, lifting his bruised gaze to Bram. Questions battered Bram's mind, but he said nothing. He flattened his lips, willing the boy to mimic his silence.

"Where did you find this abomination? Look at him. Sickly, disgusting." Folas scrambled from his chair and slammed his back against the Heptad's private door.

Two other hepta, Soira, with her severe bun and portly Jandar, hurried to join him along the far wall. Achan rose to his feet, but stayed planted at the table. Mereb, the petite Chanda, and brooding Nasir remained seated.

"Are you so afraid of one, barely more than an elfling?" Bram asked, voice sharp. "And since when do sentinels brutalize fae in the streets?"

"When they're charged to clear a vermin infestation," Siora answered from her place along the wall. "That's why we *have* sentinels."

"I would never do such a thing." Bram clenched his fists at his sides. He wanted to shake the sneering woman until she understood.

How dare they perverse his order into blind enforcers?

Killian's already slumped shoulders sagged another inch. He dropped his chin to his chest, the last of his fight draining away. Bram hoped it was from relief, not because standing took every scrap of strength he had left.

If Achan couldn't even keep the council in order, no wonder the city rotted from the inside. Bram had to put an end to this, *fast*, and get Killian out. The elfling needed Farryn's healing skills. But not in the dispensary. That would risk exposing everything.

First, get Killian free. Then, call for Farryn.

"Bram is correct. Sentinels are meant to keep the peace, not shatter it." Achan tented his fingers beneath his chin. "After such a public display, we'll need to appease those who witnessed the atrocity. Perhaps your earlier offer, Bram, would serve us better."

If it prevented more sentinel abuse, Bram would take the burden without hesitation. He could help Killian faster that way. "I can be more discreet."

Achan's mouth curled, not in humor, but in cold calculation. "I'll grant you the responsibility to dispose of this blight however you see fit. Quietly, of course.

"He is needed to find the armor," Mereb said to Achan. "There are less than three months before The Reaping."

"And five more pieces to find," Folas added, still lingering away from the table.

"Four," Achan answered. "The dryad scroll and heartstone have never left Havilar."

Bram huffed quietly at the information they had withheld. "All the more reason for me to leave now. Whatever uprising, or whatever it is, can wait until the realm is secure. Inform the sentinels to stand down until I return."

Killian lifted his face to stare at Bram. Hope sparked too bright in his bruised features. The Heptad would notice any slight connection between them.

"And then I'll deal with the menace." Bram clenched his jaw, the deception like rot on his tongue. He had to search for the rebels himself.

Otherwise, they would send others. Others who didn't hesitate to follow orders. Orders they didn't question.

The tunnels were no longer safe, but first, he had to get Killian out alive.

"How dare you—" Killian's protest cut short as a sentinel backhanded him across the face.

Bram spun and seized the sentinel's tunic, hauling him nose to nose. "Do that again, and deal with me."

"You are in the Heptad's chambers. Show proper respect or be removed." Mereb's voice made the hair on Bram's neck rise.

There was more steel beneath her kindness than he'd given her credit.

Bram released the sentinel, but didn't step back until the man dropped his gaze in defeat. Only then did Bram turn, stand at ease, and wait for the council to continue.

"Since the sword merely needs retrieving," Achan said, tone almost casual. "Three weeks should be enough to secure it from the former queen and find the heartstone. The rabble won't have time to mobilize. Any others foolish enough to surface will find a sword at their throat."

Surface? How much did he already know?

"I'm not sure I agree with that," Folas said, edging closer to his chair. He flicked a hand toward Killian. "This display could have been the spark to light a full blaze."

"We'll need to make a public show of visiting the city," Mereb said. "Ease any tensions before they fan into something worse."

It was a good plan. Bram still trusted her. She'd always been the most reasonable hepta.

Perhaps she would listen to the rebels.

Then Mereb turned her gaze on him.

Her blue eyes, once so full of warmth, held something else now.

Something hard.

Something cold.

"If you are not back within three weeks," she said. No mercy colored her tone. "We will send the sentinels to cleanse the city by any means necessary."

He stilled.

He'd been wrong about all of them.

There was *no* trustworthy member of the council.

"We don't need to worsen the problem by stirring more troubling publicity," Folas growled. "If word spreads that Saganus is in turmoil, it may spur pressure from Ha'mon. We'll be seen as weak."

Bram stepped closer, voice low and cutting. "If I fail, there's more at stake than your reputation. Or a little unrest. All Edenia will suffer if the so-called King of Mortus escapes his prison."

Folas leaned back, glaring.

"Don't be overly dramatic, Bram." Mereb shook her head, dismissing his warning with a cold smile. "We are well aware of the stakes."

"I don't want a scandal any more than the rest of you." Achan tapped his fingers against the table's edge. "But Bram is correct. The armor and heartstones must come first."

"And the moon-born," Bram added. If anyone else found them before he did, it would be disastrous.

"The prophecy only needs one." Achan said.

"We don't know that for sure." Mereb twisted in her seat to gain Achan's full attention. "The sparrow of silver fire will strike the owl from above and below when thrice the seven gather before the prime is dark . . . All we've deduced for certain is our role as the seven."

"As more are found, they should be gathered here." Folas sank back into his seat.

"Agreed," Achan said. "Three weeks. Then return."

Bram twisted, making a show of perusing Killian from head to toe. "He needs rest. And a healer if you want to quell any rumblings."

Bram left his hands loose at his sides, though every muscle coiled to move. He would grab Killian before either sentinel could react.

Killian must have sensed Achan's stare. The boy lifted his head and forced himself to stand tall, pride stiffening his battered frame.

"Did he give any names?" Achan asked the sentinels.

"No, your grace," the one who'd hit Killian answered. "Gave him a lot of chances, too."

A small blessing.

Achan gave a slow, smug grin and turned his attention to Bram. "The sentinels understand their duties. Still think you can do better? Perhaps our hopes for you were too ambitious, and we should reconsider our plans."

"I will not fail."

"That's good to hear," the High Hepta continued. "Because if you're not up to the task, someone with your skills roaming

Edenia would be too dangerous. We would be forced to ensure their . . . safety."

They had already changed him so much. What else did they plan take?

"You think you are beyond reproach?" Achan braced his hands on the council table, leaning in, his gaze boring into Bram. "I can see it on your face. You think yourself more powerful than me."

"I don't think it wise for either of us to test that." Bram's fists clenched against his thighs. The challenge bristled under his skin but he held himself back. The last thing he wanted was for Killian to see his Seeker form.

Achan ambled behind the three heptas to his right, his soft shoes whispering against the stone.

Nothing stood between him and Killian now. His voice slithered into the silence. "Are you fast enough to save him?"

Bram's body coiled tighter, like a predator ready to strike. Shadows flickered at his feet, writhing and waiting. "This is unnecessary," he said, edging his voice with warning.

If Achan moved, Bram would stop him.

The High Hepta didn't spare him a glance. His focus stayed locked on his prey—Killian.

"What was that?" Killian stared at Bram's boots, his brows knitting tight with confusion.

"That," Achan murmured, "is a threat far bigger than you."

Achan took another slow step forward, savoring every moment.

"Have you heard tales of the Seeker, boy?" Achan's words dripped with malice. "The beast lurking in the shadows of Edenia, hunting without mercy?"

Killian swallowed. Hard.

His fingers twitched at his sides, as if to reach for a weapon or raise them in surrender.

Bram didn't wait. "Leave him alone."

Darkness surged around him, curling like living tendrils, spilling across the floor to billow at the room's edges.

Achan tilted his head, his eyes gleaming. Satisfied. White light erupted from his chest.

Bram lunged. His transformation surged instantly, runes flashing, claws ripping free, horns casting twisted shadows along the walls.

But he was too late.

Too slow.

Blinding light cleaved through the air like a dozen swords.

A single heartbeat.

The searing stench of burning flesh.

A second heartbeat—broken, out of sync.

The blazing light blinked out.

Silence.

Darkness rushed over the room.

Bram knelt over Killian's body. The boy who had reminded him so much of himself. The boy he'd promised to protect.

Motionless.

Tattered.

Lifeless.

Both sentinels lay in ruins beside him, sacrificed in Achan's display. Bodies charred beyond recognition.

But Bram couldn't tear his gaze from Killian's face.

Still set in that determined expression. The one that had made Bram both proud and afraid. The face of someone too young to understand the dangers. Too eager to prove himself.

Bram's breath came sharp, ragged.

Too late. He'd been too late.

The weight of that failure crashed through him, staggering and resolute. Another face flashed in his memory—his first commander, who'd taught him that a leader's first duty was to protect the defenseless.

He'd failed that most sacred promise.

Something inside him fractured. Not just anger, though rage boiled under his skin, but grief.

Raw and overwhelming.

This boy had trusted him. Had looked at him with admiration. Had followed his advice.

And Bram let him die.

"Why would you do such a thing?" Bram's roar shook the walls, ripping from somewhere deep and primal inside him. His claws tore into the stone floor, the force reverberating through his arms. Pain sparked up his shoulders, but it was nothing compared to the hollow ache devouring his chest.

The door slammed open.

Lhoris.

She skidded to a halt, her breath catching as her wide eyes swept the scene. Her gaze locked first on Bram. His Seeker form. His claws. His horns. The blood.

Then she stared at Killian.

Bram saw the moment understanding crystallized in her eyes.

Horror. Doubt. Fear.

"What did you do?" she whispered.

Bram's stomach twisted.

Not 'what happened?' Not 'who did this?'

But 'what did *you* do?'

The accusation struck deeper than any blade could reach. After everything, his years of service, his unwavering loyalty . . . he was still the monster in their eyes. And now, with Killian's blood on his hands, how could he deny it?

He had promised protection. And delivered death.

Achan stepped forward, unbothered by the carnage. Innocent blood splattered across his silver robe—as if Killian's body were nothing more than an inconvenience.

"Go and fulfill your duties, Seeker." Achan's voice stayed smooth. Almost bored. "We'll try to keep this quiet. After all, it might spur the rebels to retaliate over your . . . *carelessness* before you return."

Bram turned to Lhoris, fists clenched at his sides. "This was not my doing."

Lhoris shook her head and slid a step backward. She didn't believe him.

Her gaze flickered to the floor then his claws.

Not to Achan. Not to the true threat.

She'd already made up her mind.

"Leave paritor," Mereb ordered, void of warmth. "And tell no one what you have seen."

Beads of sweat glinted on Lhoris' forehead; her face as pallid as cut stone. Without another word, she turned and fled.

Bram's vision blurred, fury boiling behind his eyes.

Folas sat forward, without so much as a glance at the corpses. His beady eyes met Bram's gaze with a steady, unwavering ease. "Handy that there are other moon-born to fulfill the prophecy. In case something were to happen to the one you're so fond of."

Bram went still. His blood iced his veins. They were threatening Rowena.

His hands curled into fists.

Shadows writhed violently at his feet.

"Do not touch her."

Folas smiled—a slow knowing smile

Mereb folded her hands atop the table. Her face like stone. "Three weeks, Seeker."

No warmth. No concern. No hint of the compassion he once believed she possessed.

"Do not be late."

Bram forced himself to look down. At Killian.

At the boy who should have lived.

A lump rose in his throat. His chest burned.

He'd spent his entire life serving the Heptad. Following orders. Enforcing their rule. And now, they expected him to watch as they slaughtered the innocent?

He lifted his gaze, taking in every face of the council. He would remember this. All of it.

He would return. And he would warn the rebels.

When he joined them.

15

ROWENA

By the time Rowena slipped past Havilar's boundary, the skies had deepened to violet. She turned a slow circle beneath the dense, tangled canopy. If she squinted, she could almost imagine the straight-backed, towering pines of the dryad forest behind her, but it was gone.

Here, chaos reigned. Spiraling trunks and canopies knitted together in a wild tapestry that shut out the sky.

She had entered Tixamar. Alone.

A realm of pixies she understood no better than Havilar. Would they let her leave? Or trap her like the dryads?

If she'd only traveled more. If she understood the realms better.

Dangerous thoughts. This wasn't the time for memories, or regrets. She had to live. She had to find Bram.

No matter what lay ahead.

Vines curled like living rope, braiding itself around trees with bark too smooth, too pale. The trunks twisted in wild arcs, as if they'd coiled to spite logic. Wide, waxy leaves gleamed under scattered moonlight, sheltering clusters of thorns that jutted out like hidden teeth.

Half-rotted fruit littered the ground, writhing with frenzied ants that made her skin itch just looking at them.

The air was thick with sweet decay, each breath tasting of fermented danger. A sharp musk prickled at her nostrils and settled into her clothes.

Rowena tugged at the neckline of her tunic. Skandan was cool. Mist-cloaked, even in summer.

Here the thick, sticky heat melted her skin beneath her clothes.

High above, leaves whispered in the canopy, swaying as stars winked through shifting gaps. Masah's silver light flickered with brief moments of calm before vanishing behind the leaves.

When Bram returned to the cottage . . . guilt twisted in her chest. He'd be furious she left. But she'd had no choice.

Ida had made that decision for her. Would she tell him where Rowena ended up? He would follow if she did.

Rowena believed that with every strength she had left.

If she'd thought to grab her knives when she had the chance, she would have carved marks into the trees. A path for him to follow. But now . . .

She pressed her palm against a thin, angled trunk, grounding herself against the jungle's oppressive weight. The smooth, cool bark offered relief against her heated skin. A steadying breath.

Then, a pulse of power.

Enchantment sparked from her palm in a concentrated burst, leaving behind a faint silver glow.

When the light faded, a charred handprint remained. Even if he didn't see it, he'd sense her essence etched into the living wood.

It would be enough. It had to be enough.

She would have to choose where to leave her marks with

care. She couldn't count on refilling her enchantment, not with only slips of Masah's light breaking through.

Her time in the cottage, hiding from the night skies, hadn't helped either.

She exhaled and turned toward the east. Nothing familiar waited ahead. But this wasn't the comfortable cottage.

This wasn't the time to sink into her fears. This wasn't the time to panic.

"It's time to move." Her voice shattered the stillness, and the jungle reacted.

Insects hushed. No wings buzzed. Even the breeze above failed to reach the forest floor. Silence pressed in like a held breath.

Sweat slid down the side of her face, another trickling down her back.

The air tasted thick. Heavy.

Every breath an effort.

One foot. Then the other. She pushed on.

Three steps in, her hand parted two broad leaves, and snagged straight into a spiderweb the size of a quilt. Sticky silk wrapped around her fingers. Clung to her tunic. Tangled in her hair.

She swiped and twisted and stumbled, heart hammering. The clinging strands held like vines trying to bind her. The web finally released, but she kept hopping and fussing long after.

When she realized she was free, shivers raced down her arms. She braced herself, hands on her knees, struggling to calm the trembling.

But the jungle wasn't finished.

Tiny, biting flies swarmed her, pinpricks against her neck, her hands, up her nose, even behind her ears. She yelped, slapping at her skin, flailing like a fish on the shore.

Tree roots twisted beneath her boots. She scraped her palms, pushing through the spiny underbrush. It didn't matter.

Get away. Move!

She ducked beneath an arched tree limb and collapsed, gasping for breath. The thick canopy blocked out most of the sky. Shadows blanketed the ground. She strained her ears for any sound. Any sound. Why was it so quiet?

Too quiet.

A cool drop hit her shoulder.

She froze.

Slowly, carefully, she tilted her head and glanced sideways.

A yellow-green snake slithered down her arm, its forked tongue flicking.

A whimper caught in her throat as she dropped her shoulder and jerked away. The serpent landed with a wet plop beside her foot, slithering into the leafy underbrush.

Her breathing shattered.

Her body trembled as if she stood in freezing water instead of stifling heat. Which way should she go?

The snake hid somewhere, waiting.

She swept the area, moving only her eyes, then dared to tip her gaze upward. Her stomach flipped.

Dozens of yellow-green snakes hung from the branches above, their pale scales nearly luminescent against the darker leaves.

Vines? No! Camouflaged coils, looping. Waiting.

She bolted.

Branches clawed at her sleeves. Mud sucked at her boots. Thorns sliced at her arms and legs.

Nothing mattered except escape.

Her lungs burned. Her thoughts scattered.

She hurtled through the jungle, every step a frantic plea for survival.

Predators lurked in every shadow.

Prey. She was just prey.

That's what she was. No experience from Skandan would save her now. This land would roast her flesh and toss aside her bones.

Swarm her. Swallow her.

Leave no trace she ever existed.

A glimpse of water—a river. She veered away before getting too close, racing along its edge, keeping it on her right. The ground grew steeper. Her thighs burned.

Rowena burst into a clearing and collapsed onto a patch of wet dirt, all grace abandoned.

A small waterfall tumbled into a crystal pool. A narrow creek slipped from the far side, its gurgle barely louder than her ragged breathing.

Open to the sky, the glade felt . . . safe.

Soft, spongy moss covered the ground and rocks. Fragrant purple flowers dotted the bark of a nearby tree. Respite.

Rowena buried her face in her hands as the tears came fast and raw. She gasped between sobs, unable to quiet them. She gave up trying.

Some warrior she turned out to be.

The waterfall's gentle splash gradually trickled through her panic.

Each drop steady. Determined.

Like Bram's patience.

The thought ambushed her, unwanted. Unstoppable.

Her fingers dug into the moss. Its softness so different from the thorns that had torn at her skin moments ago. Soft.

Like *his* touch when she fell apart.

Since Bram brought her to the cottage, she had been unraveling. And now, she was truly gone.

No sword. No Safi. No markings left behind for him to follow.

She had never felt so alone.

She plunged her hands beneath the waterfall, drinking the clean water, and splashing her face before sinking back to her knees.

A cluster of cave berries huddled within her reach. She plucked a handful and ate greedily, the juices sweet on her tongue.

The glade's stillness pressed against her, too similar to the cottage. Her mind betrayed her, fleeing back to that past comfort.

Bram hadn't spoken then. Not at first.

Just watched over her with those glowing eyes, his Seeker form, providing strength and safety.

Horns sharp, armor black, presence steady.

A twig snapped, somewhere in the jungle. Her head jerked up, eyes scanning.

Nothing.

But the fear remained, hovering at the edge of the clearing's fragile peace.

Still, she couldn't stop the memory now. The moments when silence stretched between them until she thought she'd scream, but then Bram had shifted, offering his steady presence Guarding her mind. Guarding her heart.

Druid form. Soft touches. Slower breathing, so hers would match.

He gave her space to fall apart, and a place to rest.

Rowena inhaled, reaching for those memories even as her ears strained for danger. She let the rhythm of the waterfall steady her heartbeat, just as Bram had once.

That's what the archways in the labyrinth had offered, too.

A place of rest. A place to listen. A place to be patient.

Her fingers curled around her imaginary dagger, willing it to appear. Rest was temporary. She would need to move again soon. Face the dangers . . . and her fears.

And that's when she noticed it.

A new rhythm. Subtle. Lighter than Bram's.

Quicker, but held in check.

Anticipation simmering beneath calm. Not an animal. She understood the difference now. There was someone nearby.

She stayed still. Eyes closed. Hands planted in the moss.

There. Again.

A golden thread, glimmering in her mind's eye, like spun sunlight caught on a breeze. It trailed toward a tree, twisting around another until both had become one.

A hidden stranger. Watching. Spying?

Rowena rubbed her palms over her thighs, anchoring herself.

Breathe. Focus.

A glimmer of curiosity met her search. Faint boldness. Easier to sense now, though her own emotions churned like a storm. She pushed to her feet and arched her back, tilting her face toward the sky.

A bitter laugh slipped past her lips.

Lungol hung high among the stars. A crescent bright and sharp.

Of course. The volatile moon. No wonder she'd fallen apart. It never gave rest. Still, perhaps that same chaos sharpened her awareness.

She caught the spy's emotion flaring; surprise, then a rising nervousness.

Pixies, the stories said, were small, winged tricksters.

She imagined sensing them would seem sharper, pinpoint jabs of emotion. She could be wrong. But the one nearby seemed her size.

She brushed the leaves from her knees. Shifted her stance to face east. All deliberate.

The rhythm faltered. Curiosity flared again.

"Perhaps it would do better for both of us," Rowena said, voice clear in the stillness, "if you introduced yourself. There are far more terrifying things in this realm than me. I'd hate to mistake you for one of them."

A pause.

The heartbeat rhythm vanished.

Rowena waited.

Then she shifted her weight, sliding closer to a thin tree with high branches, pressing her back against the bark.

There. Just as she expected.

A brush of movement. A held breath.

Cold metal pressed against her throat.

Rowena froze, not daring to breathe.

"Who are you?" A female voice purred beside her ear, too calm. "You are no pixie. And you are not Solara."

Rowena remained motionless; her gaze fixed ahead. No sudden moves.

Only a whisper. "Move your blade."

The woman complied, but only just. Enough for speech, not escape. Every motion was precise. Practiced.

"Answer."

"Skandan." Rowena kept her tone steady. Let her assume she was Telana. Unenchanted. Unthreatening.

Let her underestimate.

A scoff answered. A hard shove between the shoulder blades sent her tumbling. The slope gave way beneath her boots.

She toppled and rolled. The river ready to catch her.

A hanging vine. Her hand shot out, clinging fast, breath sharp in her chest.

"I should have known from the accent," the woman called, a

body length above, silhouetted against the moonlit slope. Her teeth flashed from a grin as she sheathed her blade.

Rowena glared, chest still heaving from the fall. "I don't have an accent. *You* do."

The woman laughed; a rich sound, rising and falling like a song.

Musical. Confident.

She had to be Solara. Rowena remembered a traveler once, years back, who had visited Taesing. He carried the same interesting rhythm. Her father hadn't let her speak with him. She'd never understood why.

"I suppose we will have to agree to disagree."

Rowena climbed the incline, accepting the woman's outstretched hand when she reached the top. "I thought you might be a pixie."

"I am from Farradar." The woman stepped back, dusting her palms on a breezy tunic that shimmered like silk. "My name is Tephra. You?"

"Rowena."

Silence hung between them. Not heavy. Not light.

Sweat trickled down both their temples, but where Rowena still fought against the heat, Tephra wore it like a second skin.

Her trousers, light blue, flowing open at the sides, and tied at the ankle, fluttered with the slightest breeze.

She couldn't be much older than Rowena, if at all. But she carried herself like someone born for power. Even here, in mud and vine, the weight of command clung to her stance.

Rowena had a throne.

She glanced at her muddy tunic. The hole in her trousers. It would be evident to no one.

"Why are you in Tixamar?" Rowena asked. "Are there others with you?" There would be safety in numbers. Unless they meant to capture. She had to stay ready for anything.

Tephra didn't answer right away. Her arms remained at her sides, open, unthreatening, but ready. "Why do you want to know?"

"This forest is dangerous."

"That doesn't answer my question." A flicker of irritation, or was it caution, twitched in Tephra's voice. "All lands are dangerous."

"I have a long journey, and I need to understand who is nearby."

"Where are you headed?"

Rowena inhaled. "Bethon."

Tephra tilted her head, as if listening to something deeper than words. "You said you are from Skandan. Yes?"

Rowena nodded, both curious, and concerned why she asked.

"That is across the Straight from Bethon. How are you so far south?"

Rowena pressed her tongue against the roof of her mouth, forcing herself to remain silent. Form a reasonable a lie.

"Trade mission. Our ship went down . . . in a storm. Wrecked. Bethon was to be our last stop," she said. "I swam ashore."

A sharp brow arched. Disbelief, clear as dawn.

Rowena met her stare without blinking. Let her think what she wanted. The truth was more unbelievable anyway—that she'd survived Havilar. That the Queen of the dryads had let her go.

To her left, the jungle thickened, shadows pooled where Lungol's light didn't reach. To her right, the creek spilled down rocks in a narrow cascade. Behind, the river. Ahead, a Solara.

Alright then.

"You haven't answered why you are here?"

Tephra glanced away. A new expression crossing her face,

calculating. "This is the best place to cross the river. We go together. It will benefit you as well, yes?"

Not an answer. Again.

Fine. Let her keep her secrets. Rowena had her own.

"How can you be sure?"

"I followed it for several leagues. There is no better."

Rowena's fingers twitched at her side. That meant Tephra had been following a similar path. Perhaps behind her for some time. Watching. Tracking. The realization prickled along her spine, raising the hairs on her neck.

"You came from the south?" She kept her voice steady, though her heart quickened.

"Yes." Another graceful arch of her brow. She would not share more.

Trust was not an option.

Rowena studied the woman's face; the curve of her smile, the gleam in her eyes that revealed nothing and promised less.

What game was she playing? And why did it matter now, with the river to cross and dangers lurking everywhere?

She weighed her choices. Time slipped away with each breath.

Go alone and risk the current. Go with this stranger and risk a knife when she least expected it.

"I will agree, if you keep your blade where it belongs. Not at my throat."

Tephra smiled, wide and unbothered. "You expect me to believe you cannot do the same to me? That your blade is not tucked away as well?"

It was. On the small table, near the bed in the cottage. She'd stopped wearing them. Hadn't even considered them when Ida offered her the chance.

She straightened. Pulled her lips into a matching grin. "I guess we'll have to trust each other, at least until we're across."

Tephra stepped closer, raising the back of her hand.

Rowena leaned back a fraction, wary.

"In Farradar, we seal a pledge this way. Hand to hand, or nose to nose." She smirked. "Hands seems better here."

"Hmm." Rowena tapped the back of her hand on Tephra's.

"There. Done." Tephra nodded toward the river. "Now, we only have to survive the river."

Without hesitation, she picked her way past Rowena and down the hill, barefoot grace moving with surety through roots and vines.

Rowena lingered for half a breath, memorizing Tephra's path. If she had made a poor decision allying with a Solara, there was no way to know.

But staying alone was no longer an option.

She followed, stepping with caution after her mysterious new companion.

The hillside leveled after another twenty feet, opening to the river's edge. Water rushed around jagged boulders, surging fast enough to swallow them whole.

"This is the narrowest part of the river for a league at least," Tephra said, already picking her way forward. "It does not look deep. We will move from stone to stone. There was a yacare earlier, back that way. There are likely more. Keep alert." She swatted her hand, dismissive. Already moving on without waiting.

Rowena caught up, eyes narrowing at the churning current. "Strong water. What's a yacare?"

"A beast. A giant lizard with skin like stone and a snout full of wicked teeth. It waits under the surface, grabs your leg, and drags you under."

Tephra lunged without warning and snatched at Rowena's trouser leg.

Rowena yelped, stumbling backward.

Tephra laughed and lifted a shoulder, unapologetic. "We are safe ... mostly. Too fast for them here."

She spoke as if death by river monster was an afterthought.

Rowena's mouth went dry. She glanced to the water's surface; dark, slick, hiding Caelus knew what. "We can't see under there. How will we know if something's close?"

"Their eyes sit atop their heads. They surface to watch the banks." Tephra stretched her back with a casual roll of her shoulders. "They do not come ashore often. They prefer slower, murky water."

Rowena studied the river. Four or five yards across. Possible. If they were quick. Only one stretch between boulders looked risky. "You've been to Tixamar before?"

"No." Tephra tugged the ties at the bottom of her trousers. "But I travel often. You learn the land quickly or you do not survive."

That did nothing for Rowena's confidence. She'd been floundering since she left the cottage.

Tephra checked the knife on her belt, then glanced over her shoulder. "Ready?"

Rowena rolled her neck. Something in Tephra's certainty set her on edge. As if the woman always had a plan, and Rowena was not sure she was part of it.

Before she could answer, the jungle silenced.

No chirps. No rustling wings. Nothing.

In Skandan, that only meant one thing. A predator had arrived.

Rowena snapped her gaze to Tephra, whose eyes had gone wide. Neither spoke.

Rowena listened, reaching inward. And there it was. A slow, heavy rhythm. A heartbeat too large to belong to anything safe. She gripped Tephra's wrist. "Move."

They raced for the river's edge. Water. Escape. Her mind offered nothing else. No plan. Just run.

Dirt blurred beneath her feet. Tephra's breathing harsh beside her. The heartbeat grew louder. Closer.

Two steps into the water, Rowena's foot hit slick stone. The world tilted. Impact knocked the air from her lungs. She slipped under the surface. Cold. Dark.

Hands seized her shoulders, yanking her upright. Tephra's face, terrified but determined, as she shoved Rowena against something solid.

"Slow down. Even now."

Rowena clung to the rock, breath coming in shudders. "Something's out there . . ."

"A huacat, most likely," Tephra said. "They hate water. We will be fine."

The words had no sooner left her mouth when a sleek feline emerged from the jungle's thick green curtain. It prowled toward the bank, fluid and silent on paws the size of Rowena's head.

The cat lapped at the water's edge, calm and unconcerned. Black fur shimmered under the moonlight. Its bobbed tail hovered, motionless. Muscles rippled under taut skin like braided steel.

Rowena didn't dare breathe. Her throat clogged with fear, thick as wax. When cats in Skandan hunted mice, sometimes they sat, licking a paw, calm, unassuming. Until a mouse believed it had gone unnoticed. Then the cat sprang. This one had the same stillness, but tenfold the size.

Rowena jerked to move, but Tephra caught her arm. "Wait," she whispered. "It's only thirsty. Do not provoke it."

"I thought it didn't swim?"

"This one does. It is a panthalyx," Tephra whispered. "It hasn't seen us."

Rowena locked eyes with her. Was she mad? Or simply fearless?

"Go," Tephra breathed, and let go of her hand. She waded with slow steps toward the next boulder.

Was this the right decision? They weren't that far from shore. A cat that size could make the leap. One wrong move, and the beast would be on them.

Stay or go?

She followed.

The water reached their thighs, tugging hard. Every step felt like climbing uphill on wet stone. The rushing current masked all sounds from shore. The beast from shore might be stalking them.

A shiver rolled over Rowena's shoulders. The water's roar seemed to soften, or perhaps her senses sharpened. Something in the air changed, a shift so subtle she almost missed it.

Then, a growl. Low. Deep. Close.

Tephra sprinted for the rock.

Rowena's ankle twisted on a loose stone. No time to cry out. She plunged under.

The river swallowed her.

Ribs slammed into stones. Her knees. Her shoulder. Her limbs pinwheeled, grabbing at anything.

Her lungs screamed.

She surfaced. A breath.

Then under again.

The world spun. Up became down. Survive.

She struck something sharp, snagging her tunic. Her whole body wrenched. Pain flashed down her arm.

And then . . . stillness.

Her face broke the surface, just enough for air. She gasped, choking. The river gurgled around her, still angry but losing strength. Whatever had caught her tunic held firm.

Then it moved.

No claws. No teeth.

Hands.

Dragging her up the bank.

She collapsed in the mud. A stick scratched her jaw. She cried out, spitting grit.

"You are safe," Tephra said, voice low. "Quiet now."

Only then did Rowena realize she was crying. She peeked through slitted eyes. They huddled in tall grass, soaked and muddy. Tephra wiped her palms clean on her tunic, calm as ever.

"The other side?" Rowena asked.

"Yes. But too far south. We need to go."

"Panthalyx?"

"Left behind."

Rowena pushed onto her hands and knees. Mud squelched beneath her palms. Behind her, the river whispered instead of roared. She sagged in place, just for a moment. "Yacares?"

"Still around," Tephra answered, already moving. She stayed low, jogging with light steps even in the muck.

Rowena didn't care about stealth. She only cared about leaving. She ran, legs pounding, heart wild, like a baurun let loose from its pen.

She would not die here.

Not like this. A fierce determination burned within her chest, a blazing promise.

She would survive. She had to.

16

BRAM

BRAM BURST through the door of the cottage in his elven form. The space, cramped yet familiar, still carried Rowena's lingering scent of wildflowers and pepper root. He was eager to find her and begin their hunt for Fidessa.

His three-week deadline allowed no room for delays.

"Rowena."

Heavy silence answered.

Blackened logs sat cold in the hearth, untouched since he'd left.

He rushed into the single bedroom, allowing himself the illogical thought she had not heard him bellow.

Everything was as before, including Rowena's dagger and the small knife she wore on her thigh. She wouldn't have left those behind on purpose. He slipped them among his own weapons to give her later.

He'd told her to wait for him. Now, he had to find her, and that would make it even harder to return to Saganus on time. And that was only for the deadline.

Then he had to warn Farryn, and tell her of Killian. It was

going to take some planning to get the rebels, and their elflings, to safety while making it appear he tried to capture them.

He scrubbed his hand through his hair, realizing he should have arrived in Seeker form. The dryads already knew who he was. He rubbed his brow and switched forms a heartbeat later.

His horns slipped comfortably from his hairline, his fingers long and clawed, flexed easily, his vision sharper, colors more intense in the light. Nothing could hide from him within the shadows.

The runes etched along his skin pulsed in a familiar hum only he could hear. He could do without the white hair, too much like the disavowed, but he'd gotten used to it. The change as easy as breathing.

The agony it once inflicted, a nearly forgotten memory. Mereb had been the one who held his hand, stayed at his side . . . apologized.

It was all a lie.

She'd been protecting her own interests, watching to see if he would comply. The Heptad was nothing he had believed them to be. And he was nothing more than their tool.

Rowena would not become one of their pawns. Neither would the others, whoever they might be. But she was his priority—if he could find her.

With mounting frustration, he hurried to fill a sling with provisions, enough for two, and strap a waterskin to his belt. That they could share.

Bram slammed open the cottage door and ducked outside. Cool evening air rushed to greet him. No one entered the forest unnoticed.

"Where is she?"

Three birds burst from the trees, startled by his bellowed interruption to the peaceful clearing. He paced, doing his best to wait. The battle already lost to his temper.

By the time he heard a branch crack at the forest's edge, he was ready to explode. He inhaled and released, twice, forcing calm into his muscles. He needed the dryad's help. Screaming at them would serve nothing.

When he turned, shoulders squared, ready to hear their reasons why Rowena hadn't stayed in the cottage ... emptiness.

It wasn't odd for the secretive dryads to hold back, but they already accepted him. These games were unnecessary.

"Show yourself."

Bram scanned the tree line. His gaze snagged on an oddly placed yew. Too uncommon for the forest, and new to the meadow.

"Do you think I can't see you? Turn and show yourself." He tapped his fingers against his thigh, waiting.

An agonizing minute passed before branches crackled, rustling the air. The tree twisted until a young dryad female stood where the yew had been. "How could you tell I was there?"

It wasn't Princess Ida who'd greeted him before. She'd been older, with a ruler's confidence. No more than a sapling, in dryad terms. Tall. Thin. Perhaps Rowena's age.

She stepped closer, a slight grin curving her lips, her eyes bright.

"You're not very good at hiding."

"I am, but it's nearly dark. Also, there has been no need of such a skill until recently." She jabbed her hand onto her hip. "Who are you? *What* are you?"

She was brave. He'd give her that. Bram sensed no fear at all. She studied his horns, perusing him like an object as she crept closer.

His jaw tightened. The anger still coiled inside him, but her open stare was ... unexpected. Different from the fear or reverence he usually encountered. He bit his lip, forcing himself into stillness. If tolerating her scrutiny would gain her help, so be it.

But when she reached out and touched his hand, a startling jolt passed between them. She jumped back a step.

The sensation gave Bram pause. Perhaps it was simply that the dryads had never left Havilar, keeping themselves withdrawn from all others.

She carried a stronger enchantment signature, yet he suspected it was something else.

Something important.

A relieved sigh left his lips that he'd changed forms. No need to test the Heptad when he had so many other issues with them.

But before anything else, he had to find Rowena. "Where is the one who can give me information?"

"She's right here." Ida entered the clearing. "Go home, Evora. We will speak later."

Evora. Princess Evora. Her enchantment level made more sense.

"But mother, two visitors in such a short time," Evora said, still caught up in her examination. "Where did you come from? Is it Skandan, like Rowena? Because she looked nothing like you."

"Evora, that is enough." Ida clamped her mouth tightly. A scowl carved deep creases along her forehead. She moved in front of Evora, blocking her continued study. "By the queen's command, I gave Rowena some training. Afterward, we led her to Tixamar. Ultimately, she is headed to the Veilrune Mountains. Now go. Our borders are closed for a reason. We will tolerate no more intrusion."

"You sent her into the jungle alone?" Fire built in Bram's gut at the audacity of the dryads to send her away.

"She is strong and capable."

"That's true." Evora slid sideways into view. "Her enchantment grew much stronger while she was here. I worried and tried to follow her, but . . ."

Ida let out a long exhale. "We sent her through the pixie lands because it was the safest way for her to travel. Would you prefer we had sent her straight into the mountains to meet with a bandit from Anomie, preying on travelers?"

That would have been handing her directly to Tanith. He had to get to Rowena before anyone else. "That was the second-best option you had, so I suppose I should be grateful for that."

Evora dropped her gaze to the meadow grasses near her feet. "I wish I could have gone with her. I still have so many questions. She is so much braver than I am."

"Go, and do not return to this cottage," Ida said to Bram, ignoring her daughter. "You are no longer welcome in these lands, Seeker. Find your rest elsewhere."

"Why send her away at all?" He would leave when he had all the answers he needed and not before. "I made myself abundantly clear that I would return."

"As did I about that being unacceptable." Ida settled her arms across her chest. "She will find the mage, Fidessa, hiding in the mountains."

"And why did she tell you she needs to find her?" The hair on Bram's neck rose. Ida was hiding something, an alliance perhaps. Or she had information she should not have.

"Alona holds the Scroll of Trust. Her knowledge of what has been and is to come is vast."

Bram growled. Things didn't add up. They'd sent Rowena into the jungle alone. On a mission to find Fidessa alone.

"Then she knows what's at stake. If the Queen of Havilar is aware of all that is happening, why wouldn't she at least provide an escort?"

"Rowena's future is still unwritten, but what she seeks is not our concern. The dryads have done our part to ensure her skills are ready for her destination. This realm will participate no further in the events to come."

"At the expense of all others. You guard your lands so completely that you are no help to anyone. If the prophecy fails, everything you fight to protect will be dust. That is how *your* legacy will be written."

"Mother?"

Ida rounded on her daughter. "Evora, leave. Now!" A wind swirled, pressing the grasses flat

Bram held steady. Ida and the queen were wrong. They had to understand that.

The whites of Evora's eyes showed bright around the brown centers. She made a noise, a blend of fear and anger, as she raced for the forest's edge.

"You can't keep her locked away forever. The time is coming and she must be involved.

"Her future is a dryad concern, not yours."

"Until it's time. Then neither you nor your mother will have a choice. You cannot hold her back or deny her the Scroll."

"That time is not now."

"Soon." He'd already lost the Sword. For the Scroll to become vulnerable, Alona would have to break her silence and return to her elven form.

Unlikely.

"The Heptad is aware that Alona is guarding the Scroll. To my understanding, they are not aware of Evora. Yet.

That is the only reason I am deferring my duties, for now. But I will return for her when it is time."

Ida flattened her lips, though her nose flared and her chest rose and fell faster.

It didn't surprise him that she'd be angry. The dryads kept themselves isolated. They were going to have no choice but to change their policies—and soon. He could offer her a little solace, but the time was upon them all. They would have to accept their part in the prophecy.

"I am dedicated to all the moon-born's safety, no matter what threats may come. For now, Havilar is the safest realm for one to hide."

Ida rolled her bottom lip, biting it. The first real sign of doubt she'd shown. "I don't know which route she has taken, but Rowena will have to cross the Awa River. She will exit near the mudflats of Aclanus."

"Within sight of Anomie. And Tanith."

The powerful dryad dropped her gaze to the ground. "It is why we gave her training. We could not allow her to draw others to our lands. We tried to help."

Bram rubbed the back of his neck. Frustrating as the dryad's decision might be, he had to move forward. He would not convince them of the importance of his duties in one night. They would have to listen. But that would be a different day.

"When did Rowena leave?"

"Before twilight. I watched her until she disappeared into the trees. As did Evora."

"My business is not finished here. I *will* return and we *will* speak further."

Bram didn't wait for Ida to reply. Rowena was navigating the jungle at night.

Alone.

She was strong; he understood that. She'd survived enslavement, a frost dragon attack, but she'd also lost her family. Her support.

Since they'd arrived in Havilar, she hadn't even taken a step outside the cottage. Now, she was adrift and unaware there were others searching for her.

The Awa River ran the length of the pixie lands. But there was only one place safe enough to cross on foot. Not that Rowena would know that. It was night beneath the jungle's canopy, and neither moon could offer her help.

It was the best place to start his search.

He closed his eyes.

The shift was as natural as breath. His skin peeled from the light, his bones from flesh. His solid form released into shadow. Part of the aether. A weightless slip into the darkness. Here, all things quieted.

Thought. Pain. Want.

He became nothing, and in that nothing, he was free.

It was like being cradled inside memory. The way he used to linger in his Primary form—pure light, refracted across the skies of Caelus, shimmering in gold and violet arcs. Returning to his elven body had once been like coming home.

Now, when he emerged, all color drained from his sight for several breaths. As if the world punished him for leaving it behind.

He emerged along the river's shore. The jungle morphed from gray to lush colors, clinging to the night, thick and damp and pulsing with life.

"Where are you?" he whispered into the air, heavy and wet against his skin. The words dissolved like breath on a blade.

Every sound, from the slow drip of dew off broad leaves to the distant cry of a night-bird, pressed in close.

Bram crouched low, fingers brushing over soft mud. He found his target. And more. The shape was faint, nearly swallowed by the jungle's hunger, but unmistakable.

Two pairs of footprints, one in boots, one barefoot. Fresh. Heading east. One smaller, the other wider, deeper.

He cleared away more leaves—three footprints. The third from giant paws; four rounded pads. A cat. Panthalyx, from the size.

His skin chilled despite the heat.

He followed the trail to the river. No signs of struggle. No claw marks, no blood. Nothing to suggest an attack.

Just . . . disappearance.

Rowena would not have been foolish enough to cross the river at night. Unless she had to. He rested his arms on his thighs as he took in the narrow track of disturbed moss weaving into the water. She'd made it this far.

Alive.

But then what?

The trail ended at the water's edge, choked in vines and low-lying mist. No sign of crossing, not even a misplaced reed.

She'd been wearing her boots when he left, so it made sense those prints were hers. But who had been without shoes?

There were five toes, not four, so an elf not a pixie. Evora had not made it this far into the jungle, according to her own account.

Bram searched along the riverbank from where he found the footprints. North for a quarter league, then south for a quarter league before returning. Nothing.

Who would have known Rowena was in the jungle?

If the information Lhoris shared was valid, both Ha'mon and Tanith could have individuals after her.

Whoever Tanith sent from her city of dregs and thieves could be shoeless. Bram still didn't understand how Ha'mon maintained influence outside his prison, but no doubt he dealt with unsavory characters as well.

Bram rolled his shoulders back and let out a long breath. It clung to the thick air before melting into the mist.

So close. Yet, not close enough.

There was more at stake now. At least for him.

Three weeks to do a task that had already taken him months. He could not let the Heptad find the rebels. Or allow more to die. He would find Rowena and the sword and return to Saganus . . . alone.

He would not deliver Rowena, or any of the moon-born, to the Heptad.

He picked his way over roots, vines, logs, and whatever the jungle kept huddled over the ground, searching for more clues. When Rowena left the jungle, she would have to skirt the mudflats of Aclanus. She would be exposed. He didn't doubt her skills to reach to Bethon—if she understood that was the best way into the Veilrune Mountains from here.

She had no knowledge of how the anarchical city of Anomie operated. If she tried to go to the mountains close to the city . . .

What instructions did the dryads give? What did they view as prepared?

He blew out a deep sigh.

There were no more signs to point anywhere other than into the river. It would waste time trying to catch up. The jungle covered trails as quickly as they formed.

It would be best to wait near the border, close to the mudflats. He'd spot her no matter where she emerged from the jungle.

A heartbeat later, he stood at the edge of the jungle, shadows rippling across his skin as he stared at the city in the distance.

Anomie.

Travelers, as dangerous as the jungle beasts behind him, trudged to the gates. Open, but not welcoming. Flanked by giant trolls, who inspected cargo and collected entry fees. Wagons sat, ready for those who couldn't pay.

He searched for golden hair among the detained, thankful to find none.

Bram's jaw tensed. He'd walked the streets of Anomie just once, after he first arrived on the continent. He thought he would find gossip. Truth or rumor didn't matter, anything to direct him toward a moon-born. Instead, he'd found himself meeting with Tanith—ousted queen, spider at the center of a web spun from ruin. Her smile still haunted him.

Inside that city churned a hive of the unwanted—disavowed druids, rejected mages, broken warriors, thieves. Every cast-off seemed to find their way there.

Rowena was strong.

Fierce.

But not ready for the corruption that lived behind those walls.

She would need him.

He would find her.

17

ROWENA

WHEN THEY WERE FAR ENOUGH from the river, Rowena collapsed onto the leaf-strewn ground, every muscle aching as the damp earth absorbed her exhaustion.

Tephra rounded on her, urgency seeping into her sharp words. "We are not safe yet. There are still dangers."

Her words filtered through Rowena's tired mind. She struggled to her knees, heart hammering as a wave of memory struck. Her father's laugh, that proud glint in his eyes when she'd found him during one of their games in the woods. She bent over, leaning on her elbows, forcing breath into her lungs. He'd been teaching her skills for the forest.

This was the jungle.

Just like then, she'd find her way to safety.

Somehow.

"What is wrong?" Tephra's voice softened. A hint of curiosity slipped through her usual edge.

Rowena kept her head bowed, as if she could conceal the turmoil roiling inside. Her mouth tasted of mud, gritty and metallic. She spat once. Then again.

She rose, swiping at her lips. "Nothing."

Tephra's nostrils flared, but she said nothing more. She spun and moved on. Faster than before.

Rowena followed, more careful of her stealth. She wasn't going to share her grief with a woman who'd half-dragged her through the river and mocked her fear of being eaten.

But she was still alive thanks to Tephra. That counted for something.

The jungle beyond the river offered no relief. Not even the dark had changed the temperature. Heat clung to her skin, heavy and unmoving through the night. The canopy cracked in places to reveal stars, but neither moon peeked through. Each vine, curling over roots, seemed like serpents.

She willed herself onward, through broad leaves hiding rotting logs, stickers, and other unknown terrors.

She quickened her pace, catching up. "Are we heading north or east?"

"Both," Tephra answered, without glancing back.

Reasonable. The river had pushed them south. They needed to correct.

Mid-thought, something prickled the hairs on the back of Rowena's neck. She slowed.

Tephra did as well.

That made her more uneasy.

There air shifted. Energy thrummed, not like enchantment, but something raw and sizzling.

Like the sky before a lightning strike.

Tephra's voice dropped. "We must hide." She ducked behind a thick tree with leaves as broad as Bram's torso.

Rowena stood frozen, confused, then dove after her. Tephra had already moved deeper into the greenery.

Crouched low, Rowena closed her eyes, searching for her.

A jolt slammed into her chest.

A burst of rage. Hostility. Hunger for violence.

Rowena gasped and dropped to her knees. She clutched her chest. Her breath came in pants. The feelings overwhelmed her.

Tephra appeared a moment later, gripping her shoulders.

"Focus," she hissed. "She will sense you."

She?

Rowena dug her nails into her palms. The pain grounded her, just enough to force the foreign emotion back. She pushed it aside, little by little, until the pressure eased. Her muscles sagged.

Tephra released her with a shove. "You are Lunara."

"From my mother," Rowena said, still catching her breath. She hadn't lied, just held back.

Tephra sneered. "I should let them take you. Perhaps then they would stop."

"Who? Who is after me?" Rowena rose, backing away.

Tephra stared for a heartbeat. She grinned, sharp and mocking. "Come and see."

She stayed low, sliding from one shadow to the next. Rowena followed, curiosity overriding her fear.

The jungle thinned; an orange glow flickered ahead.

Tephra halted, yanking Rowena behind a wide, smooth trunk.

A moment later, a weapon-clad warrior stalked past, no more than two feet in front of them.

Dressed in black fighting leather, he reminded Rowena of the panthalyx. Power rippled through his movements with that same liquid strength. Dark hair slicked back from his face into a tight bun. A sword poked over his shoulder from its place on his back; a dagger loose in his hand.

Tephra pressed a finger to her lips and crept after him.

A glade opened, unnatural, as though the jungle had bent into submission. Other warriors lounged around a low fire. Some sat cross-legged, eating bread dipped into a communal pot. Others drank, their laughter muted but sharp. The energy in the air vibrated with power, control, superiority.

Rowena had never sensed such intense emotions before. Her stomach twisted. It wasn't just power. It was entitlement. A need to dominate.

Tephra tapped her shoulder.

Rowena flinched, her nerves boiling.

She spun, ready to snap, but one glance at Tephra's narrowed stare checked her impulse. Rowena dropped her gaze, laid a hand over her chest, and forced herself to suppress the sensations rolling off the warriors.

When she raised her eyes, calmer now. Tephra scoffed. She tilted her chin toward the far edge of the glade.

Rowena followed the motion, and her breath caught.

Curled in a nest of vines and shattered trees, its sides rising and falling in a slow rhythm, slept a dragon.

Not just any dragon.

A crimson fire dragon. Its scales shimmered like embers. Claws, the length of Rowena's forearms, flexed with each breath. Its wings, half-folded, glinted with bronze along the veins.

She swallowed. Her insides shriveled.

That overwhelming dominance hadn't been the warriors.

It was the dragon's.

Without a word, Tephra and Rowena slipped back into the jungle, retreating from the warriors and their sleeping dragon.

Tephra moved like someone with something to lose, her caution sharp, every step measured.

That unsettled Rowena more than the sight of the fighters.

Who was this woman she followed? She needed to keep alert. Remember to keep herself open. Aware.

They crept in silence, ears tuned for patrols, careful not to brush a single leaf the wrong way. A grin arrived unbidden, thankful to Ida for her harsh commands when she traveled through Havilar.

Rowena assumed the warriors to be Solara. They're tanned skin similar to Tephra's and that long ago merchant. She'd never heard tales that they traveled outside of Farradar with dragons.

That coiled heat still clung to her bones. Even in sleep, the beast bore so much hostility. The frost dragon had been powerful and violent, but not like that.

What would have happened if it had awakened? Shudders rolled over her shoulders.

Only when they'd put enough distance behind them did they break into a run, sprinting through clear patches of jungle until their lungs gave out.

They stumbled into a clearing where the canopy grew so tightly woven that little else thrived beneath it. Rowena's legs trembled as she braced against a tree trunk, her palm sliding on the slick moss. Each breath burned like fire in her chest, and her shirt clung to her back, soaked with sweat and torn from branches that had clawed at her during their escape.

The absence of underbrush was a small mercy after fighting through vines that had left angry red welts across her forearms.

Her boots crunched on the thick blanket of leaf-litter; the sound unnervingly loud in her ringing ears. Every snap threatened to reveal their location.

Rowena strained to listen past her hammering heartbeat for signs of pursuit, but heard only distant bird calls, the chatter of animals, and the faint rustle of canopy leaves.

She tilted her head back, blinking sweat from her eyes as she scanned the treetops. Lungol would be gone already. She'd lost her chance at his energy for tonight. The familiar knot of anxiety tightened in her stomach.

Without the moon's power, she was vulnerable.

But they were safe. For the moment.

"This will do," Rowena said, fighting to keep her voice steady despite her parched throat. She mentally calculated how long it might take Masah to rise. Even if the bigger moon couldn't find her through the dense canopy, hopefully flying beasts wouldn't either.

Her fingers instinctively brushed the empty spot at her belt where her dagger should have been. Another loss that left her feeling naked and exposed in this hostile jungle.

Tephra dropped to the ground unceremoniously, leaves squelching under her. She covered her face with her hands.

It was the first genuine frustration she'd shown.

"Who are they?"

"The Argentry," Tephra said, staring straight ahead. "King Kyrem's elite."

Rowena shivered. The Farradar king, so she'd guessed right. They were Solara. "Why bring a dragon to the pixie lands? I thought there were treaties in place about that."

"There are, but with some exceptions. She is so beautiful."

Rowena dropped her mouth open, but quickly composed herself. That was not the word she would use for the sleeping killer. The Solara had to live with dragons flying over their lands. Perhaps that gave her a different opinion. If Rowena ever saw another dragon, it would be too soon.

"What exceptions would give them cause to be *here*?"

"To find me."

Rowena blinked. "What?"

Tephra didn't look at her. She twisted her fingers together, the gesture oddly nervous. "You've heard of the Tournament of Saints?"

"No."

Tephra drew a breath. "It is held before the Reaping. A performance, really. To keep the dragons content. The king claims it is tradition. That it honors the bond between Farradar and the dragons."

Rowena's brows knit. "By doing what?"

"Each year, women from across the kingdom compete for the dragons' favor."

Rowena's stomach turned. "An offering."

"He calls it a sacred bond. A celebration." Tephra smiled without humor. "But yes."

"And they go willingly?"

"Only the winner. And they do not have a choice." The words were flat. Practiced. "If they refuse, their families are marked. Cast out. Ruined."

Rowena couldn't understand a king sacrificing one of his subjects like that. Worse, she didn't believe such an offering would satisfy the dragons. She studied Tephra. Her clothes were too fine, her manner too polished.

"How are the competitors chosen?"

"By the king's council."

"You're one of them, aren't you? One of the competitors?"

A pause. Then a shrug. "Not officially."

That was no answer. Rowena bit her tongue.

Tephra leaned back, her voice light again. "This year, there are different rules. By the king's decree, it will be held earlier than usual and there will be two winners. One for the dragons. One for the prince."

A heavy pause settled between them.

Rowena busied herself with breaking off a couple of bananas at the edge of their resting place. She handed one to Tephra.

"Why wouldn't the king want to find a better arrangement? Another royal, or at least a noble, to strengthen alliances, or boost trade relations." That's how most of Skandan created betrothals. As Rowena understood well.

Uther's declaration of her betrothal to Daenon flashed behind her eyes.

She scrubbed the thought away.

"The prince refuses to choose a wife." Tephra's gaze flicked upward. "The king is shrewd. He is only allowing those of a certain age to be chosen."

"And that is new? How old is the prince?" The whole idea of the tournament made Rowena cringe.

"The prince is twenty summers."

The hair on the back of her neck rose. "That's the *only* reason for the changes?"

"There is a rumor of the next Burning Moon arriving with The Reaping. The king also searches for a moon-born. A weapon stronger than his dragons."

Rowena's breath caught. Bram said there were others like her. Were they being hunted? Was she? "Why would he believe the moon-born is a weapon?"

"Conspiracies abound."

"And you are the right age?" If Tephra was a moon-born, what then? Should Rowena admit she was as well? They could join together. Fight for each other.

A flutter of hope bounced around her insides.

"Old enough to be chosen," Tephra said. "But not the one they seek. Which is why I ran."

It sounded too smooth. Too rehearsed. Even so, Rowena's anticipation died like a moth swooped up by a bat. She gazed at nothing, unsure of what to believe.

A moment passed.

Then Tephra twisted, fixing her stare on Rowena. "I am heading to Aclanus. After that, we go our separate ways."

Relief and guilt tangled in Rowena's gut. She didn't want to drag Tephra deeper into her troubles. But the thought of continuing alone made her stomach clench.

Rowena frowned, her mind racing through the scattered tales she'd heard of that realm. Nothing in Aclanus but the city of Anomie and the Twisted Forest—places that haunted elfling's nightmares and trader's warnings.

Her father had once described trees there that moved of their own accord, hunting unwary travelers. "Why Aclanus?"

"There are druids in the city who can . . . help people disappear. If I can change my appearance, I can stop running. Return home." Tephra's voice held a desperate hope that made Rowena's skin prickle.

Her breath caught in her throat as Bram's face flashed in her mind; his altered features and the weight he carried because of them. Would Tephra end up the same? Marked by corrupted enchantment but without Bram's sense of purpose? "That's not something to take lightly."

"I am not." Tephra's jaw clamped tight.

"There's risk."

"There is risk in everything," Tephra snapped, her eyes flashing. "I will not live my life waiting for the king's dogs to drag me back. Did they seem gentle to you?"

The memory of rough hands and cruel voices made Rowena hesitate, the phantom pain of rope biting into her wrists. "After the tournament, won't they stop searching?"

"No." Tephra's voice dropped, hollow with certainty. "Once marked, always marked."

She didn't say she *was* marked. But the implication was there.

Rowena stared at the ground.

She hadn't expected the rest of Edenia to be crueler than what she'd experienced in Skandan and Ibern. Thrust into slavery, losing her parents, her home.

It seemed everywhere in Edenia was a realm of cages.

"Maybe just . . . wait. See if it passes."

"I have waited long enough," Tephra said. "Years."

Silence stretched again.

Rowena finally sighed. "Well, first we have to survive this jungle, anyway. This is a fine place to rest."

Tephra smirked. "With the biting, slithering, poisonous things crawling about?

Rowena let out a tired laugh, muffled by the weight of her fatigue. "No," she whispered, as if the looming jungle would add another terror if she spoke too loudly.

18

———

ROWENA

DESPITE THEIR PACT TO stay awake, Rowena jolted upright with a gasp.

Something heavy pinned her hip, its warmth shifting with a slow, deliberate weight. Her body locked; a scream trapped behind her clenched teeth. Chills chased down her spine. Careful not to move, she tilted her gaze downward, only her eyes flickering, until thick diamond-shapes came into view, undulating across her stomach. Yellow scales bordered by wavy brown bands, rippled with every breath.

A snake.

Massive. Thick as her thigh.

It slid, tasting the air with a flick of its forked tongue.

Her pulse roared in her ears.

Move. Now!

She thrust out her hand. Silver energy surged through her fingers before thought could catch up, instinct steering her. The snake's front half lifted from her body, suspended midair like a twisted ribbon of muscle. She scrambled back, elbows gouging the ground, heels skidding.

Her enchantment faltered. Too weak. She had fallen asleep without gathering strength from Masah.

A snap of twigs. Tephra jolted awake, springing to her feet.

"What in Sawel's name—"

The snake's head hovered a foot away from her midsection. Mouth agape, fangs flashing. It twisted once, then lunged. Sparks flared across Tephra's palms as she snapped her fingers together. A sharp crack split the air, followed by a blazing arc and fiery bolts that exploded from her hands, striking the snake's gaping mouth.

Golden light erupted.

Rowena twisted away, shielding her eyes behind the crook of her elbow as a wave of heat rolled over her face.

When quiet settled, she peeked over her arm. The snake's body writhed, headless, on the ground.

Tephra swayed, sweat beading across her brow, face blanched. "We must leave."

"Which way?"

Dawn had just begun to clear the stars from the sky. The jungle spun around Rowena, but her stomach had clenched to stone. Masah was gone. As was Lungol, long before.

Her reserves thinned, almost depleted.

Tephra pointed east, toward the rising sun. "That way."

Rowena didn't wait. She vaulted over the twitching carcass and ran. A shiver cascaded down her spine, urging her faster.

They stopped twice to rest and refill their waterskins, foraging nuts and berries as they trekked. The trees gradually parted, revealing a narrow ledge overlooking Sylph Bay. High enough to glimpse the water's ghostly shape far below.

They followed a narrow trail, whether carved by beasts or nature, Rowena didn't care. She only wanted out.

"Keep Sawel on your right," Tephra called.

Rowena lifted a hand in acknowledgment, panting as she

sprinted. Her body ached; her chest still burning from panic. In contrast to her enchantment, which barely pulsed. Shriveled. Sluggish.

Below, the jungle swept at a severe angle toward the bay. The greenery almost beautiful from such a high view. A thin mist from the water crept along the treetops near the shore, and birdsong floated higher with Sawel.

Deceptive.

Peace was a lie told by distance.

Movement in the sky snagged her eye.

A dark flock wheeled in the distance, swooping in a wide arc. They stayed bunched together, no matter how the wind shifted. No scattered chaos among their wings, only a precise, unnatural formation.

Rowena's gaze flicked from the ridge to the sky. "To the right," she shouted over her shoulder. "The birds. Something is off."

"They are nothing," Tephra answered.

Rowena's chest tightened. She pressed her fingers to the spot where her enchantment gathered. A whispered warning thrummed beneath her skin. She disagreed with Tephra.

A flash of white streaked across her path. A small bird, with brilliant silver stripes, darted in front of her face.

She ducked instinctively. The bird twisted midair, hovering for a heartbeat before her face.

Rowena skidded to a stop, flinging her arm wide to warn Tephra. The edge of the trail loomed too close.

"What is it?" Tephra hissed, her feet scraping the ground, nearly colliding.

"That bird." Rowena pointed, pulse racing. It couldn't be the same little white bird from Skandan. Could it? "I've seen one like it before."

"That is merely a beacon," Tephra said. "They live throughout Edenia. Usually, they are brown with silver streaks."

"It's warning us. I'm sure of it."

The bird fluttered again, dancing away from the path, then circling back, insistent. Rowena's gaze flicked to the dark flock, closer now. Wings sharp. Bodies larger than expected.

Not ravens.

Vultu.

And they were flying in a straight line toward the ridge.

She'd heard the stories. Birds driven by cruel instinct or command, circling prey until it went mad and died, then feasting on the remains. Their cries said to echo like eerie laughter.

The beacon fluttered its wings near a tree to their left, drawing them away from the open trail.

"Into the trees!" Rowena cried.

Tephra shoved between her shoulders. "Faster!"

The sky blackened with wings.

The vultu descended like a storm cloud, their cries a cacophony of whistles, trills, and guttural screeches. Sharp claws raked across Rowena's scalp, tearing strands of hair as they passed.

She ducked beneath the canopy, the green swallowing her whole.

The flock wheeled twice overhead, casting jagged shadows —then veered northeast in perfect, chilling unison.

Rowena doubled over, gasping for breath. The white beacon chirped once, twice. Then vanished into the leaves.

The second, no, *third*, time it had saved her.

Why? Who sent it?

Rowena's hands drifted to her chest, where the fading remnants of enchantment barely hummed beneath her skin.

The moons were gone. The jungle was too thick. She'd need time to recover.

"Is there any other way to get to Anomie? she panted between breaths.

Tephra, equally breathless, shook her head. "No."

Sawel had risen, but not high enough. Her enchantment had most likely faded as well.

They were both running on borrowed strength now.

And Anomie awaited.

They traveled in silence. The hush between them thickened, prickling with unspoken fears. Tephra led, avoiding easy trails and keeping them hidden beneath the jungle's heavy canopy.

Rowena was certain Tephra believed as she did: the birds had not come by accident.

Someone was hunting them, but which one did they seek?

The jungle thickened with every step. Humidity clung to Rowena's skin like a second layer, slick and oppressive. Leaves the size of shields drooped overhead, glittering with moisture. Each breath grew heavier, infused with the scent of decay and overripe fruit.

They didn't speak. There was no need.

Every branch they pushed aside snapped back with a whispering menace. Every step became a gamble; between hidden roots, stinging brush, and the threat of venom.

Sawel crept higher in the sky, but under the canopy, the light filtered in slanted rays, fractured through the trees. It offered no relief. The heated air steamed like a giant cauldron.

Rowena's tunic stuck to her back. Stray hair, damp with sweat, curled against her neck and cheeks. Her braid had mostly come undone, and her boots squelched in the jungle muck.

"How much farther?" She asked at last, pushing a branch aside with more force than necessary.

Tephra didn't glance back. "I have never been to Anomie." The words came clipped, tight.

Before Rowena could respond, something darted in front of Tephra's face, quick and silent, like a falling leaf spun wrong.

Tephra ducked. "What—?"

The thing circled and hovered midair for a heartbeat. Rowena caught a flicker of a shape, small and swift.

An elven silhouette. Less than a hand tall.

"A pixie," she breathed.

The air flashed blue—brighter than the clearest summer day. In that blinding instance, the hovering figure blurred and expanded, enchantment whooshing outward like a breath held too long. When the light cleared, a woman stood before them.

Not tall, no taller than Rowena's shoulder, but even as she blinked away the lingering spots, command radiated from the stranger's posture. This was someone accustomed to being obeyed.

Her skin reminded Rowena of polished bone carvings back home, and her hair caught the dappled light like the copper ornaments her mother once made. A narrow diadem shimmered across her brow, marking her as nobility, or perhaps royalty. Her tunic mirrored the jungle itself. Deep green fabric with threads that shimmered like dew on leaves.

"Why have you invaded our land?" The woman asked.

Her voice was smooth, almost too relaxed, but with an undertone of command that stiffened Rowena's spine.

"We mean no harm," Rowena said carefully. "Only passing through."

She stepped beside Tephra, hands open at her sides, trying not to stare. The woman had the strength of authority, and the patience of a predator.

"You were seen entering from two separate paths. North and South." The pixie's gaze swept them like a blade. "Now you travel together. And yet, you sought no audience. You carry no supplies for sale or trade. That is . . . unusual."

Rowena opened her mouth to explain, but Tephra touched her wrist lightly, silencing her.

"We met by chance," Tephra said, dipping her chin with a practiced ease. "Our paths aligned as we both seek Bethon. We did not mean to disrespect your territory by failing to announce ourselves."

The pixie's expression didn't shift. "Farradar has an agreement to travel through Panon. Few would come this way." Her gaze then pinned Rowena. "And you. You are not Solara."

"I'm Skandan. My ship wrecked off your coast." She had begun the lie with Tephra, no reason to alter it now. Tephra had learned she was Lunara, but nothing more. Since she'd already offered a lie herself, Rowena counted on her to remain silent, for both their sakes.

The pixie tilted her head. "I have received no word of a wreckage—to the *west*."

Oh no. Rowena had not considered the direction. There was no sea on the pixie's northern border, where they already knew she'd come from.

Tephra shifted slightly beside her.

Rowena's instincts sparked. This was not a conversation they were winning.

"Perhaps you should explain your experience to our queen."

Not again. No more queens with lessons and cages to keep her trapped in this horrid jungle.

"You are not the queen?" Tephra asked.

Rowena held her breath, rising onto the balls of her feet, legs taut, ready to run.

The woman spread her palms, then folded them at her waist. "I am Princess Nisha. My mother, Queen Estherah, rules Tixamar."

Rowena bowed her head, though every muscle in her body stayed tight. Tephra followed suit, offering only a shallow nod.

"We did not mean to offend, and will be on our way shortly." Rowena wouldn't stay. Princess Nisha had been too fast in pixie form; they'd never outrun her. What else could they do but run?

A gasp caught in her throat. An idea.

"We did encounter something you might find helpful," she offered in a rush. "As a show of our goodwill."

Tephra stiffened, subtle, but Rowena felt the tension between them like fraying thread. It couldn't be helped. She couldn't answer any more questions about a ship wreck that did not exist. Nor could she stay silent and risk the consequences.

"Oh?" Nisha's voice softened, though her eyes remained sharp. "Do tell me something I don't already know about my own lands."

Rowena's knees trembled. This might have been a mistake. "We came across a unit of Solara warriors," she said, voice low. "And . . . they have brought a dragon."

The air changed. Even the leaves seemed to hush.

Nisha's attention slid to Tephra. "Solara?"

Rowena cursed herself inwardly. She hadn't not thought of that. "They are not associated with us. We don't know why they are here."

Tephra rumbled a noise deep in her throat. A sound Rowena knew all too well. Anger. And rightly so.

"They are Argentry," Tephra said, her voice as smooth and cold as the pixie's. "The king's guard. I do not know why they have come. Nor do I wish to."

A long silence stretched between them.

"A dragon in Tixamar." Nisha's voice dropped, contemplative. "That is . . . necessary information."

She turned her head slightly, eyes scanning the treetops, as if she already planned her response.

"I will inform the queen," Nisha said at last. "You may go. But speak of this to no one else. The wrong tongue could cause panic. I will see to this threat myself."

It was oddly generous. And slightly chilling.

"Thank you." Tephra's jaw tightened as she spoke. "We will not linger."

Nisha's gaze swept across both of them once more. "See that you don't. I'll send a flight of troopers to ensure you've cleared our border."

She did not wait for a reply.

The air shimmered again. A flashpoint, sharp as cracking glass, and Nisha hovered in place for a heartbeat, once again in pixie form. Her wings so translucent they fractured the light into a spray of colors. Then, vanished into the trees.

Silence returned.

Rowena exhaled slowly. "She's not what I expected."

"No one ever expects a pixie to carry power like that." Tephra wiped her brow, her lips pressing into a tight white line. She set off again, without waiting or checking for Rowena.

Rowena swallowed the bitter knowledge of her mistake.

She hurried after Tephra, hoping she wouldn't be left behind.

19

AVI

Avi barely had time to react before her mother collided with her, sending a cascade of blue shimmer into the air. er usual echo, trailing like a shooting star through the dense foliage.

They ricocheted off a wide-barked tree trunk, and landed hard on a thick branch, breathless, wings twitching from the shock.

Nisha recovered first.

"Avelinah!" Already on her feet, Nisha crossed her arms, pinning Avi with a glare. "What are you doing here?"

No, are you hurt? No, are you alright?

Just that familiar, cold reprimand.

Avi sat up slowly, her back aching from the jolt. "I was just exploring," she muttered. As if she had anything else important to do. "You flew past me so fast; I thought maybe something was wrong."

Her mother's eyes narrowed. "Those women are none of your concern."

"So, they *were* from other realms?" Avi's curiosity sparked despite the throbbing in her elbow. The dark-haired one wore the loose, shimmering fabric like the styles from Farradar Avi always admired. And the taller one had golden hair, like spun Sawel light, unlike any Avi had seen before. A Telana probably. But from where?

Investigating those women would be so much more interesting than preparing the village for heartbreak.

"I said it does not concern you." Nisha's voice sharp as wind-cut stone. "Why aren't you with your grandmother?

"I didn't know it was her Ascension Day until this morning!" The words burst out before she could stop them. "Why didn't you *tell* me?"

Nisha's sigh was long and tired. "Avelinah, there has been talk of it for weeks. If you paid attention instead of floating through the canopy, you would have known."

There it was again. That undercurrent; disappointment polished like river stones.

"Now go home," Her mother continued. "Stop wasting time and help set up the ceremonial ring. Gather lorea blossoms on your way."

Avi's hands curled into fists. "But what's going to happen to her? Why—"

"I do not have time for this." Her mother took to the air in a blur, wings slicing through the stillness.

Avi could have followed her. Could have caught her easily.

But what was the point?

Her mother never changed. The crown first. Always.

Not a flicker of comfort. Not a squeeze of the hand. Not even the simple kindness of calling her Avi.

Only Avelinah. Her princess name. Her responsibility name. Avi hated it.

She sat alone on the branch, letting her feet dangle off the edge. She let the jungle's music wrap around her like a hug. Her wings drooped, heavy against her back.

How would she survive without her grandmother—the only

one who treated her like she mattered? How had she missed the signs?

There had been more visitors in fancy clothes lately. More feasts with strange foods that Avi had sneaked extra portions of before disappearing into the trees. More hushed conversations that stopped the moment she wandered close.

But everyone was always having boring meetings that didn't include her. Nothing had seemed different enough to notice.

Second in line for the crown meant no one cared if she participated. There were hundreds of summers before she would have to rule. Or so she had believed.

She closed her eyes and put her hand over her heart. Her pulse thumped wildly against her palm, even though she sat perfectly still.

Not an hour before, her grandmother had found her playing in the canopy. The heganape she had stolen an opal from might have seen it differently. But Nona had arrived and made her give the healing stone back.

She would have. Eventually.

After that, they'd gone to the grotto and strolled in their elven forms, winding around the sparkling pool as if it were any other day. Nona had worn her favorite tunic, the green one embroidered with lorea petals, and her eyes had crinkled at the corners as she tucked a strand of Avi's bright red hair behind her ear, calling it her spark, her uniqueness, not an oddity.

Avi hugged her knees up to her chest, wriggling her bare toes against the branch. Nona blended into the canopy with grace and style. Avi never even bothered to cover her feet. She liked the feeling the bark and leaves and mud.

She was one with the jungle, free.

Nona never commanded her to submit to protocol. Unlike her mother.

"My dear one," Nona had said softly, "I wish we had more

time. But the Great Guardian has summoned me. It is time for my ascension. I am to become a Warden of the Light and take my place beside Osric's throne."

"I'll be all alone." Avi had choked out the words, sounding as whiny as Peylon, but she didn't care.

She didn't care if she seemed young enough to cling to her mother's skirts. She didn't care if that meant her enchantment wouldn't blossom.

Her grandmother could not leave.

Nona had drawn her close, warmth and steadiness in her strong arms, like the hush before first light. "We all have a destined path, if we're brave enough to endure the dangers that mold our character. You must remain strong."

Avi had cried then, as tears flowed again now, quiet and bitter at the memory.

"Avi, I will never be far. Watching. You'll never be alone."

She didn't wipe the new tears away. She couldn't picture her life without her grandmother. Nona was hers. The one who taught her to shape the wind, to get dirty, to explore, to learn.

She swiped at her cheeks, but the tears kept coming.

Her mother doted on Peylon, the baby prince who could do no wrong. Her father, kind as he was, always kept too busy improving Vadara.

Without Nona . . . she had no one.

How would the village change when her mother ruled? As princess, she kept strict rules and didn't accept mistakes or excuses. Avi's days of carefree, barefooted exploring would be over.

That her time with Nona had been interrupted, stung fresh. Two of her mother's guards had appeared at the grotto, their fancy uniforms stiff and uncomfortable.

They were sweating, which was weird, since nobody sweated in the jungle unless they were outsiders . . . or really nervous.

"The crowned heir requests your presence, Your Majesty," one had said to Nona, his voice cracking like he'd swallowed a toad. His ears turned so red that Avi almost laughed.

Nona had frowned, her fingers tapping against her thigh the way they did when thinking hard. She'd given them a look that made them both step back, then told them to report to Mathas instead.

At the mention of her personal guard's name, both troopers had gone pale. Everybody knew Mathas didn't like anyone else watching over Nona. He was scary enough that even Avi had stopped trying to prank him.

Nona had squeezed Avi's hand before leaving. "Gather some lorea blossoms for the ceremony, little spark," she had said. But her smile hadn't reached her eyes.

That was when Avi knew something was wrong. Nona's smiles always glittered with mischief.

After Nona left, Avi had wandered aimlessly. Even the ruby-tails racing through the upper canopy could not tempt her to join their fun.

She'd half-heartedly picked a few lorea blossoms, but her heart wasn't in it. She'd flopped onto a branch and crushed the flowers she'd gathered, breathing in their sweet scent as it mixed with birdsong.

That's when her mother had zoomed past, flying so fast that Avi nearly tumbled from her perch.

Weird. Her mother never rushed. "Haste creates mistakes," she'd lectured a thousand times.

She acted as if a camazotz was chasing her. Avi waited a moment. Nothing emerged.

She *had* to follow. Something interesting was finally happening!

Her heart hammered against her ribs, and her wings ached from pumping so hard, reaching for as much speed as possible.

Only to find her mother calmly talking to those two strangers.

They were girls her age! Not boring old merchants with fake smiles, but actual young women.

Traders usually stayed in the south. These two, a Telana and Solara, were following the eastern ridge.

No packs, no goods.

Her mother's face gave nothing away, it never did, but she'd let them continue on their way, which was strange too.

Usually, visitors had to wait forever for permissions and escorts and all those tedious things her mother called "proper protocol."

Then her mother had flown away in a rush—straight into Avi.

Why would her perfectly composed mother be in such a hurry? And why send guards to watch over Nona; today of all days?

The feeling in Avi's stomach wasn't the usual dread of facing her mother's disappointment. This was new. A creeping sensation that made the sweet flower scent turn sour in her nose.

She needed to get home. Now.

20

BRAM

Bram flicked his fingers against his thumb, pacing in short, sharp turns at the edge of the treeline. Grit stuck to his boots.

The mudflats reeked of brine and decay. Not the layers of compacted leaves and soil like the jungle at his back, but sour stench of like bodies left to rot in the sun.

He hated this place.

The border between Tixamar and Aclanus was more of a suggestion than law. The mudflats served as a buffer, claimed by no one.

How long was too long to wait?

He calculated the distance, the time, the effort. He had to have made it to the border before Rowena.

He could slip into the shadows. Hide himself better. But in Seeker form, others tended to leave him alone. It gave him authority to question anyone. The horns. The markings. The quiet, steady hum of restrained violence.

That part, the violence, was getting harder to hold back the longer he stayed idle.

Let others wonder why he stood exposed.

Wherever Rowena emerged, he'd reach her in a heartbeat.

High above, a single vultu circled. Its silhouette crossed the morning sun, dipping lower, wings tight against the wind. It screeched once, then twice, sharp, keening sounds that made Bram's runes prickle.

That was no ordinary bird. It twisted its head mid-flight, catching Bram's gaze, first with one eye, then the other. A watcher, commanded by someone inside the walls.

Bram backed into the darkness, scanning the surroundings. Each step sent a dark flicker through his chest, followed by a ripple of heat across his shoulders.

Wards.

Anomie had corrupted the enchantment laced into its soil. Of course, Tanith would watch for incoming signatures carrying power. She was too careful. Too paranoid.

The bird flapped away with another screech, angling toward the city.

It had been a mistake to stand so far from the trees. Bram growled at himself. He should have been more cautious. His mind had only thought of making sure Rowena spotted him, not who else might.

Too late.

More vultus gathered, their rising cries like shrieks from a shattered chorus. He watched them swirl and dance above the gates of Anomie, and for a moment, it was almost beautiful. The precision. The unnatural grace.

Then a figure emerged from the gates.

A woman. Cloaked in brown robes, hem soaked with black mud. Her hood fell back as she argued briefly with the trolls at the gate.

White hair. A disavowed.

Moments later, she followed the birds—no, was led by them.

Straight toward him.

Bram forced himself to breathe evenly through his nose. Stay calm.

He recognized the woman before she reached him.

Yralissa. The Oraku from Ibern.

What was she doing here?

He stepped out of the trees in full view. Arms crossed. Body still. Waiting.

"Seeker!" she called as she slowed her approach. "I wasn't sure if you'd come this far."

She spoke as if they were old allies, meeting again on familiar ground. He didn't answer. Just let the silence stretch, long and pointed.

"I've been watching. The birds. They're mine." She stepped closer. "You're looking for her, aren't you? Rowena. I heard that she entered Tixamar. Fidessa knows too. She's searching."

Bram raised a brow. "Odd that you know that."

"Gossip is rampant in Anomie. Some call it a city of chaos, maybe so, but chaos listens."

"Spoken like someone who's lived there a while."

"I found myself here when I first left Saganus. Until I found a home in Ibern." Yralissa gave a tight smile. "After you refused to help me, I had few options. So I returned. Most disavowed come here to survive."

"You make it sound like it's Caelus-blessed."

"Hardly. But it has its uses. And now, I have something you need."

Bram narrowed his eyes. "Which is?"

"Your wait here is in vain. Rowena has already passed through. I know where she is."

Bram's muscles tensed, but he forced himself to remain still. A question about Rowena's speed niggled the back of his mind. He shoved it aside. Yralissa had sought him out. Raced across the mud.

He did not trust her, but she had known he'd come for Rowena. He would hear her out. Yet, true information was currency in Anomie.

Heat flared through his chest. He leaned closer. "Why not sell that information to Tanith?"

"Because I want to go home. Not become part of her broken court." Her nostrils flared, but she reset quickly. Her sharp tone softened. "And no one but you can restore me."

"I have already told you I *cannot*."

She closed the gap between them by a step. "My hope is that you will try anyway."

Bram said nothing. The wind picked up, rustling the grasses behind him. His focus stayed locked on Yralissa. She was like all the others.

Too many lies. Too many sharp smiles. Secret motives.

The Heptad. Mereb. Even the rebels.

She was no different.

He lifted his gaze to the sky over Yralissa's head.

"You doubt me. That's understandable." Yralissa lifted her hands as if in surrender. "I don't expect your trust. But we can help each other."

There was nothing he could do to reverse her disavowed state. It wasn't a lie. He could do nothing to help her. Her request only distracted him from his true duties. He dropped his arms to his sides. "My purpose is clear."

"If you would just give me a chance. It means everything."

Bram inhaled. A bitter taste soured the back of his mouth. He hated secrets. Hated games. Manipulation for gain at others' expense.

But if she wouldn't listen, and if she knew where Rowena was . . . He'd have to play along.

"Tell me where she is, and I'll do what I can."

"There's an old watch tower, in the Veilrune Mountains.

Rowena was taken there." Yralissa slid another step, and rested her fingers on his arm. "It's sheltered in a glade not easy to find. I know where it is."

Bram clenched his jaw. The Veilrunes matched the information Ida gave. "How did she get to the mountains from here?"

"She did not make it long after she entered the mudflats. Warriors took her before she could reach the city."

It made sense. She had to pass through this way. It was why he stood here. If Fidessa had her—and the sword? He had to find her.

"I've heard another rumor," Yralissa said, sliding closer. "That the ancient prophecy may be fulfilled soon."

"That is old gossip without value." He spoke too harshly. Too insistent. A dead giveaway. He knew better.

Yralissa's eyes widened, and she dropped her hand. "It's worth much, I would guess. Especially if Fidessa has found the girl before you."

He didn't like the way she said *the girl*. Detached. Dismissive.

Rowena deserved more respect than that.

She lowered her chin, gazing up at him through lowered lashes. He'd been too obvious.

"I'm not your enemy, Bram."

That he did not believe. He said nothing aloud. Instead, he twisted to scan the treeline. No trail. No whisper of Rowena's enchanted signature. Not a sign of her.

Nothing.

Standing here, waiting. He gambled with Rowena's safety and the rebels' lives. If he didn't act . . . if he waited, like he'd done with Killian, hoping for a cleaner way to outwit danger, someone else might die.

He wouldn't risk that again. Especially not Rowena.

"How far is this glen?"

"Far. Between the Sightless Vale and the Twisted Forest. To walk will take several days." Yralissa's lips curved.

Bram scoffed. She had witnessed his offer to Rowena in Forsa. All Primary Druids could travel through the aether. But not like he could. "I have a faster way. But it may be . . . unsettling."

She held his gaze, giving a slight nod over her shoulder. "I've managed many unpleasantries."

He held out his hand. "Picture the exact place. Hold tight."

She stepped into him quickly, too eagerly. Her hands were cold. Her smile too smooth.

But Bram closed his eyes and pulled them both into the shadows.

Darkness enveloped them.

Not the usual absence of light, something older. Hungrier. Bram had traveled as shadow more times than he could count. Alone, or with Rowena, he moved like smoke.

Effortless. Quiet. Unseen.

But something was different. Wrong.

Yralissa's presence dragged against his power. The shadows fought him, like a storm crashing against a rocky coast. It was not her presence beside him, but something deeper. As if the shadows rejected her.

Pain shot through his shoulders. His runes flared hot against his skin, a warning. An interference? His enchantment reacting to hers?

Focus. Find the target. Get through.

Flashes of light disrupted his concentration. His shadows writhed, defensively, stretching around them both.

He had to push harder. Keep them moving.

Flashes. More lights flickered in the distance.

He tightened his grip on Yralissa.

The darkness constricted.

Not against him. Against her.

A sharp cry beside him. Cut short.

Her breath came in short, panicked bursts.

One final surge of will.

The shadows fractured, expelling them with unexpected force.

Bram hit the ground hard, skidding through pine needles and wet moss. He'd gotten them through, despite the struggle. According to the images Yralissa shared, they were in the correct location.

She'd come to rest nearby, coughing, gasping. "What in Caelus was that?"

Bram rose, limbs trembling but undamaged. "It was wrong." He shouldn't have taken her with him. His gut had warned him.

He surveyed the area. High pines surrounded a glen. The sky overhead, gray, filled with light. A circular tower stood like a lone sentinel in the center.

Something pressed at the edge of his senses. A wrongness inside the quiet.

The glen held no sound. No movement except the distant sway of treetops. No birds. No insects. Nothing living but themselves.

No sound meant no warning of approach.

A few paces away, Yralissa knelt in the brush, hands braced on her thighs. Her back shook—weakness that would hinder his efforts if they faced danger.

Rowena had never had such a severe reaction. She adapted.

This one did not.

Bram rotated his shoulders. His runes itched. A low, persistent vibration just beneath his skin.

A familiar sensation. Recently.

Wards.

He crouched and pressed his fingers to the ground. The

moss was damp, but underneath, the soil shuddered with something colder. Not in temperature, but in resonance.

Rising, he circled the glen's perimeter. The runes on his forearms flickered, barely perceptible, but enough to confirm the wards stretched over the entire area.

"Yralissa."

She straightened, wiping her mouth with the back of her hand. "That was more than unsettling."

He'd warned her, but he hadn't expected his own discomfort. Better left unsaid. "There are wards in this place."

"Old ones," she said quickly. "That's why this place is used to hide those others don't wish found."

A twig cracked beneath his boot. The sound echoed too long. He scanned the glen again. The trees had stopped swaying. He took another step. A pressure leaned against his back, urging him toward the tower.

Not physically pushing him. Nothing enchanted in the usual sense. More like being called to a place that already knew his name.

A plea. Rowena?

"She is inside?"

Yralissa gestured toward the tower, her hands still trembling. "This way."

He didn't like it. The silence. The way his runes pulsed faster.

A warning. But he followed. If there was a chance, no matter how small, that Rowena was near, and in danger . . .

He had to go.

21

———

BRAM

THE TOWER ENGULFED Bram the moment his boots struck the stone floor.

A warning.

No welcome. Nothing innocent. Nothing neutral.

A scythe during harvest.

The shadows, held in check within his body, tangled. Desperate to leave, they knotted together. Locked in place no matter the effort.

Another alarm.

Nausea wracked his insides so deep it rattled his bones. He halted, bracing himself against the curved wall. A symbol, partially hidden under his fingers. He twisted his hand, exposing a faintly glowing rune.

He trailed his gaze from the firs, to a second, then a third. All around the circular room, etched into the stone. Runes. Ancient, braided.

Wrong.

Not marked by enchantment, but something deeper, stronger.

They pulsated with unmistakable energy. Primary power. Only possible from a full druid.

Recognition.

Wards did not just protect the glen, they extended to the tower as well.

What had he done?

Bram blinked. The stale air remained unmoved. No presence but himself and Yralissa. A strange tingling sensation rolled down his neck, through his arms. His heart quickened.

He twisted to face Yralissa. She said nothing, her features shrouded in darkness. No tension leaked from her as it roiled in his own chest.

She stood serene. Too serene.

A cold reality hit him.

"Oh, my dear Bram," Yralissa purred, a cat pleased with its prize. "You seem troubled."

His eyes adjusted to the low light. Rough stone underfoot. High ceiling. Solid curved walls . . . No windows. No longer a door.

This place was not warded to keep dangers out. It was to capture those within.

"What is this place?"

"An abandoned watchtower, as I said." Yralissa's stare glinted with cold satisfaction.

Bram curled his fingers into his palms, willing himself not to grab the insolent woman by the throat. "Why did you bring us here?"

"Such billowing negativity." Yralissa pouted each word, sidling across the room, out of his reach. "There's nothing to worry over."

He closed his eyes, inhaling, long and deep. Reaching within his chest where his shadows rested. He would return to the mudflats.

Nothing stirred.

He tried again, clawing inward. A distant rattle. Like the metal of a cage door. Then nothing.

His connection was gone.

Not disconnected.

Blocked.

He stared across the room. Mind blank.

Think. Reason. Form a plan.

Yralissa stood near a fireplace, cold but prepared with kindling and stacked logs. She touched her fingers to the pile, murmuring a soft, indecipherable word. Fire blazed to life, engulfing the wood.

The room burst into a flickering brightness.

She faced him, arms tucked into the sleeves of her brown robe. The flames silhouetting her posture like carved stone.

The room, now bathed in amber light, held a bed, piled with furs. Far too extravagant for a watchtower. Heavy drapes hung as if to frame a non-existent view. A high-backed chair angled toward the fireplace.

It was not a room for watching—but for waiting.

He faced the druid. "You said Rowena was here."

"I lied." She shrugged without a hint of apology. "She is nearby. I assume with Fidessa by now. That might be true."

Even disavowed, she would have access to some enchantment, but not much. Not enough to have created all of this.

Fidessa was a powerful mage, but this work was beyond simple spells or incantations.

But if they worked together . . . perhaps.

He had no time for games. She had no idea what she made him risk. "What is this? Why am I here?"

"You're so devoted to your duties. It must be exhausting." Yralissa brushed off her hands. "I've provided you a place to rest."

That was the last thing he needed. "What is it you want?"

Yralissa stood with her hands still tucked into the sleeves of her simple brown robe, her silver hair sparkling in the flickering flames. "I've already told you."

"You think this action proves you worthy of restoration?" His body tensed, senses alert for any crack, any sliver of escape. "Seems that you're only proving the Heptad's case for disavowal."

"That is naïve."

"Whatever your motive, you're meddling where you don't belong. You do not know what this delay will cost."

Rowena. Rebels. Sword. Heptad.

Faces and hopes flashed through his mind. Those counting on him. Depending on him.

Whatever self-righteousness Yralissa acted upon. She risked lives. Innocent lives.

Lives that he cared for.

"That's an interesting view. Where I don't belong." She pinched her lips, holding back more.

Then she extended her hands, palms up. The flames in the hearth danced higher.

With a shimmer, her robe melted into a gown. Emerald silk that flowed like water, cinched by a golden girdle.

"You don't understand what it means to be dismissed. Not denied. *Dismissed.* Your questions unanswered. Your presence erased."

He said nothing, his throat too thick for words.

No one would *pretend* to be disavowed.

What would be the upside to choose a solitary life of indentured servitude? He'd seen her working for the king in Ibern. An Oraku. Hadn't he?

His mind spun. She had been there when he tried to get Rowena to come with him. Standing over her when he arrived.

Not inside with the king. The Heptad said not every druid who left Saganus was stripped of their powers. Was Yralissa was still a Primary Druid?

She couldn't be. Despite her change of attire, her hair remained white.

Her eyes silver.

White runes still gleamed on her hands.

"You should understand more than anyone." Genuine pain filtered through her words.

Why? He had no connection to her or her troubles.

"Of all druids, it's you. Chosen, marked, exalted," she went on. "The perfect son of the realm."

He scoffed. She rambled like a fool. "You're speaking nonsense."

She raised her hands again, clenching them into fists. A barely contained screech broke loose. "How are you so obtuse?"

Whatever issues she had with the Heptad, right or wrong. This was not his fight.

"You trained with the sentinels, protecting the Heptad," Yralissa continued. "Now you keep their secrets. You're marked, *yes*, but they didn't throw you away just for asking *why*."

What was she getting at? She was right about one thing; he did not understand.

"If you have grievances, there are ways to handle them. But this," he gestured to the walls, the glowing markings wrapped like chains, "This is not the answer."

"Maybe not," she said. "But this will give me answers to *my* questions."

She turned her back on him and flicked her fingers. The fireplace flared higher, escaping its boundary to blacken the hearth. The air simmered with heat.

"They take our lives, the ones we're meant to have, and then toss us aside as they wish." Her hands trembled, but she forced herself back into a restrained calm, brushing her hands down her gown.

"That doesn't make this right." Bram kept his voice low. He needed to cool her temper. Get her to give him Fidessa's true location; if that's where Rowena truly was.

Then get away.

"I don't need right. I need to matter." She turned from the fire, facing him fully. A mask of calm slid into place. "You still don't get it. You've never been betrayed. Never rejected. You were so special that power was simply bestowed on you. But you can't use it now, can you?"

Her assumptions stabbed deep.

After the tunnels, after Killian, Bram did understand betrayal.

He called for his power again. His shadows remained out of reach, coiled and ready, but untouchable. Like a door barred from the inside.

Only a cold emptiness filled him.

"The best part in this," Yralissa's face brightened with a genuine, wide smile. "I didn't sever your power. You gave it to me. You stepped inside of your own will. You chose to trust me."

"You manipulated the choice," Bram answered. Though a sour taste, regret, burned his tongue.

She was not wrong.

Her smile didn't waver. "The Heptad does that every day. Consider this . . . a lesson."

The flames dipped slightly, flickering in a rhythm that made his skin crawl. They seemed connected to Yralissa's emotions.

Her anger at the Heptad ran deep. She believed he could influence them. "You want something." Something beyond being restored. He wasn't even sure she needed that.

Yralissa's eyes sparkled. "Clever. Good. I've been waiting.

Let's make this a game." She closed the gap between them, hands clasped.

"I don't have time for games."

"You will play or you will stay."

They held each other's stare. Nothing but the crackle of burning wood filled the silence.

Yralissa broke first. "Fine, I'll give you time to think about what you want. We'll talk in the morning." She slid back a step.

"I will not be staying." He hated himself for answering to her obvious ploy.

"Then solve my riddle," she said. "If you do, you leave. Fail . . . and you stay until the prophecy fails and the gates of Mortus open. Either way, I'll find out what you're made of."

Bram narrowed his gaze. "What kind of trap is this?"

"It's not a trap." She stepped backward, her gown swishing against the floor. "It's a mirror. Listen well.

Into the soil, two seeds were sown

The gardener, partial, one has grown

A tree they sprout, with branches wide

An orchard to share if not for pride

One shaped by shears, one left to wane

A love, obscured by veils of disdain

The silence divides, left untended

In mother's absence, hearts upended"

When she finished, the runes along the walls flared a shade brighter.

"You get three guesses," she said.

Bram needed to stall, think each line through. "You said Fidessa is close. What if she has Rowena?"

Yralissa shrugged. "The perhaps you should guess quickly."

"There are other issues at hand, Yralissa. There is no time for this."

She glanced around the room. "Seems you have all the time you need. I'll return for your first guess."

A blast of unnatural blue smoke curled up from the fireplace, surrounding her. The smell of sulfur and scorched sage filled Bram's lungs. He covered his mouth, stepping back as the haze thickened, and when it cleared . . .

She was gone.

The fire dimmed. The runes pulsed, like heartbeat echoes, sealed tight around him.

She didn't say when she'd return. It had better be fast.

A pain stabbed his chest. An invisible dagger through his heart.

He could have just sealed the fates of every moon-born— every living being in Edenia.

Handed them over to destruction.

22

ROWENA

"YOU SHOULD NOT HAVE TOLD of the Argentry." Tephra snapped, wheeling to face Rowena. "If the princess tells anyone, they will know they were close."

Rowena blinked, still caught in the awe of Nisha's transformation and departure. "Then we had better hurry."

Tephra twisted her lips like she'd bitten into something rotten. She muttered under her breath, sharp and guttural, too low for Rowena to catch, then spun and stormed off toward the east.

Rowena followed, pressing a palm to her chest as if she could steady her heart. The jungle behind them felt heavier now. Something unsaid still lurked between the trees.

The smell hit first.

A wall of rot and salt, thick and clinging. Rowena gagged. "Is the stench always this bad?"

"How would I know?" Tephra floated back, pointed and terse.

They slowed their pace, moving low as the trees thinned and the canopy surrendered to a gray smear of open sky.

Tephra raised a hand to halt them.

"What is it?" Rowena whispered.

"We are close. There may be guards."

Rowena's limbs ached with the need to run, to break into the open air and leave the suffocating jungle behind. But she swallowed that instinct, forcing herself to match Tephra's quiet pace.

The trees grew shorter. The soil underfoot shifted, spongier, dotted with gnarled roots and slimy rocks. Then came the nausea—sudden and absolute. Rowena clutched her middle, barely able to breathe as her vision swam.

She staggered against a tree. "What—?"

Tephra bent double, retching into the leaves. "Wards. Strong ones." She coughed, spitting bile.

Rowena wiped her mouth, her skin damp with sweat. "Witches?"

"Or mages. Or disavowed. Anomie collects them all." Tephra's voice trembled with effort, but her spine straightened. "We keep moving."

Rowena tried to admire the resilience. But her own body still tried to turn itself inside out.

Stomach rolling. Lungs kicking. Ribs aching.

She staggered forward.

"What is the purpose of wards?" Rowena coughed, still trying to clear her lungs. Were they like the warning disks and bones they hung on ropes in Skandan? But filled with strange enchantment? "Will others know we're here now?"

"We will find out," Tephra said, continuing on.

Always so confident.

Rowena rubbed away the last bit of discomfort from her chest and followed.

They crept the last few paces through a curtain of brush. Until, finally, the trees parted.

Aclanus.

A bleak sprawl of gray and brown stretched before them, as

if the land had drained itself of color. The city's massive wall loomed. Three men high, if not more, of sheer stone, ringed with sharp pickets shoved into the ground at awkward angles.

Rowena would bet all of Skandan could fit inside.

Some rooftops stretched their necks above the outer wall. An odd haze wandered among them, like a choking torc. The air reeked of ash and stagnant water.

Rowena crouched beside Tephra, using a twisted brush for cover. "That has to be the ugliest place in all of Edenia."

"Agreed." Tephra murmured.

"You still want to get help from inside there?" The idea of Tephra changing her appearance made Rowena shudder, but the view in front of them made it even worse.

Tephra darted a glance, but didn't answer.

Asta provided blessings and assistance to Rowena's father . . . or she had. Even so, her presence commanded respect. And it was given.

What would the disavowed be like inside a place that reeked of shame and squalor?

Along well-worn paths, snaking toward the opened gates, trudged elven, and many others unknown to Rowena. She couldn't guess their origin, but they made their way toward the gates in groups or couples or alone.

Heads low, shoulders rounded. Whether old or young.

No laughter. No play. No hope.

Rowena's emotions were too raw. Exhaustion. Relief. Fear. All fought for control. She could not enter that city.

"There." Tephra pointed to a small convoy arriving from the south. Five low wagons, hand-pulled, and battered. Several figures gathered near one of the carts on the muddy trail.

"They seem stuck," Rowena said.

"They are. We will blend in at the back. Join with them when they move again."

"And they will just accept us?"

Tephra raised a brow. "You can *help* with that, yes?"

Rowena blinked. She'd spent so little time soaking in rays from either moon, she wasn't sure. "I can try. But I'll have to touch them."

"Now. Hurry!" Tephra ducked back into the trees to circle toward the trail.

Apparently, the plan had been discussed, and accepted.

They emerged, exposed, onto the flats about thirty yards from the convoy. The wind slapped Rowena's face with its damp mist and foul stench. She raised her tunic to cover her mouth and nose, running like a wobbly drunkard over the rough ground.

Murky puddles, hard-packed mud, and sloppy muck stretched between the jungle and the rutted trails near the wall.

Rowena's legs burned with the effort to keep up with Tephra's speed.

Halfway to the wagons, something twitched in her gut. A flicker of her enchantment. A warning.

She slowed.

The wagon silhouettes hadn't moved. They were still. Too still.

It was difficult to feel anything beyond her heart hammering in her chest, but she strained to sense those near the wagon.

Nothing. She slowed even more, trying harder. Still nothing.

"Tephra! Stop!"

Too late.

Black wings darkened the sky, coming over the city wall. Vultu descended with a flurry of screeches. They weren't just birds—they were unnatural. Their eyes gleamed red, and their cries pierced like claws into bone.

Tephra had reached the last wagon. She spun, waving Rowena away, palms crackling with golden enchantment. "Run!"

Terror flooded through Rowena, making her gasp for every breath. But she would not leave Tephra to fight alone. Her boots slipped in the muck. She flailed her arms, struggling to stay upright.

Closer now.

The twisted forms huddled beside the wagon were not real.

Merchant clothing, stuffed with straw.

A trap.

But for who? It couldn't be for them.

A hunter's snare meant to ambush the unsuspecting before they reached the gates. Rowena growled. At herself and Tephra.

Fools. They'd raced right into danger like mindless gilrids. The trap was for them.

Black talons swooped to slash at Rowena's face. She crouched low, blocking with her arm. Pain bit into her scalp from a separate assailant. She rolled over a shoulder and rose, palms out. A thin silver stream hit one of the birds, so weak it only knocked it off course for a moment. Another circled. Then another. Rowena's enchantment sputtered, frayed like an old rope. Then it was gone.

Running would leave them more exposed. The wagon had been half-buried in the mud, so there was no space to hide underneath. Digging would take too long. The best they could do was keep moving. Dart in and out among the decoys.

Rowena rolled and kicked one bird. It fell with a thud, but hopped right back to its feet. It didn't attack from the ground, but flapped its wings, returning to the air. Only to dive once again and slice into Rowena's back.

She spun, slapping and waving and hitting nothing.

No more birds attacked.

They flew higher, circling. Not retreating, but watching.

Rowena lowered her arms, but kept ready. "Are you injured?"

Tephra, stood as she did, staring into the sky above them, breathing heavily, a bloody scratch down her cheek.

"Nothing serious," she hissed. "What are they waiting for?"

It made no sense.

They kept their focus on the birds, until the ground vibrated.

Distant at first. Then louder.

Rowena jogged closer to Tephra, instinctively taking her hand. Tephra squeezed back and twisted so they stood back-to-back.

"There!" Rowena pointed with her free hand to a herd of borelk charging in from the west.

"This way too." Tephra called.

The massive creatures stampeded around each side of the wagon with their long, slender legs nearly as tall as Rowena.

They formed a circle.

At first around all the wagons, then just the one where Rowena and Tephra stood.

Pressing ever closer.

They released each other's hand, preparing to fight.

Hooves thundered like war drums, spraying mud with every stride. Tusks, longer than Rowena's hand, erupted from their scruffy black snouts. Antlers spread over two yards wide, tangled like dead branches.

And on their backs . . . riders.

Swathed in dark cloaks, their faces hidden. Gloved hands gripped reins threaded through rings in the borelk's snouts.

Rowena froze.

Her limbs refused to move. Her mind screamed to run, but there was nowhere to go. Her feet anchored in place like stone. One of the riders reached for her.

She screamed and twisted. Too slow.

A hand clamped around her upper arm and flung her effortlessly through the air. She slammed face-first onto a borelk's back. All air gusted out of her lungs. The borelk charged, jolting her with every stride.

She gasped for sips of air only to lose them.

She scrunched her eyes tight, spots dancing like wisps behind her lids.

Foul mud splattered her face, into her mouth, flowing back out with her spit.

She couldn't see. Couldn't breathe.

Her legs flopped uselessly. Her hands scrabbled for purchase on the slick hide and coarse fur. Knuckles bruised her back where they twisted the fabric of her tunic, keeping her from falling off.

She caught glimpses of the city wall, rising higher with each pounding stride. They were heading into Anomie.

No. She couldn't. She'd rather get trampled by the herd.

Tephra?

Rowena blinked through tears, and caught a flicker of another borelk just behind her. Tephra's limp body across a beast's back. Still alive or they'd toss her aside.

Thank Masah.

The city loomed.

Fog crawled over the palisade like grasping fingers. Shapes moved along the ramparts—too many to count.

Watchers. Shadows. Weapons. Waiting.

Rowena reached deep into her chest, searching for any scrap of enchantment left in her core. But it had bled dry with the vultu. There was nothing.

She let her head drop, cheek bumping against the beast's warm hide. Her vision tunneled into a dim blur.

The city swelled closer.

No.

And then—

Black.

She fell, not in body but in spirit, as if her heart slid out from under her skin. The pounding hooves faded. The screech of vultu dissolved into silence.

She let go. The fear. The panic. Even the grief.

The last thing she felt was wind, cold, crisp, clean, curling across the back of her neck.

Soft snowflakes whispered against Rowena's cheeks, just like they did every winter in Taesing. But this time, she walked alone through the empty village.

Barefoot.

Her footsteps made no sound, left no tracks, and the surrounding forest stretched on in endless silence.

Then a voice behind her, warm as firelight.

"You aren't alone. Not if you'll let yourself be found."

She spun, searching.

The trees swayed in time with a wind that carried the scent of pine and home. A shadow stood among the trunks. Tall.

Familiar.

"Bram?" Her voice cracked.

But it wasn't him. Not exactly.

The shadow stepped forward, wearing his shape, but no warmth called to her.

His horns glinted. His eyes were dark. Distant.

"You always run away," he said, not with anger, but sorrow. "You run before anyone can follow."

"I never meant to."

"You're still running."

Rowena tried to reach for him, but the snow turned to ash

beneath her feet. The forest burned behind her, distant at first, then faster, closer.

Her home. Her mother's laughter. Her father's hand. Her hope.

Gone. All gone.

She dropped to her knees, choking on the ash.

Where do I belong?

The wind shifted. The fire vanished. The snow returned.

And somewhere far away, a woman's voice, low, soft, echoed across the dreamscape: "You must be ready to lead them."

Rowena gasped and shot upright.

Awake.

Her hands gripped the damp grass. Cool air clung to her skin. She blinked through the haze of afternoon light, the sky above pale and clean, scented with fresh dew.

No walls. No gate. No city.

Only trees.

Only mountains.

23

ROWENA

ROWENA'S RIBS gave a sharp protest, cracked possibly, bruised for sure, punishing every breath.

For several moments, she slumped, face pressed into the pine-needle dusted forest floor, dampness soaking into her tunic. The musky stink of borelk sweat and churned soil filled her nose. She tried to push off the ground, but her arms trembled under her weight, and she collapsed to her side with a hiss of pain.

Tephra lay motionless, nearby, but out of reach.

"Tephra?" Rowena choked on her words, her voice hoarse and raw. She wrestled her arms to a crawl, dragging herself to on an elbow, then sliced her hip on a rock, wringing a moan from her throat.

"She'll live," a voice said behind her, low, gravelly, and sharp as shale.

Rowena twisted, one arm curled protectively around her side, and glared up at the speaker. Hidden within the shadow of a deep hood, something about his presence made the little hair on the back of her neck rise. "Who are you?"

"One you don't want to cross, princess."

Her spine stiffened, sending pain rattling through her body. He hadn't just acknowledged her title, but there was weight behind the word.

Deliberate. Knowing. Not a guess.

If he understood who she truly was, these were not random bandits, ready to ransom wayward travelers.

She tried to sit up straighter, curling inward as cold wind cut through the trees, stinging her cheeks and exposed skin. Snow draped the treetops above, and frost clung to patches of grass. Pale clouds swirled around jagged slopes in the distance.

Her tunic and trousers, too thick for the jungle, were now far too thin for the bone-deep cold. Tephra would be frostbitten in her fragile clothing.

They weren't in Anomie.

They'd been taken into the mountains. High into the mountains for it to be this cold.

"Stay down," the rider snapped as she shifted positions. Her hands were roughly seized, pressed palm-to-palm, and bound tightly with cord. "Don't be foolish."

It was a fitting statement, really. More than he could understand.

She'd spent her life dreaming of adventure, exploring the continent. Naïve to the danger. And now here she was: tied, bruised, and discarded in an unknown forest.

If only the dryads had allowed her to stay in the cottage. She'd be with Bram, and Tephra would not be caught.

That kind of thinking would do her no good.

Rowena gritted her teeth against the pain in her side. The binding on her hands was no real prison, but it was enough. Enough to stop her from bringing enchantment through her palms. Enough to render her defenses nearly useless.

She glanced toward the borelk, who foraged under the trees like enormous shaggy boars with long delicate legs; powerful, swift legs that spirited her far from anywhere. Their hooves and antlers tore at the earth with rhythmic snorts, pawing up roots and berries. The scent of wet fur swirled with the wind.

Nearby, Tephra stirred. She rolled over with a low groan, her knees drawn to her chest. Her eyes were slits, but she was breathing. Conscious. Bound the same way. Whether it was understood she was Solara, or simply that she had been Rowena's companion, her enchantment had also been sealed from use.

Rowena exhaled with a shaky effort. The shared pain between them offered a sliver of reassurance, familiar, if grim.

Their captors moved silently, efficiently, setting up a fire pit with practiced ease. Six of them, all cloaked in heavy layers.

Some had thrown open their cloaks to aid in preparing their camp. Underneath, their garments were embroidered with geometric patterns in brightly colored thread. Reds, yellows, oranges.

Far more decorated than anyone in Taesing would wear. Heavy linen pants, baggy at the thighs, were tucked into thick leather boots to the knee. Odd.

Where were they from?

She thought she'd overheard an accent. They spoke in whispers so low it was difficult to hear anything but a stray word or two. The little she had heard came from both male and female voices, though each equally as rough.

Their emotions were as shrouded as their faces. Not that Rowena had enough enchantment to feel too much. They'd been careful to keep themselves from touching either her or Tephra unless absolutely necessary.

Once the warriors had settled themselves to other tasks, ignoring the women, Rowena whispered to Tephra. "Do you know where they are from?"

Tephra's voice rasped, breathless, laced with pain and anger.

"Panon. Belyse Castle perhaps. I've seen similar in Parsa. The king contracts their kind for quiet work."

"Assassins?" Rowena dropped her mouth open, but shut it a heartbeat later. The cold rubbed against her teeth and dried her tongue. She swallowed, once. Twice. "Why keep us alive?"

Two riders, cloaks still hiding their features, faced them, but made no move toward them. Giving them freedom to talk, and to listen, no doubt.

Their group moved with order and precision. No idle conversation, no wasted motion.

But it was a different silence that drew her attention the most. They were like the stuffed dolls from the trap, a void of emotion or energy.

It unsettled her.

There were beings, the undead Inmorti, that traveled throughout Edenia, but this seemed different. An intentional void, as if veiled.

"My mother feared Belyse," she said softly. "She called it a place where honor was buried in the name of loyalty."

Tephra nodded faintly. "My father calls it a place for smiling liars."

Rowena bowed her head, speaking into her shoulder. "They called me princess."

If the secretive bandit hadn't said her title, she might have thought they were after Tephra and not her.

She glanced at her friend, who huddled over her bent knees, rocking. Perhaps the captors made a mistake and got them mixed up.

"Are you not?" Tephra kept her gaze toward the fire, now in full bloom but too far to offer them comfort.

How had she guessed? Rowena had told her very little about herself.

"I have met Skandans before. Each time, they are hale and

hearty, with skills to survive any challenge." Tephra scoffed from amusement. "You do not. It was not hard to figure out that you are privileged."

Rowena pressed her lips tight. The insult frustrated her. They had just met. She had faced many challenges with success. "You are the one running. Perhaps they have us mixed up?"

"Mine are Farradar issues only." Tephra let out a dark laugh, short and low. "Not that it matters."

The reply left Rowena bothered. But before she could speak again, a heavy boot thudded against her thigh. "Up."

Rowena snapped her head up. "Hey!" she shouted, even as pain flared in her side.

The male did not answer. He dug his hand into her upper arm and yanked her to her feet with such ease it made her feel small.

In that fleeting moment, even through his glove, something shifted. Emotion pulsed through her.

Strong. Hungry. She wanted to hurt him. Not just that. She wanted to enjoy it. Anger boiled over like a forgotten stew. Then restraint. Sudden. Complete. Her need to inflict harm buried beneath a practiced calm.

Her stomach twisted. She recognized him, not the individual, but where he'd come from. Now she was certain they had not confused her with Tephra. They had come for her.

They were Lunara

Another arrived, dragging Tephra to her feet. They were shoved together, backs pressed against a pine, bound more tightly with rawhide cords, shoulder to shoulder. A single blanket was tossed over them to share. Heavy branches swaying over their heads would provide cover from snow or rain. They also kept Rowena away from Masah's soothing rays.

Then they were left alone.

"They are not assassins. At least not ones from Panon," Rowena whispered.

Tephra twisted her neck to glance at her. "How can you be sure?"

"Because I . . . felt it. They are from Penumar."

Tephra let out a quiet snort. "That is not a comfort."

The night grew deeper, and all but one of the cloaked figures lay down to rest. A watchful patrol near the edge of the trees. The fire was maintained, but not fed. Its warmth didn't reach them, anyway.

A fog had crept in, coiling around the branches above with a faint silver glow beneath the large moon's light.

From deep in the woods, a howl rose, thin and distant. Then another.

Unfamiliar. Not quite wolf. More like something imitating one.

Lycani.

Tephra's voice a whisper. "Which is worse? The predators in the woods . . . or the ones who tied us here?"

Rowena, too cold to even shiver, smiled with a bitter humor. "Does it matter?"

ROWENA GOT little sleep through the night. Her ribs throbbed with every breath and her back ached from where it pressed hard against the rough bark.

She tried to stay awake, but when she did doze off, her head would bob to her chin, waking her with a start. Fear surged through her from the strangers surrounded them. She could still feel the press of that gloved hand on her arm.

The little training her mother had taught . . . before her

death . . . said that she was only able to increase another's emotions that were already present. The one who'd influenced her had enjoyed control. Had yearned to inflict pain. He'd forced *his* emotions onto *her*.

A sick feeling rattled down Rowena's spine.

Had he? Was that the direction it went? Her body slumped against the bindings. The truth too heavy to bear.

Lungol sped by close to the horizon, his gleaming light fleeting and fickle, but Masah had stayed with Rowena. His comforting brilliance had infiltrated the tree branches to keep her company. A sliver of her enchantment returned. Not much, but enough to slate her thirst.

At some point, despite her efforts, she dozed off because a rattling noise startled her awake.

She jerked so violently her head cracked against the tree trunk. Stars burst through her vision. Biting pain lanced through her skull.

Based on Tephra's slow rhythmic breathing, she remained asleep. Rowena twisted her leg to nudge her companion awake.

Their Lunara captors were rising, readying the borelk for travel.

Tephra opened her eyes to slits. Her lips were tinged in purple.

Rowena called her name, but she only moaned a response. She'd gotten too cold. The frigid night air with only one blanket had not been enough.

"Someone help! She's freezing." Rowena wiggled, trying to get as close to Tephra as possible. "She needs to get to the fire."

A rider ambled over, unhurried. The Lunara stood before Tephra, staring; or so Rowena assumed since she still couldn't see their blangdang faces.

"Fire's out. Solara should wear real clothes." The rider

removed the bindings holding her to the tree and hoisted Tephra to her feet. Her legs crumpled.

He grumbled, muttering under his breath as he tossed Tephra over his shoulder.

Rowena's eyes stung, but she held back her tears. Please Osric, let her be alright. Even if they weren't actual friends, she couldn't bear to lose someone else.

The rider strode away.

Rowena strained at the cords still holding her in place. "Where are you taking her!"

"Quiet!" The Lunara twisted and yelled to Rowena. "I'm getting something to warm her."

Rowena settled back against the tree, breathing hard. If the Lunara were assassins, they didn't act how she expected. Their goal seemed to be something other than killing two young women.

A sigh of relief left her lips.

Not long after, Rowena was released from the tree, and spotted Tephra near a rider tending one of the borelk.

The riders made to haul them onto separate beasts.

"If you expect us to ride, we need a moment to ourselves behind a bush," Rowena said. "And then a bite of cheese, or some hard tack at least to keep our strength."

There were at least a couple of grumbles, but her requests were granted. Nearly. They were not allowed privacy while they took care of their morning necessaries, but they were given time to eat.

Afterward they were settled onto the borelks; allowed to sit astride, rather than tossed over like sacks of grain.

As distasteful as it was to have one of the captors seated behind her, it gave Rowena the ability to check on his emotional state.

Focused. Determined. But his only desire was to complete

his task. Until she sensed a thread of violence, restrained and coiled.

An uncomfortable pressure joined her prodding. She hesitated, exploring the sensation. Then startled and withdrew.

The Lunara knew. He had allowed her to read him. He toyed with her.

A quiet chuckle rumbled against her back. She vowed to be more careful and concentrated on her surroundings.

The heavy borelk were surprisingly fast and light on their feet, rustling through the branches, creating no more noise than a crackling fire. The group traveled without a trail, traversing through the forest as a herd. Two other riders raced ahead of Rowena's mount, while the others, ten or twelve from her counting the night before, spread behind. Wherever they headed, it would not take long to get there.

What horrors would she and Tephra face then? Perhaps their captors had spared their lives because they were delivering them to someone else? Someone who wanted to take their lives personally.

When they barreled up a steep section of the mountain, Rowena twisted her fingers between the wavy black fur on the animal's neck. It gave her some sense of support without forcing her closer to the captor at her back.

She closed her eyes, taking comfort from the rough coat weaving through her tied hands.

Despite her situation, there was a sense of peace exuding from the musky odor and refined power of the borelk's undulating muscles. The beast seemed to embody both gracefulness and ferocity. Their massive bodies and the sharp tusks protruding from the sides of their noses should have made them difficult to control, yet they gave to the bit with surprising elegance.

A wild, desperate idea flickered in Rowena's mind. So

unlikely she almost dismissed it immediately. Her fingers tightened involuntarily in the borelk's coarse fur.

Could she influence the borelk? She'd never attempted her enchantment on an animal before. Would a creature's mind work differently? If it did, she, and Tephra, might have a chance to escape.

It was worth the risk.

Her heart hammered against her ribs. She glanced at Tephra, now in a cloak of her own, riding slightly ahead and to the right. Their eyes met, and something unspoken passed between them—a shared understanding of their precarious position.

Rowena stilled her breathing, slowing it to match the borelk's steady rhythm. She closed her eyes, anxiety twisting in her stomach as she searched blindly for that thread of connection.

Nothing.

Nothing.

Then, there! A flicker of something wild and unfamiliar brushed her consciousness. Not thoughts as she understood them, but instincts. The borelk's natural drive to flee. To run. To be free.

It wasn't like an elven mind, but simpler. Unclouded by rational thought or social constraint. She hesitated, uncertain if she could, or should, manipulate such pure emotion.

But the alternative was captivity or worse.

With clumsy mental fingers, she seized that primal thread and pulled it closer. Awkwardly weaving her own desperate need for escape into it, hoping the creature would respond. For a terrifying moment, nothing happened. Then the borelk's muscles tensed beneath her. Its head jerked up, nostrils flaring.

"Hup! Settle!" The Lunara behind her growled, wrestling

with the reins. He leaned into Rowena, hissing in her ear. "Stop this, now!"

The borelk reared, front hooves pawing the air.

Rowena clung to its neck, leaning forward as the rider tumbled to the ground, yelling startled curses. The Lunara's wrist snagged on the reins, dragging him over twigs and through bushes before he lost hold.

The chaos rippled through the group. The other borelk snorted and stamped, agitation turning to panic. Bellows tore through the air, and the borelk scattered, racing in all directions.

Rowena lost sight of Tephra as the trail narrowed and wound between several large boulders. She found her again atop a boulder. As high as the borelk, crouched and waiting.

Had she jumped off? She really was fearless.

"I can't stop it," Rowena yelled, urging the borelk as close to the boulder as she could.

Tephra didn't answer. Just leapt, landing behind Rowena.

"Go," she shouted. She gathered Rowena's tunic within her fingers. Her body trembled. If one fell, they both would.

Rowena squeezed her legs around the borelk's sides, fingers dug into its shaggy ruff. The trail opened again, and the beast surged, plunging down a slope and away from the shouts and bugles.

The forest echoed with thundering hooves, seeming to rebound in all directions off the rocks. Their borelk charged forward with blazing speed. Rowena's pulse pounded through her ears, bringing a quiet focus that sharpened every other sense.

The scent of pine and moss. The stinging bite of branches whipping past her face. The thunder of pursuit rumbling through the ground like a storm.

Their stolen borelk, muscles straining, carried them higher into the mountains. The cold bit deeper as the air grew thinner.

Rowena's lungs burned. Every inhale cut like glass. Yet they pressed on, driven by the desperate need to put as much distance as possible between themselves and their pursuers.

The borelk angled toward a narrow path winding along the edge of a cliff. Rowena's inside wobbled. The animal went too fast. Rowena leaned against its neck.

Please, please, please. She pleaded in her mind, too worried about falling for any other words.

Unconcerned, the borelk raced over loose rocks, ignoring a sheer drop on one side. Rowena squished her eyes closed, trusting, hoping. Her heart hammered. Tephra leaned into Rowena's back. Possibly biting her braid based on the tugs against her skull.

One wrong step from their mount would send them all tumbling to their end.

Distant hooves from behind. The cloaked riders had found their trail. Rowena's heart stuttered.

"We can't outrun them forever," Tephra said, her voice tight in Rowena's ear.

Behind them, shouts echoed.

The pursuers were close. Too close.

The borelk was tiring. Foam streaked its muzzle. Its breath came in ragged clouds.

Then, a shadow in the rocks.

"There!" Rowena shouted.

A break.

An opening. Tight, but easy to miss by the others.

A small cave nestled among a cluster of boulders.

Rowena had to get the borelk to turn through two large stones. She leaned to her right, not far, squeezing her left leg even tighter at the same time. The animal responded, ducking through the opening.

Then they were inside. Darkness enveloped them. Cool,

damp air closed in around their heated skin. The borelk halted with a jolt, its body trembling.

Rowena slid from its back. Her knees buckled, sending her to the ground. Her ribs screamed. Her lungs felt hollowed out.

Tephra followed, collapsing hard at her side.

They were alive.

The thin top layer of soil released a scent of moss and wet rock, but underneath was frozen in early preparation for winter despite it being summer. They had to be *very* high in the mountains.

Rowena's eyes adjusted slowly to the low light, revealing the passage's rocky walls. Wide enough she could stretch her arms out and not touch the sides.

The borelk pranced, uneasy, tossing its head. Its antlers scraped dirt and pebbles to rain from the low ceiling.

Rowena rose stiffly and lifted her bound hands, speaking in a hushed tone to soothe the animal. She avoided the tusks, rubbing below a wild eye, rolling to show the white. Its face was rough and prickly compared to the thickly furred neck and slick body. She shuddered, only making the animal dart further out of reach.

"Easy," she whispered, forcing her own fears to hide. She needed this creature if they were to escape these mountains. "Easy now."

The borelk snorted, pawing the ground, but it didn't bolt. Rowena reached out again, running her fingers along its side, sending waves of calm through their connection. Its muscles quivered, then gradually relaxed.

After a rest, and no more sounds of pursuit, Rowena and Tephra made their way deeper into the passageway, leading the now-docile borelk by its reins. Their footsteps echoed in the silence, and the air grew colder with each step.

They pressed on, until a cavern opened before them, far

enough from the entrance to be hidden, but still within earshot so they wouldn't be surprised.

A pocket of safety.

Shadows crowded the walls, and near the back, a dark passage gaped. A possible escape route, if it came to that.

Bone weary, creature and women alike slid to the ground. The borelk tucked its nose against its flank, falling asleep in utter exhaustion.

Tephra rolled to her side, wriggling oddly.

"Are you hurt?" Rowena asked, concern piercing through her exhaustion. If Tephra was having fits, how would she get them both to safety?

A moment later, Tephra rolled over again, this time sitting on her knees. Her hands were free, and a blade glinted in the low light. "They did not find them all."

Relief surged. Rowena held out her wrists, grateful the instant her restraints fell away. As the cords dropped to the ground, she rubbed her raw skin and met Tephra's gaze.

"Now what?" The reality of their situation settled in. They were free, but . . . lost in mountains they didn't know and pursued by enemies whose numbers and resources exceeded their own.

Tephra's smile was grim as she turned the blade in her hands.

"Now we survive."

24

———

BRAM

BRAM PACED in front of the hearth, shadows of his horns warping across the stone walls. He'd lost count of his circuits around the room. Here, time had no meaning, no moons, no Sawel. Only the stale air of a tower carved from secrecy.

He should have seen it coming.

The trap. The runes. Yralissa.

Yralissa . . . he was done underestimating her.

Into the soil, two seeds were sown

The gardener, partial, to one has grown

Each moment stretched his thoughts taut between worry for Rowena and the maddening riddle.

With sheer force of will, he dragged his focus back to the words Yralissa had uttered.

In darkness they flourished, a feud unfurls

Roots entwined in a weft of worlds

One shaped by shears, one left to wane

A love, obscured by veils of disdain

The silence divides, left untended

In mother's absence, hearts upended

If he twisted his thinking as he imagined Yralissa's, parts of it made him wonder if he was the subject. *In darkness they flourished,* might reference his shadows.

They. Plural.

Nonsense.

A frustrated growl rumbled from his throat. Why did everything have to be so obscure?

The prophecy was a big enough riddle. It could mean Rowena or someone else, the Heptad didn't care, as long as one moon-born survived before the Burning Moon. Regardless of who was chosen to save Edenia, he had to ensure Rowena's safety.

He crossed to the wall and pressed his shoulder into the cold stone. Grounding himself.

Even now, he couldn't shake the image of Rowena trudging alone through Tixamar. Had she really made it out yet?

What would she, or did she, think of the jungle? An ache gripped his chest at the thought of her navigating the hanging vines and heat of the pixie lands. It would overwhelm her.

After holding her through her nightmares, he hated imagining her facing it alone. Or worse, being caught by Fidessa.

Nothing good was happening to her either way.

Bram hung his head. Whatever Yralissa wanted from him, he'd give. He had to get out of this tower, and find out what kind of runes could lock his powers. That was not a skill anyone else needed to learn.

He stepped closer to the fire, somehow kept stoked. Enough to hold off the chill of stone, yet not enough to make the room stifling. Another testament to Yralissa's skills.

Who was she?

He tried to place her from Saganus. She couldn't be more than five seasons his senior. But he was certain she hadn't been there during his time as a sentinel. Someone like her would have stood out. That voice, that presence, that ambition. If the

Heptad had known of her, they likely would have given her a seat on the council.

Memories sparked. Being released from the pedagogy. Declared a sentinel. One of his first assignments had been escorting a craftworker to the lazaret after being disavowed. Bram never saw him emerge. That hadn't been part of his duty.

He'd been all of fourteen summers, eager and naïve—the same as Killian.

The boy's face flashed in his mind; defiance, then shock, then gone.

Bram had rushed to volunteer when the Heptad put out the call for a special assignment. A task so important only the bravest, most sincere druid would be considered. If found acceptable, they would save all of Edenia.

He begged for the chance.

So blinded by becoming a hero, he never asked the right questions. Never asked *any* questions.

Bram kicked at a remnant of blue fog clinging to the floor near the single chair. It didn't tingle or hum with any enchantment. What was he missing? He was supposed to be the most powerful being in Edenia. That was what the Heptad told him. Another lie on an ever-growing list.

Bram barked out a laugh, loud after a night of silence. "Of course," he said aloud. Yralissa had been the Heptad's informant. The one who told them of his involvement in the battle in Ibern. When she had refused to believe he couldn't reverse her disavowed state.

All of this effort, and the reason he'd been called away from Rowena, was just because of Yralissa's wounded pride?

Why was she so intent on involving him in her troubles?

He halted, arms clasped behind his back, and stared into the fire. Orange and yellow flames danced without care, crackling and infusing the room with the rustic scent of turned soil and ash. Its warmth should have been a comfort. Here it felt like a leash.

Controlled. Contained. Another part of her plan.

The thought made him pause.

He leaned back, studying the fire more closely. Smoke curled in lazy wisps from the burning logs. A barked laugh escaped him. How had he not figured it out sooner? Yralissa hadn't ignited the fire to give him light or comfort. She'd done it to block the only exit.

The floor whispered behind him.

He waited. Silence his weapon.

Once the air chilled over his shoulders, he turned. Slow. Deliberate.

Yralissa stood near the bed, more blue fog dissipating at her feet as if it had exhaled her into being.

The only fading hint at how she entered.

"Figure it out?" She folded her arms, one brow arched.

Bram blinked. The exit? No, the riddle. He let his shoulders drop, forcing himself to stay loose.

Despite her nonchalant posture, tension pulled at the lines of her frame.

Bram tested his theory, casually edging away from the flames. If he had judged right, Yralissa would put herself between him and the only possible escape. As she had the night before.

Sure enough, she sidled to the fire, extending her hands as if to warm them.

He fought the grin tugging at his lips. "I may have deciphered a line or two, though perhaps it's hubris to say so."

Yralissa chuckled. "That is no surprise. Tell me correctly and you'll go free."

Not likely. "First, I have a question."

"I'll not give you any hints."

"Of course not." He leaned a shoulder against the stone wall, crossing one ankle over the other. Yralissa's brows pinched, just a flash, before she smoothed her features into casual disinterest once again. It was enough. He had her curiosity.

"What is it you want after this is done? When I solve the riddle, and resume my task, what will you have gained?"

"You're correct. Your hubris clouds your judgment." Her voice carried an edge as sharp as a blade. "What makes you believe that there will *be* a task for you when you leave? You're the Heptad's puppet, and your delay will not amuse them. They want to control the moon-born and the armor pieces. They will have no use for you if you fail."

"Fidessa already has the Sword of Justice, so Edenia is already at risk." He wasn't about to mention the heartstones, not if she didn't understand their significance.

Yralissa gave him a pitied grin. "Do you think me that dense? There Sword is nothing without the Lunastone. Once King Ha'mon acquires that, the first step in our plan will be complete. And you will no longer be necessary."

She was working with *Ha'mon*? The way she spoke, he expected she'd allied with Fidessa. Not the one responsible for Caelus being torn apart so long ago.

"He started the Chasm. Why would you ally with someone like that?"

"This is growing tiresome." She waved a dismissive hand. "This is your first chance to answer the riddle. I'll come by only twice more."

He pushed off the wall and raised his hands. Placating.

Before he left this confined space, he needed to learn everything Yralissa knew of the bigger plan.

"I apologize. I'm sure you have your reasons. I'm trying to understand them. You're clearly powerful if you can retain so much enchantment after being disavowed."

Her smile was sly. "You think it is pretense?"

It was a logical consideration, but he still wasn't sure it was possible.

"Ha'mon is an original Primary Fae. He wouldn't work with a disavowed. Someone with so little power."

"The king has many hands to do his bidding."

How could she be so gullible? She was far too clever, which he hated to admit, to be so blind. "If he is freed, everything will change. Tell me how you think Edenia will operate if that happens."

She tilted her head, studying him for a long moment.

"If Osric had wanted Caelus to remain whole, he wouldn't have created Edenia, or the Reaping. Why give the King of Kur time to gather followers and build an army if he was never meant to leave Mortus? That's why he helped Tanith escape. To create a realm in the above world. She prepares the way for his arrival, when everyone will be free."

"Free?" Goosebumps erupted along Bram's arms. "Have you ever met Tanith?"

"Yes." Her lips flattened.

"Then you must understand that she has a different view of her release from Mortus."

Yralissa glanced away.

Regardless of the split in Mortus, Yralissa's statements mostly echoed what Lhoris told him. Ha'mon needed his prison gates to open. If he captured a moon-born, or the armor, he would keep them from fulfilling the prophecy. Paving the way for his escape.

"The Heptad is lying." Yralissa's voice dropped, gaining intensity. "They have grown weak because the enchantment flowing into the world is fading. The two realms are meant to separate. Some claim the prophecy is a false creation by the council to keep their own power."

Bram's blood went cold. Could that be correct? He'd witnessed the council's cruelty first hand.

The rebels would be searching for Killian. Those who loved him would not have an answer to his disappearance until Bram returned. If he got there in time.

"I cannot defend the Heptad's misuse of power. On that, we agree." He hesitated, gauging her reaction. "However, there is far more at stake. Ha'mon styles himself a king, but he's a war criminal. Nothing good can come from freeing him. The Reaping doesn't help him build an army; it keeps his misguided followers from destroying the peace of our lands."

"That's the Heptad's mantra. It isn't true." She stepped closer, eyes flashing. "They are desperate. We are both proof of that."

"In what way?"

"When someone is disavowed, an apprentice prepares them for the hepta, who comes to the lazaret. It's a painful process, even more so when they are unsuccessful—as happened with me. Hepta Jandar allowed his apprentice to help him, let *her* perform the ritual to rid me of my rightful powers." She grinned. "Though, to look at me, she probably thought she'd been successful."

He'd been right. She wasn't pretending, she *had been* disavowed. But not like the others. "How much of your enchantment did you retain?"

"More than enough." Her gaze glittered with satisfaction. "We are more alike than you realize. My powers were reduced. Yours were increased. Like me, you live outside of society, unable to rule your own life any longer. They needed someone to do their bidding, someone with the power they no longer have individually. Just a guess, but I'm betting they were *all* present when they made you into this." She motioned down to his feet and back.

She wasn't exactly right, but near enough. The Triad. Not the others. His silence was his only answer. Let her assume what she wanted.

"How can you work with them? Can't you see how dysfunctional Edenia has become?" Yralissa sauntered along the curved stone wall, trailing her finger across it. "We must change things at a fundamental level. Tear down the old to build the new. The Armor and heartstones are a cage, keeping everyone except the elite in bondage. They must be destroyed if we're ever to move forward."

"And you believe Ha'mon is going to do that? He wants total power to overthrow Osric. There's no way he'll make a better world for anyone but himself." Bram crossed his arms over his chest. "You are letting emotions override logic, which will only invite more oppression."

She tipped her chin to the ceiling and let out a grumble. "You are so blinded. An indulged child in need of discipline."

Whatever points she'd made, she'd also played into his hands. If he could provoke her enough to draw power from the flames again, he might find his way out of the tower.

"*You* are acting like an over-privileged ingrate." Bram gripped one of the bed posts, his claws carving deep grooves into the wood. "You want to dismantle everything because you don't like how you were treated? There aren't enough Oraku positions for all the disavowed. They live like hermits, starving in alleyways, hiding from bounty hunters, wasting away while trying to cling to a shred of dignity. Is that what you want for Edenia? Anomie is called the city of anarchy for a reason. It's the most dangerous place outside of Mortus."

He closed the distance between them, shoulders squared and chin high. He wouldn't hurt her, but he would let his size intimidate her. She couldn't be more than five and a half feet tall.

Yralissa's eyes flashed, but she didn't retreat. "Ha'mon has more power than Tanith. He will make things better for everyone." Her fingers twitched at her sides, a subtle tell.

One more push. He just had to ensure she used the fire.

Yralissa stepped closer, fists clenched. Bram darted right, and by the height of her brows and the way her hand flew to her throat, he'd properly surprised her. As he expected, she spun and flung herself into his path, blocking his route to the fire.

When she reached toward the flames with one hand, he scooted back, giving her space. She was so predictable, he almost felt guilty. He side-stepped one way, then the other, until she twisted to use both her hands as she'd done before.

Bram curled his lip, a growl rumbling in his chest. He almost shook his head in pity. She'd accused him of being naïve, but he'd learned.

"You need to feel what it's like being second best!" She snarled; voice thick with emotion.

What did that mean?

He didn't have time to wonder. Yralissa ripped the flames into her hands. Fire answered her call, curling around her fingers like living serpents, hungry and eager.

Bram dropped and rolled over his shoulder. Flames seared the air where he's stood a heartbeat earlier. When he sprang up, he was at Yralissa's side, too close for her to cast another stream of fire.

Bram leaned his shoulder into hers, knocking her aside as he dove into the firebox. A cool tingle rolled over him. The same sensation he'd felt on arrival. He landed in a crouch, flames flickering harmlessly around his boots. It didn't matter now; his powers were no longer locked.

It took only a heartbeat to enter the shadows and slip up the chimney.

He hadn't reached the top when a force like a silent wave blew through him. It had no effect on his current form, but when Yralissa's scream followed, the entire tower shook. Stone crumbled around him, chunks of masonry falling harmlessly through his shadowed body.

A parapet encircled the top of the chimney. It collapsed as Bram emerged, the whole structure swaying beneath him before folding inward in a puff of black dust.

Hurriedly, he traveled out of the area, the crash of falling stone echoing behind him.

He landed on a recently traveled path, high in the forest. Sawel peeked over the horizon, but hadn't warmed the soil enough to thaw the morning frost. Crisp air bit his lungs as he shifted back into his elven form, drawing deep breaths.

A twinge of regret flickered through Bram. She'd played him. Lied to him. Mocked his duty and nearly trapped him forever. Irrational. Blinded by vengeance and pain. But he wouldn't wish her harm. He didn't want her buried beneath the rubble. She didn't deserve to die. Not like that.

And yet . . . he couldn't go back. Not now.

As he wavered, smoke tugged at his senses. Across the sloped rise of a northern hill, faint plumes curled into the sky. There, half-obscured by the dense forest, stood a ruined castle tucked between the ridgelines. Even from a distance, he could see patches missing from the structure, walls crumbling away. Decay and neglect had hollowed what had once been a proud stronghold.

Yralissa had said they were going near to where Fidessa hid . . . though he shouldn't believe anything she said.

He stood motionless, weighing his choices. Return to check on a woman who had imprisoned him, and aligned herself with forces intent on destroying Edenia? Or pursue the sword that might already be near his grasp?

The image of Rowena flashed in his mind; her fierce determination, her vulnerability, her trust in him despite the odds. If the sword was there, he'd be one step closer to keeping his promise.

She might even be there herself.

He didn't have time to check on Yralissa. The Sword of Justice could be within reach. He could not risk missing it.

With one last glance toward the crumbled tower in the distance, Bram turned toward the ruined castle. Whatever awaited him, he would face it.

For Rowena.

For the moon-born.

For all of Edenia.

25

ROWENA

ROWENA ONLY DOZED FOR A MOMENT, during Tephra's watch. Or so she thought. No other sounds echoed through the cave but her own breathing. The borelk's musky scent still clung to the air, mixed with fouler odors added through the night, followed by a scrape of what might have been a hoof, or tusk, against the stone.

Deep inside the cavern, they'd stayed warm from a fire Tephra created.

Why had she let it go out?

Rowena closed her eyes and concentrated on the power inside her chest. Familiar warmth flared and light bloomed from her palms, pushing back the darkness. Across the cave, the borelk lay curled near the opposite wall, its head tucked against its back hocks. Apparently, she hadn't been the only one tired enough to ignore danger, or perhaps it was a good sign they were safe.

But Tephra was gone.

A flutter of panic beat against Rowena's ribs, the ones still aching as she rose to her feet. The borelk woke with a snort, unfolding in one fluid motion, its antlers nearly brushing the cave's ceiling.

Rowena stifled her enchantment and eased closer, palms open in peace, and caught the looped reins hanging against the creature's chest. The borelk would most likely follow her back through the tunnels, and she couldn't risk losing her best way to move quickly through the mountains.

Tephra must be keeping watch closer to the opening, where there was fresher air.

Rowena glanced at the passage at the far end of the cave. Tephra might have gone through to check if it was an exit . . . doubtful though.

Rowena relaxed and led the borelk toward the cave's entrance. They hadn't gone far when the beast grew restless, stamping its hooves. Its muscled side bumped Rowena into the rough cave wall, scraping her shoulder. It was probably eager to graze after their crazed dash through the trees. She picked up her pace, warily eyeing the tusk that swung dangerously with every prance.

Distracted with her charge, she forgot her training and burst out of the cave. Dawnlight, brighter than she expected, stabbed at her eyes after all the dark.

"Did we wake you?" A male voice, amused. Familiar.

Rowena's skin pebbled. She knew that voice—etched into her memory with blades.

"I am sorry, Rowena," Tephra called.

The borelk pranced and lunged, yanking the reins from Rowena's fingers. It hadn't been hungry. It had scented danger.

The animal swiped its tusked face back and forth, lowering its antlers. When it charged, warriors, forming a semi-circle around the cave's mouth, jumped aside to let it pass. The borelk disappeared into the forest, taking with it Rowena's hopes for a swift escape.

What a fool she'd been.

Rowena released a slow breath and studied her situation.

Daenon and eight other warriors faced her. Not her cloaked captors from the mudflats. These were elven males, painted in chalk across their faces, their bare chests, arms, legs, even in their hair. Their only clothing was a strip of fabric wrapped around their waists and slung over one shoulder. Even Daenon.

More like Jotnari than Telana. Who had he aligned himself with?

One of the warriors held Tephra's tight against his chest, keeping her from fleeing. Her face was a mask of regret, but her eyes burned with defiance.

What did Daenon want with her? He'd taken her cousin as leverage, spellbound and dying, to force Rowena into finding the Sword of Justice.

None of this made sense. Rowena steadied herself, projecting more confidence than she felt. "Where is Safi?"

"So you do remember her." Daenon's mouth curled into a mocking smile. "Doesn't seem like you're even searching."

He shook his head, crossing his arms over his chalk-covered chest. "I shouldn't be surprised. Enchanted only think of themselves."

Heat surged through Rowena's veins, her fingers curling into fists at her sides. How dare he? He'd been there when her parents died. She'd cried on his shoulder. Right before he assaulted her.

"Where. Is. She?"

"You weren't even hard to find." He ran his fingertips along the chalk symbols painted on his arm, gaze never leaving her face.

"Say nothing," Tephra called, struggling against her captor's grip.

Someone else in harm's way because of her. Rowena's chest tightened, as the truth clicked in place.

"These are your men?" she asked, stalling for time.

"You didn't think I'd take my father's crown without my own warriors, did you?" Pride and mockery braided through his tone.

"Why didn't they help you in Ibern?"

"Because it wasn't time." Daenon stepped closer, his boots crunching on the frost-covered ground. "Like it is now."

"You think that makes a difference?" Rowena rubbed her palms together, calling her enchantment to life. Silver light bloomed beneath her skin, coursing through her veins. She wouldn't be taken without a fight.

One chance. That was all she needed. One break in their circle. She would not be helpless again.

Daenon spun aside just before Rowena lashed out with a thin rope of glowing silver power. She'd projected too much, and instead of striking him, the jolt of metallic enchantment slammed into a tree, spraying sharp splinters through the air.

The warrior holding Tephra took a hit to his shoulder. His grip faltered, just enough for her to wrench free.

Rowena didn't have time to check on her.

Daenon charged, his body a blur. She hurled herself sideways, landing hard, pain stabbing through her shoulder. Rolling fast, she narrowly evaded a warrior's grasp. She sprang into a crouch in time to glimpse Tephra's dark hair disappear down the trail.

Tephra hadn't looked back. None of the men followed. At least she got away.

"Let her go. She's nothing," Daenon called, stalking toward Rowena, his eyes ablaze.

He had no right to be angry; that was Rowena's privilege. "Why are you here? What have you done with Safi?"

"My hands are clean." He spread his palms, chalk dust

falling like snow from his fingers. "You're the one who let her stay trapped in that spell."

She still had time. "I had thirty days."

Daenon shrugged, smugness returning to his features. "Give or take."

"Liar!" Without hesitation or better judgment, Rowena burst ahead, slamming into Daenon and driving him to the ground.

The impact knocked the breath from both of them. Daenon recovered first, rolling to pin her. Rowena twisted, driving her knee upward. He grunted, shifting his weight just enough for her to squirm free.

She scrambled to her feet, summoning the last bits of her power. It was Too many days under the jungle's canopy, too many nights beneath pine-heavy skies, starved her of moonlight.

Silver threads flickered weakly across her palms, but she thrust them outward, desperate to ensnare Daenon.

She doubted she could lift him, but perhaps drag him down, heavier. Anything to slow him down. It would affect her too, but her body was already sluggish, plagued by aches from her earlier escape.

But the tendrils flagged, dissipating before they reached him, scattering like leaves in a harsh wind.

Daenon laughed, a cold, hollow sound that echoing against stone. "Do you really think I would fall for your tricks twice?"

Confusion rippled through her. "How—?"

He tapped a chalk symbol on his chest. "You're not the only one with friends in dark places."

The warriors formed a tight circle around them, blocking any escape. Rowena's mind raced. Her enchantment wasn't working, not just weak, but ineffective against him, specifically. How had he known to prepare for her?

Her emotions swirled. Sorrow for failing to reach Safi in time. Fury at Daenon's betrayal. Simmering anger at Bram. For taking her to Havilar, for forcing their separation, for leaving her to fight alone.

The distraction cost her. Daenon lunged, but instead of tackling, he feinted left. Rowena moved to counter, and his fist slammed into her in the ribs. Right where they were already bruised from the day before.

Pain exploded through her side. She doubled over, gasping. Daenon swept her legs from under her. She hit the ground hard, stars bursting behind her eyelids.

Daenon's boot pressed into her stomach, not enough to crush, but enough to pin her down. "Look at you," he snarled. "The great hope of Skandan. The last Lunara in the north. Not so impressive without your shadow guard-dog, are you?"

Rowena clawed at his leg, trying to push him off.

Trying to influence him. Trying anything.

Her fingers scraped against his chalk-painted skin, and sudden insight struck. The symbols. The chalk shielded him, blocking her enchantment.

She had to get it off.

In a desperate move, she grabbed his ankle with both hands and twisted hard. He stumbled, his weight lifting just enough for her to roll away. She stopped near a half-melted mound of snow. She plunged her hands into the water, barely enough to cover them. But enough to scrub away the chalk.

When Daenon charged again, she was ready. She flung the water from her fingertips, watching with savage satisfaction as it splashed across the chalk symbols on his chest and arm, smearing them into unrecognizable streaks.

For a heartbeat, surprise flashed in his eyes. She seized that moment, reaching out with her enchantment again.

Daenon faltered. His eyes widening. He hadn't expected her to break his protection charms.

"You took everything from me," she cried through gritted teeth, advancing on him. "My home. My family. My freedom."

He stumbled backward.

Rowena pressed her advantage, gathering the last drops of her strength. She focused it into a sharp point directed at his heart.

One final blow. One chance to escape.

But she'd spent too much time. The silver light in her palms dimmed, and blinked out. The connection between them snapped like a thread yanked too tight.

Daenon shook his head, surprise bleeding into renewed rage.

"Nice try."

Rowena turned, desperation driving her toward the trees.

She had to get away. Hide until the moons rose. Restore her power.

She'd barely managed three steps before Daenon's warriors cut off her path.

She veered left. Then right.

They anticipated her. She was surrounded.

With no other choice, she spun back toward the cave. If she could reach that deeper passage, there might be another way out. Perhaps she could lose them in the dark.

Rowena's breath came fast and sharp. She had nearly escaped when Daenon snagged her arm, twisting her off balance. On her way to the ground, her hand found his hair. Digging her fingers into his golden hair, she brought him down with her.

Scraped, but not broken, she hopped to her feet. Daenon wobbled on his hands and knees. Blood trickled down his temple. She kicked him hard in the ribs. He fell over with a moan.

She forced her body to move, gasping as she fought past the ache. His men loomed at the cave entrance. No way past them.

She sprinted into the darkness for the far tunnel.

There was still that passage at the back of the cave. It had to lead somewhere.

Footsteps thundered behind her. She pressed on her side where ribs protested. Her tunic stuck to her shoulder where she must be bleeding. She had to press on. She clamped her teeth tight and willed herself to go faster.

The passage was close. Almost there. She could nearly touch the opening when Daenon drove his shoulder into her back, driving the air from her lungs. The force of the blow sent her tumbling. When she hit the hard ground, the impact stole what little breath remained.

She landed on her stomach, her palms scraping raw against rough stone, a rock digging into her sternum. Shock paralyzed her.

Before she could react, Daenon's breath burned against her ear.

"You're not getting away from me this time," he growled.

His weight pinned her down. His hands wrapped around hers, keeping them apart, stopping her from summoning her enchantment.

No, no, no.

She would not be trapped in a cave with him. Not again.

Her mind screamed.

This was not then. She would not be helpless.

The moment his body caged hers, her mind yanked her somewhere else—another cave. A smaller, tighter cave.

The cave where she had hidden with Daenon; the day she lost everything.

She had trusted him then. Fled with Hann. Fled with the prince she thought noble. Instead of safety, another loss.

Trapped. Held down. Violated.

A sharp pain snapped her back.

Daenon yanked her head back by her hair, forcing her to face him.

"You think you're so special?" he sneered. "You're nothing."

Rowena clenched her jaw, choking back the fear clawing up her throat.

"I have plans to rule all of this. The northern islands and beyond." His voice was dripped with smug satisfaction as he crossed her wrists behind her, binding them with leather laces. "I've made a deal and you are my payment to seal it."

Her mind reeled. What deal? With who?

Before she could demand answers, he hauled her to her feet, locking her in an iron grip, certain her wrists were trapped tight enough to block her enchantment. She struggled, but his hold was relentless.

She darted a glance toward the passage. It was close. Just a few feet. If she could just get her wrists free.

A sound sliced through the cave.

A grating scrape.

Boots scuffing stone.

Her stomach twisted. Two heartbeats later, a figure stepped from the passage.

One of Daenon's men, followed by three more.

"Thought she'd come this way," the warrior said.

Daenon gave a sharp nod.

The last thread of hope snapped.

"This way," Daenon ordered. "Let's get going. I'm eager to be home with our prize."

Rowena's pulse pounded in her ears. It was over.

Warriors had found the passage. Others stood at the cave's mouth, blocking every escape.

And Daenon had her locked in his grasp.

All she could do now was stumble forward, dragged back into captivity.

26

BRAM

BRAM CROUCHED BEHIND A CRAGGY OUTCROPPING, breath fogging faintly despite Sawel's midday light. From his vantage, the ruined castle slumped in the clearing below, half-swallowed by forest. Moss draped the outer walls like rot, and the western tower listed dangerously, ready to topple with the next ill-tempered gust.

Though no one moved outside, a steady plume of smoke curled from the chimney on the left keep. The drawbridge lay open, granting access to the guardhouse and a closed portcullis beyond. Bram stayed hidden, for nearly a half-mark, chewing the last of the cheese he'd taken from the cottage.

Only two guards. Waddling the muddy loop of the court-yard. Too focused on their own feet. Short and stout, a club over a shoulder. Faces obscured by helmets.

Odd. Who left guards at a ruin like this? It didn't strike him as the sort of place Fidessa would suffer. He still wasn't sure where he was, or who he would face. That meant extra caution.

He'd approach in elven form. Just another traveler seeking warmth and rest, just like in Forsa, when he'd first seen her at the well. A grin tugged at his mouth. Even worn thin by slavery,

Rowena's strength had burned through. She'd been battered, but never broken.

Where was she now? He had to get back to her. If anything happened—No. He slammed the thought shut.

Whoever was inside, he needed answers. Yralissa had drawn him here for a reason. If he could learn where in the Veilrunes he was, he could make a real plan. Maybe this place was just another useless detour, but he had to be sure.

If Fidessa was here, he'd rip the sword from her hands and get one step closer to Rowena. Then to Saganus. A day spent wandering and a night trapped in the tower had already cost him more time than he could spare.

He grumbled, hating the indecision, and himself for letting it linger. He strode for the castle.

Halfway across the bridge, a voice barked from behind the closed gate. "Identify yourself."

"Just a traveler hoping to warm by the fire and escape the cold." Bram kept his voice neutral. Steady.

"From what land?" The voice rasped with a whistled lisp. Bethoni, if Bram guessed right.

"I've wandered many lands, but have roots in none." A half-truth. One that served him well before.

"Come to the door."

Bram hesitated. He expected a welcome. But the guard's disinterest scraped his nerves raw.

Too calm. Too dull.

The hair on his neck lifted. He crossed the bridge with a wary eye, hand hovering near the dagger at his belt.

The door creaked open when he was still three strides out. "Inside," the guard commanded.

"Show yourself." He wouldn't walk blind into a narrow door without seeing who called. One insignia would tell him everything he needed.

The man stepped forward, shoulders filling the doorway with bulk out of proportion to his squat height. His helmet sat low, pinching his jowled face and upturned nose, lending him a distinctly piggish look. No insignia marked his dull gray brigandine.

"Kitchen's this way." The guard jabbed his club toward a side arch near the keep's entrance, then waddled off without looking back.

Shifting to shadow now would only cause alarm, and make things harder, if the round-bellied sentry even noticed.

He muttered a curse under his breath and stepped through the door, overtaking his short-legged guide in four strides. He didn't like any of this. But he needed answers.

They rounded a corner, and the guard ducked through a low doorway, forcing Bram to bow his head to follow. The corridor beyond offered height but little width. His shoulders scraped both walls with each step. The guard plucked a torch from a metal bucket; it flared to life in his hand.

"Nice trick," Bram muttered, eyeing the sudden flare.

"Queen thinks of everything," the guard replied, with a note of pride.

"Queen Fidessa, I assume?"

The guard gave no answer. Confirmation enough. Bram pursed his lips. Of course, it was her. Only Fidessa would be arrogant enough to think she could hide in plain sight.

A nudge stirred his chest, faint, but familiar. Not as strong as when he'd felt the sword before, yet a similar resonance. Despite the gnawing misgivings, he'd made the right call to enter.

They went deeper than Bram expected, descending a stone stairwell beneath the keep.

Odd.

Kitchens were usually near an outer wall with easy access to gardens or supply carts.

Daylight flickered at the far end of the corridor, but the rock walls around them were mountain-hewn, as if this place had been carved from stone in secret.

Halfway down, a stench thick as fog slammed into him—carrion tangled with wet dog. It caught in his throat, cloying, foul enough to taste. His stomach twisted, bile creeping higher.

"What in Caelus is that smell?" He clenched his jaw, resisting the urge to cover his nose.

"Bunyip." The guard didn't even flinch.

Bram had heard of the flesh-crazed creatures. Swamp-born horrors, by all accounts. "What's one doing here?"

The guard chuckled. "Eatin' the queen's scraps."

They passed a cave-like chamber, its wide entrance sealed by iron bars. From the shadows, two glowing green eyes blinked open. The bunyip lunged, snarling, only to be yanked back by a thick chain just before it hit the light. Matted fur tangled with moss. Jaws gnashed, venomous saliva spraying as it snapped. Bram's skin prickled. Even as the Seeker, he'd rather never face one.

"Cheery fellow," Bram muttered, glancing back at the cage.

"Hungry. He'll eat soon." The guard's voice held a note of . . . anticipation.

The air dropped colder than the Frost Flats. Bram's breath fogging again as they neared the corridor's end. Strange. Why would Fidessa keep a swamp-dweller in a place this frigid? Bunyips needed heat. Moisture.

The guard stopped abruptly, raising one hand in a silent signal for Bram to halt.

"You lost?" Bram asked, scanning the shadows for any sign of danger.

The guard didn't respond. Didn't even twitch. Just stood there, motionless.

No doors.

No sounds.

Nothing Bram could sense. He slid to go around the guard—then halted.

A silhouette moved at the far end of the corridor. A woman's stride. Smooth. Confident.

He'd recognize that arrogant glide anywhere.

Fidessa.

A four-legged creature padded beside her, low and quiet.

The guard snapped to attention, banging his club twice against the stone in a theatrical salute before resting it on his shoulder.

Under different circumstances, Bram might've laughed. Not today.

Fidessa glided past the guard and stopped in front of Bram though her gaze never touched him. Instead, she crouched to scratch behind the ears of a wolossum, her fingers slow, absent, like a woman drifting through some private reverie.

Bram frowned. Of all creatures, why a wolossum? Mid-thigh tall and bear-shaped, sure, but harmless. Strict herbivores. Their rat-like snouts and long hairless tails gave them no edge.

Useless as guardians.

Just ugly.

"Do you know," she said softly, still not looking at him, "these creatures bond for life. But only if you feed them, before they learn fear."

The wolossum chirred and nuzzled her hand.

"Poor things. Once trust is broken, they never recover."

Then her gaze snapped to Bram. "Still, I find them preferable to most fae. At least their loyalty is honest."

The wolossum twisted and plopped onto its haunches, pressing against Fidessa's leg as if the world didn't exist.

Bram shoved aside his unease. Fidessa was odd; always had been. But he was here for the sword.

"Where's the Sword of Justice?"

His voice held steady, his stance firm, even as alarm bells clanged behind his ribs.

Fidessa tilted her head and cackled, sharp and sudden. "You are so deliciously dim."

The guard spun. Bram caught the motion—too slow, too heavy.

No, not slow. Repositioning.

The brute dropped his head and barreled forward, slamming into Bram's gut. He staggered back, breath knocked loose.

His hand flew to his dagger, but the second charge hit low, at the knees. Bram toppled, skidding across the floor.

Bars slammed shut behind him. Metal screamed as the lock caught.

He surged to his feet, shadows already coiling within, but then . . .

Nothing.

Not even a flicker

The shadows dissipated, leaving him fully visible, fully trapped.

Fidessa's smile stretched; teeth too white in the gloom. "Look around you, Seeker."

Bram swept his gaze around the walls.

Rough stone. Bucket in the corner.

Iron bars . . . etched with runes.

The same kind Yralissa had carved in the tower.

Cold crept into his veins. "You're working with Yralissa."

"I only trust myself." Fidessa's lip curled, half-smirk, half-snarl. "You're not the only one with friends in the dark."

She closed her eyes, fingers sinking into the wolossum's fur. Silent. Still. Then her gaze returned to Bram.

"I do hope you enjoy your accommodations. They're quite . . . secure."

Her guard snorted, shoulders shaking with glee. Beady eyes glittered under his helmet's brim.

Fidessa turned, the wolossum padding at her heels. "Oh," she said, pausing mid-step, "don't worry about boredom. I've arranged some entertainment."

Bram forced calm into his voice. "This isn't over."

"No," Fidessa agreed, not even glancing back. "But it soon will be."

Their footsteps faded. Silence closed in. Cold stone, iron bars, impossibly enough, held him prisoner.

He gripped the bars. Fire-like energy surged up his arms. He jerked his hands away with a hiss.

Eyes shut. Exhale Slow.

Another trap. And he'd walked straight into it, ignoring the guard as an unworthy imbecile.

But how had Fidessa known to prepare for him?

Yralissa had to be involved. No matter what Fidessa claimed.

Ha'mon? Could he have found a way to communicate from Mortus? Imprisoned a millennium before Bram became the Seeker.

No. That made no sense.

Someone else.

Someone who knew exactly what he was.

The list was short.

Bram paced the cell, hours slipping through the cracks of his mind. Light still bled through the corridor, dim, late. Each step echoed like a war drum. He studied the runes. Familiar. Too precise. Too much like hers.

They thrummed when he leaned in, pulsing like a second heartbeat.

He called on his shadows.

Once.

Twice.

They snapped back, burning the edges of his power.

Same as the tower.

Same twisted spell.

This wasn't just a prison. It was a message. Specifically, for him.

He flexed his hands, rage simmering, stalking the space like a caged predator.

If brute force wouldn't free him, then he'd *out-think* them.

A grinding sound split the air. Stone on stone.

Bram turned; fists ready.

Dust billowed into the corridor.

A hidden door opened from the wall.

Yralissa.

Alive. Somehow unscathed. Just a torn sleeve, wind-ruffled hair.

"Surprised to see me?" She teased. "Not very chivalrous of you to leave me buried in pile of stones."

"You seem fine." He eyed her, scanning. What were her tells? Anything that might help him understand what she wanted. How she thought he fit into her plans.

She smoothed her gown. The green one she'd exchanged for her Oraku robe. "Resiliency. One of my better qualities."

Again, he struggled to understand how she had so much power. Unless she lied. The one thing that made sense.

"You said you weren't working with Fidessa."

"It was a simple transaction. She needed bait, so I help her net the little fish. I need answers, and she provides information." Yralissa snickered and ambled closer, slow as poison. "You really were the worst choice the Heptad could have made."

Bram slammed his hands against the bars. The pain flared, but he didn't flinch. "When I get out, and I will, you'd better stay buried."

She laughed. "Such grand ambitions."

Why was she so confident? He was missing something. He clenched his fists. She was stalling.

Smug. Mocking.

Why?

"Still confused?" she cooed, making a frown. "Is this place too scary? Or are you trying to figure out how you fell for a trap for the second time in two days? It is impressive."

"I'm not caught."

Yralissa glanced at the bars, then peered up and down the hallway before returning her gaze to him with an arched brow. "Then maybe we have different definitions. You're behind bars, Seeker. If that's freedom, I'll pass."

Bram's frustration simmered. He growled his answer. "I escaped your tower. I'll escape this." He had no time for her or her games. There were more pressing matters at hand.

"I'm shocked you're still in that elven form," Her voice soured. "Where's the beast we're all supposed to fear?"

"I'm not a sideshow trick." How dare she . . .

"But you are a fabulous weapon. Shouldn't you be seen by all, not hidden away?"

"If you've nothing of value to say, leave." Bram's patience wore thin. "Unless you want me to bury you twice."

"Oh no, not so fast." Yralissa smiled, fake and mocking. "Why can't you just waft through? No shadows left to crawl into?"

He didn't answer. Wouldn't give her the satisfaction. Though he clamped his mouth so tight his teeth ground together.

"Well, then. Leave how you will. I'll wait." She took a step back, crossing her arms over her chest, mirroring him.

Despite how he tried to remain calm, her mocking fueled the anger bubbling inside him. She kept him from what truly mattered.

He grabbed the bars. Pain surged. Deeper, into his skull, into his bones.

The runes flared.

Shadows rippled up his arms. Change, he demanded of himself.

Nothing.

"Are you having troubles? That was kind of anticlimactic."

"Why didn't you come with the queen?" Bram demanded. "You've obviously helped her set this trap."

"Fidessa doesn't get to see this part. I have a gift just for *you*, Bram." She grinned, a foul taunt. "I wanted to give it to you in the tower. But you seem more of a blunt tool than a sharp mind. So, I'll help you out. Something easier. Just become the Seeker."

"I'm not entertainment." Gray shadows barely darker than the stone floor, lifted by his feet.

"I wish it was just for fun. But I have a much better reason," she said.

"I need nothing from you." Determination hardening his resolve. He would get through these bars.

She sauntered closer, running a finger down the bars with no ill-effect. "When you broke through the tower, I was a little surprised. But the tower was weak. This is iron, and I've strengthened the runes. You'll not get out of here *without* my gift."

Her admission fell flat. That much he already understood. But there still had to be someone providing her with information.

"Did you secure this gift from the same source who taught you these runes?"

She batted her eyelashes like a demure courtier. "Giving away all my secrets ruins the fun."

There had to be a way to escape without letting her win. Bram closed his eyes, prepared himself for the pain, and grabbed the bars again. The energy grew stronger. His anger grew with it, stirring something deep within.

Transform.

The shadows lapped just out of reach.

He focused on breaking the runes—slipping through.

His horns ached. His fingers stretched.

His skin burned. Veins liquid fire.

Too soon. Too wrong.

"That'll do." Yralissa patted his hand. A sharp, needle-like puncture between his thumb and forefinger.

He gasped, stumbling back.

"Midway will work even better." Yralissa's fingers rested where his had been. Her eyes gleaming with triumph. "Some secrets shouldn't stay in the dark."

"What . . . have you done?" Bram's knees buckled. His arms still trembled. His chest burned.

"I'm proving that you're not worthy."

The world dimmed.

Yralissa's voice swam through the haze.

"Sleep now. When you wake, you'll understand."

Bram's world descended into darkness.

The last thought that flickered through his fading mind—Rowena.

And how he'd failed her again.

27

ROWENA

Rowena's insides twisted, bile rising fast. She swallowed it down. She wouldn't give Daenon and his monsters one more scrap of proof she was weak.

What would it matter, though? Wasn't she exactly what they expected?

No. She couldn't think like that.

She closed her eyes, slowing her breath while her feet navigated the cave's uneven floor. Focus. Feel the ground. The air. The surrounding heartbeats.

Just like the labyrinth, she had control. She *had* to summon it. Daenon would not steal that from her again.

She opened her eyes as they rounded the final corner before the cave's mouth. At least a dozen warriors had gathered, waiting. Four more behind, with Daenon.

They were outside now. Dusk pressed in, and Rowena nearly collapsed in relief at the sight of Lungol peeking over the treetops. Sawel's fading light lingered, but it was Lungol that mattered. The smaller moon's wild energy pulsed into her every breath. With time, her enchantment would restore.

Unfortunately, time was not on her side.

The men waited, loose, relaxed in the small clearing outside the cave. Chalk-painted bodies ghostly in the dimming light. Some leaned against jagged stone; others stood with arms crossed, every face carved in bored contempt.

None thought she'd escape.

That was their first mistake.

The second? They hadn't bothered to bind her hands.

Rowena flexed her fingers. Lungol's energy tingled along her skin like tiny silver needles. Not much. Nothing like the flood of power under the full moon in Skandan.

But it would have to be enough.

Enchantment pooled in her palms, a faint glow she concealed with curled fingers.

Four warriors stood nearby, their attention fixed on Daenon, not on her.

Another mistake.

She drifted closer, feigning exhaustion. Her legs genuinely trembled, but she exaggerated it; shoulders slumping, steps faltering.

The first warrior barely glanced as her sleeve brushed his arm. Just a touch, but enough.

She slid a thread of enchantment into the contact, feeding the rage she sensed beneath his skin. His expression soured, hand tightening on his weapon.

She bumped another as she stumbled past.

That one radiated contempt, toward her, toward life. She didn't have to try hard to tip him.

Two seeds planted.

"Why can't we just kill her? Why is she so important?"

Two others grumbled. More targets.

She stumbled, letting her knee buckle. She caught herself on one warrior's forearm.

"Sorry," she murmured, eyes lowered. The picture of defeat.

The warrior grunted, shoving her away.

Too late. She'd already stirred his resentment, subtle as slipping poison into wine.

His face twisted as fury bloomed.

She'd barely regained her footing before colliding with another, taller than the rest. His hands shot out to steady her. She gripped his wrists, long enough to drag out the anger beneath his calm.

Both men clenched their jaws. Eyes darkened. The whispers around them sharpened. Cracks in the calm.

Daenon spun her hard, locking both wrists in his grip. "Stop that!"

Rowena blinked with false innocence.

Let him rage. It saved her strength.

"Someone bring the chains!" He barked into the fray.

A shiver crawled down her spine. What did he mean by *chains*?

Moments later, shouts erupted. Anger spilled from those she'd touched to those they stood beside.

Violence was in their blood. She just helped stir it.

Within seconds, three more of the chalk warriors joined the chaos. Her knees trembled with the effort. Please, Caelus let that be enough.

The men were arguing now, more interested in their grievances than paying attention to their captive.

"She is influencing you. It's Lunara enchantment," Daenon roared over the rising voices.

No one listened.

He shoved between two warriors, chest to chest, shouting. One wrong move and fists would fly.

Daenon's attempt to break it up, only made one bump into the other. That spark caught the kindling she'd laid. And the blaze erupted.

The entire group dissolved into mayhem.

Only one guard remained at her back. She threw herself into his chest. He didn't budge. Instead, he retaliated, shoving her to her knees.

Perfect. She rolled, hugging her knees to her chest, and sobbed for show.

A heavy boot slammed into the back of her thighs. Real pain burned behind her eyes.

But the man turned away, his attention lost to the brawl.

With everyone distracted, she crept slowly along the rocky slope. Once out of sight, she scrambled atop a jutting boulder. Careful and slow enough to remain silent, but fast enough to disappear. Using roots and stone, she climbed, higher, always higher. At the top, she belly-crawled to peek over the edge at the disarray below.

When they regained control, they'd search the surrounding forest. The logical, flat, easy route. She'd hide where Daenon would never expect ... right over their heads.

She inhaled deep. Tangy pine and rich soil grounded her as the dryads had taught. Their gift more valuable than she'd imagined.

Rowena lay flat against the rough stone, heart pounding. She had actually done it. Escaped. Air tumbled from of her lungs in shaky bursts, each one a promise that she was free.

The warriors shouted below, but their words scattered into the trees.

Exactly how she'd hoped.

The sun slipped behind the mountains, leaving Lungol's glow to stretch long shadows over the clearing. They shrank until they were swallowed by the trees. Her climb had angled too steep. Rowena wanted to scream.

She stayed motionless. Waiting. Listening. Until only the leaves spoke in soft whispers from the breeze. Her cheek ached from where she'd smacked into the dirt. Her ribs throbbed from lying still too long. But none of it mattered.

Rowena exhaled, slow and steady, then rose to stretch the stiffness from her limbs. They'd figure out soon enough she'd gone up instead of down.

She climbed again, quiet but quick, aiming for the next peak. A rocky outcropping near the ridge would buy her time.

Halfway there, voices rose from below. Too close.

Rowena froze, drawing shallow breaths. She had to blend into the mountain. Be stone. No reason to glance up. Time slowed. Every breath roared in her ears. Every heartbeat screamed.

The warriors fanned out below, torches flickering between the trees like fallen stars. Rowena flattened her back against the stone, willing her body to vanish. She wished to be a dryad, hidden, unnoticed, part of the forest. A tree, overlooked.

The rough surface dug into her spine. A reminder. She was still free.

For now.

She closed her eyes. Slow breaths. Calm pulse.

The dryads *had* taught her this. Stillness. Listening. The mountain had its own rhythm. Ancient. Steady. Unchanging.

She matched her breathing to its rhythm. Becoming one more shadow among many.

A loose stone shifted beneath one of the warrior's boots. The echo carried in the night air, impossibly loud. Rowena held her breath.

"Nothing here," someone called from below.

"Keep searching, she couldn't have gone far."

The voices drifted downslope.

Had they missed her? Hope flared, fragile and sharp.

"Look!" Daenon's voice cut through everything. "There! The rocks!"

Her knees wobbled. They'd seen her.

She dug her fingers into the crags, scrambling with renewed urgency. She had nowhere to go but up.

Rowena reached the outcropping and dove into a tangle of rocks and brittle shrubs. Her strength was fading fast. She had to hide. Give herself time.

Lungol's ray twinkled through the branches, nearer, but fleeting.

She scooted in tight to the boulders, knees to her chest, smearing dirt across her pale skin. She dragged broken pieces of brush in front of her like a shroud.

Below, the warriors crept closer. Through her veil of twigs and leaves, she spotted Daenon's dark outline, leading them on foot up the slope.

"Leave nothing unturned!" he barked; his voice dangerously close.

Rowena bit her lip until she tasted blood, forcing herself not to tremble as energy bled from her like water through a cracked pot.

Lungol teased, just out of reach.

Boots crunched past, just feet away, searchers kicking at rocks, peering behind outcroppings.

Rowena's pulse matched their determined footfalls. ach step a drumbeat of dread.

She closed her eyes. If only Bram was here. He'd pull her into his shadows. Take her far from this place.

"There!" a voice shouted, too close.

Rowena tensed, bracing for hands on her arms. But his shadow kept moving, pointing farther uphill.

She opened her eyes. Dare she believe? They thought she was still running.

"We've got her now," Daenon called. Heavy footfalls pounded the path above.

Rowena waited, body tense, until the echoes faded, carried upward by their own confidence.

A breath slipped from deep inside her, and her muscles turned to water, crawling from her hiding place before they circled back.

"Not so fast," a voice growled behind her.

She spun. Daenon's chalk-smeared face leered from the shadows, almost ghost-like in Lungol's pale glow.

He had stayed behind.

"How . . .?" The word died on her lips as his hand clamped around her wrist. He yanked her from the rocks, like plucking prey from a snare.

"You enchanted, always thinking you're better than everyone else," Daenon sneered, his grip tightening painfully. "But you couldn't outwit me with this little trick."

Rowena twisted, kicking his shin. Hard. It was like striking stone. But he flinched. Barely. Enough to spark hope.

"Insolent," he hissed, dragging her closer. "You think we fear the forest? You strolled into our trap."

He didn't bind her hands. Just took hold of her wrist and hauled her toward where others waited.

Not that it mattered. She had nothing left. Drained. Empty.

"No need to fear us. Not yet," Daenon said. "You've still got plenty to face where we're going."

Rowena stumbled over loose stones and twisted roots, every misstep jolting pain into her bones. The warriors loomed ahead, waiting like dark sentinels as Daenon dragged her back the way she'd come. His grip unyielding and vicious.

Dizziness blurred her vision. Her head ached. Why had she thought she could run? She'd had no more sense than a rabbit before a fox.

Three warriors emerged from behind.

"Good work," Daenon said.

It must have been their footsteps near her hiding place. She'd thought herself so clever. But she'd underestimated them. She blinked back hot, frustrated tears.

At the edge of the group, Daenon shoved her forward. Laughter followed, sharp and cruel, echoing through the dark.

"So much for your grand escape," one jeered.

Rowena stared at the ground, unmoved.

"We'll see how she enjoys running now," Daenon said, his smile like a knife. "Bring the chains."

He called for those earlier. Now what?

Chains clinked behind her, dragged across stone.

Rowena stiffened.

Iron looped around her waist. Cold. Heavy. Unforgiving.

The other end hooked to the belt of the largest warrior in Daenon's company.

"Pog isn't much of a talker," Daenon murmured, brushing a strand of hair from her face. "But he can run for days. If you fall, he won't notice. He'll just keep running . . . until you're little more than a bloody mess, barely alive."

His voice was almost tender. That made it worse.

Rowena stumbled forward, nausea rising as the chain bit into her stomach. Each step a battle against exhaustion and despair.

The warriors had set a punishing pace, gliding like phantoms over the mountain trail, open to Lungol's cold gaze.

Pog ran without pause.

The links tugged at her, every jolt a sick twist to her gut. "Is this how you've treated my cousin, too?"

Daenon scoffed, slowing to keep pace beside her. "She doesn't complain at all like you. Especially now."

His mouth lifted into a menacing grin. "That spell had some side effects. Even after she was released."

Rowena's head snapped up. Her foot caught on a loose stone. She nearly fell. "You let her go? How? That was Fidessa's spell."

Realization crashed over her like a wave. Of course. It was a ruse. The split between Daenon and Fidessa . . . a lie.

They'd been working together the whole time.

The chain tugged tight, jerking her into a forced march.

An amused chuckle came from Daenon.

"What side effects?" She asked, voice purposefully flat.

"One thing I thoroughly enjoy—she's mute." Daenon's words cut through the night air. "I don't have to hear her condescending tone anymore."

Mute? The word hit Rowena like a stone to the chest, knocking the air from her lungs. Memories flooded her mind.

Safi, who once commanded the King's Guards.

Safi, laughing at stories by the fire.

Safi, who whispered encouragement when Rowena needed it most.

Silenced.

The chain snapped taut, yanking her forward. Pain shot through her waist where the metal links bit. Pog marched ahead, oblivious that they'd begun to descend a steep slope. Rowena's boots skidded on loose stones. She tripped, skinning her palms on rough bark and jagged rock. Blood warmed her cold fingers.

"But even better," Daenon continued, seemingly deaf to her gasps and struggles, "she's developed a vicious passion for violence. She's quite the weapon."

Ice crept into Rowena's veins.

"She fights for *you*?" The question escaped before she could swallow it.

"Like a wild beast." His laugh bounced off the mountain walls, multiplying like demons in the dark. "It's really something to behold. I'd have brought her with us to find you, but she had other duties."

Rowena was going to be sick.

Her cousin had once protected the weak, stood against injustice. She'd taught Rowena that vulnerability was strength.

Now she'd become a twisted weapon for the very man who'd stolen her voice. A blade that kept his hands clean.

Something cracked. A fissure in Rowena's chest. Her heart stung with it. Eyes burned.

She blinked hard, and kept her voice even, hiding the tremor rattling through her body. "What duties?"

Daenon's smile faded, just a flicker. "Nothing that concerns you. Yet."

The path opened into a small clearing. Rowena glanced upward, seeking comfort in the familiar skies. Lungol hung low on the horizon, his energy distant. She sensed Masah's approach, a subtle vibration, the promise of his rising imminent. But something was off. The rhythm discordant, like an instrument playing out of tune.

She drew in a breath and let it settle behind her ribs.

She would free her cousin. She would undo whatever they'd done.

The promised hardened into a blade. Sharp and unbreakable.

"I don't understand," she said, refusing tears to form. "What does Fidessa get out of this? I thought she wanted to rule Ibern for herself."

"Ibern?" Daenon chuckled. "That's just the start. With the sword and heartstone, we'll have so much more."

Heartstone . . . Lunastone. Rowena's mind raced. He knew.

He *knew*.

"The sword is just a symbol." A test. "It has no real power."

Daenon barked laugh, loud and sudden.

"Is that what your precious Seeker told you?" He leaned in, breath hot against her ear. "The sword and the stone together can reshape Edenia. And when the Burning Moon rises . . . We'll be ready."

An icy chill slid down Rowena's spine. The Burning Moon. But ready for what?

She stumbled again, and this time the chain yanked her to her knees. She struck a rock, sending pain shooting up her leg. She bit back a cry. Refused to show weakness.

Pog didn't slow, continuing to drag her several paces before she could scramble to her feet.

Daenon had given her valuable information, though. Wherever he was dragging her to, the sword was there as well. And where the sword was, so was her chance to reach Safi.

Pog shifted course, turning east down a steeper path. Rowena's legs trembled with fatigue, but her will held firm.

She would find the sword. She would free Safi.

And she would make Daenon and Fidessa pay for what they'd done.

"We'll rest at the river crossing," Daenon called. "Half a mark. No longer."

Then low, so only she could hear. "Rest while you can, princess. The hardest part is yet to come."

A tremor ran through her.

She couldn't rest among these dregs. A half mark, he said. Too long. Break the chain. Escape.

As if sensing her thoughts, Daenon jiggled the links, turning one, so she could see the rune etched into the metal.

"Escape isn't an option any longer. So don't waste your strength."

She stared at the rune. That had to be what made her sick. The reason Masah seemed so far away. He'd arrived among the stars as they traveled, nothing more than a dimmed presence.

Another of Fidessa's spells, no doubt.

Rowena's thoughts turned to Bram. Where was he now? Was he looking for her? Or had he been caught in a trap as well?

She wanted to believe he was out there and that somehow, she wouldn't face this alone.

Elfling thoughts.

She'd faced struggles, but she'd handled them, more or less.

The chain pulled tight again, hard. Rowena stumbled into the dark.

Despite everything, she would get herself free.

And Safi too.

28

BRAM

Bram awoke to a foul stench curling up his nose, sharp and pungent like rotting vegetables abandoned in the summer heat. The smell coated the back of his throat, thick enough to gag.

Something rough brushed his cheek.

Unexpected.

Unwelcome.

He tried to rise. Pain exploded through his skull. A white-hot lance pulsing with every heartbeat. His hand flew to his forehead, where his horns would emerge. Instead of smooth arches, his fingers met only skin, and excruciating pain, as if his horns were trapped beneath and desperate to break free.

A groan escaped his lips, echoing against the hewn walls.

A scrabbling sound, clawed feet skittering over stone, made him tense. Every muscle protested. Pain surged through his limbs. Cold bled up from the dirt floor, sinking deep despite his leather armor.

Piece by piece memory returned. Dungeon. Cell. Prisoner. Flashes. Fidessa's trap. The rune-lined bars. Yralissa's triumphant gleam. She'd pricked his hand with something, needle or lance, he couldn't be sure. His memory frayed at the edges, murky and slow.

With effort, Bram forced his eyes open.

Darkness greeted him thicker than it should be. Impenetrable. Too long before shapes emerged.

Something was wrong.

Even in elven form, the Seeker's vision pierced the darkest shadows.

What had she done?

He rolled onto his side. Vertigo threatened to plunge him back into unconsciousness. The stench returned, worse, joined by something calloused pressing against his face.

"What you?" More grunt than speech. The voice was gravel and growl at once.

The closeness spiked adrenaline into his gut.

Something was very wrong.

He scrubbed a palm across his face, and froze. His body felt wrong. Disconnected. Like wearing someone else's boots. He turned his head to the side, and two large, bulbous eyes of brilliant yellow blinked. Slow. Watching.

A goblin. Warty, gray-green skin blended into shadow, but those eyes were unmistakable. The creature's stubby nose twitched. Teeth too large for its frog-like mouth gleamed.

What was a goblin doing there?

Bram's thoughts scrambled through the fog.

Goblins were mischief-makers and thieves not loyal to anyone.

Had Fidessa made one into a pet?

"Work Queen, not you." The goblin thumped a small fist against its sunken chest with force. Something between pride and defiance in the gesture.

"Okay," Bram rasped, barely audible. His mind clawed for

meaning, trying to piece together this new puzzle, while his body remained foreign.

Goblins didn't serve anyone. Not willingly.

Nothing made sense.

Something glinted. Silver, encircling the goblin's skinny ankle.

Not a servant then, but a prisoner. Forced.

The realization sparked a flicker of hope.

Perhaps this strange little visitor was his way out.

Bram reached for his shadows. Called to his power. Always his.

Instead, agony burst through his chest. He cried out and doubled over, clutching his sternum.

Fear crept in. A rarely allowed emotion. It uncoiled, threaded through his thoughts.

"Queen no need you." the goblin watched Bram's suffering with detached curiosity.

When the wave of pain dulled enough to think clearly, Bram lifted a trembling hand to his forehead again. His fingernails scraped against his skin, longer. Sharper. but not Seeker claws.

He scanned down. Black leathers, but his hands were wrong. Elongated fingers, but no runes. Just fragments.

A strand of hair slipped into view, not brown of his elven form. White. The realization hit him: he'd become trapped between forms. Neither elven druid nor Seeker. Yralissa had done something to fracture him.

How was that possible? Icy dread pooled in his gut. The Heptad's enchantment couldn't be undone. They were Primary Fae. Caelus-born, original power in their veins.

The goblin scuttled toward the cell bars, apparently having lost interest in the strange prisoner. Bars that no longer shimmered with runes.

"Hey, little guy, I don't want to hurt you," Bram called,

forcing himself upright. His muscles screamed. Nausea surged. The world tilted . . . then steadied. "Can you help me get out of here?"

"Queen have you. Feed Goby Bunyip," the goblin blinked, matter-of-factly, unbothered.

The bunyip's mention made Bram's skin crawl. He remembered that creature from the corridor with matted fur, venom-dripping fangs. Exactly the sort of cruelty Fidessa would enjoy.

"Goby, that's a good name." Bram softened his voice, extending his palms in a show of peace. His fingers still ached to shift, but he buried the need. "I agree. The queen is unstable. But I can keep you safe. Help me, and I'll get us both out."

The goblin's brow wrinkled even deeper. "No need you. Goby try hard."

Bram's chest clenched, but he kept his expression neutral. A thousand concerns pressed for attention. What Yralissa had done, how to get back to Rowena, finding the sword. None of it mattered if he couldn't escape this cell.

"Goby, listen." Bram leaned in, his voice dropping to a confidential tone. "Coming in here with me; that was brave. I need someone, helpful and clever, like you."

A thought occurred to him.

"Do you know where the guards keep the keys?"

The goblin's eyes popped wide. He recoiled as if struck. "Goby no help. Queen kill."

"I hate to say this," Bram replied, chest tightening. He didn't want to frighten the creature. "But she probably will kill you, anyway."

"Why?" Goby wailed, his voice echoing beyond the stone walls. "Goby good!"

Bram winced, both at the volume and the distress in the goblin's voice. He glanced toward the corridor.

Too loud. Too risky.

"It's not your fault. Fidessa is mad and cares for no one. She uses others. Then tosses them away." He held the goblin's gaze. "I'll help you. I'll keep you safe."

The words hung between them. For a breath, Bram thought he'd reached the creature. Then, Goby scampered away, disappearing down the corridor.

So much for that plan.

Disappointment settled heavily across Bram's shoulders. He rolled to his hands and knees and crawled to the side of the cell, ignoring the stones that bit into his palms. Cool stone met his back as he leaned there. Taking stock.

No escape. No power . . . Not yet.

How long had he been unconscious? The question nagged at him. Yralissa shouldn't have the strength to do what she'd done. Where had she gained such power? And more worrisome—who had taught her to use it?

Before he could delve deeper into these questions, a familiar jingling metal echoed down the corridor. Bram tensed, preparing for a fight despite his pain. But in his current condition, overpowering even one of those club-wielding sentries would be a challenge.

The sound grew closer, and then, two glowing yellow orbs. Not a guard.

Goby.

The goblin crept near; eyes darted wildly before fixing on Bram. "You keep Goby safe?" The question held equal parts hope and suspicion.

Hope surged through Bram, so fast it made him dizzy.

"Absolutely," he promised, pushing himself to his knees with one hand braced against the wall.

Without another word, Goby clambered up the bars with surprising agility, a ring of keys clutched tight. The goblin's small fingers handled them with practiced ease. The first key slid into the lock, then jammed. Goby muttered something guttural and tried another. Still wrong.

Three more attempts, each one stretching Bram's nerves tighter as he strained to track any approaching footsteps.

Finally. A satisfying click.

The door creaked open with Goby still clinging to the bars.

"That's a good boy," Bram breathed, rising slowly to his feet. His legs trembled with the effort, but held. He rolled his neck, feeling vertebrae pop between his shoulders.

Every instinct screamed to shift. Use the Seeker's greater strength. The pain wasn't worth it. Not yet.

What mattered now was escape, and finding Rowena.

Discovering what Yralissa had done. Reclaiming what was his.

"Show me the way out, Goby," he said, determination hardening his voice. "Let's escape this madness."

The goblin's sharp teeth flashed in . . . a smile? He dropped from the cell door and scuttled into the corridor.

"This way. Guard sleeping. Goby know secret path."

Bram followed.

Hope burned in his chest. Fragile. Flickering.

Whatever Yralissa had done, whatever game Fidessa was playing . . .

They had underestimated him.

And that would be their undoing.

THE WINDING PASSAGEWAY narrowed as they left the cells, forcing Bram to hunch his shoulders beneath the low ceiling. The stink of mildew and stagnant water slowly gave way to woodsmoke, roasting meat, and the earthy scent of root vegetables.

Goby paused at a junction, his nose twitching like a rabbit.

"Guards this way," he whispered, pointing left, then scuttled right. "Kitchen this way."

Bram's jaw clenched.

That first guard had promised the kitchen, and Bram had ended up in that cell. Now he was trusting a goblin. Brilliant.

"We need to get out now."

The goblin's yellow eyes narrowed, a stubborn set to his jaw. He halted.

"No food. Goby no help." He folded his arms across his narrow chest with surprising authority.

Blackmailed by a goblin.

A muscle in Bram's cheek twitched. His fingers flexed. Still wrong. Not quite Seeker's claws, not quite elven hands. The pain in his chest had dulled, but a shift might trigger worse.

He had to escape first.

"Fine," he said, sharper than intended. "But we make it quick."

Goby nodded once and scuttled ahead through a passage that grew warmer the further they went.

They emerged into a narrow corridor, light spilling from an arched doorway at the far end. Delicious smells wafted toward them, meat, herbs, roasting root vegetables.

Bram's stomach clenched.

How long had he been unconscious?

The kitchen stood empty. A stroke of luck Bram hadn't dared hope for. A wide stone hearth dominated the far wall, banked coals glowing orange in its belly. Copper pots hung from above wooden workbenches, cluttered with half-finished prep.

A cauldron simmered over the low fire, sending out mouth-watering steam.

Goby made a beeline for a wooden barrel beside the larder door.

With surprising strength, he heaved aside the heavy lid and dove in. Half his upper body vanishing. He emerged seconds later clutching an armful of carrots, leafy tops still intact.

"Seriously?" Bram hissed, keeping his voice low despite the quiet. "That's what we're risking our escape for?"

Goby darted furtive glances toward the kitchen entrance as he selected a particularly fat carrot. He skewered it with a three-pronged fork and hunched over it protectively, then tore into it with frightening ferocity.

Sharp teeth shredded the carrot. Orange pulp spattered across Goby's chin as he devoured his prize, growling softly with each bite.

"When was your last meal?" Bram asked, with genuine curiosity.

Goby's head snapped up, fork raised like a weapon, carrot strings dangling from his bared teeth.

"MINE!" he snarled, the word somehow a threat and plea all at once.

Bram raised both hands and stepped back. "I won't come near. It's all yours."

They needed to be on their way. But if he had to wait—the smell of potatoes and savory spices coming from that pot, urged Bram forward. He grabbed a bowl from a shelf and ladled in a hearty portion.

"Bread there." Goby pointed to a box with his fork. "Spoon too."

Grateful, Bram tore off a piece of crusty bread and dipped it into the stew. His mouth watered. He'd needed the meal badly.

Apparently satisfied with Bram's choices, Goby returned to his feast, demolishing three more carrots with alarming speed. When finished, he plopped onto a low stool, sighed with contentment, and wiped his chin with the back of his hand. The belch that followed echoed through the kitchen, proud and unapologetic.

Bram winced, his gaze snapping toward the doorway.

His finished his stew. More tempted, but he was out of time, Bram set the bowl beside the carrot carnage.

"We should go," he whispered. "Someone might have heard."

But Goby seemed languid, slouched on his stool, sated as a house cat. "Goby live kitchen. Get all carrots want."

"That's . . . fortunate for you," Bram muttered, trying to mask his growing impatience. "But we need to go. Now. Unless you *want* the queen to feed you to the bunyip?"

At the mention of the bunyip, Goby froze. Then bolted, off the stool, through a small door. Gone.

"Goby!" Bram whisper-yelled, torn between pursuit and escape. Following could be a trap. The goblin had intimate knowledge of the castle though. Guards were numerous, but predictable. Even without his abilities, Bram had navigated worse.

Before he could decide, Goby reappeared, struggling under the weight of a wicker basket nearly his size. Leather straps. Reinforced bottom. Multiple compartments. A well-used pack.

With single-minded focus, the goblin began filling it with carrots, selecting each one like a precious gem before adding it to his collection.

"You can't be serious," Bram muttered.

He moved to the doorway, keeping watch for approaching guards. The longer they lingered, the higher the risk.

Goby worked fast, practiced and efficient. He tucked his prized fork into a side pouch, then crept behind a cook's station. From a knife block, he extracted a large kitchen knife.

Bram's attention sharpened. Quality steel. Well-maintained

edge despite the crude wooden handle. The blade gleamed in the firelight as Goby tested its edge with a small finger, nodding with approval. Proper weapon assessment.

"Are you done yet?" Tension coiled inside Bram. Every passing second added unnecessary risks. The kitchen staff could return. The guard rotation was unknown.

Goby buckled the final strap on his pack with practiced movements. The basket appeared absurdly large on his slight frame, but he adjusted it with ease. Not his first escape.

"Now ready," he declared, trotting toward Bram with surprising agility.

Bram's gaze fixed on the knife handle jutting from the basket. "That could come in handy," he said, reaching for it casually.

Goby slapped his hand away with surprising speed. "No touch! For carrots!" He patted the basket possessively.

A faint smile tugged at Bram's lips. Goby's single-minded obsession to his carrots was oddly admirable. Focused. Consistent.

Still, they'd spent far too long.

"Which way out?" he asked, returning to the immediate need.

Goby pointed toward a narrow servant's door tucked behind flour sacks. "That way garden. No guards."

They slipped into a cool stone passageway, heavy with the scent of soil and herbs. Bram's tension eased, slightly. They were close.

His mind already raced ahead. Find Rowena. Unravel what Yralissa had done. Find the Sword of Justice.

The passage ended at a wooden door; iron hinges rust-streaked.

Goby cracked it open, peeked, then waved Bram to follow.

They emerged into a moonlit herb garden, silvered beneath Lungol's glow. The castle wall loomed just fifty yards ahead.

"Almost there," Bram murmured.

Hope kindled, small but fierce.

They crossed the garden to another door.

The way out.

Instead, it led to another passage.

ROWENA

Rowena stumbled along the trail, the chain rattling between her and Pog. The warriors moved without speed or stealth. Loud, lazy, breaking branches and snapping twigs like bonnacons through underbrush.

They laughed and chatted as if they weren't dragging a prisoner.

Rowena's thoughts spiraled.

Daenon was taking her to the hiding place he shared with Fidessa. Safi would be there too. She had to be. And the Sword of Justice as well.

If both Safi and the sword were in one place, it was her chance.

Rescue Safi. Retrieve the sword.

When she found Bram again, he would be so proud. She wouldn't just be a prisoner with regrets. She'd *done* something.

Pine needles coated the path with a sharp, astringent scent masking the stench of sweat and chalk-paint from Daenon's warriors.

They stayed beneath the trees, though Masah hadn't risen yet, Lungol still held onto the horizon.

Rowena itched for Lungol or Masah, either of them, but she needed open sky.

Twilight still clung when they broke free of the forest into a clearing. A hundred paces away, a castle loomed in the darkness. The portcullis down for the night. A shallow moat, curled around it, half-dry and stinking of brackish decay. The entire place screamed escape, not enter.

Ten paces out, Daenon called out. "Ho, to the castle!"

No reply.

A long silence stretched, until a gruff voice wheezed through the gate—nasal and congested. "State your business."

"Open the gates for your king," Daenon demanded.

Beady eyes peered through the gate before a scuffle occurred within the gatehouse. The portcullis groaned upward, and six portly guards emerged; long, snout-like noses, dressed in full garb. Helmets, brigandines, bracers, yet they seemed ill-fitted and wrong.

They carried a wooden ramp, raising it awkwardly before tipping it across the moat. It wobbled precariously, then settled. They drove long stakes into either side and signaled readiness.

"That's quite a procedure," Rowena remarked as Daenon stepped up next to her.

He grunted, visibly annoyed. A small satisfaction, but she'd take it.

"Forward!" Daenon barked, and his warriors marched with eerie precision, unlike they'd displayed earlier.

Rowena glanced over the edge of the bridge; stagnant green water rippled below. Something large nipped the surface. She shivered. For once grateful to be chained to Pog. If he didn't fall, neither would she.

The guards followed them with their beady black eyes, identical as if they were all related—or the same individual. Nothing about this castle seemed welcoming.

Inside the bailey, the castle's dilapidation became clear. One tower leaned at a precarious angle, a marvel it hadn't collapsed. Cracked walls. Ivy-cloaked stone. Of the double keeps, only the right one appeared solid amidst the decay.

From her right, Rowena saw more guards approached. But one figure made her breath hitch. Safi. Her cousin's long blonde hair, braided back, her brown leather armor, so familiar. A quiver of arrows slung over her shoulder, and a dagger at her hip.

Rowena nearly burst with relief.

"Safi!" Rowena called. Her voice crackled from urgency.

No response.

She called again, louder. "Safi!"

This time, her cousin stopped. The guards behind her stumbled as they halted as well.

Safi turned, tilting her head, eyes blank. One brow raised briefly. Then she resumed marching past the chalk warriors and out the front gate.

Rowena's heart plunged.

Safi wasn't catatonic anymore. Daenon had told the truth. But the way she'd stared at Rowena . . . as if she didn't recognize . . . or care.

"I told you she's not the same," Daenon said.

"Yes." Resolve hardened inside Rowena. Whatever they had done, she would undo. She would help Safi return to herself, unravel the spell.

Shatter Fidessa's cage.

Pog unhooked the chain from his belt and handed it to Daenon. "Your problem now." He smirked and joined the other chalk warriors heading behind the left keep, leaving only Rowena, Daenon, and the odd assembly of guards behind.

"If you think I'll be removing these, think again," Daenon said, twisting one of the links so only those around her waist stayed in place. The long section that had bound her to Pog clattered to the ground.

Daenon tugged the remaining links, ensuring they remained secure. He turned to the squat-looking guards, pointing to the discarded chain. "Handle that."

He turned back and extended his hand to Rowena as if inviting her to a ballroom. "This way, if you'll please."

"I don't—" Rowena started, then caught herself. At least she could walk without being dragged along. "Nevermind."

Daenon snorted. "Always got a comment."

She pushed through the keep's doors, with Daenon trailing. Inside, there were stark wooden floors and plain brick walls, maintained, but undecorated. The whitewash on the walls had dulled to a gray film. No rugs. No tapestries. No fires in the hearths.

Just cold.

They climbed a round staircase, crossed a hallway with arches opening to the entry and then ascended another spiral staircase.

Daenon kept prodding, corridor after corridor, stair after stair. Not a single decoration, no chairs, no curtains, no soft touches, along the way. Only stone and splinters. Only silence.

Then they stopped before a plain wooden door.

Daenon rapped three times. They waited. A pause that dragged too long. Then footsteps. Two latches clicked.

The door swung open, and Rowena stood face to face with Fidessa.

Daenon squeezed through the doorway ahead of Rowena, unconcerned she might run. The chains still at her waist made escape laughable.

"I've returned with our prize, my love," Daenon said, pressing a kiss to Fidessa's cheek.

He ruffled a wolossum's head and flopped into the only

cushioned chair. Two weasel-like creatures scrambled up his legs, wiggling and chattering in welcome.

"Splendid." Fidessa beamed at him. "And with perfect timing."

Rowena fought the urge to gag.

Like the rest of the castle, the room was stark, smelling of dust and mildew. Only one table occupied the far corner, paired with a straight-back wooden chair. Papers, quills, and an inkwell sat neatly on top, but otherwise, the space seemed barely lived in.

Except for the animals. Perched behind the desk, half in shadow, an owl ruffled its dark feathers, then settled, staring with unblinking eyes that glowed red in the candlelight.

She shivered and turned away to peer through an open doorway on the opposite wall. Inside, shelves packed with scrolls rose to the ceiling, herbs hung drying from the rafters, and a large table in the center, loaded with bottles, open books, jars . . . even crates that twitched.

It had to be Fidessa's spell room. She wouldn't waste care on comfort, only her potions, charms, and other nefarious spells.

Rowena *had* to find a way in there. She could not believe even a woman as nasty as Fidessa would cast a spell so sinister on her own daughter. There had to be a flaw. A mistake that could be undone.

"I had expected you to be chasing the Sword of Justice, or your cousin. Instead, you've been traipsing through the continent," Fidessa said, bringing Rowena's focus to the woman who had stolen everything.

"Yet, here I am. Right where I need to be, for both." Rowena's heart pounded, but she would not cower. "Perhaps *you* have played into *my* plans."

Fidessa threw her head back and laughed. The owl flared its wings, and the wolossum spun a circle before curling against her legs. "Such a naïve girl. A princess above and a peasant below, a trap I set, and both did show."

Fear skittered down Rowena's spine like spider legs.

Fidessa was not just cruel. She had gone mad.

"You think touching a bit of enchantment makes you powerful enough to defeat me? Me, a lowly mage."

The owl leapt from its perch, landing on Fidessa's shoulder. She stroked its chest with one slender finger.

"There are many eager to tear away the yoke of oppression created by the enchanted. It's only a matter of time before the tables turn."

It was basically a confession, confirming Rowena's suspicions she was working with someone else, someone more powerful. But who?

"Where shall I deposit this slave for you, my dear?" Daenon asked, rising to trail his fingers over Fidessa's shoulders.

An involuntary shiver rolled through Rowena.

She could not go back to being a slave.

Not again. Not for anyone. Especially not for *her*.

Last time, she'd survived because of Muriel and Tuck. Now with Bram gone, she had no one.

No.

She had herself. She was not helpless.

She was enough.

"In time." Fidessa's gaze pierced, never wavering. "First, I have questions for my wayward niece."

"We are no relation," Rowena said.

"Fair enough." Fidessa smiled faintly. "That makes it easier . . . no false niceties."

A sharp chuckle burst from Rowena. The idea of anything *nice* coming from Fidessa, past or present, was absurd.

"After what you've done to Safi, you expect me to believe you care about anyone?"

"You will hold your tongue," Daenon roared. "Respect your queen or suffer."

"Shh, my pet," Fidessa cooed. "I have nothing to fear from her."

She turned to Rowena, voice purring. "Besides, I intend to let Safi take care of her when I'm finished."

Rowena flinched. "Why would you make her into a killer? She is strong and intelligent, with more compassion than you could ever hold."

Fidessa ambled until she was within an arm's length of Rowena. "It may not have been intended, but if you can't see what value she holds now, you are dimmer than I thought."

"She's your *daughter*."

"Taken from me. Brainwashed by those imbeciles in Velmeg. They filled her head with nonsense to make her hate me. Even after Lendan *violated* her, she still pined for Dewan. But now," Fidessa's eyes glittered. "Now, she is mine. She understands. She will stand beside me forever."

Rowena pressed her lips tight. Her stomach churned in a knot of disgust. Fidessa didn't want a daughter—she wanted another pet, a weapon that wouldn't leave her. "What happens when she turns on you?"

"That will never happen!" Fidessa snapped, cheeks flushed red. Hate glazed her eyes.

The owl hissed from her shoulder.

Rowena slid a step back.

"She is loyal to me!"

Daenon slid to her side, fingers slipping under her long, mouse-brown hair to stroke her back. Fidessa inhaled, eyes closed, then returned her gaze to Rowena with a calm smile. The transformation unnerving.

"We've already discussed your little tricks, trying to drive a wedge between us." Her voice softened yet remained edged, like silk over blades. "If you so much as suggest she leave me, she will kill you. Without hesitation."

A weight pressed into Rowena's chest, heavier with every heartbeat. To free Safi might mean death.

Rowena had to believe her cousin was still inside her body, her mind. She wouldn't *want* to hurt those she loved. Their bond went deeper than blood.

Whatever the cost, she'd break that spell. She'd break Safi free.

"I think she's got enough to think about now," Fidessa said in a nonchalant, singsong way. "Let her ponder for a hundred years, or one, she'll never walk away this time."

Fidessa trailed her fingers along Daenon's jaw and withdrew a silver key from her pouch. "Thank you for delivering her. Take her to the servant quarters upstairs. You'll have time to wash before we dine."

"Of course."

Daenon seized Rowena's arm. "I'll return shortly."

He dragged Rowena into the hall and shut the door behind them.

"This way." He shoved her forward.

"You're a fool to believe she cares for you," Rowena said. Even if it wasn't true, which was disturbing enough, she might still sow division, despite her lack of enchantment. Besides it gave her rage somewhere to focus.

"Your days of influence are over. Besides, slavery suites you." He shoved her again as they reached a stairwell. "Up you go."

At the top, only one hallway stretched. Long and bare, with four doors on each side. All open. All dark.

Daenon marched her to the second door on the right, tripping her into the windowless room. She fell hard, knees cracking on stone. He knelt to the chains. Metal scraped. Blessed relief as they fell away.

"Enjoy your night." The door slammed. The lock clicked.

Rowena stayed on her hands and knees, letting her eyes adjust to the dark. She made out a wooden plank bet, scantly covered in straw. A chamber pot. Nothing more. Not even a blanket.

The stone walls and bare floor chilled the room, seeping into Rowena's bones. She crawled onto the bed, leaned her back against the wall, hugging her knees to her chest.

No window. No moonlight. No enchantment.

She closed her eyes, slowed her breathing. She would survive this.

Somehow.

30

BRAM

BRAM TURNED TO GOBY; an unexpected ally he still wasn't sure he could trust. "We need an exit, somewhere hidden where we can slip away unseen. Any ideas?"

The goblin's already wide mouth split into a grin, revealing sharp, jagged teeth. To anyone unfamiliar with the creature, it didn't read as joy to help, but as a predator ready to pounce. Even Bram tensed.

"Follow Goby." In a blink, the goblin dropped to all-fours and bounded down the hall.

Bram jogged to keep him in sight, scanning the halls and hugging the wall for cover. Goby was familiar in the castle. Bram was not.

After descending a winding stairwell, followed by another long corridor, before Goby darted right out of Bram's view.

"Get off!" A male voice boomed out.

"What is this?" another said, amusement beneath the words.

Goby had run into others coming from the opposite direction. Bram crept to the end of the hall and pressed his back to the stone, edging along to listen. Perhaps it was nothing, just guards.

He risked a glance.

One man held Goby by the leg, dangling upside down. The other stood watching, arms folded as if sizing up his next move.

Bram ducked back.

He recognized them. Liam and Hywel, two of the Fianna he'd fought beside in Ibern.

He rested his head against the stone, thinking fast. They'd been allies when he last saw them, and had discovered him to be the Seeker.

What were they doing here? He couldn't let Goby get hurt. Couldn't risk hesitation.

They might not know he'd been the queen's prisoner.

He inhaled, straightened, and strode into their view.

Liam startled, dropping into a fighting stance and half-drawing his sword. Hywel spun, swinging Goby still held aloft.

Liam narrowed his eyes, studying Bram's face. He straightened, hand still on his sword's hilt, but no longer threatening. "Bram?"

"What the inmorti are you doing here?" Hywel asked.

Bram let his arms fall loosely, forcing ease into his stance. He grinned. "I could ask you the same thing. Exterminators of little beasties now?"

Goby grunted at the insult.

Hywel snorted a laugh and lifted the goblin higher. "Only when they slam into us like we're bowler pins."

"What brings you to this paradise of a castle?" Liam let go of his sword, ignoring Goby's wriggling protests.

"Just passing through." Bram held Liam's gaze. He itched to lunge at Hywel and pry Goby free, but he had to remain steady. Hopefully, the goblin wouldn't bite. That would gain him a dagger through the heart.

Liam glanced at his friend. "Just drop the thing. It'll scurry off."

Hywel growled and let Goby fall. He landed on his hands, then rolled over his shoulder to glare at Hywel, hissing.

Goby flicked a glance at Bram, and he gave a subtle nod. Goby sneered, mock-lunged at Hywel, then flipped through the air and bolted.

Hywel wiped his hand on his trousers. Liam shook his head, grinning as he returned his attention to Bram.

Bram mirrored the grin, keeping the atmosphere light. But he needed more information. "So how did you find yourself here?"

Liam shrugged. "After you left Velmeg with the moon-born, Conri wanted us to help Queen Dewan clean up from the battle. Clearing rubble, repairing the gates, that sort of thing. But her warriors didn't see her as a strong enough leader."

The moon-born. Rowena. He didn't realize they had understood that part.

"King Lendan had ruled with an iron fist. After he died, his army didn't trust her softer style," Hywel added.

"Was there an uprising?"

Bram couldn't believe it. He'd had his doubts about the queen's ability to keep order. But she had raised Safi. He'd hoped that meant steel beneath the grace. He hadn't expected rebellion. Not this soon.

"A short one," Liam said. "Then King Daenon returned."

"What happened to the queen?"

"Still there," Hywel said. "Locked in her rooms, but not like she's a prisoner. Servants still cater to her. No harm done."

Bram nodded. At least she was safe. "So Daenon is in Ibern. With Princess Safi?"

"He didn't bring the princess," Hywel added. "Just an entire army of clansmen. He plans to return Ibern to the old ways— chalk warriors and all."

"That's when we left," Liam said. "Conri didn't believe that was the right path, and we had to agree. We'd prefer the princess take the throne, so we set out to find her. Which is what led us here."

"Here? With Queen Fidessa?" That's why Fidessa used that spell so casually. Daenon hadn't taken Safi. It was all a performance. No more than a mummer with a puppet.

"Yeah." Hywel shook his head. "But she's different."

"It turns out that she's got some kind of complication from that spell," Liam said. "Got in a fight with Conri and ran her sword right through him."

That didn't sound like the Safi he'd known. Not the logical, sharp leader. "Conri's dead?"

Both Fianna nodded.

"We've stayed. Thought maybe we could help," Liam said. "She's got as much right to the throne as King Daenon."

True, but an odd stance. Why would the Fianna work with Fidessa? Or her with them?

Safi might be her daughter, but that alliance only made Fidessa queen mother. With Daenon, Fidessa would become the Queen of Ibern herself. It wasn't adding up.

"I'm sorry to hear about Conri. He was a good leader." Bram wet his lips, weighing his next question. "So, you're here for the princess? Not to serve the queen?"

If he hadn't fallen for Yralissa's trickery . . . again . . . he could help Safi better than either of them. Found the sword. Ended this Ibernian mess.

When he found Rowena, she'd be able to rest. Her fears would quiet. Everything would be right.

But that wasn't the situation. Not yet.

He had to purge the poison or potion or whatever Yralissa stabbed into his veins. Then he'd come back. And truly tear this place to rubble.

"That's what drew us here, but there are other issues to

consider now." Liam rubbed the back of his neck. "Without Conri, we have to choose differently. We're the last of the Fianna. Rebuilding won't be easy."

The hair on Bram's neck rose. He couldn't point it out, not yet, but he didn't trust them. They'd fought side by side, yet, now . . . something had changed. Something that went beyond Conri's death.

Understanding hit Bram like lightning.

Daenon had claimed to hire the Fianna to find the sword. It had to have been Fidessa. Liam and Hywel served her then. As they did still.

Fidessa had the sword, but she also needed a moon-born. Which meant she wanted to influence the prophecy. Why? If she'd allied with Ha'mon or his ousted wife ruling Anomie, that created a nest of trouble.

Motion near the ceiling drew Bram's eye. Goby. Positioned on the wall with a stone in hand.

In other circumstances, he'd stop the goblin from doing something drastic, like brain an ally with a rock. Yet, the conversation had gone on long enough. If these two were tight with Fidessa, he didn't need to give them a chance to find out Bram was supposed to be in a dungeon cell.

"That sounds like it will take some time. While my heart is heavy for Conri, I'm glad to know that you two are safe. As is the princess." Bram moved to slip past them, but Hywel shifted. Casual. Blocking.

"What happened to Rowena? Last we knew, the two of you seemed thick as thieves." Hywel rested his hand across his stomach, trying not to appear that he was readying to draw his sword.

"She's safely recovering from her ordeal. I have other business to attend to that doesn't involve her." This was definitely not a topic he wanted to continue discussing.

"Interesting," Liam said. "She was quite stubborn—"

"And opinionated." Hywel interrupted.

"That too." Liam smiled, though it changed nothing about the sharp look in his eyes. "Seems she'd struggle to sit back and let someone else finish the job. Might be searching for Safi on her own."

Bram curled his fists, ready to grab Liam's throat. What did he know?

Armor jangled down the corridor, along with many pounding feet. Fidessa's guards. Heading their way.

It burned like a crucible through Bram to leave. He had no choice. They'd threatened Rowena. He had to find her first.

He tipped his head toward Goby. "Now."

The goblin understood and a stone the size of a melon flew. Hywel twisted to follow Bram's line of sight just in time for the stone to hit him directly between the eyes. Both Fianna and stone clattered to the floor.

Bram took advantage of Liam's surprise and slammed his shoulder into the Fianna's stomach, sending him into the opposite wall. While he hated to do it, Bram landed a punch to the side of Liam's face, knocking him unconscious.

"Run, Goby!" Bram raced down the hall while the goblin traveled along the wall. As they rounded the next corner to the left, groans echoed from behind. One or both Fianna were waking. "Hurry."

They'd made it halfway down the next hallway when the goblin dropped and scurried across the corridor in front of Bram. "Careful!" He stumbled to avoid kicking the goblin, who started roaming his hands over the stone wall.

"Follow Goby."

"We don't have time. Keep going."

Goby found what he searched for and used both hands to push on a single stone. A door creaked open, just like the one Yralissa had used, showing a narrow, hidden passage behind.

"Here. Secret."

Bram skidded to a stop, backtracking to darted through the opening. Goby hurriedly found the right stone on the inside and the door closed.

They stood in complete darkness, surrounded by the smell of dust, neither moving. Bram barely breathed as he listened to the approaching footfalls. Liam and Hywel. They ran past without hesitation.

Bram rested his hand on Goby's shoulder and whispered. "Will the guards know to look here?"

The goblin made a scoff-like noise. "Too dim."

Bram's eyesight adjusted to the darkness, slower than he was used to, but effective enough. "Lead the way."

Goby didn't hesitate and jogged off on two feet with a rattling gate. Bram easily kept up, making sure he stayed as light on his feet as possible. The guards might not be too bright, but Liam and Hywel were much cleverer. If they knew about the castle's hidden passageways, they might start searching for the entrance.

"Girl this way."

Bram halted. "What girl?"

"Heard talk."

"You know where Safi is being held?"

Goby shrugged "Just girl."

So it might not be her. Oddly, Bram trusted Goby wouldn't take him somewhere they'd be caught. "Okay."

The narrow walls brushed against both of Bram's shoulders and, in some places, he had to squeeze sideways. They climbed two sets of ladder-like stairs before Goby stopped.

"Girl here." Goby pointed above his head to a small peep-hole in the wall, then to a line down the wall. "Door."

Bram spied through the hole, not sure what to expect inside. It was an empty bedchamber, and he backed away quickly. Who else came through the secret passages to spy? Goby deftly climbed the wall, sticking to the stone like a lizard.

"Alone. Hide by window."

Curious about how he'd missed her, Bram peeked once more. Sure enough, the curtains were rounded where someone hid behind them, standing in the sunlight coming through the window.

While he watched, a woman with long dark hair and golden skin left her position behind the curtain and trudged into view. She had to be from Farradar. Why would a Solara be with Fidessa? Or was she?

Bram let out a sigh, defeated. The captive woman wasn't Safi.

"See. There."

"I see her, but she's not who I'm searching for." Bram kept his voice low. It was already uncomfortable to be peering through a hole in the wall.

"Goby show true."

"You did well. It's not that, it's—"

"Who is there?" The woman's voice whispered on the other side of the wall.

Bram swallowed and peered through the hole, then backed away quickly. The woman had heard them and come closer. Bram winced, unsure if he should say anything.

"How did you get behind this wall?"

The soft Farradar lilt confirmed what he'd already guessed. "I apologize. We are in the wrong place."

"Who are you?"

"No one of importance. We just made a mistaken turn. Sorry to disturb you."

"Please don't go. Do you serve the queen?"

Bram rested his back against the wall. He could hardly tell a strange woman who he really was or why he was sneaking through hidden passages.

She remained unbound, and her room boasted carpets and fine, plush furnishings. Very unlike the rest of the castle. So not a prisoner.

If she was a Farradar emissary, it might be worth learning some of Fidessa's plans. That would risk so much.

"How is it one from Farradar is working with a queen from Ibern in a crumbling castle near Bethon?"

The woman let out a noise that was amusement or annoyance. He couldn't tell. "It was not by design. But I am not a woman willing to let others dictate my life. Now, your turn to answer my question."

"I am a traveler, just passing through." He hesitated. Goby sat on the floor listening, but content, so he continued. "I've unintentionally outstayed my welcome."

This time the woman laughed, a throaty, knowing laugh as if from someone who understood the art of deception—perhaps better than he did.

"Fidessa does not offer hospitality. Unless your needs align with her goals. If you did not make a good deal with her, then you are wise to leave this place in secret. Which is why I wish to know how you found such a clandestine passage. It may be necessary for me to know of this if my deal goes awry."

"You seem resourceful, and I'm afraid I can't give you that information at the moment."

"Other girl? She know?" Goby asked, without a hint of being discreet.

"So not just a mistaken turn. Who do you seek?" The woman's voice came through the hole with clarity. Bram made sure he stayed back enough that she could not see his face.

"A princess that the queen may have locked away."

Silence filled the passage and the room. Bram had heard no footsteps or a door to indicate the woman left.

Finally, the woman whispered an answer. "I traveled with a

princess, and strange riders caught us from the north, Penumar, I believe. However, she got away."

That couldn't have been Safi. A rush of excitement flooded through Bram's veins, but he held himself in check until he could speak with indifferent clarity. "What was her name?"

"I don't think that I should share that with a stranger speaking to me through a hole in my wall."

"Fair enough. What if I guess?"

"Then I would not be responsible for telling you."

"Rowena."

"That was quick and accurate."

"Where did she go? Which way?"

Again, the woman was silent. Bram wanted to punch the hole bigger and force her to answer. They'd wasted too much time and give this woman too much information. If she called out, she would compromise his escape.

"The last time I saw her, she headed east toward the Twisted Forest. I could not warn her during my own struggles."

The Twisted Forest. Created out of Tanith's corruption. If Rowena went in there, the ever-changing landscape wouldn't allow her to leave. Most never found their way out.

"How long ago was that?"

"I've said enough."

"How long?" Bram no longer cared about anything other than getting information on Rowena's location.

"Two days, maybe three—"

The woman's door opened, cutting off their conversation. Bram dropped low, keeping his back to the wall, and gestured for Goby to get out of sight as well.

"The queen has summoned you." A male voice, but not the nasally voice of one of Fidessa's guardsmen.

If the woman was in danger, shouldn't he step in and help? Bram risked taking a peek. The man wore the garb of long ago

Ibern: a plaid wrapped around his waist and slung over one shoulder without a tunic and his hair was stiff with painted chalk. He'd gripped the woman by the arm, but she yanked herself free.

"Don't touch me, you imbecile. I know the way."

Bram braced his hands against the wall. She hadn't been a prisoner, and she seemed like a woman who could take care of herself. Goby tugged at Bram's tunic to leave. Rightly so.

Now he knew where Rowena was—or was heading, at least. And it wasn't good.

31

BRAM

IT HAD BEEN easy to leave the castle. A broken area of the curtain wall gave them a quick exit to the forest beyond. Bram paused in the shadow of ancient pines, letting his lungs fill with the clean mountain air. The scent of resin and loam replaced the dank, stale air of the castle, a physical relief that did little to ease the knot of worry in his chest.

The mountains stretched like a spine down the entire continent. Rowena could have taken any number of paths to reach the Twisted Forest.

Far too much land to cover. Especially if she had a two or three-day head start.

Bram stopped to gather his bearings, fingers instinctively rising to rub his forehead. The skin was smooth beneath his touch, but pain radiated from temple to temple across his hairline where each horn should be, but instead they were locked away, irretrievable. The constant dull ache of his failure, of Yralissa's victory.

"You lost?" Goby peered up at him, his yellow eyes reflecting what little light filtered through the canopy.

"Just thinking." Bram met the goblin's unblinking stare. He

might know a direct route. Some goblins were known to live in the Twisted Forest. "Have you ever been inside the Twisted Forest?"

"Goby home." The answer came with a surprising hint of melancholy.

"Can you take me there?"

"No." The goblin's posture stiffened. "Goby no go back."

Bram frowned. Whatever strange magic Yralissa had used, his ability to travel through shadow was locked completely. By foot could take weeks. And inside the Twisted Forest, Without the goblin's help . . . he had to find a better way. "If you can get me to the edge, I'll make sure you get a steady supply of carrots."

Goby twisted his head, staring at Bram from the corners of his eyes with open suspicion. "No trick?"

Bram shook his head. "I wouldn't do that to you."

"Queen did." There was a wealth of hurt in those two simple words.

Bram snorted. That sounded like Fidessa. "I'm not like that."

The goblin studied him for another long moment before apparently making his decision. "Town best place." He adjusted the wicker pack on his back, still bulging with his stolen carrots. "This way."

They set off along a barely visible game trail that wound upward through the forest. Sawel's late summer rays filtered through the pines in shafts of golden light, but Bram could feel the edge of winter in the air—a crispness that grew more pronounced as they climbed higher into the mountains. Ancient trees towered overhead, their trunks wider than three men standing shoulder to shoulder, their roots twisting across the path like gnarled fingers.

The forest seemed to breathe around them. Wind sighed through the branches, carrying the calls of birds Bram couldn't identify. Pine needles blanketed the forest floor in a thick carpet that muffled their footsteps. Occasionally, they passed moss-covered stones arranged in patterns that suggested these mountains had once been home to more than just trees and wildlife. Remnants of a civilization long forgotten.

As the path grew steeper, Bram found himself exerting more effort than usual. Another consequence of his altered state. Where once he could have traversed these mountains with ease, now his lungs burned and his muscles protested. Sweat beaded on his brow despite the cool air.

Goby demonstrated natural agility as he scrambled up inclines but paused at times to wait for Bram before resuming his lead. The goblin moved through loose stones and hidden roots with perfect knowledge of his foot placement never stopping to pause.

By mid-afternoon, the forest had changed. The dense stand of towering pines transitioned into a forest where firs and spruces stood further apart. Larger patches of sunlight filtered through the trees and illuminated the forest floor where purple asters and golden arnica wildflowers formed colorful displays amidst the greenery.

Twilight approached, stretching shadows across the forest floor while the sky above the canopy transitioned to an indigo hue. Ahead of Bram, Goby slowed as his goblin vitality appeared exhausted as well.

"Need rest. Food." Goby directed Bram's attention to where rushing water could be heard. "Stream there."

They left the trail to push through a low juniper thicket until they reached the edge of a mountain stream. As water flowed over polished stones it gradually cut through the mountain terrain in its steady march. The proximity to the water created a cooler atmosphere that signaled the approach of night's cold air.

"This is a good spot." Bram scanned the tiny open space next to the stream. I'll fish while you gather firewood.

Goby placed his wicker basket down gently beside a tree and then hurried off into the dense shrubbery.

Bram took off his boots and rolled up his trousers before braving the water to his knees. The cold sent tickling prickles up his legs but he accepted this feeling as proof of his survival and ongoing struggle.

He stood motionless, watching the water swirl around his calves as his eyes adjusted to the patterns beneath the surface. A flash of silver caught his attention. Trout, the spotted back nearly invisible against the stream bed. With practiced patience, he waited until the fish swam closer, then struck with the speed that remained to him despite Yralissa's tampering.

His fingers closed around the slippery body, and he tossed it onto the bank. Three more followed in quick succession, each one caught with a little more difficulty as the daylight continued to fade.

Goby returned with an armload of sticks just as Bram stepped back onto dry land. The goblin dropped the wood in a haphazard pile and eyed the fish with obvious hunger.

"Good catch." He began arranging the wood, his small fingers working fast, but without understanding of how to build a good fire.

"Not all wood burns the same," Bram remarked, kneeling beside him. "We want dry pine for kindling. It catches quickly." He sorted through the pile, selecting the smallest, driest twigs. "But oak or maple will burn longer, giving us steady heat for cooking."

Goby watched intently, absorbing the lesson. "Goby not learn fire."

"That's too bad." Bram struck his flint, sending sparks into the nest of pine needles and twigs. "Fire is a tool, like any other. Dangerous in the wrong hands, life-saving if you know how to respect it."

The kindling caught, and Bram carefully fed the growing flames. Goby's face transformed in the firelight. His usual wariness replaced by something close to wonder as the orange glow reflected in his bright eyes.

Together they built the fire into a steady blaze, then fashioned a makeshift spit from green branches. Bram gutted and cleaned the trout with his dagger, then threaded them onto the spit. The fish sizzled as their skin met the heat, filling the air with a mouthwatering aroma.

"Smell good," Goby murmured, settling closer to the fire. He pulled a carrot from his pack and held it near the flames, mimicking Bram's cooking technique.

A twig snapped in the darkness beyond their firelight. Bram's hand went to his dagger, his body tensing as he scanned the shadows.

"We have a visitor," he said quietly to Goby, who froze mid-bite into his warmed carrot.

A figure emerged with stealth from the twilight shadows. He was tall, as tall as Bram, with broad shoulders and the solid build of someone who spent his days in physical labor. Long brown hair streaked with blonde and silver was pulled back from his face, though he didn't look old enough to carry so much gray. A heavy axe hung from his belt, balanced by a long knife on his opposite hip.

But it was his ears that caught Bram's attention—rounded instead of pointed. A Lycani, one of the shifters of the Veilrunes. Wolf most likely.

"You're trespassing," the man stated, his voice a low rumble like distant thunder. His gaze swept over their campsite, lingering on Goby before returning to Bram. "These are pack lands. You don't have permission to be here."

Definitely wolf. Bram rose slowly, keeping his movements deliberate and non-threatening. "We're just passing through."

"That's not how it works." The Lycani's expression remained impassive, but Bram could sense the tension in his posture. "You speak to the alpha before entering our territory."

"I did speak with the alpha," Bram lied. A risk, but he had to dodge a territory dispute. "He granted us passage."

The Lycani's eyes narrowed, a flash of amber appearing in the brown irises. "Is that so?"

Goby tugged at Bram's trousers, trying to get his attention, but Bram kept his focus on the wolf-shifter. He couldn't afford to appear uncertain. The wolves lived by their hierarchy, respecting leaders.

The goblin made a noise of frustration, then stomped back to his basket. He plopped atop it, arms crossed tightly over his narrow chest, and huffed with clear disapproval.

"The alpha's name?" the Lycani challenged.

Bram faltered for only a fraction of a second. "He didn't give it. Merely waved us through after I explained our purpose."

"I don't see how that can be since I *am* the alpha of this territory," the man said, his voice dropping lower. "And I don't recall granting permission to a disavowed and a goblin to build fires on my land."

The silence that followed crackled like the flames between them. Bram measured the distance to his weapon, calculating his odds if this came to violence. The Lycani would be faster, stronger in his wolf form. Even at full strength, Bram would have found him a challenging opponent. In his current state . . .

"I apologize for the deception," Bram said finally, holding out his hand in greeting. "Bram. And this is Goby."

The Lycani gave a firm shake in return without changing his suspicious glare. "Bekh."

"We'll be out by morning. I'm tracking someone," Bram offered, hoping it would help cover the sting of his earlier lie.

"Someone who went into the Twisted Forest," Bekh stated rather than asked.

Bram's surprise must have shown on his face, because the Lycani's mouth twitched in what might have been a smile.

"How do you know that?"

"Call it a hunch. Your scent is . . . wrong," Bekh said. "Not entirely disavowed. Not entirely something else. And you travel with a goblin who wears a basket of carrots, like armor." His amber gaze shifted to Goby.

The goblin glared back defiantly.

That was the second time Bekh had called Bram disavowed. He understood the reason, but that's not what happened. Only the Heptad could do that. Yralissa had done something else. But what? That was the question.

"These are unusual times," Bekh continued. "The forest is restless. Strangers cross our lands with increasing frequency. But usually trying to skirt the danger, not head straight for it as you are."

"I'm looking for a woman," Bram said. "She has light hair, pale skin. An informant said she headed for the forest, and she may have passed this way two or three days ago."

Bekh shook his head. He tapped his temple. "Neither I nor my pack have seen anyone matching that description. We speak to each other across distances. If any had seen her, I would know. Especially if she has the power to do . . . whatever she did to you."

"This is not her work." Disgust at the thought of Rowena being charged with Yralissa's actions. Hope rose in Bram's chest, though. If Rowena hadn't been seen in the Lycani territory, it could mean she hadn't made it even this far.

But where was she then?

"Grimhold, a village at the edge of the forest, has a mage—powerful, wise," Bekh said. "He has helped my pack on many occasions. He might be able to guide you through the forest, if you're set on searching there."

"A mage?" Like Fidessa. Bram couldn't keep the distaste from his voice.

Bekh's expression hardened immediately. "You speak as if the word itself is poison."

"They're frauds," Bram said dismissively. "Mimicking true enchantment with potions and parlor tricks."

The Lycani's eyes flashed fully amber now, no longer bothering to hide his nature. "Not everyone is blessed with natural gifts. Some must work for their power." His lips pulled back slightly, revealing teeth that seemed sharper than they should be.

"And then use that power against the innocent." Bram crossed his arms over his chest. He may not have all his abilities, but he wasn't helpless. Not even now.

"Your prejudice is unbecoming of one who walks these lands. The mage I speak of has saved many lives, including those of my pack. He deserves your respect, not your contempt."

The rebuke landed. Bram had never considered his views on mages as prejudice. Simply a fact. Yet here was this Lycani, defending an unenchanted with more skill than himself.

How could Bram judge anyone? Was he not in need of help himself?

"You're right," Bram admitted. Wrong was wrong. "If this mage has earned your respect, then he deserves a chance to earn mine as well."

The tension in Bekh's posture eased slightly. "We will watch for your woman. If she crosses our territory, we will know of it." He gestured toward the fish on the spit. "You should eat. The night will be cold."

Without another word, the Lycani melted back into the trees, leaving only the rustling of leaves to mark his passage.

Goby hopped down from his basket and scurried over to Bram, his expression a mix of annoyance and reproach.

"What has you so angry?" Bram asked, turning his attention to the goblin.

"Goby know village," he grumbled, jabbing a finger in the direction the wolf-shifter had gone. "No need wolf."

Bram sighed, feeling the weight of the day's journey in every muscle. "I'm sorry, Goby. I should have listened to you."

The goblin's eyes widened in surprise, then narrowed suspiciously. "No one sorry. Not for Goby."

"This one is." Bram checked the fish, finding them flaky and ready. He removed the spit from the fire and offered the first trout to Goby. "There's a lot I still need to learn. About these mountains. About who I can trust." About his homeland. He met the goblin's gaze steadily. "About myself."

Goby accepted the fish with cautious hands, uncaring of the heat. His suspicion gradually gave way to something closer to satisfaction. "You learn slow. But learn."

The appraisal drew a tired laugh from Bram. "I suppose that's true."

They ate in companionable silence as night fell around them, the forest transforming into a realm of shadow and Masah's gentle glow. The fire crackled between them, a small circle of warmth and light in the vast darkness of the Veilrunes.

Regardless of the hour, they would rest, then continue to the village.

Where Bram would have to ask for help from a mage. And pray he wasn't too late to find Rowena.

For now, he had fish and fire and the unexpected companionship of a carrot-hoarding goblin.

BRAM AND GOBY finished their meal, dowsed the fire carefully, and left to find Grimhold. Only two marks later, the village appeared through the trees. A cramped collection of stone and timber structures huddled beneath the looming shadow of the Twisted Forest. Thick plumes of chimney smoke hung in the air like silent warnings, refusing to dissipate in the mountain chill.

Bram paused at the treeline, studying the settlement with narrowed eyes. The place set his instincts on edge. A malevolence, unseen but tangible, hovered. The village existed in a carved-out area of safety, yet with two borders along the Twisted Forest. Weathered buildings crowded together like they huddled for warmth, their windows dark and suspicious.

"Not good place," Goby whispered, pressing closer to Bram's leg.

A knot of worry had taken residence in Bram. He searched the buildings, too cramped to identify one from another. "We need that mage if we're going to find Rowena."

He marched ahead, shoulders back. This was not a time for indecision.

A group of villagers passed near their position; faces etched with hardship. Their clothes were practical and worn, patched in multiple places. One man spat on the ground near a building with symbols carved above its door—protective wards. Or they were meant to be. None of the markings were familiar.

False hope sold by charlatans no doubt.

"Stay close," Bram murmured to Goby.

The goblin tugged his pack higher on his back. "Goby no like."

"Neither do I."

Conversations quieted as they passed. Hard eyes followed their progress through narrow streets that stank of tannery waste and rotting vegetables. Elflings were nowhere to be seen. Probably kept indoors. If they existed.

They turned a corner and a weathered sign swayed about halfway down on the left. Its painted mortar and pestle faded but still recognizable. The apothecary.

Relief flashed through Bram, but it was short-lived. Heavy wooden shutters covered the windows, and a hand-painted sign hung from the door: *Closed until dawnlight.*

"Gone." Goby's observation unnecessary.

Bram stared at the door, frustration building in his chest. So close. Now they would have to wait until morning.

Bram had tried to keep his hopes down. The disappointment flooding through his veins proved his failure. Besides helping to locate Rowena, he'd given too much thought to getting help for himself.

A group of men emerged from a nearby building, their loud voices carrying through the street. One spotted Bram and nudged his companions, gesturing toward the strangers.

"You lost?" The question came from a stocky man with a scarred face. His beard more gray than brown, and his gaze held no welcome.

"Just passing through," Bram replied neutrally, feeling Goby press tighter against his leg. "Looking for the mage who keeps this shoppe."

The men exchanged glances. "Read the sign. Won't be around till morning," one said.

The scarred man stepped closer, sneering at where Goby huddled. The goblin slid further behind Bram.

"What's that you got there?"

Frustration and exhaustion made Bram's patience thin. He

shifted subtly, placing himself more firmly between Goby and the men. "My traveling companion."

A ripple of disgust rolled off the group. The atmosphere changed from suspicious to hostile.

"We don't allow goblins in Grimhold," the scarred man spat. "Filthy creatures. Steal anything not nailed down."

Rage flashed hot beneath Bram's skin, an emotion too sudden and powerful.

"He's with me," Bram stated. He promised Goby protection, and he would gladly give it. "We'll be on our way as soon as we've spoken with the mage."

The scarred man's hand drifted to the knife at his belt, a movement echoed by his companions. "Don't mind the disavowed. But that," he jerked his chin toward Goby, "waits outside the village."

Disavowed. Someone else who saw him that way. Before Bram could respond, a weathered voice cut through the tension. "Enough, Mason."

An elderly woman stood in the doorway of a nearby building, her face lined with decades of harsh weather. Despite her age, she stood straight as a spear, her gaze sharp as she surveyed the confrontation.

"Innkeeper," the scarred man, Mason, acknowledged her with obvious reluctance. "This doesn't concern you."

"When you threaten to spill blood in my street, it concerns me." She fixed her gaze on Bram. "You looking for a meal and lodging?"

"Yes, but—"

"Then come inside and leave these fools to their posturing." She turned without waiting for a response, disappearing back into what Bram now recognized as a tavern and inn. Two doors down from the Apothecary. Good.

The invitation would avoid the confrontation, but Bram

hesitated. Did she welcome Goby as well? Prejudice clearly ran deep in Grimhold.

Goby tugged at his sleeve. "Go wait shadows," the goblin whispered.

Before Bram could protest, Goby darted away. Out of sight in a flash. He vanished into the space between two buildings, leaving Bram alone with the hostile villagers.

Mason's expression twisted with disgust. "Smart beast. Knows its place."

It took every ounce of Bram's control not to reach for his dagger. "This isn't over," he promised quietly, then turned and strode into the tavern.

Inside, the atmosphere was marginally warmer than the village streets, though conversations quieted as Bram entered. The fireplace at the far end and a handful of torches along the walls, flickered light across rough wooden tables where a dozen or so patrons hunched over their meals. The smell of roasting meat and strong ale couldn't quite mask the underlying odor of unwashed bodies and wet wool.

The innkeeper gestured him toward a small table in the corner. "Sit. I'll bring you something hot."

Bram obeyed, positioning himself with his back to the wall and a clear view of both the entrance and the other patrons. Tired. Bored. Most only seemed to notice their own bowls. A couple twitched or darted too many glances at others. More from their own fears it seemed.

The woman returned moments later with a wooden bowl of stew and a hunk of dark bread. "Eat," she instructed.

"Thank you." Bram's gaze drifted toward the window, searching for any sign of Goby in the deepening twilight. "I need to know where—"

"Your companion will be fine," she interrupted. "The shadows are kinder than Mason and his ilk."

Bram studied her more carefully. There was something in her manner that spoke of more perception than he'd initially credited her with. "You saw him?"

"Old Meggy's lived in Grimhold for sixty-eight years," she replied, tapping her chest. "There's little I haven't seen, especially these days." She lowered her voice. "This close to Anomie, with the Twisted Forest at our backs, creatures of all kinds pass through. I help where I can."

She winked and ambled off, leaving Bram to his meal.

The stew was better than he expected. Rich with root vegetables and gamey meat he suspected might be rabbit. He tore into the bread, soaking up the broth.

"Do you get much trouble from Anomie?" Bram asked when Meggy returned with a tankard of ale.

"It's a half day's travel south. Too close to avoid its troubles." Her expression darkened. "I'd hold out to find your place as an Oraku elsewhere. That place makes this village seem like Caelus itself. No laws but the queen's. Streets are filled with thieves and killers."

She glanced around the tavern. "Many here fled from there, bringing their fears and prejudices with them. Others come lookin' for what they can take back for a profit."

Movement near the kitchen door caught Bram's attention. A flash of gray-green skin and yellow eyes, peering cautiously around the corner. Why had Goby come inside? The goblin's gaze fixed on a basket of vegetables near the hearth, where several carrots lay atop a pile of turnips.

If Goby was caught stealing . . .

The goblin darted from his hiding place, moving with speed across the tavern floor. Bram swept the room, hoping no one paid attention.

Goby's small hands closed around two carrots, tucking them under his arm in one fluid motion. But he wasn't fast enough.

One of the patrons, a thin man with a sour expression, spotted the movement and leapt to his feet with a shout.

"Goblin! Thief!"

Chaos erupted. Chairs scraped against the wooden floor as men rose, reaching for weapons. Goby froze, terror widening his eyes as he realized he'd been spotted.

Quick. A distraction. Bram upended his table.

The bowl of stew crashed to the floor, the sound and sudden movement drawing all eyes.

"My purse!" Bram shouted. "Someone's taken my purse!"

In the momentary confusion, as patrons looked between Bram and his overturned table, Goby slipped away, disappearing through the kitchen door.

Bram made a show of checking his belt, then held up his coin pouch with a sigh. "Never mind. It was just caught in my cloak."

Suspicious glares met his mock-innocent expression, but the distraction had served its purpose. Goby was gone. The alarm attributed to Bram's false claim.

Meggy's knowing gaze met his. She said nothing, but a barely perceptible nod told Bram she understood what he'd done.

After returning the table upright, and paying for his meal, as well as the broken bowl, Bram made his way back to woods near the village edge. Darkness had fallen completely now, the forest a wall of deeper shadows.

He found Goby waiting at the spot where they'd first emerged from the trees, exactly where he'd expected.

"Got food," Goby announced proudly, producing the stolen carrots.

"That was reckless." Though Bram could feign no real anger. "You could have been caught."

"Goby hungry." He shrugged, already crunching into one of his prizes. "Village bad."

"You still have half a basket from the castle." Bram sighed and settled beside the goblin on a fallen log. "But, yes, village bad."

They wouldn't find shelter in Grimhold. Bram would rather sleep rough than risk Goby anyway. Tomorrow, he would return alone to speak with the mage.

For now, they would make camp at the forest's edge, under stars partially obscured by the smoke of a village.

Goby finished his stolen meal and curled up beside him. Bram stared toward the Twisted Forest. Dark trees reaching above rooftops north of the village. He couldn't fathom that Rowena might have traveled into the ancient trees and warped magic. She could be trapped. Or worse.

The thought tightened the ever-present knot in his chest.

Tomorrow couldn't come soon enough.

32

ESME

ESME WORKED METHODICALLY, grinding dried moonflower petals into fine powder with her mortar and pestle. The work had made her rebozo too warm, and she'd tossed the striped shawl over a chair. Yellow stains spotted her blouse from the chamomile flowers, but the color would just blend into the embroidery work.

Morning light filtered through the small window above her workbench, casting golden patterns across the dried herbs hanging from the ceiling. The familiar scents of rosemary, elderflower, and mountain sage enveloped her like an old friend's embrace, bringing with them memories of countless remedies mixed and spells woven within these walls.

The apothecary had been her sanctuary for a year now. A place where villagers came for remedies yet never ventured beyond the shoppe's front. Never questioned the strange lights sometimes visible beneath the door to her private quarters. Never wondered why certain ailments healed faster than they should.

The bell jangled over the door, moments after they'd

opened. She listened. If the need was urgent, she might have to help. Gabe's greeting held no hint of concern. Another customer seeking relief from winter's approaching chill, no doubt.

Esme continued her work, letting her husband handle the front as always. His voice carried a warm authority that put people at ease. A gift she'd never possessed despite her efforts to cultivate it.

The answer came from an unfamiliar accent. Deep, melodic, with the subtle cadence of someone not from the mountains. Not from anywhere near Grimhold.

"Are you the mage of this establishment," the stranger said. "I was told he might help me locate someone."

Esme's hands stilled. Something in the voice raised the fine hairs on her arms. She set down her pestle and moved silently to the door separating her workroom from the shop, pressing her ear against the weathered wood.

"I'm Gabe," her husband replied, his tone carefully neutral. "And you are?"

"Bram." A pause. "I'm searching for a woman who may have passed through here. Blonde, amber eyes, northern accent. She would have been headed toward the Twisted Forest."

Esme's heart quickened. Travelers *seeking* the forest were rare enough to be noteworthy, but something in the stranger's tone suggested more than a simple search for a lost companion.

"The forest is no place for anyone, especially now," Gabe said. "It's never been stable, but lately it's worse. The paths shift multiple times each day. Trees appear where none stood before. Even the locals who've foraged from its edges for generations won't venture beyond the first line of twisted oaks."

"I must find her fast, then," the stranger, Bram, replied. "A Lycani named Bekh directed me to you. Said you might be able to help me track her."

Bekh? Esme's pulse quickened further. For the wolf-shifter alpha to send someone to them meant this was no ordinary traveler. The packs kept to themselves, protecting their territories from outsiders with fierce determination. For Bekh to direct a stranger to Grimhold . . . to them. It had to be for more than someone lost on the trail.

"I might be able to help," Gabe said. He kept his tone light, but she could tell he tensed. "I'll need more information. Who is this woman to you? And why does she seek the forest?"

A long silence followed. Esme could almost feel the stranger weighing how much to reveal. She pressed her palm against the door, extending her senses beyond the physical. A whisper of enchantment, the barest thread, brushed against her consciousness, then abruptly vanished, like a candle flame suddenly extinguished. Her spell didn't work. No ordinary stranger, indeed.

"She's Lunara, and her name is Rowena," Bram finally said, his voice dropping lower. "She's fleeing from someone in the mountains, and I'm concerned that either Tanith or Ha'mon's hunters might find her before I do."

A small gasp escaped Esme's lips before she could stop it. Tanith—creator of Anomie, the deposed Queen of Kur. Ha'mon —King of Kur, imprisoned under the barrows of Mortus, who had no qualms about making his queen a monster. Those names were not to be spoken if someone wanted to stay safe.

Esme's stomach threatened to reject her morning oats.

The floorboard beneath her foot creaked as she shifted her weight, betraying her presence.

"Who else is here?" Bram's voice sharpened.

"My wife." Gabe sighed. "Esme, you might as well come out. This concerns you as well."

After a deep breath, Esme grabbed her rebozo and pushed

open the door. The stranger stood tall by the counter, his druid heritage evident in his graceful posture, and an undercurrent signature of Primary power, despite appearing disavowed. Something seemed off—a dissonance she couldn't immediately identify. Perhaps it was his black leather warrior garb instead of a typical plain brown robe. Or the way his golden eyes fixed on her with the intensity of a hawk's spotting movement in the grass.

Golden eyes on a disavowed. Odd.

"You shouldn't speak those names so casually," she said, meeting his gaze directly. She finished wrapping the shawl to cross over her front and tuck in the back, leaving her hands free. "Especially not in this village. Walls have ears, and Grimhold is not kind to those who draw unwanted attention."

The druid studied her, suspicion clear in his expression. "And why would the names concern you?"

Esme exchanged a glance with Gabe, who gave a slight nod. Years of protective secrecy warred with the immediate need to establish trust. She and Gabe had helped many escaping persecution over the years. And she wouldn't stop now.

"Come to the back," she decided, gesturing toward her workroom. "This is not a conversation to have in the shoppe."

Once inside, with the door firmly closed and the small window shuttered, Esme lit three candles with a wave of her hand. She needed no incantation, no focus object like her husband. Just pure intent manifested through will. And she shouldn't have done so in front of a stranger. Where was her mind?

The druid's eyes widened slightly. "You're a witch."

"Yes." There wasn't any reason for her to lie at this point. She pulled three stools around her workbench.

"And far more powerful than me." Gabe smiled wryly. The

lines around his dark eyes, despite being only nineteen summers, gave proof that his face lit up with joy more often than hers. "If either of us can help you find your Rowena, it's Esme."

"Though he's the one who deals with the public," Esme added. "So, I'd appreciate not speaking too openly about my skills."

"If I'm not mistaken, you're still holding secrets of your own," Gabe said. "For your companion to be hunted by those from Mortus, she's no ordinary individual."

"Trust can be fickle." Bram remained standing, his hand resting casually near his dagger. "I've come based on the Lycani's recommendation, but witches and mages don't typically concern themselves with helping the enchanted."

The accusation stung, but Esme understood his caution. She didn't understand those long, pointed fingernails, though.

"I know something of being persecuted by others out of fear because of what they don't understand." She gestured to the stool again. "Please, sit. Tell me about Rowena, and why you believe she's headed for the Twisted Forest."

Reluctantly, Bram lowered himself onto the stool. "What knowledge do you have of the Burning Moon or the prophecy connected to it?"

More than he would believe. No one living within leagues of Grimhold would bring up that topic. He piqued her interest.

"Quite a bit," Esme said quietly, watching for his reaction. "The one that some believe speaks of the moon-born. Though many opinions abound about how they are connected."

Surprise flickered across Bram's face. "Most who remember anything have heard no more than whispers."

"I know of it because it directly concerns me." The words felt strange to speak aloud after so long of carefully guarded silence. Somehow, this stranger made her feel safe to do so. "As does the Burning Moon, that is arriving this coming Reaping."

Bram's eyes narrowed. "What makes you say so . . . How old are you?"

A bitter smile touched Esme's lips. The urge to tell the truth so strong, she couldn't deny it. "I was born during the Burning Moon seventeen winters ago, as was my twin brother." She twisted the simple copper ring on her finger—a nervous habit from childhood. Only Gabe knew of her birth. Until now. Never would she have believed she'd be so open, but something about Bram almost called to her.

"A moon-born witch." Bram glanced around the room as if the idea confused him.

Esme understood others believed the prophecy was only for the enchanted, but most forgot witches held some of that power as well. Tainted as it was from Tanith's line.

"Your twin is a witch as well?" Bram asked.

"Yes, but his abilities have not manifested as strongly as mine."

"Interesting." Bram's brows furrowed, seeming to be contemplating her information.

Esme's pulse kicked up like a rabbit on the run. She could have just put her family in danger. But an idea formed—one that could keep her and her loved ones safe.

"And are you moon-born as well?" Bram asked, nodding to Gabe.

"No," Gabe answered, a snorted chuckle. "I'm but a mage. Talented enough, but nothing like Esme or her brother."

"We've been careful to hide our heritage," Esme continued, hoping she had picked up on the right cues. "That is valuable information to Tanith's hunters if they discover the truth—as I suspect is the *real* reason you are concerned for Rowena."

Bram leaned forward, elbows on his knees. He pinned Esme with a stare, searching. Too long. "That is true. But if you're aware of the extra dangers, why stay in a village like this? Surely there are safer places for you."

Pain flashed through Esme's chest at the question. Old wounds that never fully healed. "My brother Ean is away searching for someone. A girl he saw once when we were elflings. We'd been abandoned in the forest, and finding her seems to give him purpose, something to hope for."

"How old were you when you were abandoned?" Bram asked.

"Seven winters." Her voice softened with the familiar old sorrow. "Our stepmother convinced our father we were cursed. That our natural mother's death after our birth was punishment for bringing witches into the world."

The memory surfaced unwanted. Her father's anguished face, hunched shoulders as he trudged away, leaving two young elflings alone among the twisted trees. Their frightened cries left unanswered as darkness fell. She and Ean tried as hard as they could to find their way home, but the forest toyed with them until they were too exhausted to go on.

"How did you get out of the forest?" Bram asked.

He seemed so genuinely interested, something inside of Esme begged to connect with him. "Gabe. The three of us had been friends before, and when he found out that we were gone, he came looking for us. All of nine winters himself."

Gabe reached across the table to wrap his dark hand over her lighter brown one. "I helped them move to the edge of the forest, where it doesn't shift that often. They still had to survive that place. She's amazing."

She hated and loved it when he praised her like that. Gabe was her rock. He and Ean were her only family, and she'd do anything for them.

"Rowena hadn't known she was moon-born when we met," Bram said. "I've met another recently who is still unaware of who she is—for now. Were you aware there were others besides you?" Bram held her gaze.

She couldn't get over his eyes. Not silver, as they should be. "I never gave it much thought, to be honest. I guess I figured it was too dangerous for us to speak of it, so I never considered there might be more."

"How do *you* know of the others?" Gabe asked. "Are you searching for them?"

Smart question. Esme needed to exercise more caution. She wasn't acting like herself. Normally, she was the one taking such care to protect her identity for the safety of her family.

"You are correct, the second Burning Moon is eminent. I was tasked by the Heptad to find the moon-born and Armor of Caelus. "

"You're a hunter?" Gabe asked.

Bram raised his hand. "No, nothing like that."

"You are not disavowed, either." Esme didn't have to ask. Somehow, she already knew.

Bram pinched his lips tight and twisted away for a long moment. "I'm not sure."

"What does that mean?" Gabe asked, leaning forward. "I would guess you'd know if your Primary enchantment had been stripped from you."

Bram scoffed. "I'm aware that something has happened. I'm just not sure what. This girl your brother searches for, is she moon-born as well?"

His voice dipped to a frosty, dangerous level with his abrupt change of subject. Esme rose from her stool, casually moving to the end of her work table. From the corner of her eye, she noticed Gabe tense as well. "I don't know. I didn't even believe she existed until a year ago."

"I apologize." Bram held up his hand. "I didn't mean to speak so harshly. It's just that . . . who I am is complicated. And I don't want to frighten you. It's just that so many moon-born have come to my attention lately. It took me months to find the first."

Gabe stood up at that, moving himself to Esme's side. "We've given you a lot of information that puts our lives at risk. We'll give no more until you explain."

"I understand." Bram rubbed his forehead. Almost as if he searched for answers. He remained silent for far too long.

Had she made a huge mistake?

When he dropped his hand, he met each of their stares in turn. "Have you heard of the Seeker?"

Gabe huffed. "From the tale to scare elflings?"

Esme bit the inside of her lip. She wasn't so sure it was just a story.

"Yes. Though the details in those stories are fabrications, the Seeker is real. Or I was until recently."

Esme twisted her ring. That was frightening. "You don't match the description. The Seeker is said to have horns and claws." She glanced at his hands again.

"Until two days ago, I did. Somehow, a disavowed, or possibly a full Primary Druid disguising herself as disavowed, poisoned me with something." Bram's shoulders rounded just a finger's width, but the slight movement made him seem so much more vulnerable.

"There are other rumors as well," Gabe said, resting his hand on Esme's back. "Like searching for the moon-born to destroy them, cleansing villages of whoever the Heptad deems unworthy . . . "

"Helping to release Ha'mon," Esme added. If any of those were true, they had just invited death through their door.

Bram shook his head, his gaze lifting to the ceiling. "I am none of those things. While my appearance can be frightening, I assure you, my purpose is to help the moon-born and gather the

Armor of Caelus, so they are ready to fulfill the prophecy, not to bring them harm."

Esme twisted to meet Gabe's gaze. She wanted to believe him. His heart seemed to match the tone of his words. But did her husband believe him? Bram had made that comment about witches and mages earlier.

Gabe rubbed his tongue along the edges of his teeth. He did that when he thought through difficult problems. He wasn't convinced. "Yet, a disavowed had the power to affect you?"

Bram huffed with a half grin. "She pricked my hand with a lance of some type that injected something. I don't know what. It halted my transition just as it began."

"That must have been painful," Esme said.

Bram nodded. "Bekh smelled something wrong with my blood. Then told me of the mage who might be able to help me, but I suspect he was actually sending me to you."

She believed him. "If I can help, I will."

Gabe rubbed Esme's shoulders. "Are you sure about this?"

She met his gaze, loving as always, and her heart warmed. She couldn't help but smile. "We do what we can to help those in need. Bram is no different."

"You are a gem bigger than that emerald Ean carries." Gabe kissed her on her temple and returned to his stool.

"Your brother carries an emerald?" Bram sat up taller.

"It's a long story, but it's a loose stone we found in another witch's possession. She had a great deal of gemstones, actually," Esme said. "Since she had tried to kill Ean, we figured taking a few of her collection was worth the pain she'd caused."

"That was a year ago," Gabe added. "We sold several of them to start the apothecary."

"And that's when he saw the girl he seeks?"

"That's when we learned she was real. He saw her years before, not long after we'd been abandoned." Esme sighed heavily. "Finding her has been his obsession. He fought the forest's changes for years. Then last year, he finally found the witch's cottage again, where he'd first seen the girl. That experience nearly cost his life. But he continues to search, convinced he *has* to find this mystery girl."

"That she needs his help," Gabe added.

"And you stay, waiting for his return," Bram guessed correctly.

"My family is all I have in this world, and they are worth everything to me," she replied simply. "Gabe and I maintain the shoppe, help where we can, and wait for news of Ean."

Bram's expression darkened with what might have been understanding. He rubbed at his forehead; a gesture that seemed unconscious each time he did it. If he truly was the Seeker and was supposed to have horns, that would make sense. Esme had dealt with severe injuries where phantom limbs haunted their past hosts for years.

"You're in pain," Esme said, lifting her hand. "May I?"

He hesitated, then inclined his head in permission. Esme reached out, her fingers hovering inches from his brow. As a witch, she had an inherited ability to access limited powers, nothing like an enchanted, but still the signature within Bram nearly flew out at her. A foreign presence entwined with his life force, something powerful, and not kind.

She drew back in surprise. "The enchantment flowing through your blood is at war with itself. There are multiple poisons battling against each other, and binding something essential within you."

Bram's jaw tightened. "Can you help?"

Esme closed her eyes, reaching deeper with her senses. The magic resisted her probe that time, slippery as quicksilver and twice as toxic.

"No." She hated to admit that. "This is ancient and complex.

Only a Primary Druid could hope to unravel it without killing you in the process."

"Farryn," Bram murmured, something like hope flickering in his eyes.

"If you know one of the Primary Fae willing to help you, then you have a chance," Esme said. "What I fear is the longer this poison stays in your system, the harder it will be to reverse. If it can be done at all."

"How long do I have before that happens?" Bram asked.

Esme held her breath. The plea emanating from his eyes nearly broke her heart. But she couldn't lie to him. "I don't know. I truly don't. The best I can say is not to wait. Go to Saganus at your first opportunity."

Bram nodded slowly, seeming to accept what she said, while also in deep thought. "I must find Rowena first."

"If she truly entered the Twisted Forest without guidance, I fear she may be lost forever," Gabe said, moving to stand beside his wife. "How long has she been missing?"

Bram clearly cared about her more than just because he'd been charged to find moon-born.

"She headed this way three, maybe four days ago now."

"And no one in the village has seen her?" Esme asked. "A woman like the one you describe would be noticed in Grimhold."

Bram shook his head. "I've asked around. No one will admit to seeing her, at least."

"We're the only village so near to the forest. If anyone had seen her there would be talk." It was the only hope Esme could offer. "It's likely she didn't make it this far."

"Then I need to find her before she does," Bram said firmly. "She could have taken another route."

"There are those who harvest all along the border. They

would mention seeing a stranger. The biggest entertainment this village has is gossip," Esme said.

"That's the truth." Gabe snorted, his half amused, half frustrated sound Esme knew so well. "If no one has seen her, then perhaps she didn't come this way at all."

Esme nodded her agreement. "What will you do?"

Bram stood, pacing the small confines of the workroom. His movements were fluid yet somehow constrained, as if the poison in his body physically fought against the bonds flowing in his veins. His expression hardened with resolve. "I won't enter the Twisted Forest. Not yet. If I get trapped inside, I'll be unable to help anyone. There's a piece of armor not far. I'll retrieve that first. Someone I promised Rowena I would help is also there. Both are in a castle high in the mountains. From that position I can keep searching."

"Safi," Esme said, the name coming to her lips unbidden.

Bram froze mid-stride, his gaze snapping to hers. "How did you know that name?"

The question startled her as much as her own knowledge.

"I . . . Don't know. Sometimes names come to me. Faces. Fragments of lives not my own." She pressed her fingers to her temples, where a dull ache was beginning to form. "I've always thought it was part of being a witch, or moon-born."

Bram rubbed his forehead again.

"It's your horns," she whispered. "Their loss is giving you that pain."

Bram's face went carefully blank. "Among other things."

The flash of raw pain in his eyes, shuttered quickly, told her plenty. "I'll prepare something that might help," she offered, turning to her shelves of ingredients. "It won't remove the poison, but it might give some relief."

As she gathered the necessary components—winterroot for

numbing, dragonberry for resilience, foxmoss for spiritual protection—Esme felt Gabe's familiar presence at her elbow.

"The armor he seeks," he murmured, low enough that only she could hear.

"Yes." She kept her voice equally quiet.

"That proves what we've deciphered from the prophecy."

Esme considered that as she mixed the ingredients, adding a drop of her own blood for potency. If the armor Bram sought was indeed one of the *seven*, spoke of in the prophecy, then perhaps there was still hope for what was to come. Those without enchantment, like Gabe, may be restored.

She turned back to Bram and handed the vial of shimmering amethyst liquid to him. "This will ease the phantom pains. A couple drops on your tongue. No more. It won't last long, a day at most, but it might help. I wish I could be sure I have the right blend. If you stayed a day or two, I could adjust it if necessary.

"Thank you." He tucked the vial into a pouch at his belt. "I must get going. I've lingered too long already, and I have a long journey ahead. And a companion at the edge of town I must collect."

"Your goblin friend from the tavern last night," Gabe said, a grin quirking his lips. "News travels quickly."

A faint smile also touched Bram's lips. "Waiting with enough stolen carrots to last him a week. Thankfully, he refuses to enter Grimhold again."

"Smart creature," Esme remarked. "This village has little kindness for those who are different."

As they walked Bram to the door, a growing certainty formed within Esme that their paths had crossed for a reason beyond chance. The prophecy was unfolding, piece by piece, drawing its players together.

Bram waited an extra moment at the threshold. "Like you,

my identity is usually well-guarded. I trust we have a mutual agreement about that?"

"Of course," Esme answered. It gave her comfort to have confided in someone who understood. She would not break his trust, nor would he break hers. Without a doubt the belief settled.

"When the time comes," Bram continued. "You and Ean will need to join the others. And he'll need to bring the emerald. It's not a piece of the armor, as far as I'm aware, but I have a feeling it's important."

"I understand," Esme said, instinctively lacing her fingers with Gabe's.

"How might I stay in touch without bringing attention to you? I may not return to this area for some time."

The unexpected kindness touched something deep in Esme's heart.

She took his hand and drew a sigil on his palm with her finger. "Focus on my name as you trace this mark. I'll hear you wherever you are. Though you'll have to trust I got the message. It only works one way."

"Does this work for anyone?" He grinned.

"It is personal, and can only be given directly by a witch," she said. "If it allowed me to contact someone else at will, I would have tattooed one on my brother."

"Worth a try if he returns," Gabe said. His grin contagious.

Esme stared after Bram as he disappeared down a side street. She turned to find concern etched in Gabe's eyes.

"He carries part of our secret now," she said quietly.

Gabe nodded, reaching out to tuck a strand of hair behind her ear. "You trust him."

A statement. He didn't question her.

"I'm not sure why." She strolled back to the workroom, mind already shifting to what needed done. "But his arrival has drawn attention. Did you see those two watching the shoppe this morning?"

"Bram asked questions at the tavern last night," Gabe confirmed. "They'll connect us to him and Rowena now."

Fear coiled in Esme's stomach. "Tanith's spies."

"Most likely." Gabe crossed to the small cupboard where they kept the maps. "We should leave tonight, after dark."

Esme nodded slowly, her thoughts turning to their carefully maintained escape plan—supplies cached in the mountains, routes memorized, identities prepared. "And Ean? If he returns to find us gone . . ."

Pain flashed across Gabe's face.

"He knows how to get in touch. I'm glad you held that back from Bram." He unrolled a weathered map across the workbench. "Besides, I fear for him if the Burning Moon comes, and he's still searching alone."

"You think we should find him first?"

"I think the two of you have a better chance of survival together than apart." He traced a path along the map's faded lines. "If the rumors are true, and Tanith's hunters are gathering, no moon-born is safe. Particularly not one obsessed with finding a lost girl instead of protecting himself."

Esme's fingers traced the worn copper ring on her finger— the only thing she had from their mother. "We'll find him," she whispered, as much to herself as to Gabe. "And then we'll face whatever comes together."

As they bent their heads over the map, studying the routes and safe havens, Esme felt the weight of change settling around them. For a year, this apothecary had been their refuge. Now it would become just another memory. Another home abandoned. Another identity shed.

In a few hours, darkness would provide the cover they needed to slip away from Grimhold one final time. Until then, there were preparations to make, potions to pack, and a lifetime of secrets to conceal.

Esme took a deep breath and began to work, her hands steady despite the worry brewing a storm in her heart. She was a survivor, first and always. So was Ean, but she'd protected herself and Ean as elflings. She would find a way to protect him again, even if it meant leaving behind everything they had built.

They would survive. They always did.

The Burning Moon was coming. She'd been right about that.

But what about the rest?

33

BRAM

BRAM LEFT the apothecary with his mind churning. The witch's words echoed in his thoughts as he moved through Grimhold's hostile streets, keeping his steps measured despite the urgency pulling at him. No need to bring unwanted attention.

If Esme was right, if that woman in the castle had lied about Rowena's destination, then he'd wasted precious time chasing shadows.

And now he'd given his identity to a moon-born, exactly as the Heptad forbade. His list of mistakes had either grown longer, or he'd finally done something right.

The Twisted Forest loomed to the north, beyond the village boundary, ancient and foreboding. Bram paused, studying the ominous tangle of gnarled branches. Even from here, he could sense the wrongness of it—paths that shifted like living things, trees that whispered with voices not their own.

No, Rowena wouldn't have entered such a place alone. Not without absolute necessity. And she would have come through the village first, just as he had. He continued to the treeline at the base of the Veilrunes, to retrieve the goblin.

"Goby?" Bram called softly, scanning the underbrush. "I'm back."

Only silence answered him. He moved deeper into the trees, searching for any sign of his unlikely companion. The wicker basket that had held Goby's precious carrots was gone, along with any trace of the goblin himself.

Something unexpectedly heavy settled in Bram's chest. A hollow sensation that caught him off guard. When had the little thief's presence become something he would miss?

"Smart creature," Bram murmured to himself, echoing Esme's earlier words. "Better off finding your own way than following me back to danger."

Still, as he turned his steps toward the distant castle, the forest seemed emptier without Goby's yellow-eyed presence scampering ahead of him.

He took a moment to use Esme's elixir, uncorking the vile and sprinkling two drops of the shimmering liquid on his tongue. A slight bitterness, quickly covered by a minty aftertaste. Hopefully it worked to diminish his headache.

The journey back would be faster now that he knew the path. If he pushed hard, minimal rests, he could reach the castle before nightfall.

Another day where anything could be happening to Rowena. Another day, Safi remained captive, and suffering. Another day, he had done nothing to help either.

If Daenon and Fidessa were working together, as he suspected, retrieving the Sword of Justice was his only hope of standing against them.

That ruinous castle could hold the key for everything.

The mountain paths grew steeper as Bram left Grimhold and its suspicions behind. Twice he paused, the sensation of being watched prickling along his spine. Each time he scanned his surroundings, catching only the faintest movement among the trees. Perhaps Bekh or one of his pack, ensuring the stranger left their territory without incident.

Or perhaps something else entirely.

By afternoon, Bram had covered more ground than he'd expected, driven by a growing sense of urgency. Esme's amethyst potion had given him relief. He'd not had a headache since he'd used it.

Without the pain, his senses had sharpened, not to their former power, but enough to give him an edge he hadn't had before.

He considered testing the symbol she showed him to thank her, but he decided against it. That was better kept for a more important reason.

It was well after dark when the castle's silhouette appeared on the horizon. A jagged wound against the Masah-lit sky. Bram approached with caution, circling wide to study the structure from different angles. Guards patrolled the main gate in greater numbers than before and torches blazed along the intact sections of the curtain wall.

Fidessa was expecting trouble.

Bram approached the broken area where he and Goby had escaped. The gap remained, though new stones suggested a recent attempt at repairs. He slipped through without incident, pausing in the deep shadows to listen.

Voices carried from the direction of the barracks; rough, guttural sounds punctuated by harsh laughter. Bram risked a glance around the corner and found Fidessa's personal guards. They were not quite elven, not quite beast. Vanasi of some type. Fidessa probably bred them for loyalty to her above all else.

Bram counted six visible guards, but the noise suggested more inside. Too many to confront directly, especially with his powers still bound by Yralissa's magic. He needed stealth, not strength, if he was to find both Safi and the sword.

The left keep rose ahead of him, its upper third crumbled away like a broken tooth. It appeared abandoned. A perfect place for him to hide.

Bram kept to the shadows, moving silently across the open yard toward the keep's entrance. As he approached, two guards emerged from the doorway, their voices low. Bram pressed himself against the wall, barely breathing as they passed within arm's reach of his position.

Once they'd moved far enough away, he slipped inside. The interior was dark, illuminated only by occasional wall sconces burning low. Dust covered much of the stone floor, yet a clear path had been worn through it, evidence of regular patrols.

Bram followed the route, hoping it would lead him to the sword. Or to answers about Rowena's true location.

The stone hallway made a hard left turn without any doors or windows. There were more guards ahead, arguing amongst themselves about something Bram couldn't decipher. He eased himself along the wall to peer around the corner. A set of stairs rose from a dead-end hall. At least six guards milled about with more lining the steps.

They jostled each other, changing positions. Some went up the stairs, some came down, and all seemed tired or bored. Though they stayed in the area.

Guarding something. Something important to require so many.

Bram tapped his fingers along his thigh. He had surprise. If he confronted them, he might beat them, even with their numbers. But if he ended up finding nothing, it would waste his time and draw Fidessa's attention.

She had to know he had left. No need to announce his return.

He waited for a heartbeat with his back to the stone, wrestling with his decision. Bram sorted through his memories of the castle as he arrived that first morning. One remaining turret, instead of four. The right keep, well-maintained and occupied. This left keep, smaller, with the top third crumbled away. It had seemed abandoned.

Then why so many guards?

Would Fidessa hide something as valuable as the Sword of Justice in such a destroyed area. Possibly.

If not for the gathered guards, he may not have had the thought.

There were no other corridors, only the crowded stairwell. He closed his eyes, visualizing how he'd battle each guard, until something tapped on his shoulder.

Bram ducked and pivoted, ready to punch, but nothing was in the hall. Then a small snicker forced his gaze to the top of the wall. Goby clung to the stone, just above where Bram had stood a moment before.

"Goby!" Bram released a long breath. "I could have hurt you."

"No see." The goblin shimmied down to the floor. "Goby help. This way."

Bram followed the fast creature as he sped down the hall on all fours toward outside. "Where are you going?"

"Follow."

Goby had known the way before. Fighting through those squealing guards would take time. He could trust his friend.

A small part of him also bristled at how the goblin had snuck up on him, but he brushed that thought aside.

Outside, Goby disappeared through a cellar door near the ground on the backside of the keep. Bram followed. Goby could steal through the castle, watching everything that went on without anyone knowing. Admirable.

They hurried to a place where walls had tumbled away, exposing a set of broken stairs, narrow, crumbling, half-concealed behind a warped door. The steps led to the top of the battlements at the front of the castle.

To the right, a walkway around the top wall. Twenty paces, and it crumbled to a pile of stones. To the left they had a solid path to where the keep cantilevered over the moat, resting against the curtain wall. They could climb along the angled walls to enter through the shattered top.

The low light made it impossible to see inside, so there would be no way to tell how many guards they might face. Doubtful they'd watch for anyone to enter from the damaged upper portion.

Bram dropped low, letting his fingers brush the stone for balance as he climbed the tilting wall. Goby scurried faster ahead and peered through a narrow window.

"No guards."

Bram craned his neck to stare at the goblin. "Are you sure?"

The few hairs on Goby's head bounced as he nodded with a wide grin.

Fidessa wasn't one to leave such a hole in her defenses. There had to be some sort of surprise inside. The jostling guards could have been a decoy to draw him into another trap.

This time he would be ready.

Once they crawled over the edge of the damaged walls, they found the main stairwell. Echoes from the growling and snorting guards travelled along the walls from the floors below.

Only one door remained closed. All others on the floor were either missing or hanging at odd angles.

Bram tried the handle.

Locked. No surprise.

He forced the handle harder and the lever snapped off in his hand. Bits of rusty dust covered his palm. Bram sighed, considering what to do. Quiet? Or fast?

He pointed to Goby. "Watch the stairs."

The goblin gave a puzzled look, but obeyed.

Bram braced himself, and charged the door, slamming against it with his shoulder. The hinges groaned, but held. He rubbed his aching arm. Changing tactics, he kicked the door, low near the broken handle.

Once. Nothing.

Again. A crack.

The third time, the door burst open. Splinters flew and dust clouded the air, as they rushed inside.

Even the bumbling guards had to have heard the crash.

The chamber was bare, except for a thread-bare tapestry hanging askew on the far wall, and a tall pedestal in the center. And sitting atop, a wooden box. Long. Familiar. The Sword of Justice rested inside.

He would have to carry the sword on his belt. Exposed.

Couldn't be helped.

He crossed the room in three strides. Eager. Relieved.

Rowena had broken the seal, so the lid flipped open with ease.

A wail erupted. High, piercing, bone-deep.

Goby bolted. Bram stumbled. He snatched the sword by the hilt, grip tight, and staggered out the door.

Its weight felt both familiar and strange. A connection to his former self that he'd feared lost forever. The metal hummed against his palm.

"Guards coming!" Goby hissed, tugging frantically at Bram's sleeve. "Lots!"

Shouts echoed from below as Fidessa's forces responded to the keening. In an automatic motion, Bram strapped the sword to his belt. "We need another way down."

Goby scampered along the battlement, peering over the edge. "There!" he pointed to where a debris slope leaned against the wall.

Not far. Not easy.

"Go," he told Goby. "I'll follow."

The goblin vanished in a blink, scrambling over the edge. Bram took a deep breath, swung over the battlement, and let go.

His legs absorbed the blow, but pain shot through his ankle.

Nothing seemed broken.

Goby appeared at his side, bouncing on his toes, excited. "Find girl now?"

Bram frowned, scanning the castle's many windows. "If she's here, Fidessa would keep her close. Controlled." His gaze settled on the right keep, where the queen's chambers were located. "She'd want her visible, but powerless."

"Kitchen," Goby said.

He could be wanting to refill his carrot stash. "Or the servants' quarters. We search there first."

Goby nodded eagerly. "Goby know way."

Of course. He knew every passage in the castle.

As they ran alongside each other, Bram in a crouch, the thought of how Goby had returned, stirred something in his chest.

"I thought you'd left," he whispered. "Why did you come back?"

Goby's eyes glowed from torchlight along the back wall of the keep. "Bram Good. Goby help."

Simple words. Heavy with meaning. He didn't deserve such loyalty as of late.

"Thank you," he managed, the words thick on his tongue.

Goby shrugged as if embarrassed, then scurried toward a narrow gap between two fallen stones. "This way."

Behind them, guards poured onto the battlements, torches

blazing as they searched for the intruders. Soon they would widen their search to the grounds below.

Bram followed Goby into the darkness, the Sword of Justice a comforting weight at his side. Safi was here, a certainty that settled in his bones.

He would get her out.

For Rowena's sake.

34

ROWENA

Rowena's second morning as Fidessa's prisoner began with the rattle of keys in her door. The idea of waking that way everyday forced her to choke down bile. She jerked upright on the narrow bed, fingers closing around the kitchen knife she'd hidden beneath her pillow, alongside the biscuits she'd swiped at dinner. When the unnamed guard entered, who all looked the same, with beady eyes too small for their bloated faces, she kept her expression neutral.

"Queen wants you," he grunted. "Follow me."

Rowena rose from the bed and tucked the knife into her waistband, concealed by her tunic. A slender hope against whatever awaited her, but better than nothing.

The guard turned down the hall leading away from the kitchen.

"Where are we heading?" Rowena asked, proud that her voice held steady despite the dread pooling in her stomach.

"Courtyard. Move." The guard prodded her with his club, forcing her to walk in front of him. A warning rather than a true blow.

"So, no breakfast today, then?" The guards didn't usually

provide any conversation worth having, but if she could get him talking a little, she might learn some piece of useful information.

"Not for you," the guard squealed with laughter, going on for much longer than necessary.

Rowena strode ahead, deciding that speaking further would be pointless. They traversed the winding corridors of the keep. Rowena did her best to memorize each turn. Down a flight of stairs, across a former grand hall now strewn with torn and faded tapestries, and through a heavy oak door that opened onto a courtyard she hadn't seen before.

Morning light spilled across the grassy expanse enclosed by the castle's crumbling walls. Unlike the main bailey where she'd entered two days before, this space felt intimate, almost like a garden carved from the wilderness. Yellow wildflowers dotted the grass. Birds called from nests tucked into crevices in the surrounding stonework.

And above it all, on a walkway connecting two sections of the keep, stood Fidessa.

She wasn't alone. Of course, Daenon stood by her side, but that wasn't where Rowena directed her gaze. On Fidessa's other side, half-turned as if wishing to disappear, stood Tephra.

"Tephra?" Rowena couldn't keep the shock from her voice. Relief flooded through her at first. Her traveling companion had survived, had perhaps come to help . . . but the sensation ebbed away when she saw the guilt etched across the Solara's face.

"Leave us," Fidessa commanded the guard, who bowed clumsily next to Rowena and retreated. The heavy door thudded closed, leaving her alone in the courtyard.

Fidessa smiled, the expression never reaching her eyes.

"I believe you two have things to discuss." She turned to Tephra. "Tell her."

Tephra's golden skin had paled to a sickly yellow. She twisted her fingers, a nervous gesture Rowena recognized from their time in the jungle.

"I made a deal with the queen," Tephra said, her melodic accent thin with strain, but carrying the distance between them like an arrow. "She will change my appearance so I can return to Farradar unrecognized—as you know I wished for."

Rowena frowned. Of course, she remembered. That's why Tephra wanted to enter Anomie. But the Lunara warriors had dashed those hopes. Guilt had settled on Rowena's shoulders for being the cause.

Each word Tephra spoke washed away Rowena's misplaced loyalty.

"You really need to be better at choosing allies," Daenon called.

He meant nothing. Rowena kept her focus on Tephra. "What did you promise in return?"

Tephra glanced at Fidessa, who nodded for her to continue.

"Information," Tephra admitted. "About the Solara moonborn, and . . . anything I can find about the lost signet ring."

"You're going to *spy* for her?" Rowena couldn't hide her disbelief. "After everything you told me about the king? About the tournament?"

"I will be careful," Tephra said, not meeting Rowena's eyes. "It is the only way I can go home."

Something wasn't right. The pieces didn't fit together. "Were you ever a prisoner? Or was that part of the act, too?"

Tephra flinched. "That part is true, mostly. I am a dragon keeper. But . . . when we were at the cave . . ."

Rowena's mind spun. Dragon keeper. What did that even mean? She'd been a fool. She had actually worried for someone who continually lied to her, and—understanding dawned like ice water down Rowena's spine.

"You were leaving. Without me."

"I thought it would be better that way," Tephra's whisper barely reached Rowena's ears. "I could slip away while you slept. And we would both be free."

"But you ran into Daenon," Rowena finished, bile rising in her throat.

"Couldn't have planned it better," Daenon added. "You can't beat us, Rowena. The high queen will rule."

Fidessa darted a glance to him, brows pinched. Rowena didn't care about their plans. Her insides churned. Everything tumbled over and over in her mind like she was back in the river, drowning. It was Tephra who saved her then. How could she betray Rowena now?

She had no sympathy for the misery that covered Tephra's face. Probably wasn't even true.

"He and his warriors were on the trail. I could not escape them. They . . . they would have killed me if I had not told them where you were."

Hollow words.

Betrayal wasn't new to Rowena. She'd felt its sting when Goetz shot her father, when her uncle had used her as a pawn. But those wounds had scabbed over. This one was fresh, bleeding, made all the worse because she'd trusted again.

And chosen wrong . . . again.

Rowena didn't yell. She didn't cry. Her mind slowed, growing numb, searching for anything that would justify what she heard. "You think betraying the Solara moon-born and turning over their armor is going to make life easier for you? You care for no one but yourself."

"I never meant for this to happen," Tephra said, her tears falling faster. "I did not know . . . you are not who they say—"

"That's enough," Fidessa interrupted, waving a dismissive hand. "I've given you what you asked. Now leave."

Tephra hesitated, looking as if she might say more, but

Fidessa's stony stare silenced her. She glanced at Rowena, regret, fear, and perhaps genuine remorse mingled in her expression. It didn't matter. Tephra turned and disappeared through a door at the end of the walkway.

"I'll follow her out, my dear," Daenon said. "As much as I'd love to watch this, I have warriors to ready for travel."

"I'll be down soon." Fidessa grinned as Daenon lifted her hand to his lips.

"Always a pleasure to watch you suffer, Rowena." A hearty laugh boomed into the air as he strode through the same exit as Tephra.

Rowena squared her shoulders. She forced down the hurt, the anger. She couldn't afford to dwell on Tephra's betrayal or her disgust of Daenon. Not with Fidessa watching her like a hawk eyeing a field mouse.

"She's quite the actress, your friend," Fidessa remarked, trailing her fingers along the wooden railing. "Though I suspect her loyalty to me will prove as fragile as her loyalty to you."

"Then why make a deal?"

Fidessa laughed, the sound like glass shattering. "She's useful, for now." She leaned forward. "As you could be, if you choose."

"I'm not interested in your deals."

"No?" Fidessa tilted her head. "Not even to save your cousin? Poor, silent Safi. She calls for you in her dreams, you know. Or she would, if she could speak."

Forge-hot anger flashed through Rowena. "You're the one who cursed her."

"I did what was necessary. She was growing . . . disobedient. Questioning my methods. Turning from me just as Uther did." Bitterness twisted Fidessa's features. "You are just like your mother. She robbed me of my husband's heart, and you turned my daughter against me."

"Safi is not gullible. You turned her away by yourself," Rowena said, her voice rising despite her effort to stay calm. Whatever Fidessa thought, her mother loved her father, and she would not disgrace either of her parents by responding about Uther. "If you want love, Fidessa, learn how to give it."

Fidessa stiffened as if slapped. "What would you know of love? You, who destroyed your father? Cast aside by your kingdom?" Her eyes narrowed to cruel slits. "Do you think yourself loved now? By that mongrel Seeker who left you behind? I said you would bring darkness into the realm, and love would not protect you. Did I not?"

The words struck Rowena's deep. The curse Fidessa had said to her the day her parents died. But she hadn't brought darkness nor had Bram left her. He was coming back.

They were only separated.

Her nails bit into her palms.

"My kingdom will remember me. They will know I could not have killed my father," Rowena shot back. "You enslave your own daughter because you are afraid no one loves you. If I have to rule alone, it will not prevent me from doing so with kindness and compassion."

Fidessa's face darkened with rage. "You know nothing of my sacrifices. Nothing of what I've endured." She straightened, composure returning like a mask sliding back into place, though her chest still heaved for breath.

"I grow tired of this exchange. Tell me where you, or your wretched mother, hid the Lunastone."

Like she knew where the blangdang stone was. The thought burned like bitter poison. She might give it to Fidessa just to end this nightmare.

"I don't have it," she said instead.

"Lying won't help you." Fidessa's fingers twitched, and a small vultu hopped onto the railing beside her. She stroked its reptilian head absently. "Your family removed the Lunastone connected to the Sword of Justice. You must know where it lies."

"I don't," Rowena insisted. "I—"

"Enough!" Fidessa's voice cracked like a whip. "I've been patient. I've been reasonable. But I have limits, Rowena." She gestured to the surrounding courtyard. "You are too difficult for gentle means. Let's see if something more physical will loosen your tongue."

The ground beneath Rowena's feet trembled. She stumbled, her heart lurching as the grass rippled like water beneath her boots.

"Here are your choices," Fidessa continued, a wicked, terrifying smile spread across her face. "Tell me the Lunastone's location, or attempt to escape what I'm about to create. If at any moment you wish to end your suffering, simply call out the stone's location, and I'll release you."

Rowena's throat constricted. She glanced desperately at the courtyard walls, the door, gauging the distance. Too far. Much too far.

What else? Think.

Negotiate.

"And if I somehow escape your trap? What then?"

Fidessa cackled, genuine amusement glittering in her eyes. "You won't. But very well, if by some miracle you reach the end with your secret intact, I'll entertain what you might want. Not that I'll have to grant it if you're dead. I have other sources, but you're here, so it would be much easier if you just tell me now."

The ground shook violently. Rowena nearly lost her balance. Something dark pushed through the soil, like fingers reaching up from a grave. Her stomach turned to water, but she forced herself to stand upright.

She felt for the knife against her back, the small blade offering little comfort, but it was something. Her pulse hammered so hard she was certain Fidessa could hear it, but she held the queen's gaze. "When I survive, you will release Safi from her service, and you will never cast a spell upon her again."

The words came out stronger than she felt, fueled by desperation rather than confidence.

For a moment, Fidessa was silent, calculating. Then her lips curled into a cruel smile. "Deal. Oh, I forgot to mention. One of my sweet beasties will be joining you."

All around the courtyard, black vines pushed through the grass, sporting long spiky thorns that intertwined as they grew. They writhed like living things, twisting upward and outward, forming walls that rose higher with each passing second.

A labyrinth of thorns growing before Rowena's eyes.

And from somewhere within its depths came a low, rumbling growl that turned her blood to ice.

The thorn hedges continued to close in around Rowena like the jaws of some ancient predator. Black branches wove tightly together, creating solid walls bristling with thorns as long as her hands that seemed to quiver with anticipation. The hedges rose higher than her head by at least half her body, perhaps more, cutting off any view of the courtyard beyond, or an escape route.

She'd been snared in a cruel hunter's trap.

With each step deeper into the labyrinth, the air grew stifling. The ground no longer covered in soft grass, but damp soil scented of mushrooms and something more disturbing—charred flesh and decay. Rowena bit back vomit. She pressed the back of her hand against her nose, trying to cover the stench as she navigated the first loop of the deadly labyrinth.

Left, then straight, then right.

That was the pattern in Havilar. Those paths had been designed for meditation and growth. This twisted creation existed for one purpose only—to break her.

Had Ida, or Alona, known she'd be here? No doubt one of them had.

Anxiety exploded from Rowena's toes to her throat, doubling her over. Her knees buckled momentarily, forcing her to catch herself against one of the walls. Sharp pain lanced through her palm as a thorn pierced her skin. She jerked back with a strangled cry. Blood welled from the wound.

"No," she whispered, pressing her uninjured hand to her chest where her heart threatened to burst through her ribs. "No, no, no."

Rolling her neck, she replayed a mantra in her mind. She could do this. She could do this.

She halted and forced herself to stand tall. Steady against the rising tide of panic. Her legs betrayed her with their trembling.

Memories of Ida's guidance floated back to her: *Focus on your breathing. Find your center. Let your awareness expand beyond yourself.*

She pressed her lips tight. Advice from her first trip through the dryad's labyrinth. How many other lessons had she ignored?

As her breathing stuttered toward something resembling calm, Rowena reached out with her senses, the way she'd learned in Havilar. She hadn't fully believed in her newfound abilities then, and doubt still lingered. Would such skills even work within Fidessa's twisted creation?

The thought that they might not, that she might be alone and defenseless, made her stumble, her momentary calm slipping away like water through her fingers.

"Stop it," she chided herself, swallowing her voice even as tears of frustration gathered behind her eyes. She would not satisfy Fidessa by showing such weakness. That was what the queen wanted.

Fear. Doubt. Surrender.

Uncertainty still remained, but Rowena allowed her awareness to expand beyond her physical body the way Ida had taught her. The moment her mind reached the thorn hedge, she recoiled with a gasp. Fear, bitter and foul like spoiled ale, flooded her mouth, coating her tongue. But it wasn't just her own terror. Something else lurked within these walls. Its rage and hunger so primal it nearly sent her backward into the thorns.

Fidessa's beastie. Definitely not sweet.

But there was something else too. A unique signature. More organized. Calculated.

Rowena couldn't separate the jumbled sensations bombarding her senses. Was it the beast, or had Fidessa placed other obstacles between her and freedom?

Anxiety plucked at her like a lyre, each string a different fear, death, failure, pain, playing a funeral dirge.

Her trembling fingers found the concealed knife at her back, its wooden handle smooth and inadequate against her palm. A kitchen blade against Fidessa's monster. She almost choked on the hysterical laughter climbing her throat.

She couldn't stay there, frozen like prey. The only path through was forward. She had to keep moving, put her fears aside, or let them drive her, but she couldn't stand still and let Fidessa or any beast stop her.

The image of Safi's blank eyes flashed in her mind. Fierce, independent Safi reduced to a mute weapon wielded by those who should have protected her. That could not continue.

Thoughts of her cousin steadied her, like finding solid ground in quicksand. Rowena squared her shoulders and moved forward, keeping to the center of the path, scanning every shadow for movement among the thorns.

As her confidence grew, so did her pace. The rhythmic crunch of soil beneath her boots became a heartbeat. Left foot, right foot, left foot, right. The fear remained, but now it rode alongside her determination rather than drowning it.

Then came the grinding.

The sound started low, almost imperceptible, like dry bones shifting beneath the dirt. Rowena froze; the hair on her arms rising. The rasping grew louder, and the hedges, the living walls, grew thicker. The thorns lining the pathway elongated, stretching toward the center like reaching fingers, narrowing.

Fidessa was changing the rules. Perhaps not. Rowena hadn't asked if there were any. Wasn't that another lesson from the dryads? What the queen had told her to do? *The one you seek is in the Veilrune Mountains. But when you arrive, remember to ask the right questions.*

She'd set herself up for failure before she started, but she would not give in. Let Fidessa have her fun, playing with her like a half-dead mouse. She was still half-alive, at least.

Rowena pressed on, her path becoming serpentine as it forced her to weave between the advancing spikes. Each adjustment of the labyrinth carried a message—Fidessa was watching. Worried she was adapting. Not giving into her fear enough.

The realization brought a grim satisfaction that warmed through her chest for a brief moment. Each time Fidessa changed her trap, it meant Rowena was getting under the queen's skin. Making her nervous.

Rowena was surviving.

Her satisfaction vanished in a heartbeat. Focused on a dense cluster of thorns ahead, Rowena ventured too near one side. A spike snagged her tunic, slicing through fabric and into the flesh beneath with hungry ease. She hissed in pain, jerking away only to feel the thorn tear deeper before releasing, like a barbed hook ripping free.

Warm blood trickled down her arm, soaking into what remained of her sleeve. The smell hit her nostrils, metallic and wrong in this place. The thorns seemed to respond, quivering more eagerly, straining toward her as if drawn by the scent.

Rowena halted along the center of the path, crouched low, heart thundering, waiting for the motion to stop. She pressed her hand against the wound, wincing as pain radiated up her arm. The cut wasn't deep, but it stung, a scorching reminder of how easily these walls could tear her apart.

When she rose, the world tilted. Had she twisted when she jerked away from the thorn? The path behind looked identical to the path ahead, both stretching into darkness. In Havilar's open labyrinth, the rows were clearly outlined, allowing her to check her position. Here, with walls that seemed to scrape the sky, she couldn't tell which direction led forward and which back.

Panic regained its hold. Getting lost meant death. Either by the thorns or by the beast. Her breath came in shallow gasps, useless for filling her lungs.

Stop. Breathe. Center.

Rowena squished her eyes closed, forcing herself to still her mind. If she couldn't trust her sight, she would have to trust her instincts. With a renewed sense of calm, she refocused on the pathways, and turned to the right. She squared her shoulders and struck out at a slower pace, shoving indecision aside, trusting she'd chosen correctly. The thorns kept growing, but rushing meant mistakes. Mistakes meant blood. Blood would draw the beast.

Slow. Steady. Careful.

She cycled through the words in her mind with each step.

The roar, when it came, seemed to shake the very ground beneath her feet. Guttural and bloodthirsty, leaping over her head along the top of the hedges and bouncing through them like discordant wails from all sides.

Rowena's legs wobbled.

The monster stalked closer, furious and huge and hungry.

Her instincts screamed at her to run, hide, protect herself. That would only deliver her into the beast's jaws faster. From somewhere deep inside, she found reason.

Prey ran. Prey died. Prey she was not.

One foot, then the other. Focus.

If the labyrinth followed the same pattern she'd practiced in Havilar, a right turn would arrive soon, proving she still followed the outside ring. The thought renewed her determination. She rose onto the balls of her feet, expecting confrontation rather than fearing what may come.

Her breathing steadied. With each careful step, she glanced over her shoulder and then peered ahead, alert for movement coming from either direction. The knife gripped tighter in her palm; a reminder. If she had to fight, she would.

Safi. Safi. Safi. The name became her heartbeat, her reason to continue. The image of her cousin's face, hardened into that of a stranger, violence made flesh, haunted her.

But that one flash of recognition, that moment of connection beneath the spell, told Rowena that the real Safi remained somewhere inside.

If, *when*, Rowena made it out of this labyrinth alive, Safi would be free. Whatever consequences she'd suffered, whatever trauma she'd endured at her mother's hands, whatever it took, they would find the woman inside.

Rowena would not fail her again.

The path curved right as she'd expected, and for a single moment, relief eased the tension in her shoulders. She exhaled a hopeful breath. Her intuition had been correct.

Then a figure stepped into view.

Rowena's breath seized in her chest. Her feet refused to move.

"Conri?"

The name escaped her lips in a strangled whisper. Her knees nearly buckled beneath her. The Fianna leader stood before her; his massive frame nearly spanned the width of the path. But something crawled along her spine, a warning that made her skin turn to gooseflesh.

His eyes, always so expressive, crinkling at the corners when he laughed, were dull, lifeless. The same vacant stare Safi had given her, looking through her as if she was nothing but air.

Conri bent his knees, readying to charge.

"Don't," Rowena pleaded, the word catching in her throat. "It's me, Rowena. Remember?"

Her voice sounded small, elfling-like in her own ears. The same desperate tone she'd used when begging for her father to believe she hadn't shot that arrow.

Fidessa's snare had caught Conri before, during the battle in Velmeg. Had she done it to him again? Or was this another of her cruel tricks? Rowena's heart slammed against her ribs so hard it hurt.

The wall to her right swished and rustled. She twisted sideways toward the sound, her body coiled tight, expecting the thorns to be closing in once more. Instead, the branches spread apart with a bizarre offering. A strung bow with a single arrow slid through the gap, landing at Rowena's feet with a soft thud that might as well have been thunder.

Time seemed to stop.

The bow, so simple an object to most, but sent bile rushing up Rowena's throat. The world narrowed to that curved piece of wood, her vision tunneling until nothing else existed. She stood once more in the middle of a battlefield, the metallic stench of blood filling her nostrils, the chaos of combat swirling around her as she took aim at a warrior charging her father. Then came her father's face as he turned, confusion pinching his brows as an arrow, not hers but he thought so, pierced his heart.

Her father's blood. His accusing eyes. Her scream that filled the breach between them.

The memory choked her, crushing her chest like a vice. She couldn't touch the bow. Couldn't relive that moment. Her palms grew slick with sweat, her mouth dry as desert sand.

"Conri, please," she whispered, little more than a desperate exhale. "Hear me. Don't do this."

The man kept his blank expression, his hands folded into fists, his knees bent. But as pain gave way to her survival instinct, something tugged at the edges of her awareness.

He wasn't right.

Conri's red beard, normally full and bushy, grew in sparse patches. His arms, which had been able to lift a fallen tree with ease, seemed oddly uniform, without definition between forearm and upper arm. They rounded instead of bent at the joints. His knees did the same.

Rowena had a doll once, crafted from bundled straw. No matter how she'd tried, its limbs had never bent naturally. They'd always looked . . . like Conri's did now.

Let the truth reveal itself. Another lesson from Havilar.

She peered at Conri again, her pulse gradually slowing as understanding dawned beneath her terror. This thing, whatever it was, wasn't the man who'd protected her in Ibern.

This was a trick. A ploy by Fidessa to make her relive her greatest heartbreak. She'd picked at Fidessa's raw wound by telling her that Safi didn't love her. Now Fidessa was returning the favor, forcing Rowena to confront her own unhealed pain about her father's death.

But it wasn't real. Not Conri. Not her father. Not her past.

With that realization came clarity that burned through her fear like dawnlight through fog. Rowena lowered herself to a crouch without taking her eyes from the Conri-thing, dropping the knife, her fingers finding the bow and the loose arrow. Each touch against the wood sent shivers of memory through her body. In one fluid motion, she stood and nocked the arrow, drawing the string back to her cheek.

Her stomach twisted itself in knots. The stance, the tension in the bow, the weight of the arrow. It was all too familiar. Sweat trickled down her temple, stinging her eye. Her arms trembled so badly she feared she'd miss at this close range.

"I don't think you're Conri," she said, forcing each word past the cork in her throat. "If you are, you'd better let me know right now."

In the distance, the beast roared again. Closer this time. The bellow vibrated through the soles of her boots.

The Conri-thing charged, its movements jerky and unnatural, confirming Rowena's suspicion. Still, her finger hesitated on the string. The face, like his despite its wrongness, made her heart ache with grief.

Rowena blew out a shaky breath, tears blurring her vision as she released the arrow.

Everything went silent as she watched it arc through the air and plunge into the thing's neck. The bow slipped from her fingers, numb and clumsy. She never heard it hit the ground.

Instead, the earth beneath her feet shuddered violently. The Conri-thing froze mid-stride, its blank eyes widening, appearing almost surprised. Its body shook, but it never reached for the arrow. Then it exploded with a thunderous boom that shook the growing walls and beyond.

A scream ripped from Rowena's throat as she dropped into a low squat, arms covering her head as debris pelted her from all directions. Splatters like heavy rain plopped to the ground, some striking her arms and back with stinging force.

When the noise stopped, she unfolded herself and stared in shock at the devastation, her breath coming in ragged gasps. Rust-colored chunks of clay littered the path and stuck into the thorns like grotesque fruit. The smell of wet earth overwhelmed her nostrils, so that she could taste it on her tongue.

A golem. She'd been right. It hadn't been Conri at all, but a clay idol made to appear like him. A mage's trick, designed to prey on her guilt and fear.

And she'd defeated it.

The realization washed over her in a wave. She half-laughed, half-sobbed in relief. The emotional armor she'd worn for so long cracked, just a little. Bits of pain and anger and hurt she'd carried for years loosened their grip on her heart, leaving her lightheaded and trembling.

Fidessa, Uther, Daenon, Goetz . . . they had taken so much from her. Her home, her crown, her freedom. But standing here, covered in globs of clay and blood, Rowena understood something important: she was still capable. Still fighting. Still alive.

She lifted her face to the sky, knowing Fidessa would be watching from somewhere above the snarled pathways.

"You will not beat me!" she screamed, her voice raw with emotion and fierce with determination.

The words echoed through the labyrinth, carrying with them the weight of a promise, to herself, to Safi, and to whatever future waited beyond these walls of thorns.

Rowena retrieved the kitchen knife and held it before her like a talisman. The beast still lurked somewhere ahead, and the exit remained hidden. But for the first time since entering this nightmare, she believed she might survive it.

One step at a time, she moved forward into the darkness.

35

EVORA

EVORA TRACED her fingers over the bark of a young ash tree, feeling its life force pulse beneath her touch. She'd been avoiding her mother since the confrontation with Bram in the meadow four days earlier. Not out of fear, but because her thoughts had become a tangled thicket, she couldn't navigate.

You guard your lands so you're no help to anyone. That's what Bram had said of Havilar, his words sharp enough to pierce the protective shell she'd never known she wore.

"If the prophecy falls . . . all will be dust," she whispered to herself.

What prophecy?

The words had lodged within her like thorns, impossible to remove without pain. She'd always believed Havilar to be a sanctuary—a place of safety and beauty. But what use was a sanctuary if it turned its back on the world beyond?

Doubt had crept in, slow and insidious as morning mist.

A whisper of movement caught her attention, and Evora flattened herself against the ash's trunk. Her mother glided through the forest, radiant as always, with two other dryads in her wake.

They spoke in hushed tones, their words carried away by the breeze before Evora could catch them.

She held her breath until they passed, then exhaled slowly.

This hiding, this uncertainty, it wasn't like her. Yet since Rowena had departed, something had shifted within her, like soil after heavy rain. The outsider had shown her a glimpse of something foreign yet compelling: a life defined by freedom, not tradition.

Evora pushed away from the tree and returned to her private hideaway within a small hollow between two large stones under the roots of an ancient cedar. Inside, spread across her moss-cushioned floor, lay the materials she'd been gathering in secret: flexible pine branches, strips of bark, delicate vines, and an array of needles, leaves, and smaller twigs.

She sat cross-legged before her creation, a cloak unlike any garment worn in Havilar. Dryads had little need for clothing beyond that formed naturally from their magic when they shifted into elven form. But this was something different.

Evora lifted the cloak, examining her handiwork critically. The pine branches formed a flexible frame, with the bark strips woven through to create a sturdy foundation. She'd attached clusters of needles, leaves, and moss in overlapping patterns that mimicked the forest floor. When worn, she would appear as nothing more than a shifting collection of forest debris to the casual observer.

"Not perfect," she murmured, "but it might be enough."

She'd confessed to Bram that she wasn't particularly skilled at disguising herself in tree form. The admission had been embarrassing. Dryads prided themselves on becoming one with the forest. But her yew form was too distinctive, with its dark needles and red berries. Too easily remembered, too easily tracked.

This cloak would be her solution. A way to blend without transforming.

Evora rose, swinging the cloak around her shoulders. It settled with a soft rustling, heavier than she'd anticipated, but not uncomfortably so. She secured it with a vine fastening at her throat and moved to the small pool of water near her refuge.

Her reflection stared back, transformed. Where Evora's copper-tinted skin and moonless-sky hair normally gleamed, there was now only forest muted in greens and browns, textured and layered. She shifted from side to side, watching how the cloak moved with her. If she kept her movements slow and deliberate, she would indeed appear as nothing more than a drift of wind through underbrush.

A smile curved her lips. She was invisible. A fierce pride welled up that surprised her. She was a step closer to freedom.

The real test came later that afternoon. Evora followed her mother at a distance, moving from shadow to shadow, her cloak gathered close. Mother stopped occasionally to tend to young saplings or converse with other dryads, never once glancing back to where Evora concealed herself.

When Mother finally returned to her willow form that evening, Evora felt a surge of elation. If she could remain undetected by her own mother, the most perceptive dryad in Havilar, she could surely venture beyond their borders unnoticed.

The thought sent a thrill through her, equal parts terror and excitement.

That night, she did not root with the soil. She lay on the ground, staring through gaps in the branches overhead at stars barely visible through birch, maple, and linden leaves. Rowena had spoken of open skies in Penumar, of stars that burned so bright and numerous they created patterns across the heavens. Evora had never seen such a sight. The dense canopy of Havilar, beautiful as it was, hid much of the night sky from view.

What else might she have missed? The question pulsed within her, insistent as a heartbeat.

By dawn, her decision was made.

Evora packed lightly, a small drinking gourd, a pouch of dried berries like what Rowena had eaten, and her cloak, now folded into a compact bundle she could carry on her back. She left no note, knowing she would return before nightfall. This wasn't a departure, merely an exploration. A test of her own courage.

The border between Havilar and the Veilrune Mountains lay to the north, marked by no fence or wall but by a subtle shift in the forest itself. The ancient giants of Havilar, trees that had stood since the Chasm, gave way to younger growth, still impressive but lacking the immense power of her homeland.

Evora paused at this invisible line, her heart pounding against her ribs like trapped birds' wings. No dryad had crossed this boundary in her lifetime. Mother had always insisted it was too dangerous. That the outside world held only those who would harm them or take advantage of their powers.

"They would harvest our enchantment as readily as they harvest our cousins' limbs for timber," Mother had warned, her voice tight with old anger.

But Bram hadn't harmed Rowena. He had protected her. Besides cutting trees to use for shaping structures or burning them, Evora closed her eyes, unable to comprehend such a terror, those were stories just to scare saplings. They had to be.

Evora took a deep breath and removed her cloak from her back and wrapped it around her, pulling the hood over her head, so she was securely hidden. She stepped across the boundary, moving with slow, deliberate steps as she'd done near her mother. No need to take the risk of being caught so close to her goal.

The change was immediate, though subtle. The forest felt . . .

quieter somehow. Less aware. Far away. In Havilar, she always sensed the consciousness of the surrounding trees, a constant murmur of life and growth. Here, the trees still lived, still stretched toward Sawel, but their thoughts were simpler, their awareness muted.

She continued forward, keeping her cloak wrapped around her. Though there seemed to be no one about, caution had been ingrained in her since she'd been a sapling. Then there was her short-lived stint in the pixie lands. She shivered. Caution couldn't hurt.

The forest here was different. Pines dominated where Havilar boasted greater diversity. The underbrush was sparser, the canopy less complete. Shafts of morning sunlight penetrated to the forest floor, creating pools of gold among the shadows.

Evora moved from tree to tree, touching each one briefly, introducing herself in the silent language of the forest. They didn't respond as the trees of Havilar would, but she felt a faint acknowledgment from each, like the sleepy recognition of one not fully awake.

She traveled for perhaps an hour, her excitement growing with each new discovery. Flowers she'd never seen before carpeted small clearings. Birds with unfamiliar songs darted through branches. Once, a small herd of caprea crossed her path, so intent on their own journey they didn't notice the dryad frozen against a pine trunk.

The further she went, the bolder she became. She removed her cloak, folding it carefully and strapping it to her back. What need had she for concealment here, where no one knew her face? For the first time in her life, Evora was truly on her own. Free to explore.

The thought made her laugh aloud, the sound startling a pair of squirrels who chattered indignantly from a nearby branch.

"My apologies," she told them, still smiling.

She continued onward, following a hill's gentle upward slope. Perhaps from its crest, she might see farther into these mysterious mountains. Perhaps she might even glimpse one of the Lycani. Stories told of wolf-shifters, brutal and cunning beings who roamed the mountains. Surely, from a distance, observation would be safe enough.

The trees thinned as she climbed, allowing ever more sunlight to warm her skin. Evora tilted her face upward, closing her eyes to savor the sensation. In Havilar, sunlight was filtered through layers of leaves, its heat diffused and gentle. This direct warmth was different, more intense, more immediate.

So absorbed was she in this new pleasure that she failed to notice the subtle signs around her. Distinctive marks on trees, the tracks in the soft earth, the slight change in the forest's scent.

"Why have you invaded my lands?"

The deep voice cut through her reverie like a blade. Evora's eyes snapped open as she twisted one way, then the other searching for the source, her heart lurching painfully in her chest.

A man stood mere paces away, tall and broad-shouldered, with the solid build of one who lived by physical strength. His cropped brown hair, streaked with sunshine and silver, despite a face that appeared not much older than her own. His ears! Rounded rather than pointed like her own.

So amazing. So unique. So Lycani.

For a moment, Evora couldn't breathe, couldn't think. Every warning her mother had ever given her crashed through her mind in a deafening cascade.

The wolf-shifter's eyes narrowed, amber flecks glinting within the brown depths. "You ward your lands so my kind cannot enter, but you deign to travel through my territory?" The question held equal parts anger and disbelief.

Evora straightened, calling upon every moment of watching her mother had ever taught her. Fear would only provoke a predator.

"I mean no disrespect," she said, her voice steadier than she felt. "I was merely exploring."

"Exploring." He repeated the word flatly. "Does your queen know you've crossed the boundary, dryad?"

"I'm not—" Evora began, then stopped. Denial was pointless. Her copper-tinted skin and forest-embroidered clothing marked her heritage as clearly as his rounded ears marked his. "No, she doesn't."

The Lycani circled her slowly, his movements fluid and controlled. Evora turned with him, unwilling to present her back, and careful to keep from twisting into her yew form.

"Do you have a name, explorer?" he asked, a hint of mocking in his tone.

She hesitated, then decided that anonymity was lost to her, anyway. "Evora."

"Princess Evora," he corrected, surprising her. "Daughter of Princess Ida. Granddaughter of Queen Alona."

Shock rippled through her. "How do you—"

"We may be unwelcome in your forests, but we're not ignorant of those who rule them." His mouth twisted in what might have been a smile or a grimace. "I am Bekh, alpha of this territory."

Alpha. The leader. Of all the Lycani she might have encountered, she had to stumble upon their chief.

"I did not come to spy," Evora said, the words tumbling out before she could consider them. "I only wanted to see something new. I've never left Havilar before today."

Something in Bekh's expression shifted—surprise, perhaps. "Never?"

"Well, once. To the pixie lands, but the jungle was too

strange. So many noises. It was overwhelming. I panicked. Then Mother retrieved me and I had to go back. But that was the only time. I promise I've never been to your lands before this." She wrapped her arms around herself, suddenly feeling the chill of the mountain air despite the sunlight. "The border is . . . forbidden to us."

"Hmm." He grumbled something else, but Evora couldn't understand him.

"It's not my doing," Evora said, frustration flaring unexpectedly. "I don't understand why we ward our lands. I don't understand why my mother and grandmother refuse to speak of the outside world except in warnings." The words carried more heat than she'd intended, years of unacknowledged questions surfacing at once.

Bekh studied her, his head tilted slightly to one side. "You speak too much."

She'd heard that once or twice before. "I believe in being honest, and that requires giving all the details. If I didn't, you might not understand that I really meant no harm by being here. I snuck over the border and will go back after I've looked around a bit."

He rubbed his fingers over his forehead when she finished. "You don't know, do you?"

"Know what?"

He shook his head slowly. "Your people have much land. Abundant, fertile land that never knows drought or fire. We have these mountains, growing more crowded each season as Telana encroach from the east and Lunara from the north." Bitterness edged his words. "We could live among the trees of Havilar in peace, taking only what we need. But your queen refuses all discourse."

Evora frowned. "That doesn't sound like my grandmother. She's stern, but fair."

"Fair?" Bekh's laugh held no humor. "Ask her about the Lycani delegation that came seeking sanctuary fifty years ago. Ask her what *fairness* they received."

Evora faltered, uncertain. Surely Grandmother would have mentioned such an event in her many lessons on Havilar's history. Unless . . . unless it was something she preferred not to remember.

The doubt must have shown on her face, for Bekh's expression softened a fraction.

"You truly know nothing of this," he said, more statement than question.

"No," Evora admitted. "But I would like to. Do you have scrolls I could read? Or a lesson master who I could speak with? I learn very quickly."

For a long moment, Bekh was silent, assessing her with that amber-flecked gaze. Around them, the forest seemed to hold its breath.

Evora fidgeted with the straps of her pack, squeezing her upper lip between her teeth to remain silent. The agony of waiting for the Lycani to speak nearly drove her mad.

"You should return to your lands, Princess," he said finally. "These mountains are not safe for one who knows so little of them."

The dismissal stung more than Evora expected. "I am not helpless. The trees still speak to me. Their voices are soft, distant, but I'm sure we'll be able to communicate just fine, given time."

"You said you were leaving."

"After I explore some more and—"

"No!"

She flinched at his commanding tone and volume. All words jammed in her throat, so she stood motionless, staring and blinking.

"You are ignorant. And ignorance is more dangerous than weakness. Leave my lands."

He was right, of course. This brief taste of the world beyond Havilar had shown her how little she truly knew. The thought humbled her, but strengthened her resolve to learn more.

"You're not wrong. That's why I want to learn. To see other realms. Explore. You can help me. Tell me about your lands. Where do you live? Do you root with the soil or sleep on the ground like the Lunara?" she asked. "What do you eat?"

Bekh's eyebrows rose in surprise. "Do you ever stop?"

Evora pinched her lips together and lifted her chin.

His nostrils flared, and he crossed his arms over his chest.

She narrowed her eyes, holding his stare and trying not to giggle. She did love to talk, but she was a dryad. She could remain quiet and steady for days. He couldn't beat her at that game.

Except he didn't seem to be playing.

Heat crept through her chest and over her arms. Sweat formed on her brow. It took more and more strength to continue. It wasn't fun any longer, but he'd been rude. She wouldn't back down.

Her body trembled, but she forced herself to stay upright.

Stop this!

The command entered her mind, just as her mother or grandmother did. It was *his* voice.

"How?"

Bekh lunged, shoving Evora against the trunk of a nearby tree. So shocked by his action, she held her breath, as if she had any left. Her eyes seemed to have opened too wide to close. "Do not challenge me," Bekh growled.

"I'm not . . . I . . . I didn't mean to." Her voice wavered, sounding squeaky in her ears. Perhaps the stories were true.

"Lower your eyes," he growled, the sound more wolf than man.

She wasn't staring, not really. Her fingers twitched against the tree behind her. A flicker of calm. A touch of home. A pine. She blinked once, then many times, finally able to look away from those torrent-filled eyes.

A moment later, Bekh was several paces away, his back to her. His shoulders were raising and lowering as if he had to catch his breath. What had she done to deserve such anger?

Nothing.

"I don't understand what just happened, but I didn't like it. Don't do that again!" Evora pressed her palm against the pine's trunk with an internal thank you.

"Follow me." Bekh didn't turn to face her, but his voice carried as if he still stood in front of her.

"How did you speak to me like that? My grandmother does that, but that's because she stays in her oak. And my mother does it at night sometimes while she's rooted. Was it because you were angry?"

Bekh made a very loud grumbling sound from his throat. He spun, slowly, to face her. "Lycani are linked mind to mind with their alpha. Now, as I said, follow me."

Evora listened, parsing out his words for a moment. "Where?"

"Your mother will be searching for you, and I don't want her in my lands."

The reminder of Mother sent a jolt of alarm through Evora, but it was quickly replaced by a surge of defiance that surprised her with its intensity. She would not return home like a scared sapling this time.

She straightened her spine, squaring her shoulders. "I am not going back yet. It's my decision what I do."

Bekh raised an eyebrow, assessing her with that penetrating gaze. "You would defy your mother? Your queen?"

"I'm not defying them," Evora said, though the words felt hollow even to her own ears. "I'm making my own choice for once."

"And how long will that last? I will not have my lands overrun with dryads searching for you."

She gestured to the surrounding forest. "This is the first time I've seen anything beyond Havilar's borders. The first time I've spoken with anyone who isn't a dryad or a sanctioned visitor. There's so much to see and learn."

She took a step toward him, emboldened by her own resolve. "You said I'm ignorant, and you're right. How can I ever hope to lead my people if I know nothing of the world beyond our trees?"

"And you believe a few hours in wolf territory will remedy generations of isolation?" There was a hint of amusement in his tone. Not the fun kind, but the taunting kind. He was beginning to frustrate her.

"It's a beginning, at least." She'd hoped to have a few days before she was forced back home. Enough time to get a real experience. "When it comes time to join the soil, I will be missed. But I will not go back until I decide."

Bekh studied her for a long moment, not meeting her gaze, his expression unreadable. Then he inclined his head slightly. "We shall see."

He turned and began walking deeper into the forest, his movements fluid and silent despite his size. After a few paces, he glanced back over his shoulder.

"Are you coming, Princess? These woods grow dangerous after dark."

Evora hesitated only briefly before following, her heart pounding with equal parts fear and exhilaration. With each step away from Havilar, she felt both the weight of her decision and a strange, unexpected lightness. As if she'd shed a skin that had grown too confining.

The mountain forest deepened around them as they climbed higher, the trees changing subtly, more rugged, more resilient against the harsher climate. That must have been why Bekh was so tall and strong to live in such conditions.

"You didn't answer me. How did you speak to me like that? Back there . . . in my mind?"

Bekh scoffed. "Here I was thinking you'd finally accepted silence."

"I like to think, and I have a lot of questions. Silence is beautiful, but so is conversation. It's okay to enjoy both."

"Debatable."

Still not an answer to her question. Perhaps he preferred to speak that way, make her discover the answer herself, like her grandmother always did. That was fine. It was familiar, an unexpected piece of home. Maybe they weren't as different as she thought.

Sawel began casting long shadows through the trees, when Bekh stopped at a small clearing backed by a cliff face. A narrow opening in the rock revealed a cave entrance, partially concealed by hanging vines.

"My patrol will pass by here at nightfall," Bekh said, gesturing to the cave. "You can shelter until morning."

Evora bent over to peer inside. When she rose, Bekh was striding away. "You're not staying?"

"I have other responsibilities." Only simple fact. "The pack has questions about our . . . visitor that I must address."

His pause was loud enough before he slowly turned around. She was more than a visitor. She was a dryad, daughter of those who had rejected his people. Yet he had shown her kindness. Well . . . tolerance.

"What will they want . . . your patrol?" she asked. She was tired after all the traveling, so she'd definitely be rooting with the soil. It wasn't a great time to get to know them.

Bekh's mouth quirked in what might almost have been a smile. "They will be curious. Few of them have ever seen a dryad up close."

"I'll be rooted, so it would be better to meet them at dawn."

Bekh pinched his brows, as if confused. His kind must be like Rowena.

"Do you sleep on the ground? Or do you have a dwelling? I met a Lunara, well, she was half Lunara and half Telana, very interesting. She slept on the ground overnight in our lands, but she said she normally used something called a bed."

Bekh closed his eyes and inhaled. "If you need help, call out. Someone will come." He gave a quick nod, then turned to leave again.

"Wait," Evora called after him. "Will you be back?"

"Perhaps." With that cryptic remark, he slipped into the forest.

"Until the sun rises!" Evora yelled, hoping he heard her wishes for his evening rest.

She settled at the cave entrance as twilight descended, wrapping her cloak around her shoulders against the mountain chill and sitting on a soft bed of moss. She'd root after a while. The forest here felt so different from home—wilder, less controlled, yet vibrant, with a different kind of life. Owls called to one another in the gathering darkness. Small creatures rustled in the underbrush.

For the first time in her life, Evora couldn't sense the trees around her as extensions of herself. These pines and firs acknowledged her presence but kept their own counsel, their life force more distant from her own.

The strangeness of it should have frightened her. Instead, she found it exhilarating.

Somewhere in the distance, a wolf howled—a long, haunting call that seemed to embody the very essence of these mountains. Another answered, then another, the chorus building until it seemed the very air vibrated with their song.

Bekh's pack.

Evora closed her eyes, letting the sound wash over her. Mother would be frantic by now, perhaps organizing search parties. Grandmother would be disappointed. They might even think she'd been taken against her will.

Guilt tugged at her conscience, but not enough to drive her back to Havilar.

Not yet.

36

ROWENA

Rowena picked her way through the clay debris, the remnants of the false Conri squishing beneath her boots. Each step made a wet, sucking sound that turned her stomach. Her heart pounded from her victory over the golem, but the labyrinth wouldn't allow her even a moment to catch her breath. Already the thorns were stretching inward again, quivering with what seemed like anticipation, narrowing her path like a closing fist.

The bow lay where she'd dropped it, half-buried in rust-colored clay. Rowena stared at it, her throat tightening. Touching it had made her relive that horrid day. Even so, she stooped to retrieve it. The weight of it an accusation. Still, she slung it over her shoulder, wincing as it pressed against her cuts. One arrow had been provided, and used. If there were other threats ahead, she'd need every advantage, no matter how it made her skin crawl.

Her gaze swept the thorny path ahead, searching for movement, for danger. With the golem destroyed, the way forward seemed clear, at least for the moment. But the momentary relief did nothing to quiet the dread coiling in her stomach.

That growl. That bone-shaking, primeval sound that had

echoed through the labyrinth, hadn't come from a clay figure. It still echoed in her memory, chilling her bones. Whatever created that sound was flesh and blood and hunger. Something alive. Something hunting. Something that could be tracking her right now.

A chill tapped along Rowena's spine like icy fingers, raising the fine hairs on her arms despite the sweat that made her tunic cling to her back. She tightened her grip on the kitchen knife until her knuckles ached, the worn wooden handle slick in her palm, and pressed onward, snatching up the arrow on her way.

The labyrinth pathways twisted more sharply now, doubling back on themselves in dizzying spirals, leaving her frustrated. Each time she thought she was making progress toward the center, or perhaps the exit, another turn would bring her face-to-face with what seemed like the same patch of thorns she'd already passed.

The thorns grew ever more aggressive, forcing her to hunch and weave through gaps barely wider than her shoulders, the spikes sometimes catching at her clothes or grazing her skin. The way the pathway's wound back and forth was the only similarity to the labyrinth in Havilar. Everything else proved dark, dangerous. Deadly.

Fidessa toyed with her. Wearing her down like a hunter exhausting prey before the kill.

A thorn snagged her hair and yanked so painfully at her scalp that tears sprang to her eyes. Rowena hissed a curse, carefully disentangling herself strand by strand, wincing as each pull sent a fresh wave of pain to her scalp. Her forearms bore a lattice of scratches, some deep enough that blood sent thin rivulets down to her fingertips. The scent of her blood seemed to excite the thorns; they quivered when she passed, reaching for her as if alive and hungry.

Perhaps they were. This was Fidessa's creation. It followed the cruel logic of its creator's mind.

She rounded another corner and halted so abruptly her ankle twisted slightly, sending a jolt of pain through her leg. The path ahead widened into a small clearing, roughly circular and perhaps twelve paces across. Unlike the rest of the labyrinth, this space was open to the sky above, though the black thorns still surrounded it like a crown of deadly spikes.

At the center of the clearing stood a solitary tree, its bark bleached bone-white, its branches twisted and bare like arthritic fingers reaching for the sky. It was dead, or appeared to be, yet it emanated a strange power that made the air around it shimmer like heat rising from sunbaked stone. Leaves scattered the area around the trunk, old and crunchy, as if this was an ancient place, forgotten by time.

The sight should have been ominous, yet Rowena felt an inexplicable pull toward the tree. Like a whisper calling her name, though no sound reached her ears. Before she could question the impulse, a voice, achingly familiar, called out from the other side of the clearing.

"Rowena! Help me!"

Safi's voice, high with terror and pain.

Rowena's heart lurched so violently she pressed a hand to her chest. "Safi?"

She took a step into the clearing, the leaves crackling beneath her boot, then froze. The scream had sounded genuine. Not like the flat, emotionless golem-Conri. But Fidessa had already proven her mastery of deception. This could be another trap, designed to lure Rowena into the open where whatever beast stalked the labyrinth could find her.

"Please! She's coming back! I can't—" Safi's voice cut off in a strangled cry that made Rowena's blood run cold.

Caution warred with desperation in her mind. If there was even the slightest chance that it was the real Safi, that Fidessa had placed her cousin in the labyrinth as the ultimate test of Rowena's resolve, she couldn't ignore it. She couldn't live with herself if she abandoned Safi to save herself.

She moved forward, knife clutched so tightly her fingers had gone nearly numb, every sense straining for signs of danger. Each snap of a twig echoed like thunder in her ears. The white tree loomed larger with each step, its twisted branches casting strange shadows across the clearing despite the absence of leaves. Shadows that seemed to shift and move of their own accord, as if alive.

"Safi?" she called, her voice cracking. "Where are you?"

Nothing. The silence stretched, broken only by Rowena's own heartbeat thundering in her ears and the soft crunch of her footsteps on the scattered leaves. An unnaturally loud sound, like a warning bell announcing her presence.

She had nearly reached the tree when a soft sound like wet leather stretched over stone came from behind her.

Rowena spun. Knife raised. Her pulse galloping until she grew lightheaded.

Emptiness. The path she'd taken into the clearing remained empty, yet her skin prickled with the certainty of being watched. She could sense it, a presence, weighing on her like a physical touch, heavy with predatory intent. Like the panthalyx that stalked near the river in Tixamar, but darker, colder. Less animal and more . . . something else.

She backed toward the tree, unwilling to turn her back on the empty path again. One step, then another, her legs threatening to buckle beneath her. The bark pressed against her shoulder blades, smooth and unexpectedly warm, like fevered skin. The contact sent a jolt through her, not quite pain but something equally jarring. A sense of *wrongness* that made her stomach clench and bile rise.

Rowena flinched away from the tree as if she'd been burned, spinning to face it instead. Up close, she could see that what she'd taken for bare branches were, in fact, intricate patterns carved into the white wood. Symbols she couldn't read but which tugged at the edges of her memory, like glimpsed once in a dream and half-remembered. She'd seen these before, hadn't she? In one of her grandmother's books, perhaps, or carved into stones near the bay in Skandan.

"Safi?" she called again, her voice thin with fear as she circled the tree, scanning for any sign of her cousin.

The clearing remained empty. No sign of Safi, no hint of where the voice had come from. Had it been real at all? Or just another of Fidessa's cruel illusions?

Another sound. A low, rumbling growl that seemed to vibrate through the ground beneath her feet and into her bones. Closer now. Much closer.

Rowena whirled, knife ready, only to find herself still alone in the clearing.

Not alone. A voice whispered in the back of her mind with icy clarity. *Hunted.*

Something hit the top of her head, like a heavy raindrop. When she touched the spot, her fingers came away wet and sticky. The sight of the dark fluid made her stomach heave. She looked up, seeking the source, her neck creaking with tension.

Nothing but the reaching branches and open sky. She backed further away, into the shadows of the thorn hedge, her shoulders hunched as if she could make herself smaller, less visible to whatever lurked.

Another drop landed on her cheek, warm and thick, sliding down her skin like a tear. This one she didn't touch, but its scent reached her, dense and musky, mingled with something fetid and wrong. Like carrion left to rot in the sun.

Slowly, dread building in her chest, until she could barely breathe, Rowena raised her eyes again.

It clung to the thorns above the clearing, its massive body somehow supported by the twisted vines despite its obvious weight. A wolf-like snout pulled back in a silent snarl, revealing yellowed fangs longer than Rowena's hand. Shaggy fur matted with what looked like pond scum covered its body, green-tinged slime dripping from its coat to patter on the clearing floor.

Its eyes were the worst. Luminous green orbs that held no emotion beyond hunger and mindless rage. Eyes fixed on her with such terrible intelligence that she felt exposed, already torn open and consumed.

Rowena froze, a scream locked in her throat. Her lungs burned with the need for air, but she couldn't make herself breathe, afraid that the slightest movement would trigger the creature's attack. Her mind raced, cataloging details with frantic precision even as her body refused to obey her commands to run. Not a wolf, despite the muzzle shape. The limbs were wrong, too long, too sinuous, ending in webbed paws tipped with curved claws that dug into the thorny vines. Its body seemed almost boneless, flowing over the thorns like liquid dressed in fur.

Never in her life had Rowena seen such a creature, yet some primal part of her recognized the threat it posed. This was a predator evolved for one purpose: to kill.

A beast she had believed to be a myth. A creature from the most terrifying elfling tales. A bunyip.

The beast shifted, thorns gouging its flesh and drawing thick, dark blood that mingled with the slime coating its fur. It seemed not to notice the wounds, its gaze fixed unwaveringly on Rowena, pinning her in place as effectively as physical restraints.

She needed to move, to run, to hide, to fight, but terror held her motionless, her muscles locked in place. The kitchen knife clutched in her hand seemed pathetically inadequate, an elfling's toy against this monster. One arrow, then the bow, would be useless. Her enchantment, what little she had, would burn away in moments, but she would run herself dry on purpose in the face of such a beast.

The white tree seemed to pulse with strange energy, yet it offered no cover, no escape. Her only option was back into the narrow, thorny pathways. And somewhere in that labyrinth was the exit.

But first, she had to survive this monstrosity. If she could make her body obey. If she could just breathe.

The bunyip's muscles bunched, preparing to spring. Rowena twisted and threw herself sideways just as it launched from its perch, its massive body sailing through the air. She screamed, raw and sharp, as claws raked into her flesh. Rowena rolled to her side, just enough to free her arm, muscles burning with the effort. The knife flashed, held in a white-knuckled grip. She slashed wildly. The blade connected, slicing across the beast's foreleg.

It howled, so piercing Rowena clamped her hands over her ears in agony. Her momentary lapse in staying alert gave the bunyip time to lash out with its uninjured paw, catching her across the shoulder and sending her sprawling toward the tree. Her knife flew from her grasp to land several paces away.

Unlike the black thorns surrounding the clearing, the tree seemed solid, heavy. If she could break off a branch, fashion some kind of club or spear . . . Her fingers scrabbled against the bark, seeking purchase, a weakness, anything she could use.

The bunyip's enraged howl snapped her attention back to the immediate danger. It lunged without warning, crossing the distance between them with a single bound.

Rowena rolled as the beast pounced, its body uncoiling through the air like some terrible spring. She narrowly avoiding being pinned under its massive weight. The beast landed beside her, shaking the ground with enough force to rattle her teeth. Its jaws snapped closed on empty air, inches from her face. The stench of its breath, rotting meat and something sour, made her retch.

She reached for her enchantment, no thought, no aim, just a thrust of her hand toward the bunyip's face. The bunyip reared back, shrieking. Green ichor sprayed from an injured eye, sizzling where it struck Rowena's skin like droplets of liquid fire.

Rowena scrambled away, stretching for her knife. Her fingers had just closed around the handle when the air shifted, silence floating for a moment. The beast had leapt. With strength born of desperation, Rowena flipped to her back, and with her blood-slicked hand, drove the knife deep into the creature's chest.

As the blade sank into matted fur and flesh, something surged within Rowena. Her enchantment, responding to her struggle like molten silver. It flowed through her veins, down her arm, and into the bunyip through the knife's connection. The power burned as it left her, scouring her from the inside.

A scream, more rage than pain, erupted from the beast, so close that spittle sprayed her face. It reared back, taking the knife with it embedded to the handle. Rowena seized the moment to scramble away, her palms slipping in the loose dirt as she dragged herself toward the white tree, putting its trunk between them once more.

Hot rivulets of blood ran down her arm and back. The burning in her wounds was a distant concern, masked by her thundering pulse and frantic will to survive.

The beast curled back on itself with unnatural speed, its green gaze locking onto her and never wavering. A low growl rumbled from its throat, wet and hungry. Its maw opened wider, revealing row upon row of serrated teeth. Saliva hung in strings from its jaws, sizzling where it struck the ground like acid.

It wanted her dead, no question.

Through vision blurred by sweat, she spied around the tree trunk, keeping the bunyip in her sight. It stopped to paw at the knife in its chest. Darkened patches surrounded the puncture wound where fur hung like it had melted from her enchantment, revealing raw, blistered skin beneath. Howls of frustration echoed off the walls of thorns.

Rowena should run. Take advantage of the beast's distraction to flee down one of the pathways. Her legs trembled, urging her to move, to escape. She couldn't rely on her enchantment lasting much longer after being kept away from the moons for so long. And without any other weapon, she'd be defenseless.

The beast's speed would surely overtake her in the narrow confines of the labyrinth. She could attempt to climb the thorns, but they would tear her to shreds. And the creature had already proven its agility to navigate them.

Her choices evaporated when the bunyip abandoned its attempts to remove the knife and charged straight for her, its ruined eye a mass of green ichor, the other blazing with murderous intent. Each massive paw struck with enough force to shake the ground under her feet.

No time. No weapon. Nothing but her own body and whatever scrap of enchantment she could still muster.

The beast leapt. Time slowed to a crawl. Everything clear. Each individual tooth sparkled in its gaping maw, the green glow of its remaining eye, the knife still protruding from its chest. Rowena planted her feet, feeling the soil compress beneath her boots, and thrust both arms forward, drawing on enchantment deeper than she'd ever reached before.

A stream of silver light, razor thin, but blindingly bright, left her hands, aiming for the creature's open maw. It wasn't just her enchantment, but something of herself, torn free and hurled as a weapon.

The beast swallowed the shimmering light deep into its throat. For one suspended moment, nothing happened. Then the bunyip shuddered, arching its back in an unnatural angle, and fell. Its momentum carried it forward, driving Rowena to the ground beneath its massive weight.

Pain exploded through her body as they landed together, her head cracking against the packed soil. Stars burst across her vision. The beast thrashed atop her, its death throes violent and desperate. Claws raked her legs, her sides, anywhere they could reach.

Rowena kicked her legs, heels digging into the soil with grim determination. Her forearms jutted under the broken jaw, keeping the jagged teeth from finding her flesh despite the bunyip's frenzied struggles. Blood, hers and the beast's, slicked her hands, making her grip treacherous.

After what seemed like an eternity, the creature's movements slowed. Its single remaining eye, fixed on Rowena with undiluted hatred even now, gradually dulled like a doused fire. The weight pinning her grew heavier as life drained from the massive body.

With one final, shuddering breath that washed over her face in a fetid wave, the beast went still.

Rowena lay trapped beneath its bulk, her own breathing shallow and rapid. Every inch of her body throbbed with pain, an abundance of different hurts all screaming for attention. Both the creature's caustic green blood and her own crimson soaked the ground beneath them, pooling around her body in a sticky mess.

She had killed it. The realization came slowly, filtering through the haze of pain and exhaustion.

A hollow victory. The thought formed with bitter clarity as

the realization of her situation settled over her like the weight of the beast itself. Her chances of survival seemed even less likely now. She lay there, only able to snatch shallow breaths. Badly wounded and weaponless and pinned beneath a monster's corpse.

Trapped in Fidessa's twisted labyrinth.

Fidessa had never intended for her to survive this challenge. She'd been clear about that; a moment of truth, where she'd hoped to learn of the Lunastone's location. Of course, the queen had stacked the odds impossibly high, certain Rowena would break.

Despite everything, Rowena still lived. The thought kindled something warm in her chest, something that pushed back against the encroaching darkness.

With renewed determination, she began the painful process of freeing herself from beneath the beast's body. Each movement sent waves of agony through her torn flesh, but she gritted her teeth and continued, tasting blood where she'd bitten the inside of her cheek. Inch by excruciating inch, she dislodged herself, leaving smears of blood on the packed earth as she crawled clear.

Rowena collapsed onto her back, staring at the open sky above the clearing. Her vision swam, the clouds above blurring and doubling. Darkness crept at the edges, beckoning her with promises of relief from pain. It would be so easy to let unconsciousness claim her. To drift away into blessed numbness.

Not yet. Safi waited. Freedom waited. Somewhere out there was Bram.

With tremendous effort, she rolled onto her side, swallowing a cry as wounded flesh protested. Then pushed herself to her knees, arms shaking with the strain of supporting her weight. The world tilted like a ship in a storm, but she fought through the dizziness. She crawled to the white tree, using one hand for balance, and pulled herself upright, swaying.

The beast's corpse lay sprawled before her. Beyond it, she could see two pathways leading out of the clearing. This had been the center, the heart of the labyrinth. No archways of silent contemplation in this tortured creation, no guideposts of reflection. One way would lead her out to victory. She would win Safi's freedom and her own.

But which one?

Rowena closed her eyes, reaching out with senses beyond the physical, the way she'd learned in Havilar. Exhausted as she was, she held little expectations. Except, awareness filled her, sharper, more focused than before, as if the battle had burned away some barrier within her, leaving her raw and open to the currents of enchantment flowing through her.

One path called to her. Not through sound or sight, but through a *rightness* that resonated deep within her chest. She opened her eyes and fixed her gaze on the right-hand path, certainty blooming despite her wounds and exhaustion.

Gathering the last reserves of her strength, Rowena staggered toward it, each step sending fresh jolts of pain through her lacerated body.

Behind her, the white tree seemed to whisper, a sound just at the edge of comprehension. She twisted to listen, wincing as strained muscles protested, but the words, and the tree, faded away, leaving nothing but the dead bunyip in the clearing and her own labored breathing.

Whatever Fidessa had planned next, Rowena would face it. She had survived the beast that should have torn her apart. She would survive this labyrinth.

And then Safi would be free from her mother's control.

Rowena didn't doubt Fidessa had more tricks to play, but that no longer mattered. Something had changed within her, deeper than the physical wounds, more profound than mere determination. A certainty had taken root, flowering through her veins.

She would survive. She would triumph. She would reclaim everything that had been taken from her, and more.

The knowledge carried her forward, one painful step at a time, into the waiting darkness of the labyrinth's final challenge.

37

BRAM

BRAM'S LUNGS burned as he and Goby raced through the winding corridors of the keep. The Sword of Justice, secured at his hip, felt heavier than it should. Not from its physical weight but from the burden of what it represented. After everything he'd endured to find it, the blade was finally in his possession.

And now the challenge of leaving the castle.

"This way," Goby urged, scampering ahead with surprising speed for his short legs. "Guards not know."

They ducked into a narrow servant's corridor; the ceiling so low Bram had to bend nearly double. The piggish guards pursuing them wouldn't fit through such a confined space. A rare advantage of Bram's current altered state.

Before Yralissa's poison, he would have simply melted into shadow and bypassed walls entirely.

There would be time for anger later.

The corridor opened into what appeared to be a disused pantry, dust thick on empty shelves. Goby scurried to a half-hidden door on the far wall, motioning urgently.

"Door close. Hurry!"

Bram followed, grateful for the goblin's knowledge of the

castle's hidden pathways. Without Goby, he'd have never left his cell. The irony wasn't lost on him.

The closest ally for the Seeker others feared was a creature most dismissed.

They emerged into a stone-flagged hallway that Bram recognized as part of the castle's main keep. Sunlight streamed through narrow windows, giving glimpses of the outside. Freedom lay just ahead, through a courtyard, then the outer walls, and beyond that, the forest.

Bram allowed himself a moment of cautious optimism.

The optimism died as two figures stepped around the corner ahead, blocking their path.

"Bram," Liam greeted him, his voice deceptively casual. "Fancy meeting you again."

Beside him, Hywel rested his hand on the pommel of his sword, his expression sour. He jutted his chin toward Goby. "And still with *that*."

Bram halted, instinctively positioning himself between his former allies and his new one. These men had fought alongside him in Ibern, had shared meals and battle strategies and watch duties.

But that had changed.

The Liam and Hywel from before had searched for the sword without understanding the consequences. Now they served with a different purpose. All former camaraderie forgotten.

Bram replied carefully. "Last I knew, the Fianna served the realm."

"The Fianna have always served the purse." Liam's smile didn't reach his eyes. "Alliances shift."

"And you've chosen Fidessa?"

Hywel scoffed. "The mage is useful, but it's the king we serve."

It had been Daenon. Interesting.

"And that sword belongs to him," Liam added.

Bram's hand moved to the sword at his hip. "This is stolen property."

"And now you've stolen it." Hywel's lip curled. "Thief to thief. Who's to say which is right?"

"This sword has a rightful wielder," Bram insisted. "It is not a trophy for a would-be tyrant."

"Strong words from someone who seems disavowed." Liam's gaze swept over Bram's altered appearance with unconcealed suspicion. "What happened to the mighty Seeker? Was the fearsome shadow form just an act? Perhaps you're just the druid's spy."

The accusation stung more than Bram would admit. He hadn't considered how his current appearance might be interpreted by others. How vulnerable it made him, not just physically, but politically.

"You know nothing of who or what I am," Bram said, his voice low. "Or what I've endured."

"What we know," Hywel cut in, drawing his sword with practiced efficiency, "is that you have something we've been paid to reclaim."

Goby tugged frantically at Bram's tunic. "Bad men. Go now!"

Bram assessed his options.

A narrow hallway. Outnumbered.

One option.

"Goby," Bram said quietly, not taking his eyes off the Fianna. "These bad men will take your carrots."

The goblin's yellow eyes widened with understanding. He reached into his basket, fingers closing around something hidden among the carrots.

"Now!" Bram commanded.

Goby hurled his knife at Hywel's face. The warrior reeled

back, cursing as the blade narrowly missed his eyes. In the same moment, Bram surged forward, shoulder-checking Liam into the wall with enough force to stun him momentarily.

Goby twisted between Hywel's feet until he fell.

"Run!" Bram shouted, grabbing Goby and sprinting past the disoriented Fianna.

Behind them, Hywel's furious shouts echoed down the corridor, accompanied by the pounding of boots as they gave chase. Bram pushed himself harder, ignoring the way Goby flopped around in his arms.

They burst through a heavy oak door into blinding sunlight. Bram squinted, momentarily disoriented by the sudden brightness. They stood in what would have been a large courtyard, except a twisting wall of black vines and deadly looking thorns rose from the center.

What was it? It almost breathed as if alive. The thorns contorted this way and that, never remaining still.

Goby wriggled free, jumping to the ground, but stayed pressed next to Bram's leg.

The Fianna had not followed them through the door. Another trap?

Not this time.

Movement from an open walkway above caught Bram's attention. In the center stood Fidessa.

Her expression shifted from surprise to fury as she recognized him. Beside her stood several guards, already nocking arrows at her command.

"Halt, or die where you stand," Fidessa called down, her voice carrying easily across the courtyard.

Bram smirked. The guards' arms already trembled from the strain of their drawn bows. Fidessa really should have chosen more formidable protectors.

"Stay behind me," he murmured to Goby, who clutched at Bram's trouser legs with surprising strength.

"You surprise me, Seeker," Fidessa said, leaning against the wooden railing with feigned casualness as she admitted knowing his secret. "Or should I say, former Seeker? I didn't realize Yralissa had found you again after her first debacle. Her work is very impressive."

Bram ignored the taunt. "Where is Safi?" he demanded. "I know she's here."

"My daughter is no concern of yours." Fidessa's gaze dropped to the sword at his hip. "That, however, is another matter. Return what you've stolen, and perhaps I'll consider letting you live."

Bram shifted his gaze to Fidessa's hands. Her fingers twitched as if she readied to cast. "This sword was never yours to begin with," Bram replied, keeping his voice neutral. "You've stolen enough already, including Safi's will."

Something dangerous flashed in Fidessa's eyes. "You understand nothing of what I've done, or why."

Bram's fingers tightened around the sword's hilt. "You use others as tools for your own ambition. You twist and break them until they're unrecognizable, even to themselves."

"And you're different?" Fidessa laughed, the sound brittle. "The Heptad's attack dog, sent to collect their prizes? Their weapon, bound by oaths and enchantments? We're more alike than you care to admit, you and I."

The words penetrated deeper than he expected. His breath caught, an involuntary response he couldn't suppress. A cascade of unwanted realizations struck with precision: the Heptad's careful manipulation, the way they'd shaped his ambitions as an elfling, how they'd directed his loyalty, his purpose, his very identity.

For a disorienting moment, he saw himself through new

eyes. Not as the skilled Seeker, but as what Fidessa claimed. A weapon aimed at others. A tool crafted for someone else's purpose.

A scream cut through his thoughts, distant, but unmistakably female, filled with pain and defiance.

Rowena.

The recognition hit Bram like lightning, instantly changing his focus. Impossible. Yet he knew that voice with absolute certainty. Rowena was here, somewhere in the castle. Not headed for Twisted Forest as that woman had claimed, but here, within these walls.

And in danger.

"What have you done?" he demanded, his voice dropping to a dangerous pitch that revealed more than he intended. "Where is she?"

"Surprise." Fidessa's grin grew wider, triumphant. "I told you I'd arranged entertainment. I feared you would miss it, but you've arrived in time."

"If you've hurt her, you won't live another day." Bram clenched his fists. The claim wasn't hollow. Nothing would protect the queen if he had to fulfill that promise.

And that didn't disturb him as it should have.

"She's currently enjoying my hospitality in the form of a little challenge." She gestured to the massive thorn hedge behind Bram.

He turned and felt his breath catch. Rowena was inside that?

The thorny vines, black as midnight, gleamed wickedly in the sunlight, each thorn longer than a man's finger. It had grown even taller.

Another scream echoed from within its depths.

"Rowena!" Bram shouted, already moving toward the wall of thorns.

"I wouldn't if I were you," Fidessa called after him, amusement lacing her voice. "Those thorns are poisoned. Only Rowena must enter. One scratch and you'll experience a slow, painful death."

Bram scanned the solid-looking wall, searching desperately for an entrance. The thorns continued to grow, twisting around each other in a macabre dance, forming an impenetrable barrier.

"Goby, stay back," he ordered, drawing the Sword of Justice from his belt.

The blade gleamed in the sunlight, its silver surface catching the light like liquid moonlight. Bram didn't know what would happen if he wielded it, but he had no choice. Its power sent a subtle vibration traveling up his arm, a whisper of potential that strengthened his resolve.

Without further hesitation, he thrust the sword toward the wall of thorns, expecting resistance. Instead, something extraordinary happened.

The thorns nearest the blade trembled, then parted like curtains drawn aside by invisible hands, creating an opening just large enough for a man to pass through.

Behind him, Fidessa gasped. "Impossible."

Bram didn't waste time questioning this unexpected development. "Goby, find somewhere safe to hide," he instructed. "I'll return when I can."

The goblin nodded reluctantly, backing away toward a shadowed corner of the courtyard.

"You're a fool," Fidessa called down. "Even with the sword, you won't survive what waits inside."

Bram spared her one last glance. "I've survived worse than your games, Fidessa."

Then he stepped through the opening onto a pathway. The thorns closed behind him immediately, sealing him inside a deadly labyrinth.

The path ahead twisted and turned, black thorny walls rising on either side like the jaws of some massive beast. The air within grew heavier, charged with something that raised the fine hairs on Bram's arms.

Another scream echoed through the maze, closer now. Rowena's voice filled with determination even through her pain.

Bram tightened his grip on the sword and pressed forward. Every instinct urged him to run, to search frantically, but he forced himself to move methodically. Rushing would only lead to mistakes. Mistakes that could be fatal.

The sword seemed to guide him, the thorns parting wherever the blade pointed. It was as if the weapon recognized its purpose, or perhaps it recognized Rowena, sensing her presence close by.

The thought gave Bram a flicker of hope. If the legends were true, if the Sword of Justice truly was intended for righteous purpose, then perhaps it could lead him to her.

"Rowena!" he called again, his voice echoing strangely in the confined space. "I'm coming!"

Only the rustling of thorns answered him, but Bram pressed on. Somewhere inside, Rowena was fighting for her life. And this time, he wouldn't fail her.

No matter what form he wore, no matter what powers he'd lost, one truth remained unchanged. He would protect her. Or he would die trying.

Sword raised, determination burning in his chest, Bram ventured deeper into the heart of the labyrinth.

38

ROWENA

SWEAT CLUNG to Rowena like a second skin as she staggered forward. Her nostrils tainted by the putrid bunyip's scent. Her encounter with the beast had left her battered and bleeding, each step a stubborn refusal to surrender.

She was alive. And still moving.

The path ahead twisted, narrowing until the thorns on either side touched across the middle. Rowena turned sideways to navigate the gap, wincing as a thorn snagged her already torn sleeve. The thorns seemed more aggressive now, as if sensing her weakness and pressing their advantage.

From somewhere ahead came a sound that didn't belong to the labyrinth. The rhythmic crunch of boots on packed earth. A new obstacle.

Rowena froze, her hand reaching for a weapon she no longer carried. Her knife remained embedded in the bunyip's body. Her enchantment a wavering flicker, so she wasn't completely defenseless.

The footsteps drew closer. Rowena pressed herself against the thorny wall, ignoring the sharp points that dug into her back. If this was another of Fidessa's creations, she would face it head-on. She refused to die, cowering in fear.

But something different bubbled up inside her chest. Her skin tingled. Feelings she'd had before, when she'd sensed the Sword of Justice. It couldn't be that.

A figure rounded the corner, tall and lean, with a sword gleaming silver in the filtered sunlight. For a heartbeat, Rowena didn't recognize this stranger with white hair and haunted eyes.

Then recognition struck her. But was it really him or another of Fidessa's tricks?

"Bram?"

His head snapped up at her voice, disbelief and relief warring across his features. "Rowena."

He took a step toward her, then halted, his eyes widening as he took in her bloodied state. "You're hurt."

A laugh bubbled up from Rowena's chest, half hysterical with exhaustion and relief. It was really him. She barely recognized him, but he was here. In the most terrible place possible, they'd found each other again. She couldn't get her feet to move, to run to him, to fall apart in his arms.

Because those times were gone. Instead of a joyous reunion, they would have to survive.

Something like shame flickered across Bram's face. He pointed to himself. "It's a long story."

She hated that he sounded so unsure, as if he expected her rejection. Where was the Seeker who had all the answers and could whisk them away in barely a breath's time? After they survived, because they would, they would share their stories.

He closed the distance between them, shoving the sword under his belt to free his hands. "What happened to you? Where are you injured?"

Rowena waved away his concern, though the gesture sent pain lancing through her wounds. Too many to distinguish one from another. "I'll live. There was a beast—" She broke off, not trusting her own memories. Had it been real? Or another of Fidessa's illusions, like the Conri-golem? The blood soaking through her tunic provided her with the painful answer.

She wanted to reach out, touch him, prove he was real. She held back. He held the sword. Where had it been?

"We need to get out of here," Bram said, his gaze darting to the thorny walls around them. "The sword cleared a path, leading me here, to you. If we follow it—"

A grinding sound interrupted him, the now-familiar noise of thorns growing and shifting. The already narrow path constricted further, the black vines twisting toward them with unnatural speed.

"Fidessa," Rowena spat. "She's pushing them faster."

"She can see us?" Bram asked, lifting the sword hip-high.

"I don't know how, but she always seems to know exactly where I am." Rowena backed away from an aggressive thorn that lunged like a striking serpent. "She's been manipulating this labyrinth from the start."

Bram raised the Sword of Justice, its silver blade catching the light. The nearest thorns recoiled, as if repelled by its presence. "Let's move. I came in from the western edge. If we backtrack—"

The grinding intensified, drowning out his words. The path behind Bram sealed itself completely, black thorns interweaving to form an impenetrable wall. At the same moment, Rowena spun as the thorns behind them did the same.

Trapped. The shrinking section of the path allowed the thorns to advance from all sides.

"Use the sword!" Rowena urged, pressing closer to Bram as the space contracted around them.

Bram circled, and she turned with him as he swung the blade in a wide arc, creating momentary space as the thorns shrank back. But they advanced again almost immediately, more determined than before.

"It's not working," he growled, frustration clear in his voice. "Something's different."

Rowena's mind raced. What had changed? If the sword had allowed Bram to enter the labyrinth, had cleared a path for him . . . how would it lose its power now?

Unless . . .

"I made a deal with Fidessa." The realization crystallized. "If I escaped the labyrinth, she would release Safi from her service."

Bram's eyes widened with understanding. "She never expected you to survive. Now that we're together—"

"She will not allow me to escape," Rowena finished.

The thorns pressed closer, forcing them to stand back-to-back in the shrinking space. One vicious spike darted forward, aiming for Bram's exposed side. He twisted to avoid it, but not quickly enough.

The thorn pierced his leather tunic, sinking deep into the flesh beneath his ribs. Bram's face contorted in pain, a harsh gasp escaping his lips. He stumbled, the sword slipping from his grasp.

"Bram!" Rowena spun, catching him as he sagged against her, her own injured body protesting the added weight. She eased them both to the ground.

Blood blossomed around the embedded thorn, staining his tunic a dark crimson. His face had gone alarmingly pale, beads of sweat forming on his brow.

"Poisoned," he managed through gritted teeth. "She wasn't . . . bluffing."

Horror washed through Rowena. Many of the thorns had torn at her flesh, but none of them did this. Fidessa. Again.

The thorn remained embedded in his side, still attached to the wall. Each slight movement seemed to drive it deeper, causing fresh blood to well around the wound. With trembling hands, Rowena reached for the base of the thorn, intending to break it free.

"Don't," Bram gasped, catching her wrist. "Might poison you."

It was doubtful the poison would affect her, since it hadn't so far. But Fidessa kept changing course, so she would be cautious. Ripping out the thorn might cause the wound to bleed more freely. But leaving it meant he remained tethered to the wall, unable to move as the surrounding space continued to shrink.

"Can you expel the poison? Or heal it? Like you've done for others." Rowena's hands trembled. She had never imagined Bram being hurt.

He shook his head, not meeting her gaze. His jaw worked back and forth as if he wanted to say something else, but didn't.

"The sword," Bram said, his voice weakening. "Take it."

Rowena stared at the sword. The sword her mother had smuggled out of Penumar, and Uther had stolen after he destroyed her family.

"Take it," he repeated more urgently. "You can go . . ."

"Not without you."

Bram pressed his lips to a pale line. With obvious effort, he nudged the sword with his foot. The hilt was mere inches from her fingers.

It called to her. An irresistible urge that pulled her like it was tied to her by a string. She'd take it and make sure they both found the exit.

The moment Rowena's fingers closed around the sword a strange sensation traveled up her arm. A warmth spread through her body like sunlight after a long winter. The blade seemed to pulse in her grasp, resonating with the well of enchantment within her.

Without conscious thought, she swung the sword at the thorn piercing Bram's side.

The blade connected with a sound like crystal striking crystal. Light, brilliant and silver, flashed at the point of contact, momentarily blinding her.

The thorn broke off with a sharp crack, still embedded, but no longer connected to the wall. But then the severed vine . . . transformed.

Where the black, vicious spike had been, a deep red rose bud appeared, unfurling before her eyes. The petals opened with impossible speed, revealing velvety depths. The transformation spread rapidly from the point of contact, racing along the thorny tangle of vines like wildfire.

Everywhere the change touched, deadly thorns became tight rose buds that blossomed into full, lush blooms. Their sweet fragrance filled Rowena's lungs, replacing the musty decay of the labyrinth. The grinding noise that had haunted her journey ceased, replaced by a gentle rustling like whispered secrets as the transformation continued in all directions.

"How . . .?" Rowena breathed, staring in wonder at the sword in her hand. The metal was alive against her palm, warm and singing with power.

Bram slumped, one hand pressed to his wounded side, the broken thorn still embedded in his flesh. Blood seeped between his fingers.

"The sword," he managed through gritted teeth. "It's your hands that must wield it."

It made no sense. Fidessa was playing games. That had to be it. Then she recalled . . . something. Something else from the dryads.

"The queen told me, but I didn't understand." The dryads *had* known she would face this labyrinth of thorns. What had she said? "The blade that cuts may also heal."

"Because it's from Caelus," Bram answered, his voice strained.

She hadn't realized she'd spoken the words aloud. "Did you know it would do that?"

Bram huffed a pained chuckle that ended in a wince. "Not at all, but I should have guessed."

No one could think such a thing possible. He couldn't have known, could he? As the Seeker, did he have that knowledge? She still didn't understand; not really. But, seeing death become life, roses bloom from thorns, could it really be because of her? The thought made her dizzy, frightened, and exhilarated all at once.

The transformation continued to spread outward in all directions, thorns becoming roses with each passing second. Where before the labyrinth had been a claustrophobic nightmare of twisted black vines, it was becoming an extraordinary garden of climbing roses, their perfume growing stronger with each breath.

"We need to keep moving," Rowena said, shifting her stance to better help Bram to his feet and support his weight. Her own injuries protested, but she pushed the pain aside. "Can you walk?"

He nodded grimly, though the motion cost him. "The exit should be clearer now."

Together they moved forward, Rowena wielding the sword in one hand while supporting Bram with her other arm. His body warm against hers. Before, the paths had been confusing and ever-changing, but now they stretched before them, straight and clear. As they walked, the roses seemed to sense their approach, blooms turning toward them and vines drawing back from the path. Where thorns had once reached hungrily for her flesh, the stems now curved away, creating a passage wide enough for them to walk side by side.

"How did you find me?" Rowena asked as they navigated the transformed labyrinth. She wanted to know more about what he'd been through, how or what had changed his appearance, but she held those questions for later. When they had a quiet moment. If that ever came.

Bram kept his voice steady, yet there was still a strain. "Someone told me you'd headed to the Twisted Forest. Went to Grimhold. Came back. I didn't know you were here until I heard your scream."

"I've only been here two days. Daenon found me." Because she'd trusted someone she shouldn't have.

"They were together the whole time," Bram said, coming to the same conclusion she had. "How did you end up in here?"

"He and his warriors, wearing chalk like ancient times, dragged me to Fidessa. She is convinced I know the Lunastone's location. She's desperate to find it."

They walked in silence for a moment. The roses continued to bloom around them, their perfume growing stronger with each step.

Rowena led the way with the sword held before her. With a simple light tap, its power continued to transform any remaining thorns they encountered, creating a clear path toward what Rowena hoped was the exit.

Ahead of them an opening appeared. The stone wall of the castle peeking through as if Sawel shined all her light on it at once.

Relief washed through Rowena. "We're almost out."

As they approached the exit, Rowena braced herself for one last trap. Fidessa wasn't one to admit defeat easily. But nothing barred their way. The roses parted, forming an archway of blossoms that framed the exit.

They stepped through together, emerging into the open air of the castle yard. Rowena blinked at the brighter light, trying to clear her vision while maintaining her grip on both Bram and the sword.

As her sight adjusted, she became aware of figures surrounding them. Fidessa's pudgy guards, staring in obvious shock at the transformed labyrinth.

And above them all, on the walkway where Rowena had last seen her, Fidessa remained. Her expression was unreadable from this distance, but the rigid set of her shoulders betrayed her fury.

"You've lost," Rowena called up to her, raising the sword so that sunlight gleamed along its blade. "I escaped your labyrinth, as we agreed. Now release Safi."

For a long moment, Fidessa said nothing. Then, with deliberate slowness, she turned her back and disappeared through a door at the end of the walkway.

"Coward!" Rowena shouted after her. "Face me!"

But Fidessa was gone.

The guards remained, however, forming a loose circle around Rowena and Bram. Uncertainty was clear in their postures—their queen had departed without orders, leaving them to decide whether to attack or stand down.

Bram straightened beside her. One hand still pressed to his wounded side but his stance firming. "We need to find Safi," he murmured. "And quickly."

Rowena nodded, tightening her grip on the sword. The blade hummed in her grasp, as if eager for what came next.

"I've fulfilled my part of the bargain," she announced to the assembled guards. "Regardless of whether Fidessa honors hers, I'm claiming my cousin's freedom. Anyone who stands in my way will face the consequence."

She raised the Sword of Justice, its silver surface reflecting the golden sunlight like a beacon. Behind them, the labyrinth of roses seemed to pulse in response, petals rustling in a nonexistent breeze.

For a heartbeat, no one moved. Then, with a sound like a sigh from the soil itself, the rose labyrinth collapsed. The roses released their hold on one another, scattering petals over the grass like crimson snowflakes; stems dissolving into silver motes that drifted skyward.

The guards exchanged glances, their uncertainty growing. One by one, they backed away, lowering their weapons.

Rowena didn't waste time questioning their actions. With Bram still leaning against her, she moved forward. The Sword of Justice held ready in case the guards changed their minds.

They reached the keep's entrance unchallenged. Bram paused at the threshold. His breathing labored but his gaze clear.

"That was helpful. I'm not sure I could handle even those sloppy fighters right now," Bram said. "

Rowena glanced down at the blade, still humming with energy in her grasp. "This feels . . . right," she admitted. "Like it knows me."

"Maybe it does." Bram straightened, wincing but determined. "We should find Safi. And then we need to get out of this castle before Fidessa rallies her forces."

Rowena nodded, her resolve hardening. She'd escaped the labyrinth, transformed thorns to roses, and forced Fidessa to retreat. But there was still no victory until Safi stood with them.

Together, they entered the keep, the sword still lighting their way with its silver glow. Whatever challenges awaited them next; Rowena would face them with new confidence.

The sword had chosen her.

39

ROWENA

As THEY MOVED through the castle's winding hallways, anxiety settled like a stone in Rowena's stomach. They had escaped Fidessa's thorns, but Safi remained imprisoned somewhere in this fortress. Enchanted, silenced, transformed into a weapon against her will.

How would they find her? Bram still held his side, and didn't appear he could fight. Most likely he would anyway, but what damage would it cause?

Not only that, but how would she be able to help anyone. She'd spent no time with either moon for several nights. Her enchantment seemed far enough away to be non-existent. Her only option would be to rely on her weapons training, and hope it was enough.

"This way," Bram murmured, leading them down a narrow corridor. He moved with purpose despite his injury, though Rowena noted how he favored his right side, where the thorn had pierced him. The wound had stopped bleeding, at least. She hated that he had another injury because of her. When he'd obviously been through something terrible while they were apart.

She wanted to ask about his pain, but the words caught in her throat. Everything about him seemed different now. Not just his altered appearance, with the white hair and long nails that hovered between elven and Seeker, but his manner as well. He was more guarded, more hesitant.

Or perhaps she was the one who had changed.

The sword at her hip felt like a physical manifestation of this shift. She had wielded it in the labyrinth, had discovered its power, *through her*, to transform thorns into roses. It should have been a moment of shared triumph. Instead, it brought more questions.

"I think we're close," Bram said, interrupting her thoughts. He paused at an intersection his gaze distant as he tried to orient himself. "There was a woman, it didn't seem she was a prisoner, being held in quarters near here. I saw her when . . ." He trailed off, a shadow crossing his face.

"When what?" Rowena prompted.

"When I followed Goby through a passage inside the walls," he finished, unwilling to elaborate further. "Her chambers were comfortable, but guarded. It might be the same area where Safi stays."

Rowena studied him, noting the tension in his jaw, the way he avoided meeting her eyes. Whatever had happened to him in this castle had left scars that ran deeper than the visible changes.

"Do you want to talk about it?" she asked. She tried to make her voice sound casual.

"About what?" As if he didn't understand her meaning.

"Whatever happened to you. Why you're . . ." She gestured at his altered appearance.

Bram's expression closed off, cold. "Not now."

The rejection stung more than it should have.

She was being irrational. They still had danger ahead of

them. They were sneaking through the castle. It wasn't time for a deep discussion about their feelings.

"We should keep moving," Rowena said, filling the awkward silence. "Fidessa won't remain hidden for long."

As if summoned by her words, a series of shouts echoed from somewhere deeper in the castle. Guards mobilizing, no doubt. Time was running short.

"The chambers were this way," Bram said, gesturing down the left passage. "If we hurry—"

A scuffling sound interrupted him as a compact figure darted from the shadows, brandishing an axe nearly as large as its own body. Rowena's hand flew to the sword, drawing it in one fluid motion.

"Whoa!" Bram stepped between them hand raised toward Rowena. "It's alright. He's with us."

Rowena hesitated, studying the creature. A goblin with bulbous yellow eyes and grayish skin, clutching the oversized axe with determined intensity. Strapped to its back, a wicker basket bulging with what appeared to be . . . carrots?

"Rowena, this is Goby," Bram explained. "He helped me escape my cell and find the sword. Goby, this is Rowena."

The goblin darted glances without meeting her eyes, focused on the sword in her hand. "Big sword," he muttered. "Other girl?"

"One of them," Bram assured him, reaching for the axe. "May I?"

Goby relinquished the weapon with obvious reluctance. "Got from guard. For Bram."

"Thank you." Bram's voice held genuine warmth as he accepted the axe. "I knew you'd find somewhere safe to hide."

Watching the ease of their interaction struck Rowena. He spoke to this small goblin as an equal, as a friend.

He had found someone else to protect. The thought

bombarded her, and she shamed herself over the petty jealousy. What right did she have to begrudge either of them this unlikely alliance?

Bram twisted and stared at the sword. "This might be a good time to remember that the sword must not draw blood."

The hilt grew cold in Rowena's palm, her fingers icy. The way it reacted to her. The roses. She had forgotten. She could have done something terrible.

She swallowed. Nothing had happened. Everything was still fine.

She secured the sword through her belt.

"Thank you."

"Ah, but I have a surprise." Bram sat the axe head on the ground, resting the handle against leg. He twisted with a hiss, removing something at his side. His wound needed care. "I believe this is yours?"

He held out the dagger she'd left in the cottage. A slight lift to the corner of his mouth was like a ray of sunshine. She took it gently.

"Your knife is in my sling as well. Hopefully you won't need either, or leave them behind again, but now you have a weapon you *can* use."

He'd not given up. He'd believed they would reunite. A twinge of guilt pricked at her heart. There were moments, too many, where she had not been so sure.

Rowena needed to put the dagger where the sword was, but it became awkward.

"Here, let me help," Bram said.

He leaned in close and helped remove the sword, brushing her waist with his fingers. In the hallway, without all the must and grime from the thorn labyrinth, his charred oak scent filtered through, like a revitalizing incense. She lifted her eyes to study his face. So close. Runes, so light they barely showed, edged his temples. They were brighter in his Seeker form.

Bram had gone still.

She shifted her gaze and met his. The world slipped away. Only this moment existed.

She glanced at his lips, warm, full, familiar—

"Woman this way," Goby announced.

They both leaned away, startled, having forgotten the goblin, who pointed down a different corridor than the one Bram had indicated.

"Goby show."

Bram cleared his throat. "We can strap the sword along your back, so it's out of your way."

"That would be helpful." Rowena turned and pulled her braid over her shoulder. When was the last time she'd paid attention to her hair? She plucked a broken leaf from among the flyaways.

Bram's fingers on her back sent tingles through her. Her knees threatened to turn to sand.

"There," he whispered into her ear, his breath warm on her skin.

Moons. She'd missed him.

When he stepped back, she kept her face to the wall an extra heartbeat or two. Until the heat sweeping through her faded.

"The woman I saw?" Bram asked Goby, returning to their task at hand. "The chamber was this way."

Goby shook his head, hard enough to rattle his body. "That lady gone."

"Gone?" Bram and Rowena exchanged glances.

"Tephra?" Rowena thought aloud. How would Bram know her? "She left before Fidessa built the thorn walls."

"Other lady." Goby insisted, tugging at Bram's tunic. "Still here. Goby know."

"You've met a lot of ladies, it seems." Rowena snickered, allowing herself a moment that wasn't filled with dread.

Confusion flickered across Bram's face, then he understood, shaking his head. "You have no idea."

Goby huffed.

"It could be Safi," Bram said to Rowena. "Worth investigating."

"Lead the way," Rowena told the goblin. Bram had done well, the sword rested comfortably along her spine as if part of her. The dagger was a much better size on her hip.

Goby scampered ahead, agile despite his awkward burden. Bram and Rowena followed, her muscles tense, keeping her steps light and ready through the corridors.

Some of them seemed familiar to Rowena, but she hadn't traveled them enough to be sure.

The goblin led them past several unmarked doors, then stopped as sudden as if he'd hit a wall before one that appeared identical to the others. He pressed a finger to his lips, then gestured for them to wait. With remarkable stealth for such an ungainly creature, he approached the door and pressed his ear against it.

After a moment, he shook his head. "No sound. Maybe sleeping."

Bram reached for the handle, but Rowena caught his wrist. "Wait," she whispered. "Check for a spell."

"How would we know?"

Rowena hesitated. "Let me try."

She closed her eyes, extending her awareness as she had in Havilar, feeling for the telltale resonance of magic. There was . . . something. A faint hum, like distant bees.

"There's an enchanted signature here." She opened her eyes, disappointment flaring. "But I can't tell if there's a spell or not."

"Only one way to find out," Bram said grimly. He positioned

himself between Rowena, no longer holding his side. The blood no longer seeping through the hole in his tunic. He tried the latch.

It opened without resistance.

The room beyond was not the lavish chamber Bram had described. Instead, they found themselves in Fidessa's room. Empty and dark. The hallways *had* been familiar.

"Behind that door is Fidessa's spell room."

"Are you sure?" Bram asked.

"I was in here yesterday."

"The spell she used on Safi could be in there. We might find out what went wrong. It could help her recover," Bram said.

Rowena closed her eyes. It made sense. But would they be wasting time getting to her?

"We might not be able to get back here later," Bram said, answering the objections that had to be all over her face.

It made sense. "Let's hurry."

They jogged across the darkened room. No pattering feet, or shuffling feathers moved. Hopefully, all of Fidessa's pets had gone away with her.

Rowena opened the unlocked door to the room she'd gotten a glimpse of the day before. Jars of dried herbs, vials of colored liquids, and stacks of parchment covered every surface. A large table dominated the center, covered with open scrolls held down by various small objects—crystals, stones, and what looked like bones. Shelves on each wall held oddities and more jars, boxes, and glass bottles.

Rowena exhaled and stepped inside.

Bram followed more cautiously, axe held ready, and closed the door behind them. "Wow."

"There might be something here we can use, but how will we know?" Rowena moved to the table, eyes scanning the scattered documents. "She was clearly in the middle of something."

With cautious fingers, she unrolled one scroll. Arcane symbols covered the parchment, interspersed with text in a language she couldn't read. She tried another, finding similar indecipherable markings.

Bram joined her at the table while Goby explored the room, poking into corners and sniffing at jars with overt curiosity.

"Careful Goby," Bram said.

"Goby is." As soon as he spoke the words, the goblin tipped over a jar with his foot.

Not good. They had to hurry.

"Can you read any of this?" Rowena asked, pushing a scroll toward Bram.

He shook his head. "Some of it looks like the old Primary language, but twisted somehow. Corrupted."

Rowena continued searching, moving aside scrolls to reveal others beneath. One caught her eye, not for its contents, most were incomprehensible, but for a symbol drawn at the bottom. A crescent moon, rocking on its back, cradling a triangle inside its curve. The remnant symbol.

"Look at this," she said, gesturing for Bram to see. "On the bottom looks like a signature, too. Correspondence?"

Bram leaned closer, studying the mark. "That's definitely the remnant mark. These names, though. They have to be code names. Look at them."

He spread out several scrolls, holding them open against the table.

"Taleweaver?" Rowena asked. "Sounds like someone admitting to being a liar. This one is just signed Z."

"This one says Thornheart. A little ironic." He rubbed his side, then lifted the parchment higher to examine it closer, letting the others curl around themselves again. "We should take some of these with us. I'll work on deciphering them later."

"Do you think Fidessa's working with others?" The realization sent a chill down Rowena's spine. "Or just has spies?"

She thought of Tephra's revelation that others were hunting moon-born, that they sought to either control or destroy the prophecy. "What if it's her allies—a cadre?"

They fell silent, both absorbing the implications. If Fidessa was part of an organized effort to find and control the moon-born, their quest had just become more complex.

Rowena's gaze fell on another scroll, this one detailing what appeared to be a ritual of some kind. At its center was a rough sketch of a stone—oval-shaped and colored black. Three wavy lines stacked atop each other were drawn next to it.

"The Lunastone?" she murmured, a sense of recognition despite never having seen the onyx heartstone before. The empty setting in the sword's hilt was oval-shaped.

Bram moved to her side, studying the illustration.

"Everyone keeps asking me about the Lunastone. Fidessa tortured me for its location. But I've never even seen it." Frustration colored her voice. "Why do they all think I know where it is?"

Bram frowned, reading the more legible text surrounding the image. "This mentions a connection between a stone and a silver vessel. I bet she's trying to decipher the prophecy."

The theory made a certain sense, though it offered little practical help. "Rituals and vessels . . . it seems so destructive."

Bram's expression softened. "People fear what they don't understand."

The comment hung between them, laden with unspoken meaning. Was he speaking of the Lunastone or her? Or what had happened to him?

"Bram," Rowena began, unsure if she should question him again. Though it was a quieter moment.

"I don't want to discuss it." His voice was flat, final, not giving her a chance to ask her question.

"But maybe I could help. My abilities are growing stronger. If I understood what happened—"

"I said no." The words came out harsher than he seemed to intend. He sighed, running a hand through his white hair. "I'm sorry. It's just . . . not something I'm ready to talk about."

The rejection stung, but Rowena swallowed her hurt. Pushing would only drive him further away. She'd wait. She'd made it known she would listen when he was ready. It wasn't right to push. Instead, she nodded and returned her attention to the scrolls.

She selected another one at random, this one containing a detailed illustration of a dragon, not the fire-breathers of legend, a frost dragon. Clear enough that it triggered her memories of the one in Ibern. How she'd somehow influenced it to stop fighting them. This one was leaner, with frost-like patterns decorating its scales and very few feathers on its wings.

"A frost dragon?" Bram said, glancing over her shoulder.

Rowena nodded, though something about the illustration struck her as different from the creature she remembered. The dragon in the drawing seemed smaller, with a pattern of scars across one wing. "Is it the same one? Everyone thought they were extinct until that one attacked us. Could there be more?"

"Possibly." Bram moved to examine another section of the table. "If Fidessa was behind the attack in Velmeg, it would make sense she'd have information about the dragons here."

That explanation didn't sit right with Rowena. The drawing seemed more like a study than a battle report. Detailed observations of the creature's habits and physical characteristics, notes about its diet and behavior. Drawings and calculations. Almost like the records of a caretaker, not a commander.

Goby's excited chittering interrupted her thoughts. The

goblin had discovered a hidden compartment in the shelf and was pulling out a stack of rolled scrolls, each with wax bearing a crescent-and-star symbol.

"More secret messages," Rowena murmured, taking one from Goby. "Sealed ones."

Bram nodded, gathering several of the scrolls. "Here," he said, turning to Goby. "Room in your basket?"

The goblin's eyes popped wide, seemingly horrified by sharing space with his carrots, but after a moment's consideration, he nodded, though the way he twisted his lips, it was begrudgingly. "Goby help. Goby good."

Together, they stuffed as many scrolls as they could fit into Goby's basket alongside the vegetables. They chose all the ones bearing the crescent-and-star seal, while they also focused on documents that seemed to detail enchantments or spells.

"Look at this." Bram held up a scroll covered in diagrams of what appeared to be iron bars etched with runes. "There were ones like this in my cell. They blocked my powers."

Cell? Blocked his powers? A chill rolled over Rowena's neck. She moved closer, studying the intricate patterns. "Do you know what they mean?"

"Some of them." Hope flickered in Bram's eyes, there and then gone. He rolled it tight and stuffed it into the basket.

As they worked, their familiar connection rekindled, tentative, fragile, but real. The awkwardness that had plagued them earlier faded as they focused on the common goal. They moved around each other with the unconscious coordination of partners who had once face more than battles together.

Yet beneath the surface, questions remained. Rowena felt the weight of them as she worked, stealing glances at Bram when he wasn't looking. His movements were less fluid than before, his confidence dimmed. The Seeker she had known, powerful, assured, sometimes terrifyingly intense, seemed buried beneath layers of doubt and pain.

They were both changing. Him by force, her by choice. Growing apart even as they stood side by side.

The thought brought a hollow ache to her chest. She had spent so much of her life alone, first as an elfling without siblings and then through slavery. Finding Bram had been like discovering a kindred spirit. Someone who understood duty and sacrifice, who saw her for who she truly was. As she saw him.

Now, that connection felt tenuous, strained by all they had endured apart.

"I think we've found enough we can use," Bram said, interrupting her reflections.

Rowena nodded, rolling up the scroll she'd been examining. "Fidessa might re—"

A soft click from the door silenced her mid-word. They froze, exchanging alarmed glances as the latch turned.

Someone was entering the spell room.

40

BRAM

Bram moved with silent precision, positioning himself beside the door as the latch lifted. He gripped the axe tightly, ready to strike the moment whoever it was stepped inside. Across the room, Rowena had drawn her dagger, its silver blade catching the lamplight as she crouched behind the spell table.

Goby scrambled beneath the table, yellow eyes wide with alarm, one hand protectively clutching his basket of carrots and stolen scrolls.

The door swung inward with deliberate slowness.

Bram tensed. He had no desire to add unnecessary bloodshed.

A woman slipped into the room.

Practiced. Purposeful.

Dark hair. Light, gauzy trousers with open sides.

He recognized her immediately.

The woman from the hidden room, the one he'd glimpsed through the peephole while navigating the secret passages. The one who had spoken of a princess escaping into the Twisted Forest. She appeared unarmed, though Bram knew better than to assume that meant harmless.

She had lied to him.

Bram stepped forward, grabbing her wrist and twisting her arm behind her back in one smooth motion, not enough to hurt, but enough to hold her. She reacted instantly, dropping her weight and attempting to break his hold, but he countered, using his strength to pin her against the wall. His side screamed from the effort.

"Who are you?" His voice was low and dangerous.

The woman stilled, recognizing the futility of resistance. "I could ask you the same," she replied, her accent marking her as unquestionably Solara.

"Tephra?" Rowena emerged from behind the table, her blade lowered but not sheathed. Her tone contained a complex mixture of emotions Bram couldn't fully decipher. Anger, certainly, but also hurt, confusion, perhaps even a reluctant concern.

"This is who you traveled with?" Bram asked, not relaxing his hold.

"Unfortunately." Rowena approached slowly; her eyes fixed on the Solara woman. "This is Tephra, the Solara, who betrayed me to Daenon."

Tephra flinched slightly at the accusation, though whether from guilt or mere discomfort at her position, Bram couldn't tell.

"I did what was necessary to survive," she said, a hint of defiance threading through her words.

"Is that why you lied to me?" Bram released her, but moved in front of the door to block an escape. "You told me Rowena had gone to the Twisted Forest."

Tephra's eyes widened fractionally. "You expected the truth when you were peeking at me from behind a wall?"

Rowena made a sound in her throat, but said nothing.

Goby chose that moment to crawl into the open.

"That is one of Fidessa's pets!" Tephra called.

"Not pet!" Goby spun and scrambled back out of sight under the table. "Work kitchen."

Rowena let out an amused huff. "You're the beastie Cook worried about."

"Cook nice."

"You are trusting *that,* but slam me against the wall?" Tephra sneered, glancing toward the darkness where Goby hid.

"He's proven himself a trustworthy friend," Bram replied. "You, however, need to explain why you lied about Rowena's whereabouts?"

Tephra's nostrils flared. "Why does anyone lie? Survival. To buy time." Her gaze shifted to Rowena. "I knew Fidessa would send someone after you. I thought that might be who he was, and if he searched the forest first, it might give you time to escape."

"How considerate." Rowena's voice dripped with sarcasm. "Especially after you led Daenon straight to me."

Confusion creased Bram's brow. He glanced between the two women, trying to piece together their shared history. "When did you meet?"

"In the jungle," Rowena confirmed, not taking her eyes off Tephra." After I left Havilar. We crossed paths when her own escape went awry."

"I helped you cross the river," Tephra pointed out. "Kept you alive when that snake nearly killed you."

"Only to abandon me while I slept, then trade my location to Daenon when you were caught." Rowena slammed her dagger into its sheath. "Tell me, was betrayal always your plan, or was it a convenient afterthought?"

Tephra glanced at the door, then rolled her eyes at Bram. "I was trying to get home," she said, her voice suddenly tired. "Back to Farradar. You never understood what was at stake for me."

"You told me you were running from your home," Rowena challenged. "What could have changed your mind enough to trade your freedom for mine?"

"The Tournament of Saints." Tephra's words emerged like stones, heavy with meaning Bram didn't fully comprehend. "It needs to end. So many others will still participate. I have to go back."

The declaration hung in the air between them. Bram saw something flicker across Rowena's face, a reluctant understanding, perhaps even empathy, quickly suppressed.

"I struggle to believe you had such a change of heart," Rowena said. "You're still in Fidessa's castle. She freed you, so if returning home was so urgent, why linger?"

Tephra's jaw tightened. "I need some information. A safety net if Fidessa does not hold up her end of our bargain."

"What deal did you make?" Bram asked, already suspecting the answer.

"Becoming a traitor," Rowena answered.

"To provide *information*," Tephra countered.

"She is going to tell Fidessa about the Solara moon-born." Rowena's lip curled as if she wanted to spit. "And the location of their signet ring."

Bram and Rowena exchanged glances. Fidessa's network of informants and allies in the scrolls. All focused on the moon-born and the artifacts connected to the prophecy.

"She's helping someone else," Bram whispered, more to himself than the others. Of course. Fidessa didn't have the resources or the power for the amount of ambition she had. But who?

"How did you prove to her that you could get that information?" Rowena asked Tephra.

"I told her what she wanted to hear." A hint of pride entered Tephra's voice. "Half-truths mixed with untruths. Enough to maintain her interest without revealing anything truly valuable."

"A dangerous game," Bram said.

"Life is dangerous." Tephra's gaze shifted to the table littered with scrolls. "I came back for something I saw earlier. A scroll describing a frost dragon's connection to Farradar. I have never heard of such an interaction."

Bram recalled the scroll Rowena found with detailed illustrations of a frost dragon. The one they'd assumed was connected to the attack in Velmeg.

The open sky. The frigid air. Realization dawned.

"That's what's at the end of the dungeons," he said. "Fidessa has a frost dragon."

Tephra nodded. A smile, smug and knowing. "He's not a captive. He stays because he chooses to."

That explained the scroll. It was detailed care notes. How had Fidessa gotten attached to a dragon?

"She sent him to attack us in Velmeg," Rowena said, her expression darkening at the memory.

Tephra shook her head. "No. That one was different. One of the wild ones from the northern mountains. Fidessa was as surprised by that attack as you were."

"It wasn't completely wild. Someone called it to the village. Who? Was it Fidessa?" Bram demanded.

"I don't know." Tephra's eyes shifted to the scrolls again. "But I suspect the answer might be in one of those communications. Fidessa has many allies."

Silence fell between them, each lost in their own thoughts. The Solara woman made no attempt to escape, seemingly resigned that she couldn't get past him.

"Fidessa said she gave you something. Is that the way to disguise yourself?" Rowena finally asked.

"Yes, and I will return to Farradar," Tephra confirmed.

Rowena studied Tephra for a long moment.

"Why are you really here?" she finally asked. "In this room, right now, when you should be miles away?"

Tephra's gaze dropped to the floor. "I came back for those scrolls, as I said."

"And you just happened in here at the same time we arrived?" Bram tensed. She could be in there just to stall them. With others waiting outside when they try to leave.

"I was hiding in the other room," Tephra answered.

"The door was unlocked," Rowena said. "Why didn't you come in yourself?"

"I did." Tephra grinned. "Then I wanted to check the desk in the other room, but you showed up."

"Why come back?" Bram did not like political games, and this one played them with far too much ease and skill. "You've got a scroll in your waistband. Or did you think it didn't show under your tunic?"

Tephra met his stare. "To warn Rowena that Fidessa has allies in other realms. Those searching for her are too strong."

"I'm aware of the others," Bram said, more curious about the scroll she stole and the information it contained.

"You are?" Rowena snapped her gaze to him, brows pinched.

He only nodded, hoping she would understand his reluctance to share more in that moment.

She flattened her lips, seeming to understand, then turned her attention back to Tephra. "And you're telling me this for what? Forgiveness?"

"Information." Tephra stared at the sword peeking from Rowena's back. "I saw him take the sword. And now you have it. I know it's connected to the prophecy somehow. I thought perhaps . . ." She trailed off.

"Thought what?" Bram kept his attention split between her face and her hands. Crucial tells happened in both places.

"I thought if I warned you about the danger, you might not come after me."

"You said you're not a moon-born," Rowena said. "Is that a lie, also?"

"That is true."

Bram catalogued her lowered pitch, the change in her vocal pattern. No defensive posture shifts. Her claim seemed genuine, whatever that was worth. "What is in the scroll you have?"

"A communication from the king of Farradar, detailing his hunt for the moon-born. I thought it might help me understand what I'm facing when I return home."

"Show me," Rowena demanded.

"No games," Bram added, maintaining visual contact with the knife poorly concealed on Tephra's thigh. The metal caught candlelight through the gap in her trousers; an amateur mistake. If she intended to use it, she'd have positioned it for a cleaner draw.

Tephra slowly reached into her waistband, Bram tensed, ready for multiple counter scenarios, but she only withdrew a tightly rolled scroll sealed with red wax bearing a sun insignia. She extended it to Rowena, who took it without allowing skin contact. Smart.

"I meant what I said about the danger," Tephra said as Rowena broke the seal. "They're hunting all moon-born. Including you."

Rowena unrolled the scroll, her eyes scanning its contents. Her expression remained carefully neutral, but Bram saw the slight widening of her eyes, the almost imperceptible tightening of her jaw.

"It's true," she said quietly, passing the scroll to Bram. "This one is written very clearly. The king of Farradar knows I'm the Lunara moon-born. He's ordered his men to capture me, alive if possible, dead if necessary."

Bram read the scroll quickly, his anger mounting with each line. The document was cold, clinical, discussing Rowena as if she were an object to be acquired rather than a person. "How could they know this? How did you know it said this?"

"It has been more than a month since she was exposed," Tephra said. "Ample time for letters to reach all the realms. And I have my ways."

"I'm not safe anywhere," Rowena said. "None of us are."

Bram rubbed his hand over his jaw.

A month. Exposed.

The same timeframe since he'd found her. He'd been so arrogant to think he could find the moon-born without resistance. That his presence alone would prevent intrusion to his plans.

He still believed leaving Evora in Havilar was the best option. But maybe he should have insisted Esme and Gabe come with him? And what of her brother? The moon-born were becoming like scattered cats. And he could no longer sense any of them.

Tephra's shoulders tensed. He should have noticed her tell faster. She twisted in a fluid motion that caught him flat-footed. Her hand darted to the table, fingers closing around a scroll.

Bram adjusted his stance too late. He lunged, but she moved faster than he calculated. He missed the angle to cut off her retreat. She ducked under his extended arm, and was through the doorway.

She'd taken a scroll. Whatever information it held; they needed it back.

"Tephra!" Rowena shouted, scrambling around the table. Goby popped out from under the table, nearly tripping Bram as he raced through the door.

They burst into the corridor just in time to see Tephra disappearing around a far corner. Bram sprinted after her, aware of Rowena close behind and Goby speeding along the wall.

The chase led them deeper into the castle, down twisting corridors and passed abandoned chambers. Tephra clearly knew the layout almost as well as Goby. Yet Bram's longer stride allowed him to gain ground until they found themselves in a familiar hallway—the same dungeons where he had been imprisoned.

"She's heading for the dragon den," Bram called back to Rowena.

They passed the empty chamber where the bunyip had been kept. Bram kept his gaze straight, ignoring his own previous cell. The air grew noticeably colder as they ran, their breath visible in small clouds. Ahead, the cool blue-white of daylight shined like a beacon.

The corridor ended abruptly in a massive opening cut into the mountain itself. A natural cavern gouged bigger by giant claws. The far side opened to the sky. A sheer drop visible beyond the stone ledge.

Tephra stood at the edge; the scroll secured in her belt. She wasn't alone.

The frost dragon curled along the cavern's floor. Its massive body covered in scales that shimmered like new-fallen snow. Unlike the terrifying beast that had attacked them in Velmeg, this creature had an almost regal bearing, its movements graceful despite its size. Its bright pink eyes fixed on the newcomers with obvious intelligence.

"Stop," Bram commanded, slowing his approach with his arms stretched out to catch either of those behind him. Startling a dragon was never wise.

Tephra glanced over her shoulder. "I meant what I said about the warning. Whatever our past, I don't wish either of you harm."

"You stole that scroll," Rowena accused, pulling her dagger with a steady hand.

"Yes." Tephra didn't deny it. "Because it might save my sister's life. Wouldn't you do the same for Safi?"

The question struck home. Rowena's expression flickered, lowering the sword a fraction.

"Have you seen Safi?" she asked instead. "Where?"

"The same hall where your friends spied on me," Tephra replied, placing a hand on the frost dragon's scaled leg. The creature shifted at her touch, unfurling massive wings that caught the light like feathers infused with polished silver, except for the jagged scars crossing through one wing.

Goby peered around Bram's legs. "Big dragon," he observed with wide-eyed wonder.

The frost dragon's maw swiveled toward the goblin, nostrils flaring as it scented the air. The bird-like feathers around its neck fluffing out straight before relaxing between massive spikes on the creature's spine. For a moment, tension crackled through the cavern like ice breaking over a frozen lake. Then, inexplicably, the creature settled, its posture relaxing as if it had determined they posed no threat.

"He won't harm you unless you attack first," Tephra said, noticing their wary stances. With remarkable ease, she climbed onto the dragon's back, settling between two ridge-like scales. The beast shifted beneath her, wings extending further in preparation for flight.

Tephra leaned forward, whispering something. The creature tensed, then launched itself from the ledge with surprising grace. Powerful wings caught the air, carrying Tephra up and away from the castle.

Bram and Rowena stood at the cavern's edge, watching until dragon and rider were little more than a speck against the afternoon sky.

"Can we trust anything she said?" Bram finally asked, keeping his voice level despite the strategic complications Tephra added.

Rowena sheathed the dagger, her expression troubled. "She betrayed me more than once. She may well have done so again."

"And now she's gone." Another variable outside of their control.

A sigh escaped Rowena's lips. She hesitated, struggling with what she wanted to say. "I understand why she did what she did. Not everything. I don't forgive it, but I understand it."

Bram nodded, clenching his teeth. He couldn't figure Tephra as an ally or a threat, and it represented a liability. His instinct needed clarity, defined threats. More so now.

"Goby, show us the way to where she said Safi is being held," he said, turning away from the ledge, refocusing on the objective at hand.

"Goby know." The goblin spun back toward the dungeon hallway. "Told before."

They retraced their steps through the dungeon corridor, Goby alongside with his basket of scrolls and carrots still securely fastened to his back.

"She not bad," the goblin observed unexpectedly. "Scared. Like Goby was."

Bram glanced down at his small companion, struck again by the goblin's perceptiveness. "Sometimes fear makes people do things they later regret."

"Sometimes regret makes them try to fix what they broke," Rowena added softly.

The observation hung between them, laden with meaning that extended beyond Tephra.

They continued in silence, each lost in their own thoughts. Whatever lay ahead, truth or trap, ally or enemy, they would face it as they had faced the labyrinth, side by side.

41

ROWENA

ROWENA TWISTED to stare at the empty den at the end of the hall. A curious emptiness settling in her chest. There was no satisfaction in watching her betrayer escape, but no rage either. Only a hollow acknowledgment of trust's brittleness.

"We should go," Bram said beside her, his voice drawing her back to their immediate concerns. "Fidessa will notice her dragon's absence soon enough."

Rowena nodded, turning back to the dark corridor. The chill air of the dragon's den had seeped into her bones, making her wounds from the labyrinth throb with renewed pain. Yet something else tugged at her memory. Something they'd passed in their headlong chase through the dungeon corridors.

"Conri," she said suddenly. "He's in one of the cells."

Bram's expression shifted with recognition. "The one lying on the floor when we ran past?"

Rowena nodded. "We can't leave him here." The thought of abandoning anyone to Fidessa's mercies was unthinkable, but especially Conri. A man who had fought beside them, who had shown honor even when it cost him. She hoped that his slumped form, didn't mean they were too late.

"Which one?" Bram rushed to the closest one, but the door rattled and opened to an empty space.

It's one of these close to the end, Rowena continued. The cold lingered even as they moved away from the dragon's den. The air held a dampness, heavy with the scent of mildew and stone. She'd been so focused on Tephra she hadn't noticed the stench before.

"There," Bram pointed.

Rowena rushed forward, peering through the bars, pulling on them just in case. "Conri?"

Two cells from the dragon den, his form lay curled on the floor of the barred chamber. No raised bed, or even clean straw, just a bucket in the corner. She had to strain to see if he still breathed, ready to give up when she finally saw his back move with a shallow breath.

"He's alive." She released a deep breath, not realizing she'd been holding her own as she watched.

"Goby, check to see if the keys are still in my old cell," Bram told the goblin who peered through the bars from a position he held high on the wall. Goby scurried along the stone, not taking time to jump to the floor.

"Goby get."

While Goby retrieved the keys, Rowena crouched to better see through the bars. "Conri," she called softly. "Can you hear me?"

The figure stirred slightly, a pained groan escaping. Even in the dim light, Rowena could see this was indeed the Fianna leader, though barely recognizable from the proud warrior she had known in Velmeg. His red hair was matted with dirt and blood, his massive frame diminished by what must have been weeks of inadequate food and water. Bruises in various stages of healing mapped his visible skin like a grotesque atlas.

Seeing him so reduced stirred a protective fury in her chest and beneath it, a disquieting twist of guilt. She had shot what she hoped was not Conri in the labyrinth, had felt relief when the golem exploded into clay fragments. And here he was. Suffering but alive.

His eyes fluttered open, bloodshot but alert, recognition dawning slowly. "Princess," he rasped, his voice rough from disuse or screaming or both. "Should've known . . . You'd find trouble."

A startled laugh escaped Rowena's lips. Even broken and imprisoned, Conri maintained his wit. "It does seem to follow me," she agreed. "We're going to get you out of here."

Goby returned with the keys, proudly holding up a large iron ring jangly with various sizes of metal keys. "Still there. Guards dumb."

Bram took them with a grateful nod, quickly identifying the one that matched Conri's cell. The lock turned with a protesting groan, and the door swung open with a creak that echoed down the corridor.

Rowena entered first, kneeling beside the fallen warrior. Up close, his condition broke her heart. Beneath the dirt and dried blood, his skin was swollen and bruised. His breathing came in shallow pants, each one clearly causing him pain.

"Can you stand?" she asked, though she already knew the answer.

Conri attempted to push himself upright, his massive arms trembling with the effort. He managed to rise halfway before collapsing back with a grunt of pain. "Not . . . my best day," he admitted.

"I've got him," Bram said, stepping forward. He crouched beside Conri, positioning himself to take the larger man's weight on his uninjured side. "Put your arms around my shoulders."

With Rowena's help, they maneuvered Conri into position, draping his arms over Bram's shoulders. Bram stood slowly, bearing

Conri's weight across his back like a human cape. The position forced him to hunch forward to maintain balance, and his own pain.

"Not too heavy?" Rowena asked, noting the strain in Bram's expression.

"I'm fine," he insisted, though the tightness around his eyes suggested otherwise. The wound in his side from the thorn must have caused him agony under the additional burden, but he made no complaint.

"Thank you," she said quietly, recognizing the sacrifice. If they were attacked in this state, Bram would be at a severe disadvantage, yet he carried Conri without hesitation.

They moved slowly back up the corridor, Rowena ahead of the men with dagger in hand, ready for the first sign of danger. Goby trotted in front, occasionally glancing back at Conri with undisguised curiosity.

"Man big," the goblin observed. "Bigger than Bram."

A weak chuckle rumbled through Conri's chest. "Taller . . . maybe," he conceded. "Right now . . . feel as strong . . . as newborn kitten."

"What happened to you?" Rowena asked as they navigated the narrow passage. "We were told you died fighting Safi."

Pain that had nothing to do with his physical injuries flickered across Conri's face. "Not . . . fighting," he corrected. "Trying to reach her. Spell took . . . her mind. Not her fault. And goons also helped."

She really had been the one to hurt him. The simple absolution spoke volumes about Conri's character. Even after whatever Safi had done to him because of Fidessa's spell, he harbored no resentment toward her, only understanding.

No doubt the "goons" were the guards Rowena had seen leaving with Safi when she'd arrived at the castle. Rowena hadn't heard any gossip about Safi's return when she worked in the kitchen. There'd been a lot of chat about Fidessa's pets, and her grubby guards, but when Rowena had asked about her cousin, the kitchen had fallen silent.

"We try to avoid her as much as we can, miss," the kindly cook had told her. The fear in the room had made the already warm room stifling.

They reached the junction where the dungeon corridor met the main hallway. Rowena paused behind Goby, considering their next move. They needed to be cautious with Conri in his weakened state.

"Turn east," Bram said. "That's the way to the rooms."

Rowena nodded, about to turn in that direction when Goby suddenly tugged at her tunic.

"No, no," the goblin insisted, pointing toward a different corridor. "Faster. Woman this way. Goby know."

"You've seen Safi?" His voice came out in a low grunt. He wouldn't be able to carry Conri very far.

The goblin nodded vigorously. "Silent lady. Mad eyes."

"He's been trying to tell us all along," Rowena realized, guilt threading through her. They'd assumed Goby was referring to Tephra whenever he mentioned "the woman," never considering he might mean Safi.

"Lead the way," Bram said, shifting Conri's weight slightly for better balance.

Goby hesitated; his earlier enthusiasm dampened by obvious fear. He stared directly at Bram. "You promised. Protect Goby."

"I gave you my word. I'll keep you safe," Bram said.

"She won't hurt you while we're there," Rowena assured him, though the promise felt hollow. If Safi was as deeply violent as Daenon had described, could any of them truly predict her actions?

After a moment's consideration, Goby nodded reluctantly. "Goby show. This way."

He led them down the corridor he'd pointed out, moving with the furtive caution of someone who had learned to navigate hostile territory through painful experience. The passage was narrower, less traveled, with dust gathering in corners and cobwebs spanning the ceiling. A servants' route, perhaps, or one abandoned.

"Clever," Conri murmured, his breath warm against Bram's neck. "Avoiding . . . main halls."

"Goby knows this castle better than its builders, I think," Bram replied, his voice strained from the effort of carrying the larger man.

The goblin preened slightly at the praise, his chest puffing out. "Goby smart. Know all ways."

Rowena grinned despite her worry. How would she get Safi to listen? All accounts said she no longer remembered anything of her true self. Would she even know who Rowena was.

They continued through the winding passage until it opened into a more familiar corridor. The one where they had found the spell room earlier. The realization sent a chill down Rowena's spine. They could have been right next to her while they searched those scrolls.

There was also the concern that Fidessa had returned to her room. No one said a word, they barely breathed, as they stalked down the hall. Every ear tuned to the slightest sound.

Goby approached a nondescript door, indistinguishable from the others lining the hall except for the heavy iron lock securing it. He pointed, then quickly backed away, shaking his head.

"Lady there. Goby stay," he whispered. With that, he retreated several paces, clutching his basket of carrots like a shield.

Bram carefully lowered Conri to the floor, propping him against the wall. The Fianna leader's face had gone gray with pain during the journey, but his eyes remained alert, fixed on the door with a mixture of hope and dread.

"She's in there?" his raspy voice more than a whisper.

"We'll see," Rowena answered, approaching the door cautiously. Unlike the spell room, this one radiated no noticeable magic. At least, none she could sense. Yet something about it raised the fine hairs on her arms, an instinctive warning that danger lurked beyond.

She pressed her ear to the wood, listening for any sound from within. Nothing. No footsteps, no breathing, not even the rustle of fabric.

"I'll go first," she said, placing her hand on her dagger. Its weight had become familiar in her hand again. "If she's not herself, I stand the best chance of reaching her."

Bram seemed as if he might argue, but he must have recognized the resolve in her expression. He nodded, though concern remained evident in his eyes. "Be careful. We don't know the full state of her mind."

Rowena gestured to Goby, who reluctantly approached just close enough to hand her the key ring before scurrying back to safety.

After trying several keys, Rowena found one that fit the lock. It turned with a heavy click that seemed unnaturally loud in the quiet corridor.

Bram took the heavy lock after Rowena removed it. "I'll give you a moment or two first, but yell if she tries to attack."

Rowena nodded, removing the dagger. Not to use against Safi, never that, but as an anchor, something solid. And to be ready in case other guards were with her.

Bram pushed the door open, and Rowena stepped through alone.

The chamber beyond was surprisingly comfortable—not a cell, but quarters befitting a highborn lady. A large bed with silk hangings dominated one wall, beside it a polished vanity littered with perfume bottles and combs. A sitting area held plush chairs arranged around a small table, while bookshelves lined the far wall. Sunlight streamed through tall windows, casting golden patterns across rich carpets. Nowhere else in the castle had there been such luxury.

But the beauty of the room did nothing to soften the wrongness filling Rowena. This space was a cage, gilded and comfortable, but a cage nonetheless. And unlike the dragon, its occupant was not here by choice.

At first glance, the room appeared empty. Then a whisper of movement caught Rowena's eye. A shadow shifted near the window, where heavy curtains created a pool of darkness despite the afternoon light.

"Safi?" Rowena called softly, taking a careful step forward. "It's me. Rowena."

The shadow detached itself from the curtains. Safi stepped into the light, and Rowena's breath caught in her throat.

Her cousin's beauty remained, but it had been transformed into something cold and terrible, like a statue carved from ice.

Safi wore a simple tunic with trousers of dark leather, practical garments that allowed free movement. Her light brown hair was pulled back in a severe braid, emphasizing the sharp angles of her face. But it was her eyes that truly revealed the plaguing side effects. Where they used to be gentle and reassuring gray, like the first hints of twilight, now they were utterly devoid of emotion, as if someone had drained away everything that made Safi herself, leaving only an empty vessel behind.

In her hand, she held a sheathed sword, positioned so that it could be drawn in an instant.

"Safi," Rowena said again, lowering her own weapon to

appear less threatening. "It's Rowena. Your cousin. Do you remember me?"

No response came. Not a word, not a change in expression. Only a subtle shift in posture that spoke of deadly readiness. The kind of stance Rowena had learned from seasoned warriors who'd seen many battles.

"I've come to help you," Rowena continued, taking another cautious step. "To break whatever Fidessa has done that still has its hold on you."

At the mention of her mother's name, something flickered in Safi's empty gaze, gone so quickly Rowena might have imagined it, but she was certain she hadn't. Somewhere behind those vacant eyes, Safi still existed, still fought against the spell that bound her.

"Your mother doesn't own you," Rowena pressed, watching closely for any reaction. "No one does. You are your own person, Safi. You always have been."

This time, the reaction was unmistakable. Safi's fingers tightened around her sword hilt, her jaw clenching as if fighting some internal battle. Her eyes, those terrible, empty eyes, seemed to swim with momentary confusion before settling back into blankness.

Rowena took another step forward, close enough now that she could see the rise and fall of Safi's chest, the pulse beating rapidly at the base of her throat. Signs of internal struggle, of emotions fighting to break through a hardened barrier.

"Do you remember Velmeg?" Rowena asked, her voice gentle but insistent. "The battle against your father's forces? We stood together then. You chose your own path alongside of me."

Safi remained motionless. Her expression unchanged. Yet something told Rowena her words were reaching through the breach, finding purchase in whatever part of Safi remained her own.

"I'm making my choice now, to stand alongside of you," Rowena continued. "I believe in you. Fight, Safi. Fight whatever that spell left behind."

Without warning, Safi drew her sword in one fluid motion, the blade cutting the air between them with a menacing whisper. The steel gleamed in the light. Rowena didn't move her own weapon. Her feet remained planted. Something inside her, something new and unfamiliar, kept her still as she locked eyes with Safi.

"You won't hurt me." The words rose from somewhere deep in her chest, warm and certain. Her heart beat strong and steady against her ribs, not the frantic flutter that would have seized her just weeks ago. "You're stronger than her."

For a long moment, they stood facing each other. Safi with her sword raised, Rowena with her guard deliberately lowered. The air between them heavy with unsaid words. Rowena could almost see the battle raging over Safi's face.

Then, with agonizing slowness, Safi lowered her weapon. Not the dramatic surrender Rowena had imagined. No clattering steel or collapse to her knees, but a deliberate choice, muscles fighting every inch of the way.

A tear slipped down Safi's cheek, catching the light as it fell.

Rowena's chest tightened, her own eyes burning in response. That single tear meant more than all the words they'd ever shared. It meant Safi was still there, still fighting.

"Safi," she whispered, stepping forward with her hand outstretched, fingers trembling as she reached across the space between them.

Her cousin didn't recoil from the touch. She stood perfectly still as Rowena's fingers brushed her cheek, catching the tear before it fell. Other than the dampness on her skin, there was no outward acknowledgment of emotion. Her expression remained blank, her posture rigid.

But she hadn't attacked. Hadn't retreated. Those choices, small as they were, represented battles won.

"I'm going to help you," Rowena promised, her voice thick with her own unshed tears. "We're going to take you away from here and break the remnants of this wickedness. You'll be free again."

The door opened behind her. Rowena glanced over her shoulder at Bram cautiously stepping into the room. "Rowena? Is everything—"

He fell silent as he caught sight of Safi, standing motionless with her sword still in hand.

"It's alright," Rowena assured him without taking her eyes from Safi's face. "She's fighting through the bonds. She recognized me, I think."

Safi's gaze shifted to Bram, her eyes narrowing fractionally. The only indication she registered his presence at all. Her hand tightened on her sword hilt again, muscles tensing as if preparing to strike.

"No," Rowena said firmly, sliding between them trying, unsuccessfully to block his taller frame from sight. "He's a friend. He's here to help."

The tension in Safi's posture didn't ease, but neither did she attack. Her eyes remained fixed on Bram, tracking his every movement with heightened awareness. It reminded Rowena of a predator assessing potential prey. Calculating, methodical, utterly without mercy.

"She's not going to let me near her, is she?" Bram asked quietly.

"I don't think so," Rowena admitted, glancing over her shoulder. "She seems to view you as a threat."

"Or Fidessa specifically instructed her to view me as an enemy." Bram remained in the doorway, making no attempt to enter further. "Can she leave this room? Will she follow you?"

Rowena turned back to Safi. "We need to leave, Safi. This place isn't safe." She held out her hand. "Will you come with me?"

For several heartbeats, Safi didn't move. Then, with the same deliberate slowness with which she had lowered her sword, she stepped forward. She didn't take Rowena's outstretched hand, but she positioned herself at Rowena's side, clearly indicating her willingness to follow.

"She'll come," Rowena said, relief washing through her. "But I don't think she'll tolerate anyone else getting too close."

"Understood." Bram backed out of the doorway, giving them space to exit. "We should move quickly. The longer we stay, the greater the chance of discovery."

Rowena nodded, then turned to Safi once more. "We're leaving now. Stay close to me."

She led the way out of the chamber, acutely aware of Safi following like a silent shadow. The moment they entered the corridor, Safi's posture changed subtly, becoming more alert, more predatory, her gaze sweeping the hallway for potential threats.

Goby pressed himself against the far wall, yellow eyes wide with fear as Safi emerged. "Lady scary," he whispered, clutching his basket protectively.

To Rowena's surprise, Safi's gaze lingered on the goblin for a moment, her head tilting slightly as if in curiosity rather than aggression. It was the first flicker of her old self breaking through.

Conri had struggled to his feet with Bram's help, leaning heavily against the wall for support. At the sight of Safi, something like joy broke through the pain on his face.

"Princess," he greeted her, his voice stronger than before. "Good to see you ... still fighting."

Safi's reaction was immediate and unexpected. She stepped

forward, placing herself between Rowena and Conri, her sword half-raised in warning.

Rowena raised her hand quickly. "Conri is our ally. He won't hurt me."

The words seemed to register on some level. Safi lowered her sword, though she maintained her protective stance.

"She's guarding you," Conri observed, a sad smile touching his lips. "Even through the fog clouding her mind . . . She's protecting those she cares for."

The realization struck Rowena with painful clarity. Fidessa's spell hadn't completely erased Safi's nature. It had warped it, twisted her protective instincts into something cold and lethal, but not erased them entirely. Even now, with her will suppressed, and her voice silenced, some essential part of Safi remained.

"We need to move," Bram reminded them, his gaze darting down the corridor. "Goby, is there a safe way out of the castle from here?"

The goblin nodded, though he kept his distance from Safi. "Goby know way. Through kitchens. Guards never look there."

"Lead the way," Bram instructed, offering his shoulder to Conri once more. The Fianna leader accepted the support with a grateful nod, though his eyes never left Safi's face.

As they prepared to move, Rowena caught Safi's gaze, holding it steadily. "We're going to fix this," she promised quietly. "Whatever Fidessa did to you, we'll undo it. I swear it."

No change came to Safi's blank expression, no acknowledgment that she understood. But as they set off down the corridor, Goby leading, Bram supporting Conri, Rowena beside her ensnared cousin, Safi fell into step with a precision that spoke of choices made, however small and difficult.

They moved as one strange, damaged family, bound not by

blood or oath but by something perhaps stronger. The shared experience of breaking and beginning to heal.

42

BRAM

BRAM WATCHED Safi with equal parts fascination and dread as they moved through the castle's winding corridors. She maintained a precise distance from Rowena. Close enough to protect, far enough to maneuver if attacked. Her movements were fluid yet mechanical. She lacked the natural hesitations and adjustments of someone guided by conscious thought rather than instinct.

Occasionally her gaze would sweep over him, cold and calculating, before returning to scan their surroundings. Each time, her assessment held weight. She judged him not as a person, but as a potential threat to be neutralized if necessary. He had faced many enemies as the Seeker, but few had unnerved him like this empty-eyed version of Safi.

Bram adjusted his grip on Conri. The Fianna leader had insisted on walking under his own power, but after just a few dozen paces, his strength had failed him. Now he leaned heavily against Bram's shoulder, his breathing labored with each step.

The kitchen had been bustling with activity, so they couldn't sneak through. Instead, Goby had managed to get a package of dried meat, cheese, and hard tack for them. He also returned with three waterskins hanging across his shoulders.

"Cook nice." He handed everything to Bram who handed them to the others.

While grateful for the nourishment, especially for Conri who chewed on some of the meat, it had been a dangerous task. Any of the servants who'd seen Goby leave with supplies could alert the guards.

"How much further now, Goby?"

"Not far," Goby assured him, scampering a few paces ahead before waiting for them to catch up. The goblin had taken to a pattern of darting forward to scout, then returning to the group's slower pace. "Down stairs. Gate after."

Bram frowned. "We'll be exposed going out through the portcullis. Is there no other way?"

Goby's ears drooped slightly. "Other ways blocked. Guards everywhere. Cook said."

"They know we're leaving," Rowena said, her voice low. "Fidessa will have mobilized every guard in the castle."

She was right, of course. Fidessa had known they would attempt to free Safi after her agreement with Rowena. Their window for escape was rapidly closing.

"We need to move faster," Bram decided, glancing at Conri. "Can you manage a quicker pace?"

The Fianna leader nodded grimly. Though sweat beaded on his pale forehead, he did seem stronger after some food. "Don't slow for me," he insisted. "If necessary, leave me."

"Not happening," Bram replied flatly.

He meant it. The thought of abandoning Conri to Fidessa's mercies was unthinkable. The man had suffered enough at her hands already. Whatever their path forward, they would face it together.

They descended a narrow spiral staircase, Goby leading the

way, with Rowena and Safi following. Bram and Conri followed last, navigating the steps with painstaking care. Each jarring movement sent fresh waves of pain through Bram's side, where the thorn had pierced him. The wound had stopped bleeding, but the poison lingered in his system, a constant ache that flared to agony with sudden movements.

At the bottom of the stairs, Goby paused, pressing himself against the wall as he peered around the corner. After a moment, he beckoned them forward.

"Go quick," he whispered.

Conri straighten slightly beside Bram, summoning his remaining strength for this final push. "Ready?" Bram asked quietly.

Conri gave a tight nod. "Born."

As they approached the outside door, Goby suddenly ducked behind Bram's legs, yellow eyes wide with alarm. Bram followed his gaze to find Safi staring directly at the goblin, her head tilted with what appeared curiosity again.

"Lady watch Goby," the goblin whispered, clutching Bram's trouser leg. "Why?"

Indeed, Safi's blank expression had shifted subtly. Her eyes tracked Goby's movements with something closer to interest than hostility. As if trying to solve a puzzle she couldn't quite understand.

"I think she's curious about you," Bram said, surprised by this deviation from her otherwise stiff behavior.

Goby peeked around Bram's leg, meeting Safi's gaze briefly before ducking away again. "Goby friend," he yelled.

For the briefest moment, something like confusion flickered across Safi's features. There and gone in a flash, but Bram caught it. Then her attention shifted back to Rowena, her protective vigilance resuming as if the interruption had never occurred.

"It's a good sign," Rowena whispered. "She's still here, still thinking."

Bram nodded, though he wasn't entirely convinced. Curiosity about a strange creature didn't necessarily indicate a return of Safi's true self. Still, any crack in the shell encasing her, however small, offered hope.

"Almost there," he reminded them, focusing on their immediate task. "Goby, lead on."

The goblin edged forward, motioning for them to wait as he took another careful look out the door. After a moment, he gestured frantically for them to follow.

"No guards," he whispered. "Hurry!"

They moved into the open-aired bailey as quickly as their burdened pace allowed. It was not that vast a space. Twenty yards, a few more perhaps, to the portcullis. The bridge still in place. Good.

Except the space was eerily empty—no guards, not even the usual duo making their rounds. The silence raised the hair on the back of Bram's neck. It felt deliberate, like the silence before an ambush.

"I don't like this," he murmured to Rowena. "It's too quiet."

She nodded, one hand resting on her dagger. "We're so close."

Goby already waited midway to the iron gate. The others followed, reaching him just as a figure stepped from the guard towers, tall and slender, draped in a cloak of deep green. Brown hair loose around shoulders that seemed too narrow to bear the weight of the power she wielded.

Yralissa.

Bram instinctively placed himself between the Fianna leader and the disavowed druid. Goby ducked behind Conri. Safi and Rowena positioned themselves beside him. Safi's posture shifted subtly, her hand moving to grip her sword, though she left it sheathed. Rowena did the same with her dagger.

Ready. Capable.

"Leaving so soon?" Yralissa called, her voice echoing against the castle's stone at their backs. "And after all the trouble, Fidessa went through to arrange your accommodations."

Bram's mind raced, calculating their options. The bailey had multiple exits where it broke down. If they could reach one.

Movement to their right interrupted his thoughts. A dozen warriors wearing cloth that wrapped around their waist, then slung over their shoulders, secured by belts, their skin painted with chalk that gleamed white against their flesh. Each carried a spear in one hand and a round shield in the other.

Daenon led them, dressed in the same garb. They blocked an escape from that direction.

At almost the same moment, figures appeared on their left. Liam and Hywel, swords drawn, followed by several of Fidessa's grunting guards.

"What now?" Rowena asked, her voice steady despite the dire circumstances.

Before Bram could respond, the sound of slow, deliberate clapping drew all of their attention behind them. Fidessa stood in the doorway they'd exited, staring with an expression of amused contempt.

They were surrounded.

"Well done," she called. "You've managed to free both my daughter and my prisoner. Impressive, if ultimately futile."

Fidessa's gaze lingered on Safi, something like genuine pain flickering briefly in her eyes. "I have freed her bindings, but she will return to me."

"Don't count on that," Rowena replied, her hand looping through Safi's arm in a gesture of defiance.

Good strategy.

Fidessa's smile tightened. "Guards," she commanded, "secure the princess and the Seeker. Kill the others if they resist. My daughter can take care of herself."

Rowena shuddered.

The chalk warriors moved first, advancing in perfect formation, spears lowered.

"Find a place to hide out of the way," Bram told Conri, drawing his axe. It felt laughably inadequate against the array of enemies surrounding them, but it was all he had.

Then too many things happened at once.

Safi, who had stayed motionless beside Rowena, suddenly exploded into action. Without warning, without even drawing breath, she charged the line of chalk warriors, her sword flashing from its sheath in a silver arc. The first warrior fell before he could even raise his shield, her blade opening his throat with surgical precision.

"Safi, wait!" Rowena called, but it was too late. The spell-cursed woman had engaged the warriors, moving among them with terrifying efficiency. Where a normal fighter would show hesitation, fear, or even battle-rage, Safi displayed nothing but cold, mechanical precision. Each strike measured, each movement economical.

Bram admired the skill. Was that how he'd been viewed when he fought as the Seeker? He would again, no matter what.

Yralissa raised her hands, blue fire bloomed between her palms. Bram spun to face her just as she hurled enchantment their way.

Bram dove sideways, the fire scorching the soil where he had stood moments before. In his former state, he would have melted into shadow, reappearing behind Yralissa before she could blink. Now, he was forced to rely on his reflexes, still quick, but painfully elven. And with every step, his side reminded him of the thorn he still bore. A vulnerability he couldn't afford.

He rolled to his feet, sweeping his gaze over the battle. Liam and Hywel were approached from the left while more of Fidessa's guards spilled in behind them. Rowena. Where was she? The flash of her dagger in his side vision confirmed she had engaged. Alive and fighting.

Yralissa advanced, power crackling around her fingertips like lightning contained in flesh.

"You should have stayed in your cell," she said, her voice carrying despite the din of battle. "At least there you were useful."

"To whom?" Bram demanded, angling himself toward a set of barrels against the curtain wall, marking potential cover. "The Heptad? Fidessa? Or whatever darker powers you serve now?"

A smile curved Yralissa's lips. "I serve the truth, Bram. Something the Heptad has hidden from you since birth."

Another wave of blue fire shot toward him. Bram ducked, feeling the heat of it sear the air inches from his face. Stone cracked and blackened where the flames landed on the keep.

What did this woman have against him? She acted as if she needed something from him, yet tried to kill him at the same time.

Hers was not ordinary enchantment. Yralissa wielded a power that rivaled the High Hepta himself. An advantage he could no longer match.

He had to adjust. Adapt. Attack.

"How?" Bram called, circling with the druid.

"Power was never the issue," Yralissa replied. "Access is the key. Enchantment comes from Caelus, Bram. The Heptad merely gatekeeps the Primary Spring."

Yralissa lunged forward, her right hand sweeping in a fluid arc that sent a wave of dirt erupting from the bailey ground.

Bram leapt sideways, narrowly avoiding being crushed as stone and soil shot upward. Before he could regain his footing, she twisted her left hand, and the surrounding air turned frigid. Ice crystals formed on his eyelashes, his breath clouding before him.

"You're still wondering how I can command earth and fire, water and air with equal ease?" she asked, pacing a wide circle around him. Her smile held no warmth. "While you were learning to be the perfect Seeker, I was learning what the Heptad tried to hide from everyone. The boundaries between elements are constructs designed to keep us weak."

Bram gripped his axe tighter, fighting through the pain in his side. Every instinct demanded he shift into shadow, escape, reposition, attack from behind, but the pathways to that power remained closed, locked behind Yralissa's enchantment.

He had to block out all distractions. Pain . . . Rowena.

"Achan taught me more than he intended," she continued, her voice dropping to a more intimate tone. "Late nights in his chambers, demanding I recite incantations while he . . ." She let the words hang, satisfaction gleaming in her eyes at Bram's expression. "Oh, does that disturb you? The great High Hepta, using a young paritor for his pleasure before casting her aside for someone newer?"

It did. The revelation struck at the foundation of his training, his purpose. The Heptad held a place of honor, gifted their positions from the Grand Guardian, Osric. Their corruption wasn't just a tactical concern but a betrayal of everything he'd served.

The moment of distraction nearly cost him. A shard of ice, razor-sharp and longer than his forearm, shot toward his chest. Bram twisted, the projectile slicing through his sleeve and drawing a line of fire across his biceps. Moderate pain, but nothing he couldn't handle.

"It bothered me, but I learned from him," Yralissa said, "and then I learned from others what the Heptad keeps secret."

Understanding dawned. "The Astaroth," Bram breathed. The forbidden sect of druids who dabbled in spells and enchantment deemed too dangerous by the Heptad Council.

"Clever boy," she mocked, her hands weaving a complex pattern before her. The air between them shimmered, distorting like heat rising from sunbaked stone. "They recognized the potential of my mind when Achan could only see my body. They showed me that the elements are merely separate aspects of all enchantment flowing through the Primary Spring."

Bram ducked behind a fallen portion of the wall as waves of scorching heat pulsed from her fingertips. Stone cracked audibly from the temperature shift. The axe in his hand felt increasingly useless against such power.

The cacophony of battle surrounded them. Safi's relentless assault on the chalk warriors, Rowena fighting somewhere, the clash of metal and cries of the wounded creating a backdrop to their deadly dance.

"What do you want from me?" Bram called, searching frantically for an advantage. "If you meant to kill me, you would have done it already."

Yralissa paused, her head tilting slightly. "Kill you? No, Bram. I need you to understand." Her voice hardened. "To see what they've kept from you. What they've kept from both of us."

She thrust her arms forward, palms out. The ground beneath Bram's feet turned to mud, sucking at his boots. He struggled to pull free as Yralissa closed the distance between them, her steps sure and steady on the unstable ground.

"Finish my riddle, Bram," she demanded, standing close enough now that he could see the flecks of gold in her green eyes. "What links us?"

"I don't know what you're talking about," he growled, finally wrenching one foot free of the muck.

Disappointment flashed across her features. "After everything, you still can't see it." She sighed. A sound so genuinely mournful it gave him pause. "Perhaps you need a reminder of the cost of ignorance."

Her hand shot out, faster than he could react, and pressed against the wound on his side. Pain exploded through Bram's body, searing and all-consuming. He felt something move beneath her fingers. The remnant of thorn still embedded in his flesh, twisting deeper.

"Some wounds never heal," Yralissa whispered, her lips close to his ear as he doubled over in agony. "Let this one always remind you of me."

Through the haze of pain, Bram's hand found her wrist. He squeezed with all the strength he could muster, forcing her fingers away from the wound. His other hand swung the axe in a desperate arc.

Yralissa leapt backward, but not quickly enough. The blade sliced across her shoulder, drawing a line of crimson against her green cloak. She hissed, more in surprise than pain, her free hand moving to the cut.

"You still have fight in you," she observed, a hint of approval in her voice. "Good."

The momentary connection, her hand on his wound, his grip on her wrist, had created something unexpected. A resonance hummed between them, like tuning forks vibrating in unison. Through it, Bram felt a flicker of . . . something. Not his power returning, but an awareness of it, like seeing light from beneath a closed door.

An opportunity? Or something more fundamental?

Yralissa felt it too. Her eyes widened slightly, something like hope flashing across her features before hardening once more into determination.

43

ROWENA

Rowena spun, her dagger a quick flash in her hands as the pig-faced guards closed in. Their squat bodies belied surprising speed. Some with curved blades whistling through the air and others brandishing spears as they pressed their attack. She parted one strike, ducked another, the rhythm of battle settling into her muscles despite the chaos surround them. The Sword of Justice remained strapped to her back, a comforting weight but useless in this fight.

She would not allow it to draw blood and risk the fall of the prophecy.

Beyond the guards, at the far side of the bailey, Safi tore through the chalk warriors with expert precision, her movement unnervingly fluid. Last Rowena saw, Bram was locked in combat with Yralissa. Why her dead uncle's Oraku had a reason to be here, fighting, was a question for another time.

Goby and Conri had disappeared from view, hopefully finding shelter from the worst of the fighting.

A shout from behind, was Rowena's only warning. She turned, catching a flash of movement as Fidessa ambled forward from front doors of the keep. The queen's arm rose in a fluid arc, something small in her palm.

Recognition dawned an instant too late. The stone left Fidessa's hand, arcing through the air directly toward Rowena. The weapon she remembered from when Rowena had faced Fidessa in Ibern. When she'd trapped everyone near Rowena, Safi, the Fianna, still allies then, and so many others, forcing them into an immovable state that would have eventually killed them, if Bram hadn't stepped in to help.

Rowena tried to dive clear, but one of the guards blocked her path. The stone struck the pebbled dirt at her feet, shattering with a sound like broken glass. Green fog erupted outward, enveloping her legs in a sickly mist.

The effect was immediate. Numbness spread up her calves, her knees locked in place as the charm took hold. Rowena's muscles strained against the paralyzing effect, panic rising in her throat as the guards advanced, sensing easy prey.

Through sheer force of will, she twisted her upper body, her dagger slicing the air before her. The nearest guard stumbled, avoiding the blade by inches. It bought her precious seconds, but the fog continued to climb, reaching her thighs now. Each affected muscle becoming useless as stone.

Fidessa approached slowly, satisfaction evident in her regal features. "Did you think I'd forgotten how you escaped last time?" she called. "I've improved the formulation. This mist won't dissipate so easily."

Rowena gritted her teeth. The last time it had been Bram, not Rowena, who'd quelled the charm. His shadows had silently spread across the ground, overpowering Fidessa's mage trick to free everyone. This time, she wouldn't have his help.

The Sword of Justice remained strapped to her back, its weight a reminder of what was at stake. She still struggled to believe she'd play a part in fulfilling the prophecy, but after what happened with the thorns turning to roses, she understood how precious the sword was to protect.

"I escaped you before," she managed, her voice strained. "I'll do it again."

Fidessa's laugh was cold as winter frost. "Look at you. Trapped like an insect in amber. Just as you were always meant to be."

The queen gestured subtly with her left hand. The air around Rowena stirred, then erupted into a gale-force wind that tore at her hair and clothing. Dust and debris swirled around her, stinging her eyes and obscuring her vision.

With her lower body immobilized, the wind's force nearly toppled her. She fought to stay upright, focusing on Fidessa, using her outrage to spur her strength.

Fidessa used the fingers of her right hand to twist in an odd pattern. She was weaving a spell. Keeping the wind roaring and adding something new at the same time.

The sword vibrated on Rowena's back. The shaking force grew stronger as the sword shifted slightly higher as if it struggled against being drawn.

Rowena gasped. That was Fidessa's aim. The spell she worked was to retrieve the sword while Rowena stood helpless.

That was a mistake.

Without hesitation, Rowena sheathed her dagger and reached back to remove the blade from her back. Though it couldn't draw blood, its significance made it too dangerous for Fidessa to steal again.

Rowena drove the sword into the ground before her, gripping the hilt with both hands. The blade sank deep into the soil, creating a small anchor against the howling wind.

"My hands will not leave this blade. It is bound to me and I to it," Rowena whispered through gritted teeth. "If I fall, it will mean more than my life. It risks the lives of all in Edenia. I will not let that happen."

Frustration flashed across Fidessa's face as her summoning spell met resistance. The effort rattled through Rowena's hands and up her arms, but she remained steady, the sword firmly within her grasp. Her connection stronger than the queen's magic.

Sweat beaded on Rowena's brow as she focused on parts of her that could still move. The mist had reached her waist now, advancing with inexorable patience. Soon it would claim her completely.

"Justice," Rowena whispered, the word nearly lost in the wind. That was the sword's purpose, its name.

Something stirred in the metal, a warmth spread up her arms, countering the creeping cold of Fidessa's spell. For a breathtaking moment, the green fog receded an inch, two inches down her thighs.

"Impossible!" Fidessa hissed, her concentration broken. The summoning spell dissolved.

Rowena was free. The sword had responded to her.

In that moment, everything became clear. She was part of the prophecy, in what way she didn't know, but that she was involved solidified in her mind and heart. The sword could not draw blood because it was meant to break bonds, create freedom. That mission took root within Rowena. She understood now.

She was moon-born, keeper of a piece of the Armor of Caelus. And she would protect the Sword of Justice with her life.

Rowena stood firmly now, Sword of Justice driven into the ground before her, one hand maintaining her grip on the hilt. With her free hand, she drew her dagger once more. The dual stance, awkward, limiting, but she would not release the sword. Not even for a moment.

"My hands will not leave this blade," she'd promised. But something low and fast launched itself at her hip. She saw the creature. Its black mask contorted with fury, its knee-high body striped and muscled. A rabberine.

That's when Rowena realized the literal interpretation of her vow might get her killed.

The creature's teeth found purchase in the fabric of her trousers. Blood welled around its muzzle, vivid red against her skin.

Pain shot through her, hot and immediate. Rowena brought her dagger down, driving the rabberine back, but her awkward stance made the blow glancing at best. A second rabberine circled, looking for an opening to join its companion's attack. The blood soaking into its partner's fur the only thing keeping it at a distance.

She needed both hands to fight effectively. Yet releasing the sword might allow Fidessa another opportunity to summon it.

As if reading her thoughts, Fidessa's lips curved into a cruel smile. "Trapped by your own stubbornness. How fitting."

A shadow passed overhead, large and swift. A vultu circled the bailey, its leathery wings stretched wide. The rat-like face turned toward Rowena, beady eyes gleaming with malevolent intelligence.

"You see," Fidessa called. "Even when you think you've found an advantage, I have three more to counter it."

As if responding to some silent command, the vultu folded its wings and dove, talons extended, toward Rowena's face. With one hand anchored on the sword, evasion was awkward. She slashed with her dagger, catching the creature across its belly. It shrieked, banking sharply before circling for another attack.

"How many creatures do you need to fight your battles, Fidessa?" Rowena called, the taunt thinly masking her frustration at her self-imposed limits. "Were you always this afraid to face me directly?"

The queen's composure slipped, anger flashing in her eyes. With a sharp gesture, she dismissed the wind spell. The sudden absence of pressure left Rowena swaying, the sword, still deeply embedded in the soil, keeping her upright.

"I have never feared you," Fidessa replied, her voice dangerously soft. "I simply recognize vermin for what they are—best dealt with by other vermin."

Something had to change.

She had promised, but perhaps she didn't need to be so literal. The sword was bound to her. That was the true meaning. Its essence tied to hers through the prophecy. She didn't need physical contact to maintain that bond.

Moon-born. The acceptance strengthened her resolve.

In a fluid motion, Rowena wrenched the sword from the ground and returned it to the sheath on her back, securing it firmly. Now, with both hands free, she faced Fidessa with renewed determination, her dagger held before her.

"Call them off," Rowena demanded, swinging her dagger in a defensive arc that kept the second rabberine at bay. "Or have you fallen so far that you need beasts to fight your battles?"

Something flickered in Fidessa's expression, wounded pride perhaps, or a vestige of the regal bearing she still clung to. With a sharp whistle, she commanded the rabberines to retreat. They did so reluctantly, blood still dripping from the first one's muzzle.

"You mistake practicality for cowardice," Fidessa said, drawing closer now that Rowena was mobile again. "A queen uses every resource available to her."

"Is that what you told yourself when you used your own daughter?" The words left Rowena's lips before she could reconsider them, sharp as any blade.

The blow struck true. Fidessa flinched visibly, genuine pain flashing across her features before being masked by cold fury.

"You know nothing of what I've done for Safi," she hissed. "Nothing of what it means to protect a child in a world that would destroy her."

"You mean like my mother tried to do for me? To protect me from living in a world like you've created." She gave her life. And still Rowena ended up a slave.

"It's not the same. Your mother never understood the plight of others. She had everything handed to her. Even when your father pledged his love for her, she toyed with the emotions of his brother. Stripping him of the love he could have had for me, because he pined for her."

This was not about being a mother. Or about love. Love was two-sided, reciprocal. She didn't care to share her love, just have others shower her with theirs. It was selfish.

"You bound her will to yours," Rowena countered. "Stripped away everything that made her herself."

"I made her strong!" Fidessa's composure cracked, her voice rising. "Ensured she would never suffer as I did. Never be weak, never be used!"

The naked emotion in the queen's voice caught Rowena off guard. This wasn't the calculated manipulation she'd come to expect from Fidessa. This was raw pain, the wound of old trauma still festering beneath her carefully constructed facade.

"You became the very thing that hurt you," Rowena said, her voice softening despite herself. "You did to Safi exactly what Uther did to you."

The words hung in the air between them, heavy with the truth that Fidessa had likely never allowed herself to admit.

"You know nothing of what Uther did to me," the queen whispered, her voice barely audible above the din of battle surrounding them. "Nothing of what it means to be stripped of everything, dignity, hope, a future, and be expected to smile through it all. He promised me everything, then fought for her."

"You made me a slave. I'd say I understand loss of dignity."

Fidessa leveled a glare at Rowena, silent, vicious. Then she stretched her hand out behind her, pulling her fingers to her palm in a gesture of invitation.

Movement behind the queen caught Rowena's attention. Brown shapes with leathery skin and under-bite jaws emerged from the shadows of a collapsed guard tower. Stinkbroods, at least five of them, snorting and pawing at the ground as they prepared to charge.

Rowena shifted her stance, ready to move at the first sign of attack. The Sword of Justice remained secured across her back, its weight a reminder of her purpose. She could feel its presence, like a warmth between her shoulder blades.

"You were rejected," Rowena said, desperately playing for time as she fought the spell. "By Uther, by Safi. Even your dragon left with Tephra."

The mention of the dragon struck deeper than anything else. Genuine anguish twisted Fidessa's features, a glimpse of the wounded woman beneath the queen's mask.

"He was all I had," she said, something vulnerable entering her voice. "The only creature that ever chose me freely. I raised him from a hatchling, before Uther, before any of this."

The stinkbroods inched closer, waiting for their mistress's command. As they moved, they released puffs of noxious gas that formed a visible trail behind them.

"And now you have nothing," Rowena pressed, searching for any advantage in Fidessa's moment of vulnerability. "Nothing but power built on cruelty."

The queen's eyes flashed. "I have more than you could understand. More than you will ever have."

With a sharp gesture, she commanded the stinkbroods to

attack. The creatures charged as one, moving with the single-minded aggression that made them such effective weapons. Their gas created a choking cloud that stung Rowena's eyes and burned her throat.

Now unencumbered by her one-handed limitation, Rowena moved with the fluid grace of her training. Her dagger flashed, driving back the first stinkbrood as she pivoted to avoid another. The Sword of Justice remained secure on her back, a presence she felt more than saw, its energy pulsing in time with her heartbeat.

The contrast between her and Fidessa had never been clearer. While the queen commanded creatures to fight for her, keeping her own hands clean, Rowena faced danger directly. While Fidessa bound others to her will, stripping away their freedom, Rowena fought to break those bonds. The Sword of Justice could not harm living beings because its purpose, her purpose, was liberation, not destruction.

Across the bailey, the sounds of battle crashed against her ears—too distant to help, close enough to taunt. Bram and Yralissa's conflict had intensified, elemental magic scorching the air between them. The acrid smell of burned stone and soil carried on the wind. Safi had cut through nearly half the chalk warriors, her masterful destruction unceasing despite the blood that now stained her clothing. Somewhere, Goby's voice called out in alarm, the goblin's high-pitched cries adding to the cacophony.

Pain exploded through her arm as a stinkbrood launched itself upward, teeth clamping onto her wrist. She cried out, the sound strangled in her throat. Her dagger nearly slipped from her grasp, her fingers instinctively tightening despite the fire racing up her arm. Blood, warm and wet, trickled down her palm. Behind her, hot breath and the stench of rot warned of another creature circling, teeth snapping at her back.

She was becoming surrounded, outnumbered by Fidessa's creatures. The dagger helped, but she needed a longer reach. There were too many. But unlike before, she was not helpless. She moved with purpose, with understanding of who she was. Moon-born, keeper of the Sword of Justice.

A spear lay on the ground, abandoned by one of Fidessa's portly guards. Rowena scooped it into the air with her boot and snatched it at the same time returning her dagger to her hip.

Fidessa watched with cold satisfaction, her momentary vulnerability hidden once more behind the queen's mask. "Did you really think you could defeat me in my own castle?" she asked. "That you could take my daughter and escape unscathed?"

"She's not yours to keep," Rowena gasped, fighting through the pain to maintain her stance. "She never was."

"Everything here is mine," Fidessa replied, her voice hardening. "Including you, little slave. Did you forget so quickly? Did you think a crown and a fancy title would erase what you truly are?"

The words struck deeper than Rowena wanted to admit. How many nights had she lain awake, wondering the same thing? How many times had she questioned whether she could ever truly escape her past?

But she knew the answer now. The Sword of Justice had chosen her. Not despite her past, but because of it. Who better to wield a blade that broke chains than someone who had worn them?

"I know exactly what I am," she said, meeting Fidessa's gaze unflinchingly. "I'm the one who will break your power. Not just over me, but over everyone you've hurt."

Something in her tone must have registered with Fidessa. The queen's eyes narrowed, a flicker of uncertainty crossing her features.

"Bold words for someone surrounded by my creatures," she replied, though her voice lacked its earlier conviction.

The vultu dived again, talons raking across Rowena's shoulder. Fresh pain bloomed, warm blood soaking through her tunic. One of the stinkbroods climbed her paralyzed leg, scratching her flesh with toenails like iron.

Rowena dislodged the foul beast with a swift thrust of the spear's shaft.

Fidessa stepped closer, close enough that she was nearly within reach. "I could kill you now," she said, an odd hesitation in her voice. "End this resistance."

"But you won't," Rowena replied, sudden understanding dawning. "Because deep down, you recognize yourself in me."

The queen flinched as if struck. "You are nothing like me."

"Aren't I?" Rowena challenged, even as she drove back another stinkbrood with the spear. "We were both taken, both used. The only difference is what we chose to do with our pain afterward."

For a breathless moment, something like recognition flickered in Fidessa's eyes. Then her features hardened once more, walls slamming back into place.

"Enough of this," she snapped. "I grow tired of your prattle."

She summoned the remaining stinkbroods to her side. They formed a perimeter around Rowena, their gas creating a noxious barrier that made each breath a struggle.

"When this is over," Fidessa continued, "when your friends are dead or captured, you will return to your proper place. Perhaps I'll even let you serve Safi once I've reclaimed her."

"She'll never return to you willingly," Rowena said, fighting to keep her voice steady as the stinkbroods closed in. "You know that, don't you? That's why you had to bind her will, because your own daughter couldn't bear to stay with you otherwise."

Raw pain flashed across Fidessa's features, there and gone in an instant. "She is young. Foolish. She doesn't understand the world as I do."

"Or perhaps she understands too well what you've become."

Fidessa's hand rose, perhaps to strike Rowena, perhaps to summon another creature, but a new spear sailed over Fidessa's shoulder, silencing one of the stinkbroods. Fidessa spun to witness what Rowena could view easily.

Safi stood amidst a circle of fallen chalk warriors, her sword dripping red onto the hard dirt. Her gaze had found them. Found her mother with her hand raised against Rowena. Something flickered in those empty eyes. The faintest spark of recognition, of awareness.

"She sees you," Rowena whispered, hope flaring despite her dire situation. "The real you."

Fidessa's attention wavered, her gaze locked with her daughter across the bailey. In that moment of distraction, Rowena felt the Sword of Justice pulse with energy against her back. Not a plea this time, but a certainty.

"And you underestimate what I'm willing to do to protect what's mine," Fidessa yelled, all queenly decorum gone. Her hands moved in quick patterns as she attempted another spell. Wind gathered around her fingers, coalescing into a visible distortion in the air.

She hurled the concentrated gale toward Rowena.

The impact drove Rowena back several paces, her boots scraping against grit as she fought to maintain her footing. Her wounded leg threatened to buckle, the accumulated injuries taking their toll.

Around them, the battle raged unabated. Chalk warriors and squat guards clashed with desperate fury. Yralissa and Bram's conflict had scorched a section of the bailey wall, stone blackened by unnatural fire.

And through it all, Safi continued her silent advance, cutting through any who stood in her path. Her trajectory had shifted, Rowena realized with a jolt. She was moving toward them, toward her mother.

Fidessa had noticed as well. Something like fear flickered across her features.

"My daughter returns to me," she said, though her voice lacked conviction. "As she always will."

"Look at her, Fidessa," Rowena urged, gesturing toward Safi's blank expression, her prowling movements. "Is this what you wanted for her? Is this protection?"

For a moment, just a moment, doubt crept into the queen's eyes. She looked at her daughter, really looked, taking in the empty gaze, the blood-spattered face devoid of emotion.

"I did what was necessary," Fidessa whispered, but the words sounded hollow even in Rowena's ears.

The vultu screamed overhead, diving once more toward Rowena. She was ready this time, her spear flashing upward in a precise arc that sliced across the creature's wing. It shrieked, careening into a wall before righting itself and limping back into the air.

The remaining stinkbroods charged again. Their wall of noxious fumes rising between Rowena and Fidessa. Fatigue pulled at Rowena's limbs, each movement requiring greater effort than the last. The battle was taking its toll, draining her strength with each passing minute.

Across from her, Fidessa showed similar signs of exhaustion. The queen's spells came slower now, her gestures less precise. Maintaining control of so many creatures while casting her own magic was clearly straining her limits.

They were at an impasse, both weakening, neither willing to yield.

"We can end this," Rowena offered, her spear pointed defensively as the stinkbroods circled. "No more blood needs to be shed today."

Fidessa's laugh held no humor, only bone-deep weariness. "It's far too late for that. Far too late for both of us."

With a final, desperate gesture, she summoned what power remained to her. The air between them shimmered with heat, distorting Rowena's vision. The remaining stinkbroods moved to flank her, cutting off any avenue of escape.

Rowena stretched her fingers and reset her grip on the spear, preparing for whatever came next. Despite her exhaustion, despite the pain of her wounds, she would not yield. Not to Fidessa. Not to anyone.

The bailey echoed with the sounds of conflict. Metal on metal, cries of pain, the guttural commands of Fidessa's guards rallying for another assault. Through it all, Rowena remained acutely aware of Safi's approach, of the reunion that seemed inevitable now.

Mother and daughter. Queen and princess. Both broken in their own ways, both casualties of a cycle of pain that seemed without end.

As Rowena squared off against Fidessa once more, gathering her strength for what might be their final confrontation, a new sound cut through the din of battle. Hoofbeats. Approaching fast from the direction of the portcullis.

Reinforcements had arrived. But for which side, Rowena couldn't tell.

The battle was far from over.

44

ROWENA

THE HOOFBEATS GREW LOUDER, an organized rhythm that cut through the chaos of battle like a blade. A sound Rowena recognized with a chill of dread. Borelks. She risked a glance toward the portcullis, her sword still raised against Fidessa and her menagerie of protectors.

Her view was cut short by a strike from one of Fidessa's guards. She parried, driving her blade into the gap beneath its crude armor. The guard fell with a squeal, but two more took its place, their jowled faces contorted with bloodlust.

Held at bay by her spear, she twisted to face the new threat.

Black-cloaked figures poured through the portcullis, at least a dozen of them, their faces hidden beneath deep hoods. The Lunara riders. The group that had taken Rowena and Tephra prisoner in the mudflats, treating them like cargo. Their massive beasts' tusked, boar-like heads bobbed with each powerful stride, their massive antlers scraping the spikes of the raised iron gate.

They made no immediate move to join the fray. Instead, they dismounted, sending their borelk back over the bridge. A smart move. The space was already too full for them to maneuver well.

Then, with practiced precision, the Lunara formed a tight line on foot across the bailey's entrance. Silent. Watching. Assessing.

"Friends of yours?" Fidessa asked, her voice tight with exhaustion as she gestured toward the newcomers.

"Not mine," Rowena replied, equally wary. Why were they here?

The sounds of their arrival momentarily drew the attention of all combatants in the bailey. Across the packed-soil expanse, Safi halted, sizing up the new arrivals. Many had fallen to her relentless blade, their white-painted bodies scattered across the bailey like broken dolls. Yet Daenon had kept his distance, sacrificing his men to stay out of her range.

A fresh wave of anger built in Rowena's chest. Using his own men as fodder to wear Safi down before engaging her himself. Coward.

Near the closest crumbling section of the wall, Conri had joined the fight, wielding what appeared to be a broken spear shaft against two of Fidessa's guards. Goby darted between their legs, tripping one with a well-placed shove before scampering back to Conri's side. Despite his injuries, the former Fianna leader fought with the desperate skill of a man with nothing left to lose.

And Bram? Her gaze found him locked in combat with Yralissa, elemental enchantment crackling between them as they fought each other. The disavowed's green cloak billowed with an unnatural wind, her hands tracing sigils in the air that left shimmering trails of light.

They were all fighting their own battles, too far apart to aid one another. Divide and conquer. The oldest strategy in warfare, and they'd walked right into it.

Rowena paid for her distraction when one of the stinkbroods lunged, teeth scraping her already injured leg. Pain lanced up her thigh, hot and immediate. She staggered, nearly losing her balance as she swung the spear in a desperate arc, missing her target.

Another stinkbrood snarled and leapt, all knotted muscles and spittle and that god-awful stench. Gaseous trails clung to their wake like ghostly entrails, making her eyes water. She raised the spear, but a blur of gray and black striped fur intercepted the creature in midair.

Rabberine.

Two of them, slinking from behind a shattered barrel. One chomped down on the stinkbrood's neck, the other dove for her. She thrust her spear. The iron point bit deep, and the creature tumbled to the ground with a final, gurgling whine.

Blood flowed freely down her leg now, soaking her boot and leaving dark spatters on the dirt. Rowena gritted her teeth against the pain, forcing herself to remain upright. To show weakness before Fidessa would be fatal.

Though Fidessa seemed to welcome a moment of respite. The two of them circled each other, allowing Rowena peeks at the rest of the action in the bailey.

"When are you going to fight for yourself instead of sacrificing all of your pets?" Every step sent fresh pain lancing up Rowena's thigh, but she forced herself to ignore it.

"I've only just begun," Fidessa replied, though the strain in her voice belied her confident words. The queen's face had grown pale with exertion, the complex spell work clearly taking its toll. "Your friends are losing. Surrender now, and I might show mercy."

Rowena forced an intentionally cold smile. "When have you ever shown mercy, Fidessa? To your enemies or your loved ones?"

Fidessa's expression hardened, her exhaustion momentarily masked by fresh anger. "Do not presume to judge me, little slave. Not when you know nothing of the choices I've had to make."

There was that word again. Slave.

"I know enough," Rowena countered, shifting her weight to her uninjured leg as she squared off against the queen once more. The vultu circled overhead, waiting for Fidessa's command to strike again.

Movement from the edge of the bailey caught Rowena's attention. Liam and Hywel, the two remaining Fianna who had once been allies, charged Conri from behind, swords drawn.

"Conri, behind you!" Rowena called, but her voice was lost in the din of battle.

To her surprise, the two men didn't immediately attack Conri. Instead, they engaged Fidessa's guards, harrying him, their blades making quick work of the creatures. For a moment, it almost appeared they were helping him.

Then Rowena understood. They weren't trying to kill Conri; they were trying to get past him.

To reach her.

Hywel dispatched the final guard with a brutal upward thrust, then turned toward Rowena. Their eyes met across the bailey, and she saw nothing there but cold determination. Whatever bond had once existed between them had clearly dissolved.

"Your would-be rescuers seem to have their own agenda," Fidessa observed, a brittle smile curving her lips. "How inconvenient for you."

Indeed, the Lunara warriors remained at the edge of the bailey, their hooded faces turned toward the various conflicts but made no move to intervene. Their stillness was almost more unnerving than overt hostility would have been.

The queen raised her hand once more, perhaps to command the vultu's next attack. Instead, a rabberine lunged from behind an upturned cart, aiming for Rowena's throat. She pivoted, bringing her spearhead down so hard it nearly drove through the creature, pinning it to the ground. The movement sent fresh pain shooting up her injured leg, but she pushed through it, letting go of the embedded spear to ready her dagger for the next attack.

"I don't need anyone to save me," Rowena replied, her voice steady with resolve despite her exhaustion. "I'm capable of fighting my own battles."

Something like grudging respect flickered in Fidessa's eyes before hardening once more into determination.

"Then fight this." Her hand waved through the air in a simple pattern.

The ground beneath Rowena's feet shifted. She leapt aside just as the gritty soil cracked, an opening just wide enough for Rowena.

The jump landed her on her injured leg, sending pain surging up her thigh. She backpedaled, only to find her path blocked by the remaining stinkbroods, their leathery bodies forming a living barrier as they circled her.

Liam and Hywel had made significant progress across the bailey, cutting down anything in their path as they stalked toward Rowena. Their purpose was clear in their focused expressions. The Sword of Justice was their target, and they would not stop until they claimed it. Or died trying.

"The sword," Hywel called as he drew near enough to be heard. "Hand it over, and this ends now."

"It stays with me," Rowena said, bravado covering her fears.

She found herself caught between multiple threats. Fidessa's spells and creatures from one side, the advancing Fianna from another. Exhaustion and pain threatened to overwhelm her flagging strength.

Yet she refused to yield. Not to Fidessa, who had imprisoned her body. Not to Hywel, who sought to take the one weapon that might protect those she cared for. Not to her own limitations, when so much depended on her ability to keep fighting.

"If I were you," Fidessa said, her voice dropping to a near-whisper, "I'd start questioning who my real enemies are."

With renewed determination, Rowena charged the line of stinkbroods, catching them off guard with her sudden aggression. Her dagger sliced through two of them before they could react, creating a narrow path that she immediately exploited.

Rowena's injured leg threatened to buckle with each step, blood flowing freely down her calf to pool in her boot. Her breath came in ragged gasps, each inhalation burning in lungs taxed beyond their limits.

A flash of movement to her left from Safi. Her cousin had cut through the last of the chalk warriors in her path, leaving only Daenon to face her.

The newly crowned king finally engaged, his spear spinning in practiced arcs that forced Safi to check her advance. Unlike his men, Daenon moved with precision, each strike aimed to wear down rather than kill. He was playing a longer game, preserving himself while the others exhausted their strength.

At the sight of Safi fighting alone, surrounded by enemies on all sides, something twisted in Rowena's chest. Even as she faced the same.

"You did this to her," she said to Fidessa, unable to keep the accusation from her voice. "Made her a weapon without will or choice."

"I protected her the only way I knew how," Fidessa replied, her voice cracking slightly. Her perfect composure slipped, revealing a tightness around her eyes, a tremor in her hands. "You think I wanted this? I did not anticipate complications."

The queen's words didn't match Rowena's experience with her. Instead of cold calculation, Rowena heard the echo of her own father's voice when he'd kept her from traveling with him "for her protection." The familiar justification of someone who misjudged control for care.

The glimpse of vulnerability vanished as Hywel broke through the last line of guards separating him from Rowena. His blade danced with precise arcs that spoke of decades of training. Liam flanked him, their coordinated approach leaving Rowena with few options for escape.

"We don't want to kill you," Liam called, his voice carrying over the din of battle. "Just surrender the sword."

Rowena rolled her shoulders, confirming the comforting presence of the sword along her spine, its power pulsing in response. The sword wasn't just for any Lunara. It had *chosen her*. They were one and no one would take it from her again.

"Never," she replied, the word simple but absolute.

Hywel's eyes narrowed. "Then I'll take it from your corpse."

Cold certainty told Rowena she couldn't keep fighting on multiple fronts for much longer. Her muscles burned with exhaustion, each breath coming shorter than the last. She could not stop Hywel from achieving his goal.

She reached for any remaining enchantment. Some flickered. Too far. She couldn't reach it.

Fidessa lowered her arms, appearing content to allow Hywel to take over the fight.

Hywel lunged forward, his blade forging a deadly arc toward her neck. Rowena parried. The dagger redirected Hywel's sword, but the impact sent vibrations up her arm that left her fingers tingling to near numbness. She lunged in close, preventing Hywel another swing of his longer blade. She swiped with dagger, aiming for Hywel's midsection, but he leapt away.

The air shifted behind her. Fidessa had renewed her attention. The queen would not let this opportunity pass. With Rowena distracted by Hywel, her back was exposed to the queen's attacks.

Fidessa gave a sharp whistle. The vultu responded immediately, diving from above with talons extended. Simultaneously, her remaining stinkbroods charged from different directions, cutting off any avenue of escape.

Trapped between Hywel's blade and Fidessa's creatures, Rowena made a desperate choice. She feinted toward Hywel, then reversed direction, throwing herself toward Fidessa instead. Her pets wouldn't dare attack their master.

They switched their target mid stride, turning their rage against Hywel instead. It kept him occupied while her surprise maneuver caught the queen off guard.

For a moment, they stood nearly face to face, close enough that Rowena could see flecks of gold in Fidessa's gray eyes, the fine lines at their corners that spoke of age carefully concealed.

Rowena could sink her blade into Fidessa, finishing her reign of destruction once and for all. She shook her head.

"The difference between us," Rowena said, her voice low but fierce, "is that I will not become like those who hurt me. I won't perpetuate the cycle."

Something flickered in Fidessa's gaze, recognition perhaps, or the barest hint of respect. Then her features hardened, hands rising to cast another spell.

Hywel must have dispatched Fidessa's beasts faster than she expected. She heard his approach too late, sensed the whistling arc of his blade only when it was already descending toward her exposed back.

Time seemed to slow. Rowena couldn't turn fast enough to block the strike. Her body, already pushed beyond reasonable limits, would fail her at this crucial moment.

This was how it ended. The thought came with crystalline clarity.

Then movement exploded across the bailey. The Lunara riders, silent observers until that moment, leapt into the fray with a coordinated charge. Their cloaks billowed behind them like wings of darkness, hoods falling back to reveal stern, determined faces.

The whisper of steel cutting through space filled the air. A blade intercepted Hywel's less than a hand's width from Rowena's neck. A nick trickled blood down her collarbone.

But she still lived.

Rowena slid her gaze to the Lunara, revealing weatherbeaten features framed by dark hair shot through with silver. A scar bisected his left eyebrow, giving him a perpetually questioning expression.

Why save her? Or had he simply wanted to claim the kill for himself?

Her dagger came up automatically, though her arm trembled with exhaustion. She had no more time to question the unexpected intervention. She flung her blade toward Liam while his attention was divided. He dodged, but not quickly enough to avoid a shallow cut across his chest.

The Lunara twisted from Hywel's slumped body to stand at her side.

"Why are you helping me?" she demanded of the Lunara warrior.

"Orders," he replied tersely, not taking his eyes from his opponent. "The king wants you alive."

Before she could question him further, Fidessa launched another attack. The vultu dove from above while the last rabberine charged from the opposite direction.

The Lunara spun, his blade a silver arc that caught the rabberine mid-leap. The creature fell with a gurgling cry, but the vultu dove undeterred.

The black bird's talons raked across Rowena's shoulder, tearing through fabric to score lines of fire across her skin. Warm blood trickled down her arm, making her grip on the dagger slippery and uncertain.

Gritting her teeth, Rowena lashed out with a backhanded strike that caught the creature's wing as it swooped for another attack. The vultu shrieked, spiraling toward the ground before righting itself with obvious difficulty.

"We fight together," he said, his raspy voice carrying no emotion she could discern. "For now."

"Why fight like this? Where's your enchantment?" she managed to ask with the sword still raised between them despite her shaking arm. If she had access to hers, she wouldn't hesitate to put an end to the bloodshed.

The rider didn't answer immediately. Instead, he gestured to his companions, who had formed a protective circle around Rowena, their backs to her as they faced outward against the various threats surrounding them.

"There will be time for explanations," he said. "For now, know that we are here to ensure your safety, and the sword's."

That was it. She held the Lunara's piece of armor. She glanced around the Lunara encircling her. Any one of them could spin and steal the sword from her back. They claimed to be helping, but she worried it was only until they had what they wanted.

Liam, seeing his companion fall, abandoned his assault on Rowena to melt back into the ongoing conflict. He engaged Safi directly, while Daenon hung back.

Despite her altered penchant for violence, Safi showed signs of fatigue. Her movements, while still precise, had lost some of their fluid grace. Blood stained her clothing in multiple places, though Rowena couldn't tell how much was her own and how much belonged to the many opponents she'd dispatched.

Liam pressed his advantage, forcing Safi back toward the collapsed section of wall where escape might be impossible. The Fianna warrior's blade was a blur that required all of Safi's concentration to counter.

Behind them, Fidessa had recovered from her momentary surprise at the riders' intervention. Her expression hardened as she watched her daughter's struggle, something like genuine fear flashing across her features.

For the first time, Rowena wondered if Fidessa's concern for Safi might be genuine in its own twisted way. If beneath the control and manipulation lay some vestige of maternal love, however warped by trauma and power.

"Your friends need assistance," the lead rider observed, following Rowena's gaze.

"Then fight with them," she replied, frustration mounting as her body refused to respond as it should. Her injured leg had begun to tremble visibly, threatening to give out entirely.

The rider shook his head, his expression solemn. "Our orders concern you and the sword alone, Princess. The others must fend for themselves."

Cold anger flashed through Rowena's chest. "You helped them before!"

"Only to secure our position here with you." His gaze swept the battle, uncaring.

Rowena took a step toward Safi, determined to aid her despite her own injuries. Immediately, two Lunara moved to block her path, their expressions impassive but their intent clear.

"As I said, the king requires that you live," the Lunara next to her said, his tone firm.

"Then help me, help them," Rowena snapped, attempting to push past them. Her leg buckled, dropping her to one knee. She refused to drop her dagger, catching herself with her free hand to keep herself from complete collapse. "Use your enchantment!"

Across the bailey, Liam had gained the upper hand. His blade sliced across Safi's sword arm, drawing a line of crimson that spilled down to her fingertips. She didn't cry out. Couldn't, given her mute state, but Rowena felt the pain as if it were her own.

"Safi," she called, her voice cracking with desperation. "Keep fighting!"

Whether Safi heard her or simply found some reservoir of strength, her cousin rallied. Her movements became faster, more aggressive, forcing Liam to give ground.

Encouraged, Rowena turned to the lead rider once more. "If your king wants me alive, then help all of them, or I swear by all of Lungol's chaos, this sword will never be seen in Penumar." It wasn't much of a threat from her position on the ground, where they could easily disarm her of the blade.

She didn't care. If they were truly there just to help, then this was how they could prove it.

"Penumar and the Lycani have a treaty we cannot use enchantment within the Veilrune Mountains."

She met his gaze unflinchingly, letting him see the determination in her eyes.

After a long moment, he nodded. "Very well. Six, in pairs, assist her companions. The rest of you remain."

Relief washed over Rowena as six cloaked Lunara broke from the protective circle. Two raced toward where Safi fought. Four went the other direction to help Bram and Conri. The remaining Lunara warriors maintained their position around Rowena, keeping Fidessa from coming near.

Liam, seeing the approaching riders, abandoned his assault on Safi and turned, sprinting out of sight behind the keep. Daenon, with only two other chalk warriors at his sides, growled into the air. Before the Lunara reached him, he spun and followed Liam's path away from the fight.

Fidessa remained where she stood, her creatures, only one stinkbrood and the vultu, gathered protectively near her. She made no move to attack, though her gaze followed the Lunara with calculated wariness.

And beyond her, Bram appeared to have the upper hand in his conflict with Yralissa. He seemed distressed, but she could not help. Rowena had reached her limits. Her heart clenched so tight it seemed no bigger than a pebble.

She swept her gaze to the others. Safi stood unmoving among the fallen chalk warriors. Conri and Goby had taken shelter near a collapsed section of wall, the Fianna leader leaning heavily on the goblin's shoulder despite the creature's diminutive size.

Bram, Safi, Conri, Goby, all pushed to their breaking points, all fighting their own desperate battles for survival, because of her.

Despite the sword on her back, despite the crown she claimed, despite everything she had endured and overcome, she lacked the power to protect those who had risked everything to stand with her.

In that moment, surrounded by enemies and uncertain allies, Rowena faced the coldest truth of leadership, that sometimes, no matter how desperately you fought, it wasn't enough.

45

BRAM

BRAM RECOGNIZED the cloaked warriors who'd arrived on the borelk. Lunara from Penumar.

They'd come for Rowena, surely. Or the sword. Both.

He didn't have time to piece it all together. They seemed to fight alongside her. Hope flared that her mother's realm had arrived to help.

Yralissa launched another attack, this time drawing moisture from the air itself to form a whip of water that lashed toward his face. Bram ducked, rolling beneath it, coming up with his axe raised defensively.

"You're not as impressive without your shadows, are you?" She circled him. "Just a failed experiment now."

Bram shifted his weight, ignoring the burning pain in his side. Behind Yralissa, through the chaos of battle filling the bailey, he caught glimpses of Rowena fighting.

She was holding her own, but the Lunara seemed to be aiding her. Allies.

He could focus on his own battle.

But the thought provided little comfort. Every instinct screamed at him to go to her, to fight at her side. Instead, he was trapped here, facing a disavowed druid with powers he could no longer match.

"I had such hopes for you," Yralissa said, her voice almost conversational despite the deadly intent behind her words. "We all did. The perfect vessel. Achan's pride and joy."

The High Hepta's name hit like ice water. "You worked with Achan?"

She scoffed with a sneer. "Worked with him? I was a paritor." Her fingers twitched, and a ripple of energy grazed Bram's shoulder, making his muscles spasm. "Before he found someone new, he fancied better."

The High Hepta's cruelty went deeper than he'd imagined. He'd seen how Achan treated those under his command, but this . . .

Yralissa was older than Bram, perhaps late twenties to his early twenties, but the lines around her eyes spoke of hardships beyond her years. What had Achan done to her?

"Whatever he did to you," Bram said, dodging another burst of energy, "this isn't the way to—"

"Save your breath." Her face contorted with rage. "You know nothing of what I endured."

She struck again, this time with a wave of enchantment that caught Bram squarely in the chest. Pain lanced through him, driving him to one knee. His transformed body, caught between forms, was more vulnerable than he'd realized.

He reached instinctively for his Seeker abilities, forgetting for a heartbeat that they were beyond his grasp. The attempt sent agony shooting through his veins, as if his blood had turned to molten metal.

Adapt. Find another way.

"We're the same, you and I," she said, circling him again. "Both used by the Heptad. Both twisted into shapes that suited their purposes."

"I'm nothing like you," Bram spat, forcing himself upright despite his pain.

"No?" She laughed, the sound brittle as winter ice. "You were their perfect weapon, valued. Their Seeker, hunting those who stepped out of line. I was discarded. But we share more than you know."

Yralissa continued, as if giving a lecture rather than trying to kill him.

"The Primary druids have access to all the elements, but they insist on following Osric's rules for keeping them separated: fire isolated from water, earth from air. It keeps them weak and dependent on each other. But the Astaroth see the truth. That a single druid can be more powerful if they channel all elements together. It is Ha'mon's way."

Another water whip transformed mid-strike, solidifying into a spear of ice that Bram barely managed to deflect with the flat of his axe. The impact sent vibrations up his arm.

"While you were earning the Heptad's approval, I was learning their secrets," she said, her attacks becoming more fluid, transitioning seamlessly between elements. "While you were becoming their perfect Seeker, I was discovering who we really are."

Something in her emphasis made Bram pause. "We?"

"Enough games," she snarled. "It's time you learned the truth."

"What truth?" Bram kept the sword between them, using it to block another burst of enchantment. The metal vibrated in his hands, growing hot to the touch. It wouldn't withstand her enchantment for long.

"They took everything from me. My identity. My purpose. My body." Her lip curled. "But not my mind. I *remember*. I remember who we are, who they are."

She struck again. Not with elemental power this time, but

with physical force—a kick to his wounded side that dropped him to one knee. Pain radiated through him, momentarily blinding in its intensity.

When his vision cleared, Yralissa stood over him, one hand extended. Not to attack, but as if offering to help him rise.

"We were both abandoned," she said quietly. "Both left to the Pedagogy's mercy. But she only fought for you."

Confusion warred with pain in Bram's mind. "What are you talking about?"

"About who you are. Who we are." Yralissa's expression shifted, grief momentarily replacing anger. "Finish my riddle, Bram. The one I gave you in the tower. Who am I to you?"

The riddle. He'd been too focused on escaping to give it proper thought. Something about shared blood, about forgotten bonds . . .

"Our mother lost everything in her battle for you," Yralissa continued, something raw and vulnerable breaking through her carefully controlled expression. "She was disavowed and cast out of Saganus for her efforts. But for me? She gave me up without a struggle."

The words hung in the air between them, heavy with meaning. Understanding dawned, cold and shocking as plunging into winter waters.

It couldn't be . . . *two seeds were sown . . . one left to wane . . . in mother's absence . . .*

"No," he whispered. "You can't mean . . ."

"I am your sister, Bram." The words fell like stones into still water, ripples of revelation expanding outward. "First born. Left behind and forgotten."

Sister. The word echoed in his mind, foreign and impossible.

Denial rose instantly to Bram's lips, but died there as pieces began falling into place. The resonance he'd felt when they touched. The way she'd always seemed to know more about him than she should. "That's not possible."

"Isn't it?" Yralissa's smile held no joy, only bitter vindication. "We share the same mother. A Primary Fae who broke covenant. She bore me first, gave me up to the pedagogy like expected. But when you came along, something changed. She fought for you, though she ultimately failed."

The battle raged around them, seemingly distant now despite its proximity. Bram struggled to process what she was saying, to reconcile this revelation with everything he'd believed about himself.

"You're lying," he said, but the words felt hollow.

Yralissa knelt before him, their faces level. "Look at me, brother. Really look. What do you see?"

And he did see it then. The shape of her eyes, similar to his own. The specific angle of her cheekbones. Small details he'd overlooked, dismissed, or simply never noticed. Why would he?

"Why tell me this now?" he asked, his voice barely audible above the chaos of battle.

"Because you need to understand what we're fighting for," she replied. "The Heptad, the rebels, even Fidessa, they're all pieces in a game whose rules you don't yet comprehend."

A scream from somewhere in the bailey jerked Bram's attention away. Rowena. He couldn't see her through the melee, but the sound of her voice in distress sent fresh urgency coursing through him.

"This changes nothing," he said, forcing himself back to his feet despite the agony through his side. "Whatever we might be to each other, your actions are your own. And they've brought nothing but suffering."

Hurt flashed across Yralissa's face, quickly masked by cold fury. "You still don't understand. Even now, you cling to their lies."

She raised her hands, power gathering around her fingertips once more. "If you won't listen to reason, perhaps pain will teach you what words cannot."

The attack came without warning. Not one element this time, but all of them combined into pure Primary enchantment. A wave that struck Bram like a physical blow, driving him back several paces. It felt familiar, reminiscent of the spell she'd used to bind his powers, but different in its intent.

This wasn't meant to contain or transform. It was meant to reveal.

Images flashed through Bram's mind. A woman with blurred features, indistinct. The Heptad's chamber where figures sat in judgment. A baby crying, its wails echoing off the walls stacked with books and scrolls. His memories? Hers? He couldn't tell, the distinction between them muddled under the onslaught of shared consciousness.

He fought against it, struggling to maintain the boundaries of his own mind. This was another trick, another manipulation. It had to be. Yet the images held a ring of truth he couldn't entirely dismiss.

With tremendous effort, Bram pushed back against the intrusion. Not with power, that remained locked away, but with sheer will. The connection between them wavered, thinned, then snapped like an overextended thread.

"How did you?" Yralissa stumbled backward, surprise evident in her expression. "You must understand! The rebels, the Heptad, our family is connected to both."

The words made him stagger. The Heptad? How? And the rebels . . . how did she know about them?

Everything he thought he knew about his past, his purpose, was unraveling. The rebels fighting against tradition, Yralissa's desperate need for recognition, Rowena's lost family, Safi's imprisonment. All of it connected in ways he was only beginning to understand.

His place in all of this chaos suddenly seemed less certain than ever.

Around them, the battle raged on.

Yet Bram stood frozen, the world narrowing to this impossible revelation.

A high-pitched whistle cut through the air, followed by a wet thud. Yralissa gasped. Shock replaced her anger as she stared at an arrow protruding from her shoulder, blood already staining her cloak a deeper shade of green.

Bram's eyes darted to the source of the arrow. One of the Lunara at the edge of the bailey, bow still raised. Several fought in pairs, helping. Others formed a ring around Rowena.

Bram's eyes met Yralissa's, pain and fury warring in their depths as they began to close.

Sister. The word felt foreign, impossible. Yet he believed her.

She struggled to maintain consciousness. He needed the rest of her story.

A clash of steel behind him snapped Bram back to the present. A duo of Lunara stalked closer.

Rowena needed him.

But so did Yralissa, his *sister*.

Bram charged with his axe raised to stop a Lunara sword from adding to Yralissa's injuries.

46

ROWENA

FREED FROM IMMEDIATE PRESSURE, Safi stood for a moment, swaying slightly as if reassessing her surroundings. Then, to Rowena's surprise, she advanced directly toward Fidessa.

The queen's eyes widened as she recognized her daughter's approach. "Safi," she called, her voice carrying a note Rowena had never heard from her before, something almost like fear. "Stand down."

But her cousin gave no indication she had heard. Her blood-spattered face remained expressionless. Her movements slow yet purposeful as she cut down the first pig-like guard who moved to intercept her.

"She cannot hear you," Rowena called to Fidessa, understanding dawning cold and clear. "She no longer recognizes you."

Genuine anguish twisted Fidessa's features. "Safi!" she called again, desperation edging her voice. "I command you to stop!"

The order had no effect. Safi continued her inexorable advance, dispatching another guard with brutal efficiency. Her sword moved with the precision of a killing machine, untroubled by emotion or hesitation.

For the first time, Rowena truly understood the horror of what Fidessa had done to her daughter. She had created a weapon that could not be controlled, could not be recalled once set in motion. A perfect soldier with no capacity for mercy or restraint.

Only Fidessa remained fully engaged, her focus entirely on Safi's approach. The queen's expression had transformed from confidence to growing horror as she realized her daughter had turned against her.

"What have I done?" she whispered. The words barely audible across the distance separating them.

It was the most vulnerable Fidessa had ever seemed, stripped of queenly arrogance, faced with the consequences of her own actions. For a fleeting moment, Rowena almost felt pity for the woman who had caused so much suffering.

Then Daenon reemerged from the shadows near the keep. His stride longer and more insistent than Safi's, he blocked her path, to protect Fidessa.

With a short sword in one hand and a spear in the other, he stretched out his arms. "You are the king's weapon. Stand down."

Arrogance. It would be his undoing.

Safi halted.

No! He couldn't have that kind of control over her.

Rowena lunged. She had to break through to her cousin before Daenon stole her away again.

A hand, gentle but firm, grabbed Rowena by the elbow. "Her battle is her own."

Rowena flinched and pulled away. Her jaw clenched, and she spoke through bared teeth. "He is responsible for her pain, mine, and many others. I will not allow him to hurt her again."

"Her battle tactics give her the advantage."

Who was this man to stand there so casually speaking as if

this were no more than a game during a celebration feast? "That is not a risk worth taking."

"Medraut?" One of the Lunara behind Rowena said the name as if awaiting an order.

The Lunara twisted his lips.

"Lunara dogs," Daenon spat. "Think you can take my prize?"

"Silence, traitor," Medraut called back, his posture shifting subtly from diplomatic to threatening. "Your crimes against the crown are known."

Crimes against the crown? Rowena filed the information away. There was clearly more history between these factions than she understood.

Daenon's laugh was bitter. "The true leader will rise. The prophecy will fail."

Medraut twisted to give a curt nod to one of his men behind Rowena.

Motion behind her gave the only hint that the ring of Lunara had created a gap. One that she could use. She spun and slipped through.

"Stop her!" Medraut's unmistakable voice called.

Despite how her foot dragged because of injuries, she made it to within striking distance of Daenon before anyone could grab her.

"She is not yours to command," Rowena said, venom entwined through her words.

Daenon shifted his stance to keep both herself and Safi in view. "You're a fool to believe there's anything but violence left in her. It will be my pleasure to witness your death. Finally."

"She won't hurt me." A flutter of apprehension rolled through Rowena's stomach. She had to believe she could still reach Safi, the woman she was, not the brute she'd become.

"Let's see," Daenon said, a sneer lifting one side of his mouth, staring at Safi directly. "Kill her."

He stepped backward, clearing the area between Rowena and her cousin to meet face to face. Rowena wanted to drop her sword, let Safi see that she did not intend to fight. But that would only allow Daenon to swoop in and steal it.

Safi stood motionless, unaffected. Then she arched a single brow and her lips curved ever so slightly.

A challenge.

Rowena's muscles tensed. She would defend herself, no more.

Safi darted her eyes toward Daenon, then pinned Rowena with her stare.

Not a challenge, an offer.

Fight their mutual enemy together.

Rowena choked back a sob of relief. Her intuition had been right. Her cousin remained inside despite whatever held her captive to violence.

"I accept." She let a smile bloom on her face as she spun to face Daenon.

His eyes bulged in shock as they both charged.

Safi reached him first. Her blade singing through the air so fast, the king had to drop and roll out of the way.

Right toward Rowena.

Daenon hopped to his feet, feinted toward Safi, then pivoted to strike at Rowena.

She anticipated the maneuver, ducking in closer, aiming her dagger for just under his ribs, forcing him to twist out of the way. The blade missed him by inches, leaving Rowena stumbling from her momentum.

Daenon blocked another strike from Safi, then leapt into the air, twisting and hurled his spear at Rowena.

The spear cut through the air. Its trajectory true. Safi lunged forward, but she was too far to intercept.

Rowena tried to dodge, but her exhausted and damaged body betrayed her. She stumbled, ankle twisting beneath her.

A dark blur crossed before her. A Lunara. He threw himself into the spear's path. The weapon struck him in the chest with a sickening thud. He landed heavily on the hard ground. Blood bloomed around the wooden shaft protruding from his body.

"No!" Medraut's anguished cry cut through the stunned silence.

Chaos erupted anew. The Lunara charged Daenon's position, their disciplined formation dissolving into vengeful fury. Daenon and his remaining warriors disappeared into the keep, the Lunara in pursuit.

Rowena knelt beside the fallen rider, her hands hovering uselessly over his wound. The spear had penetrated too deeply. Nothing could be done.

The man's eyes found hers, clouding already with approaching death. His lips moved, forming words too quiet to hear.

Rowena leaned closer.

"Long . . . live . . . the sparrow," he whispered.

His body went slack. The light faded from his eyes.

Rowena sat back on her heels, the rider's blood warm and sticky on her hands. He had died for her. A stranger.

The sparrow. The name her mother used to call her. The word from the prophecy.

The sparrow of silver fire will strike the owl from above and below

A chill ran through her, despite the warmth of battle.

Safi knelt beside her, a steadying hand on her shoulder. Her cousin's face was grim, her eyes asking a question Rowena couldn't answer.

She dropped her chin, too exhausted to hold back her tears. Safi's fingers gave a light squeeze, and then she was gone.

Rowena remained on the ground, numbly staring at the dead warrior.

Until a cry from across the bailey drew her attention.

Safi had reached Fidessa, her sword raised for a killing blow. The queen stood unmoving, the last of her guards fallen around her, as her own daughter prepared to end her life.

"Safi, no!" Rowena called, scrambling to rise. She could not let her kill Fidessa, deserving as it was, it would be a regret Safi would carry for life. Once she recovered.

The sword began its downward arc, a flash of steel in the afternoon light. Fidessa made no move to defend herself, her expression a complex mixture of resignation and despair.

Finally on her feet, Rowena could only watch.

Then Safi froze, her blade stopping mere inches from her mother's throat. For a breathless moment, everyone in the bailey seemed to hold perfectly still, watching mother and daughter locked in a moment of mortal decision.

Slowly, almost imperceptibly, something shifted in Safi's blank expression. Her sword arm trembled visibly, caught between the binding spell's command and some deeper resistance.

"Safi," Fidessa whispered, her voice carrying in the sudden silence. "My daughter."

The words seemed to reach something in Rowena's cousin. Her sword lowered a fraction, then another, the trembling in her arm intensifying as she fought against her unknown prison.

Hope flared in Rowena's chest. If Safi could break through the side effects, even momentarily, it meant she might still be saved.

The Lunara warriors had formed a loose perimeter encompassing Rowena, their fallen warrior, and Safi, neither advancing nor retreating. They watched the unfolding drama between mother and daughter with inscrutable expressions, their hands still resting on their weapon hilts.

Then all eyes turned skyward as a massive shadow passed over the bailey.

47

BRAM

THE LUNARA LOWERED their weapons before Bram reached them. He skidded to a halt. Like all the others, he raised his gaze to the skies.

A new threat.

He scanned the grounds. Rowena was next to Safi. Safe for the moment.

He staggered back to Yralissa. Her revelation pressing down heavy on his shoulders. Each breath like shards of glass slicing through his lungs. The tender truth now laid bare before him. Sister. The word ricocheted within his mind, foreign and yet resonant, awakening a primal urge he hadn't known he possessed. The need to protect, to shield her from further harm.

Yralissa lay on the forest floor, the arrow jutting from her shoulder like an accusation. Her face was pale, a stark contrast to the dark soil around them, yet her eyes burned with a defiance that refused to be dimmed. Bram's heart twisted at the sight, a tumult of emotions churning within him, anger, confusion, an unfamiliar longing to connect.

"Stay back," Yralissa hissed, her voice a brittle whisper,

breaking the silence that hung between them. "I don't need your pity."

The poison within Bram's veins pulsed in response, a cruel reminder of his current impotence that *she* instilled. Why had she done such a thing? She could have confided in him, told him the truth instead of playing all of her games. He could no longer shift, no longer reach for the power that had once flowed so freely through him. Yet, it wasn't power he sought now. It was understanding.

"I didn't know," Bram said, his voice raw, stripped of pretense. "I didn't know any of it."

Yralissa's laugh was bitter, a sound like cracking ice. "Ignorance is a luxury you've always had, brother. You were kept safe, cherished. While I . . ." She faltered, the words crumbling under the weight of her anger and hurt.

Kneeling beside her, Bram assessed the wound with practiced efficiency. The metallic scent of blood stinging his nose, but given the flow it had most likely avoided any major vessels. It was significant, but a non-fatal injury.

"Let me help," he said, the words emerging less as a combatant and more as something raw and unfamiliar. He glanced at the arrow. It would be too damaging to pull it out, he'd have to push it through. "Please."

She flinched; her distrust obvious. But there was a flicker, barely perceptible, of hesitation. A potential opening.

"I've learned much about taking care of myself."

"But I'm here now. Your brother," he said, the designation both foreign and correct. "I owe you that much."

Yralissa's defensive posture shifted, just a fraction. The walls she'd built disappearing, but then her inner storm returned with cold fury. She huffed, a harsh disgusted sound, slapping away his hands.

With a grimace, she grasped the arrow herself, breaking off

the shaft with a swift, brutal motion. A mix of admiration at her exceptional pain threshold. She was a fighter like him. She screamed as she pushed on the shaft, trying to force it through on her own.

Bram grabbed her hand. "You can't get it out of your back alone." He waited, holding her gaze as strongly as he held her hand, giving her time to accept his words.

She gave a curt nod and turned her face away.

Bram slid his hand behind her shoulder, lifting her from the ground. With a quick motion, he yanked the arrow free and tossed it aside. "There. It came out clean."

Her face, contorted before she pressed her hand to her shoulder.

Her fingers glowed with the white brightness of the Primary Fae, ethereal. The air shimmered around her wound, the flesh knitting together under her touch, becoming smooth and whole.

Another reminder that she was not the disavowed she claimed. Another reminder of what he had lost.

The Seeker's presence within him whispered, far away and faint and brief. A painful illusion of the power he once wielded, but could no longer touch.

They sat there in silence, two souls adrift in a sea of unspoken words. The surrounding battle seemed to hush, silent for their moment together. Though thoughts of Rowena needled their way in. She was fighting alone. He needed to get to her. But he had to stay. . .

"We have other family," Yralissa murmured, breaking the silence that had settled over them. "More than just our mother."

Bram paused, his hands stilling. "What do you mean?"

"I never wanted this," Yralissa murmured, her voice softer now, the edge of her anger dulled by exhaustion. "I just wanted to know why I wasn't worth it."

Bram's chest tightened, the weight of her words settling

heavily. "You were worth it," he said fiercely. "More than worth it. From what it seems, she fought for me because she was broken after losing you. She couldn't do it again."

"A pretty but useless delusion. They won't acknowledge me," she continued, bitterness lacing her words. "They'll use me, but they won't offer the tenderness of their care. They want to see you succeed, Bram. You're their bright hope."

His heart ached at the raw vulnerability in her voice, the sense of abandonment he could now feel echoing within him. The weight of their shared history pressed upon him.

Yralissa turned her face toward him, her expression unreadable. Yet something in her eyes had shifted. A glimmer of hope, a fragile thread of connection that wavered, then snuffed out like the last bit of candle left too long to burn.

"I need time," she said finally, her voice barely more than a whisper.

Time was not something they had, at least for now. As the shadows lengthened around them, the battle had quieted in the distance, but he felt the enormity of what lay ahead. The rebels in Saganus, his mother's legacy among them, the family Yralissa so desperately needed but couldn't reach. Each piece of the puzzle fell into place, forming a picture of a world fraught with peril and potential that he knew nothing about. Blinded by twisted trust and misplaced loyalty.

He thought of Rowena and the devastation wrought upon her family, the way Fidessa's spell had twisted Safi into a creature of violence. Their stories intertwined with his own threads of a tapestry woven by fate. Bram felt the crushing weight of it all, the realization that he was not just fighting for himself, but for all of them.

A darkness descended upon him, cold and unfamiliar from what it had been, the shadows coiling like serpents in his mind. He understood now, for the first time, what it truly meant to lack power in a world where others possessed it. The vulnerability and helplessness of Rowena's previous position as a slave to both Uther and Fidessa that had once been foreign to him shredded his illusions of heroism.

Power is not given to wield over the weak, it is given to help empower them to rise and become strong themselves.

But even amidst the chaos, a resolve began to form within him. Even if he couldn't wield all his powers, he would find a way to make things right, to bridge the chasm that had formed between him and all those he loved.

Yralissa watched him, her expression torn between anger and something softer. "You think you can fix this?" she asked, her voice laced with skepticism.

"I have to try," Bram replied, the conviction in his words surprising even him. "For you, for us, for everyone who's been hurt."

A silence stretched between them, heavy with unspoken promises and the ghost of what might have been. Yralissa opened her mouth to speak, but the words were stolen by a deafening screech that tore through the skies overhead.

The entire bailey of the castle vibrated with the sound, a primal, terrifying cry that seemed to shake the very bones of the earth. Bram's heart leapt into his throat, his eyes darting upwards as a shadow passed over them, blotting out the sun.

In that moment, the urgency of their situation eclipsed everything else. A fragile bond flickered between them—a promise of redemption, of reconciliation, of hope.

Then it shattered.

"This isn't over," she promised, her voice strained.

Before Bram could respond, she pressed her uninjured hand to the ground. The hard-packed dirt beneath her shuddered, then burst into blue flame that swallowed her from sight. It disappeared as quickly as it rose, leaving no trace of Yralissa.

He stood there, swaying slightly from pain and exhaustion, her final words echoing in his mind. *This isn't over.*

She'd never given him a name—not of their mother or their family. Had she really said they were connected to the Heptad? Her words fuzzy in his mind, but fear ricocheted through his chest. Please not Achan.

Questions of blood and family would have to wait.

Sister or not, Yralissa had made her choice. And he had made his.

With a final glance at the void where Yralissa had been, Bram turned toward the fray of battle, axe raised, scanning the skies.

The air seemed to shimmer slightly, growing colder. Frost formed on the ground, on the castle stones, spreading outward in delicate patterns. Fog slipped from the lips of every warrior.

Bram frowned. Understanding dawned just as another screech split the air above the bailey.

The frost dragon had returned.

48

ROWENA

THE AIR in the bailey shifted, turning bitterly cold in an instant. Rowena's breath clouded before her face, and frost crackled across the dirt beneath her feet.

A prickling sensation crawled up her spine. She turned her gaze to where Fidessa huddled on the ground, a strange calm settling over the mage's features. No longer the frantic desperation of a cornered animal, but the serene confidence of someone who had just played her final card.

And won.

"Something's wrong," Rowena murmured, more to herself than to Medraut beside her.

The Lunara commander followed her gaze. "The mage—"

His words dissolved as another roar split the air above them. A sound Rowena had heard only once before, in Ibern, when she'd faced death from the air.

Every living being stilled. Even Fidessa's stinkbrood silenced mid-snarl. The vultu held itself like a stone statue.

Rowena's insides rebelled, twisting and writhing to get away, making her want to vomit. Not again. She'd fought one of the dragons before. This one somehow seemed bigger. It loomed over her, blotting out the confidence she'd built, the strength she'd gained. Her breath became shattered grasps for life, frantic and shallow.

As the frost dragon descended from the sky like a thunderous god. All white with whiskers like giant icicles, threatening to impale those who ventured into its path. Those fuchsia eyes Rowena could never forget, just as piercing and eerie as before.

Except not. These didn't scan for prey or radiate hate.

Combatants from scattered to avoid being crushed beneath the dragon's bulk, some sent like tumbleweeds from the force of the beast's downdraft. Rough hands dragged Rowena to safety as a talon the length of her forearm gouged the soil where she'd been standing.

Her gaze remained fixed on the creature whose landing rattled her teeth when its feet slammed against the dirt. The beast snuffed the ground and the air, its gigantic maw making a slow arc from side to side, searching. Finally, halting its pink stare on Rowena. She swallowed hard.

It was the dragon from the dungeon lair. The one Tephra had ridden away. Had she sent it back, or did it return to Fidessa on its own?

The dragon snorted, sending dirt clods into the air to rain over Rowena's head. Then it turned away from her and calmly ruffled its silvery feathered wings before folding them against its scales, sparkling with iridescence from Sawel's light. Indifferent to anyone or anything within the bailey except Fidessa.

Only she had remained in place, still sitting on the ground, but her face transformed by an emotion Rowena never expected to see there—hope.

"You came back for me." Fidessa's laugh rang out, high and triumphant.

The reason it returned made no difference. Mage and beast ignored everyone else to reunite.

The dragon lowered its massive head, intelligent eyes fixing on Fidessa with what appeared to be deference. The beast exhaled, a gust of freezing mist curling from its nostrils, while a rumble emerged from its throat, as loud as a roar but as gentle as a purr.

Fidessa didn't cackle as she did when she taunted. Her smile, her laughter, were filled with genuine joy. She approached the dragon without fear, one hand extended to stroke the snowy-white scales of its muzzle.

"I thought you abandoned me too," she cooed, the hushed words carrying across the silent bailey. Her features softened into something almost beautiful. "I'll never doubt you again."

She stroked the dragon's muzzle with familiar ease, and the massive beast leaned into her touch like an overgrown cat seeking affection. Ice crystals formed where her fingers touched the scales, spreading in delicate patterns before dissolving again.

Safi had backed away at the dragon's arrival, her sword raised once more, but her posture was now uncertain. Her expression held a flicker of confusion, perhaps even recognition.

Bram made his way to Rowena, with his arms hanging limp at his sides. Yralissa nowhere in sight. Rips and scorch marks left parts of his clothing torn in ragged strips. He'd fought hard, but his presence beside her provided a strength she desperately needed. Her indecision and fear melted. She inhaled deep, prepared to let his charred oak scent wash over her, but something new stung her nostrils. A whiff of something bitter and tangy she couldn't place.

She shook her head slightly and steadied her shoulders. Too much had happened to both of them while separated, but it would have to wait until later. Now, their enemy still held the most power.

"What now?" he asked quietly, his gaze fixed on the dragon and Fidessa.

"I don't know," Rowena whispered back.

"A bond." Medraut's voice was tight with suppressed alarm. "The mage has a life-bond with the beast."

"What does that mean?" Rowena whispered. Fidessa had grown attached to a variety of animals since Rowena had lived with her in Ibern, but Medraut made it sound like her affection garnered more than their loyalty.

"Dragons imprint easily in their early years." Medraut's hand hadn't left his sword hilt.

"We fought one in Ibern," Bram said. "It was assumed to have come with the Jotnari who attacked us."

"This one stared at me, like it remembered," Rowena said. From the corner of her eye, Bram twisted to stare at her. He appeared to be in deep thought, but he said nothing before turning away.

With shaky movements that belied her usual regal bearing, Fidessa climbed up the dragon's leg, seating herself on its back between two massive spinal ridges. The creature shifted, adjusting to help her settle with the ease of long familiarity.

"You've taken my daughter from me," she called, looking down at Rowena from her new vantage point. "You will feel my pain."

"Safi is no prisoner. She is now free to choose her own path!" Rowena shouted back, frustration boiling over. "Unlike my family or those left to rot in Taesing because of you!"

But Fidessa was beyond listening. At some silent command, the dragon unfurled its wings to their full span, the movement creating a blast of frigid air that forced Rowena to shield her eyes.

The dragon launched itself skyward with a powerful thrust of its hind legs, wings sending another blast of icy air across the bailey. Rowena shielded her eyes against the swirling ice crystals, watching as the dragon and rider ascended toward the clouds.

As it rose, Fidessa gave one final glance to those watching in stupefied silence. No longer a queen in hiding, trying to regain her power, but something more complex. A woman with renewed purpose. Purpose that could prove more dangerous than the beast she rode.

For a heartbeat, Rowena grew numb.

Then she remembered Safi's blank eyes, the countless cruelties Fidessa had inflicted on those under her power, and the moment of weakness passed. Whatever pain had shaped Fidessa into what she was, it didn't excuse what she'd done to others, especially not to her own daughter or Rowena's mother.

The dragon circled the bailey once, then veered north over the mountains. Fidessa a small silhouette against its gleaming scales. Below, Fidessa's other pets scurried away. Her guards were already out of sight.

In their wake, an uneasy stillness settled over the bailey. The Lunara warriors maintained their positions, blades still drawn but no longer actively engaging any opponents. Rowena's pulse pounded in her ears, filling the sudden quiet with its thundering rhythm. Her muscles ached from battle, each breath carrying the metallic tang of blood; her own as well as from others. Victory should have felt triumphant, but instead a hollow uncertainty bloomed in her chest.

Her gaze found Safi standing alone, sword hanging limply at her side as she watched her mother's departure. The vacant expression on her cousin's face twisted something deep inside Rowena. What did freedom mean to someone still controlled by a spell gone wrong?

Rowena took a step toward her, wincing as pain shot through her injured leg, but determined to bridge the distance between them. Whatever came next, she wouldn't let Safi face it alone—not after everything they'd survived together.

Behind her Medraut sheathed his sword. "The battle is over for now. Gather Naal and prepare his body for the trip home. Healers help those with injuries the best you can. Aatos, take two others and gather the borelk. We leave at moonrise."

The Lunara disbanded, following their commander's orders. Tension built throughout Rowena at the thought of leaving.

Fidessa hadn't been defeated. She'd escaped, again. In doing so, she'd taken a piece of the storm with her, but it would return.

Rowena looked at the ruined bailey. At the scattered corpses, the Lunara, the scars burned into the stone walls.

Not victory.

Not peace.

Conri emerged from his shelter behind a broken cart, leaning heavily on Goby's shoulder. Together, they picked their way across the battlefield, joining Rowena and Bram in the center of the bailey.

"Well, that could have gone worse," Conri said, his voice rough with exhaustion but touched with grim humor. He pressed a hand to a bloody gash on his thigh. "Those chalk dregs fight dirty."

"Here, let me help." One of the Lunara approached, several waterskins that he handed out to each of them. "I have healing skills."

Conri eyed him warily but allowed the treatment. The Lunara warrior murmured soft words over the wound as he worked, his hands glowing faintly with silver enchantment.

Rowena watched, impressed despite herself. The Lunara were clearly more than simple soldiers. Their enchantment had a quality she'd never seen before. Silvery, and similar to her own, yet different in ways she couldn't pinpoint.

"You can heal others?" she asked.

The warrior glanced over his shoulder with a grin. "Not exactly. A small bit of enchantment can force the wound to stop creating pain. The injury must heal naturally or have a true healer's care later"

"You're hurt as well," Bram said.

Rowena glanced down at herself. Blood soaked through her sleeve from several cuts, her shoulder ached from the vultu's talon strikes, and her leggings were torn at the knees from multiple falls. The rabberine bite on her calf throbbed with dull persistence, probably her worst wound. The rest were mostly superficial. "It's nothing."

"Even small wounds can fester." Medraut gestured to another warrior, who handed him a small pack of healing supplies. "Allow us to tend to you before we depart."

"He's right. You should let them help." Bram's voice was tight and his eyes flashed with either frustration or anger. She couldn't tell which. He held one hand pressed to his side where the thorn had broken off in the labyrinth. His white hair, so strange against his transformed features, was matted with dust and blood, but his eyes were clear and alert. She wanted to ask what Yralissa had done to him. But her throat was tight, and the words didn't come.

"Only if you let them help you as well," she said instead.

He shook his head. "My injuries will have to wait for a druid healer, I'm afraid."

What had he suffered? Not just in the battle?

She wanted to refuse help as he did, to maintain this last shred of independence, but exhaustion won out. She lowered to the ground, keeping her injured leg straight and extended her arm silently, allowing the Lunara leader to clean and bind her wounds.

As he worked, she studied Medraut more carefully. She couldn't tell his age, more than thirty summers she guessed, with some silver streaking the dark hair at his temples. His face bore the weathered lines of someone who spent most of his life outdoors, but his hands were surprisingly smooth for a warrior.

"The dragon was unexpected," he said conversationally as he finished with her arm and moved to the bite on her calf. "Though perhaps it shouldn't have been."

"Fidessa has a fondness for animals, it seems. That was an affinity she kept hidden when I lived with her," Rowena replied, wincing as the healer applied a stinging salve to the puncture wounds.

"Such bonds are rarely seen in these days." Medraut's expression turned thoughtful.

"She's full of surprises." Rowena couldn't keep the bitterness from her voice. "Most of them are unpleasant."

"How did you survive the first encounter?" Medraut asked.

Rowena made a half-humor grunt. "I grabbed hold of the dragon's tail and influenced it to leave."

"It was quite the sight," Bram said, meeting her gaze with a tender smile.

Medraut's eyebrows flicked upward. "The ability to influence creatures is a skill few Lunara have."

Rowena bit the inside of her lip, saying nothing. She hadn't known if it was possible then, or that it was a rare skill. She'd done similar to the borelk during her time with the other troop of riders.

The Lunara leader finished wrapping her leg and rose, towering over her. "You will learn much in Penumar to help you hone your skills."

"Penumar?" Rowena asked.

"King Geraint would prefer you come willingly. But we are prepared to use force if necessary."

The blunt statement, given after he tended her wound, reminded Rowena that these warriors were not allies, regardless of their intervention against her enemies. They served the King of Penumar, who had his own agenda for her and the sword she carried.

"Why would he think I'd come at all?" she demanded. "After tying me up and treating me like a captive?"

Medraut rubbed a finger under his nose. "The king sent several troops in different directions. If you were mistreated, it was not by me or any with me."

"How do we even know you are working with the king?" Bram asked.

"My apologies. There has not been a moment to introduce myself officially or state my purpose for being here."

Rowena had gathered his name from overhearing his men. But nothing gave her information about why they'd come.

"I am Medraut, captain of the Lunara Guard, and by order of the king, requires your presence in Penumar."

The words hung in the air, heavy with implication. After everything they had endured, the battles fought, the bloodshed, she faced another king who viewed Rowena as a game piece to be moved at their will.

She exchanged glances with Bram, seeing her own exhaustion and wariness reflected in his eyes. Neither of them was in any condition to fight another battle, especially against fresh opponents who had just demonstrated their martial prowess.

49

ROWENA

Rowena clutched the dagger in her bloodied hands, trembling with exhaustion. The weight of the blade seemed as heavy as a war hammer now the rush of battle faded. She understood she would have to go to Penumar at some point, but not like this, not now, when everything was falling apart. The king didn't need to force her. "Why now?" she asked the Penumar captain, fighting to keep her voice steady.

Medraut's face revealed nothing. Just another expressionless soldier delivering orders. "Are you not aware of your heritage?"

Rowena's grandmother's stories echoed in her memory. Their whispered conversations by candlelight when she was small. "My grandmother and mother fled during an uprising from the current king's father. Who killed his father and older brother, who was my grandfather, Prince Aimon Vaara. The Sword of Justice was his father's, and should have been my grandfather's, then my mother's, and now mine."

The words came automatically as she picked up a scrap of bandaging, her muscles moving on instinct as she wiped her dagger clean. She'd do a better job later, when her hands stopped shaking.

"Hmm," Medraut said. "King Virion Metsa, was *our* uncle. My father is Prince Pahat, his youngest brother. Your mother was my cousin, as is the current king."

Rowena's hands froze mid-swipe, her tired mind struggling to catch up. "The usurper king changed the family name as well?" That detail had never appeared in her grandmother's carefully recited histories. The stories that had painted her grandfather as a hero and her great-uncle as a monster.

Medraut stiffened. "It was a fresh name for a revived land."

"Or a way to clear away the memories of previous rulers," Bram added.

Rowena's surname, Olvesdottir, reflected Skandan tradition, but her mother had carried the name Vaara. The last one to do so, apparently. "Even if we are related by blood, I still see no reason to go with you."

He'd actually made a better case for her to stay away.

"The High Father Osric granted the Sword of Justice to the Lunara. However, it is missing the Lunastone. King Geraint knows where it is. He believes only the moon-born can retrieve it."

The revelation struck Rowena like a blow to the gut. The King of Penumar had found the very object Fidessa had tortured her to reveal?

Anger flashed hot in her chest, burning through the fog of exhaustion. "Others have tortured me for information about the heartstone," she said, her voice low. "While he knew where it was all along?"

"The king has his reasons," Medraut replied, offering no further explanation. "Reasons he wishes to share with you."

Rowena looked at her companions. Bram, exhausted but standing tall; Safi, trapped in her internal prison but showing the first signs of breaking free; Conri, beaten but unbowed; and Goby, loyal despite having every reason to flee.

They had fought together, bled together. Whatever came next, they would face it as one.

Which meant the decision about where to go next would be made by all.

"I will not go alone," she said to Medraut, making it clear this was a condition, not a request. "All of us or none of us. And that is a decision we must make together. By ourselves."

The captain studied their ragged band, his expression giving nothing away. "That was not part of my orders."

"Then your mission fails here," Rowena replied, slipping her hand behind her back to rest against the Sword of Justice. "My companions and I will not be separated again."

For a tense moment, it seemed another conflict might erupt. Then Medraut gave a curt nod. "Very well. The king desires your presence most of all, but your companions may accompany you. It's getting late and we will travel upon moonrise. You have a half mark, no longer," Medraut said. He snatched a fallen arrow and jammed it into the ground, where Sawel's light created a shadowed line in the dirt. He scraped a line to designate a half mark, then spun to join his other warriors.

Rowena met Bram's gaze, her heart pinching at the expression he wore, like he had more bad news to share.

The Lunara warriors had taken any belonging from the fallen they deemed of use and packed them out to the borelk. Rowena could view the animals across the bridge from where she stood. A strange mixture of emotions washed over her. Relief at surviving the battle. Wariness of what awaited them in Penumar. Curiosity about the king's reasons, and where the Lunastone was.

But the strongest of all was a growing sense of determination. The prophecy was unfolding. The Burning Moon approached, and with it, decisions that would shape not just her fate, but that of all Edenia.

"I'll gather the others." Bram turned, then hissed as he grabbed his side.

Rowena rolled over, having to push herself to one knee before standing. By the time she straightened, Goby had trotted over to Bram.

"Goby help?"

"Can you ask Conri and Safi to come over here?" Rowena asked. "We have some things to discuss."

Goby's eyes widened, and he twisted his neck to stare at Safi.

"I'm sure that she'll come if you let her know I asked."

"Ask Conri first," Bram said, his face pale. "He'll help you."

Goby seemed too dazed to move, but shook himself and jogged to Conri.

"That thorn in your side must be removed," Rowena said, hobbling over to Bram. "Can I see it?"

"I'll be alright." He gave her a poor attempt at a smile. "Though if you want to try that pain relief technique the other Lunara did for Conri, I'll let you."

That was terrifying. He had a poisoned thorn impaling who-knew-what inside his body, something in his blood keeping him from shifting to his Seeker form, or at least that's what she guessed, and she had depleted her enchantment to a trickle.

"You don't have to. I shouldn't have said that."

"No! I just don't want to hurt you more." She licked her lips. "It would be an excellent skill to learn. I just haven't been able to connect to whatever amount of enchantment I have left."

She couldn't reach it the last time she tried, but if it was possible, for Bram, she'd make it happen.

"I'll give it a try."

Bram raised his shirt to show the puncture wound. The thorn had worked its way deeper so that it no longer showed. Only angry skin torn into a ragged circle remained, tinged in black and dribbling blood down his side.

Rowena swallowed. Just a brief glow. Sure.

Conri and Goby arrived just then, with Safi trailing.

"Here," Conri said to Bram. "Brace against me. When the other Lunara did that to me, it made me want to punch him at first. But then it was great."

Safi stepped around Bram to stand at Rowena's side.

"He will not punch me," Rowena said to her. She fought the grin that tried to form. "At least I hope not."

"Never," Bram said.

Rowena inhaled a deep breath and let it out. "Ready?"

Bram nodded, and Conri leaned against his opposite side, one arm around his shoulders. Goby wrapped his arms around Bram's legs in his attempt to help.

Rowena pressed her palm over the injury and closed her eyes. Once again, a remnant of enchantment flickered in the distance. She concentrated on touching it, visualizing her fingers stretching. It was too far.

She exhaled, letting her body relax. Instead of forcing the situation, she sat still, allowing herself time to rest. To connect with her surroundings. The dryads had prepared her for more than the labyrinth, that was clear.

A tingle of warmth touched her palms. Enchantment rising in a thin thread. She peeked through her lashes to find not only her hand glowing, but Bram's skin as well. She glanced up at him.

Bram's eyes pinched closed and his knuckles went white where he grabbed a torn piece of his tunic.

"I'm hurting you?" She pulled back, but he grabbed her wrist. "Please don't."

From that point on, she darted her glance from his face to the wound, unsure how long to continue. When she could feel her meager reserves coming to an end, a wave of dizziness washed over her. She had to let go.

Woozy, she wobbled on her feet, and within a blink, Safi had a hold of her under her arms to keep her from falling. The sensation only lasted a moment or two.

She patted Safi's hand. "Thank you."

Her cousin let go and handed her a waterskin before stepping away.

Conri eased away from Bram, who rolled his neck and let out a sigh. "That was very helpful. I can still feel it, but not as sharp as before."

Rowena slumped back on her knees. The threat of tears stung the backs of her eyes. Her mouth too dry to form words. She drank a gulp of water.

"I'm so glad to hear that."

After a few moments to gather themselves, the group moved over near the curtain wall to sit on some barrels.

Rowena didn't see any reason to draw things out. "The King of Penumar sent Medraut to retrieve me. He knows where the Lunastone is and believes I'm the only who can get it."

Bram had his duty to collect all the armor, the corresponding heartstones, and the moon-born. If Rowena went with Medraut, she would help Bram, as well as learning more about her mother's side of her heritage, and the enchantment she shared with them.

"You want us to head to Penumar?" Conri's face was pale with exhaustion, but determination burned in his eyes. "After everything?"

"If that's what we all decide," Rowena answered, a warmth spreading through her that Conri wanted to stick with them. He didn't have to, but it gave Rowena relief that he said so himself without her having to ask. She glanced toward the Lunara warriors as they prepared to depart. "And we only have half a mark to decide."

Conri held her gaze. "Do you think their enchantment can free Safi from whatever has a hold on her?"

Rowena glanced at Safi. She didn't seem to acknowledge what Conri asked. "I'm not sure."

"A druid healer would be the best option," Bram said.

"Medraut would know if King Geraint has an Oraku," she said.

"That won't do," Bram said. "She needs more than a disavowed's help." Something in his eyes gave Rowena the impression he had more to say, but had held back. His battle with Yralissa had been difficult, that much was clear.

Conri jutted his chin to the ground. "Will they welcome the little one in Penumar?"

Rowena trailed her gaze to where Goby sat. A carrot pierced on the end of a fork though he didn't eat it. "I've never been to Penumar to know what it's like. The warriors haven't seemed to mind him."

"I won't leave him behind," Bram said. "No matter where we go."

"He helped me today. I owe him my life, so I'm with Bram on that," Conri added.

Such a funny little creature. Rowena had heard no one mention goblins in a good way. Goby was living proof that prejudice was a snake that could slip through the thinnest cracks even for those with good intentions.

"Okay," Rowena said. "But is that alright with you, Goby? Do you want to travel with us?"

"Travel Bram. And Conri." He slid his eyes to Safi without moving his head. "Keep Goby safe."

"There's another factor to consider," Bram said.

"The other moon-born and armor," Rowena guessed. "This will help with that as well."

Bram stared at the ground a little too long. She'd guessed wrong. Her hands trembled. Whatever he needed to say, it couldn't be good.

50

BRAM

How was he supposed to explain? No one, not even Rowena, could understand what it was like to be a druid.

"Whatever it is, Bram, just tell us," Rowena said. The way her eyebrows knit together gave away her concern.

Bram took a breath. His headache had returned, throbbing with each heartbeat, unaffected by Rowena's help to his side. He'd use more of the elixir later. The memory of those underground tunnels in Saganus flashed in his mind. The children hiding from sunlight, Farryn's daughter clinging to her hip, whispering that he was "scary."

"When the druids called me back to Saganus," Bram began, his voice tight, "they were concerned that I had lost track of my duties."

"Because of me." Rowena's gaze dropped to the ground.

Bram reached for her hand but stopped himself. "In part, yes. But I defended that. They never forbade me to have a relationship."

Conri chuckled, and Rowena's ears turned pink. Heat stretched across Bram's chest.

"The bigger issue was my involvement in the battle at Velmeg," Bram continued.

"They saw that as taking sides," Conri guessed, wincing as he shifted his weight.

Bram nodded. "The Heptad believes they must remain neutral in realm affairs. They made me wait while they deliberated, so I went into town." His expression darkened as he recalled the streets strewn with litter, the run-down homes. He squeezed his fists. "Saganus has changed. There's poverty, a curfew. The druids seemed . . . afraid."

"Of what?" Rowena asked, her brow furrowed.

"Of the Heptad," Bram said.

Safi shifted her position, her impassive movements stilling as she seemed to listen more intently.

"While I was in town, I ran into an old friend. Farryn," Bram continued. "She's a healer I grew up with in the pedagogy."

"The pedagogy?" Rowena asked.

Bram's jaw tightened. "It's how all druid elflings grow up. We're given to the vivens at three days old and raised communally, to ensure we're all of equal status and ready to fit into our best position when we leave on our prime day." The words came out more bitterly than he'd intended.

"No mother or father or brothers? Sounds horrible," Conri muttered.

"It's what we knew," Bram replied, though doubt crept into his voice. "Farryn invited me to visit. When I returned to Aethercrest, I found they wouldn't meet with me again until morning."

"Aethercrest? I thought you were in the town?" Rowena asked.

"That's the name of the ziggurat where the Heptad lives. Their Tower of Enlightenment rises from the top." Bram paused, remembering how the massive structure had once held all the druids and symbolized wisdom and protection. Now it felt like a monument to control. "They also told me they were sending someone to retrieve you, Rowena."

"Ida made me leave right after you left. If they came, I missed them," she said.

Something loosened in Bram's chest. "I learned that later." He took a deep breath, the pain from his missing horns flaring. "With the extra time I visited Farryn."

Bram's mind drifted back to those underground tunnels, the smell of damp earth and tallow candles, the wide-eyed children who had never seen a dawnlight.

"Farryn showed me something I didn't expect," he said, his voice dropping. "There's an underground rebellion in Saganus. Families hiding from the Heptad."

"Hiding? Why?" Rowena leaned forward.

Bram's throat tightened as he remembered Mila's whispered *scary* and the fierce protectiveness in Farryn's eyes as she held her daughter.

"They want to raise their own elflings," he said. "The pedagogy . . . It's not just tradition. It's enforced. When parents resist, there are consequences."

"What consequences?" Conri asked, his expression hardening.

"They are disavowed," Bram admitted. "I never questioned it. But Farryn . . . she has a daughter. Mila." His voice caught on the name. "A little girl with light brown curls."

Rowena's eyes widened, seeming as surprised as he had been.

"There are elflings down there who have never seen Sawel, Masah, or Lungol," Bram continued. "They've spent their entire lives hidden away, because their parents kept them, and that breaks the rules."

"This can't be right," Rowena said, shaking her head. "The Heptad cares for the Primary Spring and ensures safety for everyone in Edenia, enchanted and unenchanted alike. How could they do this?"

"I've been asking myself the same question," Bram replied. "The rebels asked for my help. They wanted me to speak to the Heptad on their behalf." He laughed bitterly. "As if they would listen to me."

"What happened?" Rowena prompted when he fell silent.

Bram's jaw clenched. "One of the older elflings, Killian, followed me when I left. I thought I'd seen him safely back, but when I met with the Heptad . . ." He closed his eyes, seeing again the boy's terrified face as the sentinels dragged him in. "They'd found him, and beaten him for information about where the others were hiding."

"Did he tell?" Conri asked.

"No." Pride and grief mingled in Bram's voice. "He didn't say a word."

Goby had stopped fidgeting with his carrot, his yellow eyes fixed on Bram's face.

"I tried," Bram continued, his voice strained. "I transformed, but the High Hepta moved faster. He killed Killian. And the sentinels who had brought him in." The memory of the boy's body crumpling to the floor flashed before his eyes. "To make a point."

Rowena reached out, her fingers brushing his arm. "I'm so sorry, Bram."

"He rests in the hero grounds now," Conri added.

Bram nodded once, acknowledging her sympathy and Conri's belief, unable to speak for a moment.

"The Heptad gave me three weeks to return to Saganus," he finally continued. "When I arrive, they expect me to help them root out the rebels."

"But you're planning to warn them instead," Rowena said, her voice soft but certain.

"Yes. I gave my word to Farryn, to all of them, that I would try to help." He held Rowena's gaze. "There are innocent families in those tunnels. So many elflings."

"What happens if you don't make it back in time?" Conri asked.

"They will *cleanse* the island of all rebellion," Bram said, the words bitter in his mouth and memory. "They were very clear about that."

"So, if we go to Penumar, you might not make it back to save those druids," Rowena said, her fingers worrying at the edge of her sleeve. "But if we don't find the Lunastone, then the prophecy is in danger."

"Yes," Bram answered.

"Whew," Conri blew out a deep breath. "Either way ends in death."

Rowena's face clouded with conflict. "How much time do we have left?"

"Just two weeks now," Bram said.

"And how long would it take to reach Penumar, get the Lunastone, and then travel to Saganus?"

Bram calculated quickly. "Three days to Penumar, if we push hard. If retrieving the Lunastone takes only a day or two . . ." He trailed off, the numbers not adding up in their favor.

"It would be close," Rowena finished for him, her voice tight with worry.

"Too close," Bram agreed. "And that's assuming everything goes perfectly."

"Which it never does," Conri added. "Something always goes wrong."

Rowena's expression hardened with determination. "I believe the King of Penumar does know Lunastone's location. It's part of the armor, which means we need it to fulfill the prophecy."

"I don't doubt that," Bram said. "But my promise to the rebels—"

"Is important too," Rowena finished for him. "I understand, Bram. Truly."

She looked away. Her profile outlined by the fading light. Bram could read the struggle on her face. The desire to do what was right for the prophecy, for him, for everyone. The same need twisted inside of him as well.

"There's another factor to consider," Bram said, his voice lower. "The Heptad ordered me to bring each moon-born and piece of armor to Saganus as I find them. They claim it's for safety, but after what I've seen," He shook his head. "I'm not convinced that's their true intention."

"You think they want to prevent the prophecy from succeeding," Rowena said, not a question. A realization.

"I don't know what they want," Bram admitted. "But I no longer trust them."

Safi eased closer to Rowena and put her hand on her shoulder. When Rowena met her gaze, there was a determination there. "You'll come with me?"

Safi nodded, just once, but it was enough for Rowena to have to blink back tears. Even Bram had to look away. If Safi could recover from her struggles, perhaps he could as well.

"That's settled then," Conri said, pushing himself up from the ground. "Wherever it's decided that we go, we'll all be going together. The little guy and I already said that, right, Goby?"

"Goby go."

"You two work it out and let us know which way we're heading. I, for one, need to find the kitchen because I am starving."

"Goby knows." He grabbed his pack and slung it over his back, and turned for Conri to follow him into the keep.

Conri chuckled and the two of them ambled off.

A moment later, Safi squeezed Rowena's shoulder and

followed them. As she got close, one of Goby's carrots fell out of his pack. Safi picked it up and tapped the goblin on the shoulder with it. He startled so much he lost the entire pack with the scrolls and many other carrots spilling out.

Safi bent down and helped him gather them and settle his pack into place. The three of them disappeared through the keep door.

"I think there's hope for her after all," Bram said, watching the unlikely trio.

"I never doubted."

Bram's heart hammered in his chest. It was just the two of them, and he wasn't sure how she felt about what he'd shared, his new appearance, his loss of power. She might not feel the same way about him, but he had to take a chance. He slipped her hand into his.

She twisted to face him. "Whatever we do, it has to be together. Agreed?"

"Agreed."

"Can I ask you a question?" Rowena asked, entwining her fingers with his.

The simple act made his pulse race. He could sit like this, with her, forever. But there were so many things they still needed to talk about. He braced himself. "Of course."

"Are you able to travel like you used to?"

He closed his eyes, reaching for that skill even as he knew it was futile. "No." The admission hurt more than he expected.

"That's alright. I just want to know what happened to you, whatever it was, whatever you can or can't do . . . it doesn't matter to me."

Relief washed through him at her words. Her opinion meant so much to him.

"When Tephra sent me to the Twisted Forest in search of you," Bram began, then shook his head.

"You didn't go into that place, did you?" Alarm flashed across Rowena's face.

"Thankfully, no. I met a mage and a witch, however. They run an apothecary in Grimhold, just on the edge of the forest. The witch, Esme, is also a moon-born."

"A witch? Interesting. I think I might have found the dryad moon-born as well. I said nothing though because I don't think she knows anything about the prophecy."

"Evora," Bram said.

"How did you know that?"

"I went to the cottage as soon as I returned. She introduced herself."

"That doesn't surprise me. She is very curious."

Bram laughed. "Yes, she is. She is safest inside Havilar. It's the reason Queen Alona is insistent about not having visitors. I'll deal with her when the time comes."

"What about the witch, Esme? Where is she?" Rowena still held his hand, rubbing her thumb on his occasionally. He struggled to concentrate on their conversation sometimes.

"Esme is still in the apothecary. She is very adept at hiding her identity. And a talented healer, too." Bram reached into his waist purse and pulled out the vial of elixir Esme had made for him. "She gave me this to help with my headaches. It works well. She tried to help me more, but my condition was too strong. Yralissa injected something into my blood that only a Primary Fae can help with—if anyone can. Esme told me that the longer I go without help, it may be harder to separate out the poison."

"That makes sense. And now you have the thorn as well. It's good that your friend Farryn is a healer." Rowena stared at their conjoined hands.

"There's a lot to be said for getting the Lunastone before someone else does. If we don't help the king, he may decide to send someone else after it. Then we may never get hold of it," Bram said.

The door to the keep banged open, and the other three strode toward where Bram and Rowena stood. Goby had a bounce in his step as he walked between Conri and Safi.

In that moment, watching them approach, a sudden clarity struck Bram. Regardless of what happened, whether they went to Penumar or straight to Saganus, whether he regained his Seeker form or remained elven forever, he finally understood what the rebels had tried to show him.

For the first time in his life, Bram had a family. Not of blood, but of the heart. Their differences blended into a cohesive whole that he could never have on his own.

He would do anything for them.

The realization brought an unexpected peace. Perhaps being caught between states wasn't weakness. Perhaps it was where he was meant to be. The bridge between worlds, between duties, between past and future.

Whatever path they chose, they would walk it together. And that, Bram realized, was a kind of strength he had never possessed as the Seeker.

MAP OF EDENIA

To view this beautiful map in full color
www.kellynjane.com/edenia-map

ACKNOWLEDGMENTS

This book has been an adventure, to say the least. I'm not a person to rush. Not at work. Not at home. Not at play. Unless it's the grocery store—I speed through that place. So, in 2022, when I hurried to get the second installment of the Enchanted Series finished, literally typing on my laptop as I walked onto an airplane, it crushed me. It was not the story I wanted to tell. I had to start over.

Since I began this new edition, one thing after another has assaulted my life—illness, financial pressures, grief—and it seemed that forces were at work to prevent me from ever finishing. There were times I wanted to give up. I thank my Lord for the faith to keep going.

Thankfully, during this time, I've surrounded myself with those who I trust. Voices that provide sound advice *for me*. They helped me persevere and believe and finish. The entire Tales of Edenia will be different now—better—because of where I am on my journey now. I owe an enormous debt of gratitude and thanks to so many.

Thank you, John Truby and your Truby Story Program, for challenging me to grow. I became a better storyteller because of the push you gave me to dig deeper, find the golden nuggets, and never expect less of my story or myself. The confidence I gained with you is immeasurable. The Writer's Room mentorship changed me forever. Thank you to my fellow writers, my friends, who gathered in the room with me. I am so grateful for the friendship we share: Rachel Funk Heller, Sarah Crowne,

Tom Watts, Allen J. Mummert, Judith Blazer, Gina Anjou, Gérôme Ordoño, Rob Thesman. And Jocelyn Lindsay, who deserves a medal for listening to me, propping me up, swimming with me in the deep end, and overall being there when I needed a hand or a hug.

Nina Schuyler, thank you for helping me fall in love with every glorious sentence. Our monthly writing sessions in your Swimming in Style group bring me as much joy as they do knowledge. Margie Lawson, I am so grateful for your EDITS system. It is the rock tumbler to bring out a polished story. Thank you, Lisa Hall-Wilson, for helping me build skills for deep POV writing. That will take me a lifetime to master.

Arielle Bailey, I cannot thank you enough for your help in those early days. You helped me pull apart and reshape this book in a way that put me on the right path. Mark O'Bannon, thank you for not forgetting about me when I dive for weeks at a time into my "cave" and can't make our get-togethers. Every email reminds me I'm not alone on this writing journey. Jo, at Enchanted Quill, thank you for editing this massive story.

Jaci Miller, your friendship means the world to me. I am so grateful we walk this journey together. Ashley McLeo, who would have thought a small meeting in a coffee shop to talk about marketing, would lead to a lifelong friendship. You inspire me. My writing partner, my travel buddy, my friend.

I could not have a more supportive family who gives me the encouragement and love that I need to pursue my love of writing. Craig, Audrey, Sydney, Stephen, and Bailey—you inspire me to be my best every day. I love you all so much.

ALSO BY KELLY N. JANE

Enchanted Shadows

Rune of Secrets

Rune of Thorns

Rune of Blades

The Viking Maiden Complete Series

Ingrid, The Viking Maiden

Amber Magic

Realm of Fate

Arcanum (A Viking Maiden novella)

The Viking Maiden series eBook box set

The Royal Quest Series

Dragon Prince

Dragon Magic

Dragon Mates

Dragon Betrayal

Dragon Crown

Dragon War

The Royal Quest box set eBooks 1-3

The Royal Quest box set eBooks 4-6

ABOUT THE AUTHOR

Kelly is a USA Today bestselling author who writes royally epic fantasy where fate is forged in prophecy, kingdoms are shaped by intrigue, and reluctant heroes must rise to meet destiny. Her elaborate secondary worlds are rich with myth, magic, and slow-burn romance, blending character-driven storytelling with high-stakes adventure.

A lover of sassy chihuahuas and bobbed-tail cats, her coffee mug is always full, and she believes dessert goes with every meal. When not in front of her keyboard, she's probably reading, painting, playing with yarn, or lost in her imagination.

www.Kellynjane.com

www.ingramcontent.com/pod-product-compliance
Lightning Source LLC
Chambersburg PA
CBHW061530190726
48289CB00004B/992